Baltimore, Maryland, 1974. Special Agent H. Thomas Moore of the Towson Office pursued a group of five men who committed 23 known bank robberies across the Eastern Seabord from Maine to Florida. This story is based on the life of the alleged leader.

Some Kind of Crook

SOME KIND OF CROOK

Based on a true story

W.D. BURNS

Bad Ass Outlaw
Publications

BAD ASS OUTLAW PUBLICATIONS
4216 Riverview Lane
Lorian, OH 44055 www.badassoutlawpubications.com

This book is an original publication of Bad Ass Outlaw Publications.
This book is based on a true story. The publisher does not have any control over and does not assume any responsibility for author or third party
websites or their comment.

SOME KIND OF CROOK
Library of Congress
Copyright 2010
TXu001692272 revised 2015

Editing, typesetting and cover design by J.D. Williams
(www.behance.net/jdwilliams)
All rights reserved.

ISBN: 978-0-9962651-1-9

Printed in The United States of America

10 9 8 7 6 5 4 3 2 1

SOME KIND OF CROOK

INDEX

Chapter 1	SWEET REVENGE
Chapter 2	LUCKY NUMBER FIVE
Chapter 3	VEGAS ON MY MIND
Chapter 4	COUNTRY JUSTICE
Chapter 5	WEST VIRGINIA BLUES
Chapter 6	GHOSTS OF YESTERYEAR
Chapter 7	THE BOLERO CLUB
Chapter 3	THE BIG FISH
Chapter 9	DYE PACKETS
Chapter 10	POCKET MONEY
Chapter 11	ARMY BLUES
Chapter 12	PET PARTY
Chapter 13	TRUE LUST WITH LOVE
Chapter 14	THE ESCAPADE
Chapter 15	SECOND TIME AROUND
Chapter 16	MOMMA'S BOY
Chapter 17	MORNING GLORY
Chapter 18	ALL MONEY AIN'T GOOD MONEY
Chapter 19	THE GOOD, THE BAD, AND THE UGLY
Chapter 20	TROUBLE BY THE NUMBERS
Chapter 21	THE GREAT OUTDOORS
Chapter 22	THE HUNT
Chapter 23	THE GREAT ESCAPE
Chapter 24	BAD DAY RISING
Chapter 25	LADY JUSTICE
Chapter 26	IT'S A BOY!
Chapter 27	EASY PICKENS
Chapter 28	THE SEARCHES
Chapter 29	THE HONEYMOON SUITE
Chapter 30	UNLUCKY THIRTEEN
Chapter 31	THE TRIP
Chapter 32	ONCE BITTEN TWICE SHY

Dedication

To my beautiful wife, Bonnie. For without her I would have never known the meaning of true love.

Acknowledgements

Special thanks to Colleen Brown, for without her assistance this book would not have been possible. Props to my Editor in Cheif and friend, Ronnie Jones.

CHAPTER ONE
SWEET REVENGE

Asheville, North Carolina, 1975. Some days are better than others. This wasn't one of Bill Hooker's better days.

Bill and Red Miller, his partner, had departed Baltimore early, beating the Monday morning traffic. They'd risen early, hastily packing a few things, and hit the road. As usual, their destination was unknown: their future, uncertain. Each of them carried only a hundred dollars, and each shared a common goal, to find and rob a bank.

As they traveled, Bill admired the beauty of North Carolina in the Autumn. The trees swayed in a gentle breeze, their leaves colorful and abundant, the air carried a crisp snap, pleasantly cool.

Throughout the previous week, Bill had cased nearly two dozen banks, but for one reason or another he had decided not to rob each and every one. Sometimes, it was the location. At other times, the scarce amount of money that he saw in the teller's drawer when he purchased a Money Order made it unworthy of the risk. And sometimes, it was just a gut feeling, an instinct that he relied heavily on.

Red, on the other hand, figured there was a bank on every corner. He wasn't as particular as Bill.

After Bill was paroled by the State of Maryland, he made five trips to Florida in search of his wife and daughters. Finding his wife, Dayle, remarried and his daughter not knowing who he was and calling her husband daddy, it broke his heart. How could he tell his daughters that he was their daddy? He couldn't do that to them.

Bill had turned twenty-one in prison. In Anne Arundel County, the police had told him that they rode around in marked cars, wore uniforms, and asked what does a criminal look-like? Bill bought a yellow panel truck, wrote THIEF WAGON in big black bold letters across the sides and back and installed a police scanner. Night after night he heard the dispatcher announce, "yellow panel truck seen leaving scene." It was the police who had made a game of it, Bill reasoned. That game ended with their going home to their families and Bill going to prison. Bill met John Brady and studied law with him in the Anne Arundel County Jail. John had come off death row and set a precedent in the United States Supreme Court Brady v. Maryland. More commonly known as Brady material. John also wrote the book Between Life and Death. Bill met Lennard Hall in the Baltimore County Jail. Lennard had also come off death row and set a precedent in the United States Supreme Court setting guidelines on search and seizure. When Bill was charged with murder in Baltimore City, the detectives in Anne Arundel County seized upon the opportunity to write all of their unsolved burglaries off on Bill. On a plea agreement, the charges were reduced to eight burglaries. Bill pled guilty to two and nolo-contendre to six. When Judge Evans sentenced him to serve 8 eight-year consecutive sentences, Bill spoke. "Your Honor, I thought nolo-contendre meant not guilty." To that, the judge replied. "Son, ignorance of the law is no defense. You were represented by an attorney."

On Eastern Shore, in Talbot County, Bill was charged with storehouse breaking, and conspiracy. He made a plea agreement for a concurrent sentence. The prosecutor asked the judge to hold sentencing over until Bill's co-defendant. Butch Geoheigan, went to trial. When Bill objected to the continuance, stating that he had made no agreement to testify against his co-defendant, the black robed judge stood up and announced that all of his trouble came from the western side of the bridge (the Cheasapeake Bay bridge) and sentenced Bill to serve three years consecutive to the sixty-four years. Without any hesitation, Bill picked up the metal water pitcher sitting on the counselor's table and hurled it at the judge.

To further his education, Bill became an avid reader, using Reader's Digest to enhance his vocabulary. He obtained his G.E.D., and he gave all of the time back with the exception of five years. While in prison, at camp he worked in Governor Marvin Mandel's mansion. On work release, he became a supervisor for Eskay Poultry in Cordova, Maryland, in their Quality Control department. After serving two and one-half years, he was paroled. Bill felt the police had taken advantage of his ignorance of the law and his lack of education. Having lost everything he cared for, he reasoned that if you wanted popcorn, you go to a popcorn stand. If you wanted pussy, you go to a whorehouse. And, if you wanted money, well then, you rob a bank.

They entered the City limits of Asheville at about one o'clock Thursday afternoon. Time and money were running short. Neither had any desire to go home broke, it would be disgraceful.

The last robbery they'd pulled had been in Bristol, Tennessee, six weeks previously. They had, more by accident than good planning, hit a good score there. They'd anticipated a fairly small amount of money -- enough to party the weekend away, but instead they walked away with over one-hundred thousand dollars. And today they were broke.

"You know, Red, me and money just don't get along."

"What do ya mean? You love money."

"True, but it must not love me."

"Why do you say that?"

"Cause I can never keep it around!" The sound of their laughter followed them on the wind as they tooled down the highway. Bill wasn't good with money. In one year he'd lost thirty-one thousand dollars in Las Vegas, bought nine new cars, and made more than his share of financial blunders. When broke, he'd jest, "they make it every day in Richmond!"

Red, somewhat better with money, had invested in a business. He'd purchased the Log Cabin, Pineville West Virginia's only watering hole. Together, Bill and Red had bought a double wide house trailer to live in. It was a luxurious mobile home; sporting two bedrooms, a large bath, and a fully equipped horseshoe shaped wet bar. The home was being set on a permanent foundation in Oceana, West Virginia, just fifteen minutes from the newly purchased bar. The lot, adjacent to a stream on a beautifully scenic piece of land was ideal. But Bill had reservations about living in West Virginia nonetheless.

Red, however, didn't seem to have any regrets about leaving Baltimore.

"This is it, Bill. I retire after this one." Red commented.

"Sure. You'll never rob another bank, Right."

"I mean it. I've got a new home, a new business, and a fresh start on life. I'm through with it."

Sure it's easy for you to say that, Bill thought. You're a redneck if there ever was one. You'll love West-By-God-Virginia. But what about me? I'm leaving my roots behind, everything I know, everything I love. Fond memories swept Bill back to Baltimore, The girls he knew, the Bolero Club -- his favorite hangouts the Wee Hours, The Block and Blaze Starr. It wasn't an easy decision to leave, and Bill wasn't happy with it.

"You know, there's one good thing about this move," Bill said.

"What's that?" Red asked.

"I won't have to look at H. Thomas Moore's fucking grin."

"Yeah. Special Agent of the Eff-Bee-Fucking-Eye. I hate that bastard too. I sure won't miss him."

Agent Moore was becoming a serious threat to the partners. Just a few weeks past, Moore's senior partner, Special Agent O'Neil had almost came to blows with Bill. Moore and O 'Neil had visited Bill's home and had, none too nicely, questioned his live-in girlfriend, Judy Osborn, leaving her in tears.

The phone rang at the Bolero Club. The owner, Earl Murphy, a stout Irishman in his fifties, quietly passed the message to Bill.

"That was Judy. She wants you to come home. Two F.B.I. agents, Moore and O'Neil were there, hasslin'her. She's really upset." They were standing next to the pinball machine, located near the front door of the bar. Bing! Bong! The steel ball left the flippers and bounced between the flashing targets. A touch of the finger sent the ball careening off the bumpers, amassing points on the digital scoreboard. The machine held a certain mystique for the men. Every day, they tested their skill, betting hundreds of dollars, cursing, and often drinking to excess. It became a ritual, a part of their daily lives.

When Earl whispered the message in Bill's ear, he ran out the door, not even finishing the game, pausing only to toss a twenty dollar bill on the bar, a tip for Joyce, the barmaid. She smiled and waved as he left in a hurry.

As he drove home, Bill thought about Joyce. They'd been involved briefly, but quickly came to the conclusion they were better off as friends than lovers. But she would always hold a special place in his heart. It had been Joyce who'd taken care of him when, because of an arson job gone wrong, he'd received burns over sixty percent of his body. She'd tried to nurse him, but the damage had been too severe, and he'd ended up in the hospital. It had been his first arson and, if he had his way, it would be his last. The torch job had been on Frank Kalita's store, Stitch and Save in Glen Burnie. In a way, it had been a success. The building was totally engulfed in flames before the police or fire trucks arrived.

Bill met Frank through an ad placed in the local newspaper. One morning Bill was having breakfast, sipping coffee, and reading the morning paper when the ad caught his eye. Acting more on instinct than anything else, he called the number listed. Bill had no previous sales experience and Frank hired him without a background check. Within three weeks, he became the top salesman, earning upward of seven hundred dollars a week in commissions. It was through Frank's wife, Linda, that Bill met her sister, Judy.

Before Judy, there was Jean Staubs. Along with her two children, Donna and Roland. They shared an apartment on Pratt streel in Baltimore. But the inner city, with its senseless violence, was no place to raise children. So they'd moved to a rural area in Anne Arundel County, renting an apartment in Glen Burnie off Crane Highway. Later, they went their separate ways.

* * *

There were three after hour clubs in Baltimore. The Wee Hours, Hector's, and Susie's. Bill, along with a crazy Greek, Gus Valakos, ran The Wee Hours.

Gus had an insatiable lust for women, but Bill trusted him to look after Jean while he was in prison. Bill had never intended to have a relationship with Jean. But events had thrown them together...

Jean was living with a man, Johnny Campbell. He was thirty-six, an ex-prize boxer, and a full time hustler who also owned two sub shops. One in the city, the other in Hampton. Bill met Johnny in one of the clubs on the strip, the Blue Onion on Howard street.

At the time, Bill was hustling men's suits. His friend, Rich Boblitz owned a discount store in Glen Burnie. Using his credit card, he'd pay nineteen ninety-five for a suit, then change the price tag to fifty-nine ninety-five, then sell the suits in the clubs for half price. It was a lucrative business, since he never intended to pay the bills in the first place.

All of Bill's newly acquired friends thought he was crazy.

He frequently gave presents to the gorgeous dancers at the Corral, the Pink Pussycat, the Inferno, the Two o' clock Club, and The Blue Onion, and Kay's. The latter was run by Bill's best friend, Tommy Bruno.

The doorman, Tony Cordell, was an imposing figure, He wasn't a big man, maybe five eleven, a hundred and ninety pounds. But he stood erect, with no arch in his back, and he always wore turtleneck sweaters with suit jacket. Tony was quiet spoken, never raising his voice, but once committed to a fight, he never lost.

It was Tommy who took Bill aside and told him that Johnny Campbell was no good, that he sold drugs to kids which wasn't tolerated amongst seasoned gangsters. Kids were sacred. If you had a beef with another man, you could handle your business and other gangsters wouldn't bat an eye. But harm a child and you were marked for life.

Tommy added that Johnny also mistreated Jean and her kids. Bill decided that he would offer her help. But he couldn't have known how it would turn out.

December 13th, 1968. Friday, the thirteenth. A day for bad luck. For Johnny Campbell, it was the worst, and the last day of his life.

Johnny was in the process of beating Jean half to death when Bill stopped by.

"Please, Johnny, no more. You're killing me." Bill heard Jean plead. Johnny was enraged, ignoring her pleas. He continued to beat her brutally, saying. "Don't beg bitch, it'll only make it worse."

When Bill knocked on the door, Johnny yelled. "Go away! We don't need it, whatever it is." The sound of flesh slapping flesh was loud. He knew what it meant, Johnny was beating Jean again. He tried the door and it opened, so Bill stormed into the house like the charge of the Light Brigade, right into Johnny's professionally trained fists.

"Look here, it's your lover boy," Johnny said, dropping into a boxers crouch, fists held ready. Though Bill was only twenty, slim and easy going, he had all the heart in the world. He waded in, determined to beat Johnny like he was beating Jean. Johnny waited for Bill to make the first move, a big looping right hand that Johnny easily slipped. He came back with a quick left-right-left combination that rocked the younger, smaller man in his shoes.

Heart and determination wasn't enough against the experience Johnny had gained in the ring. Bill was taking a thrashing; for every punch he landed, Johnny landed three. Finally, head reeling, his vision blurred, his knees ready to fold up and dump him on the floor, Bill pulled his pistol.

Johnny just laughed. "You won't use it. You ain't got the guts."

"Take one more step and I'll blow your ass away!" Bill warned. Johnny charged, intent on beating Bill to death. Bill stepped back and pulled the trigger. The bullet hit Johnny in the chest, killing him before his body hit the floor.

The Baltimore Sun wrote: SLAYING OF SUB SHOP OWNER LINKED TO LOVE TRIANGLE. Another head line screamed: MAN TRIES TO SEE EX-GIRLFRIEND SLAIN AFTER BREAK-IN. But the hoopla only lasted until the next big story. Then Bill was -- at least -- temporarily forgotten. The shooting was later found justifiable and recorded "Homicide. No Disposition."

* * *

Prison had added a bitter arrogance to Bill's previously easy going personality. He'd taken a man's life; lost his young wife and family. He'd turned twenty-one and matured to manhood behind steel bars and concrete walls. He wasn't a criminal before entering prison, but he was one when he emerged. Unlike before going inside, now he had nothing to lose.

It started with the insurance job on Frank Kalita's store, Stitch and Save. Arson definitely wouldn't be one of Bill's better traits. Frank had told him that Amoco white gas wouldn't leave a tell-tale lead content for the fire department's arson investigator to find. It had all seemed easy enough to Bill. Douse some gas around the walls and floor, toss a lighted book of matches in through the front door as they stepped outside and, presto, no more Stitch and Save.

Bill, along with Judy's brother, Danny, left the Bolero Club early in the morning, armed with two five gallon cans of white gas. Bill parked his black 1975 Monte Carlo two blocks away and entered the store with a key that Frank had given him. When they left, Bill was to twist the lock out of the front door to make it look like a break-in.

It took only minutes to drench the store in gasoline. The rolls of fabric and bins of zippers, lace and buttons would burn fiercely. All was ready. All they had left to do was twist the lock out of the front door, toss the lighted pack of matches inside, and run like hell. But Bill, a novice at arson, had neglected to extinguish the pilot light on the furnace. The fumes hit the flame and the gas went up in a roar. The would-be arsonists were engulfed in a churning inferno. Before they could reach the front door, Danny screamed, over and over, "Oh my God, Oh my God," as Bill pulled him from the store. The flash fire had disinigrated Bill's pants from his waist to his boots. A black leather jacket had saved his chest from serious burns. The stench of burning flesh filled the air as Bill, in agony himself, pulled Danny to the car. Driving to Red's apartment was a nightmare. Danny held his burned hands in front of his face and cried in pain: the flesh peeled off of Bill's hands and stuck to the steering wheel. Both men were badly burned and in severe pain by the time they reached Red's apartment. Red was to drop Danny off at the hospital. Before they left, Bill told Danny, "Tell the cops that you were standing on a corner and a group of black guys threw some gas on you and set you on fire." Danny assured Bill that he would tell them just that. Instead, he snitched.

Bill laid on Red's living room floor, shivering with pain.

Red walked back into the room and asked, "Are you cold?"

"Nuh-no."

"Hot?"

"Nuh-no." Red shook his head, not understanding why Bill couldn't tell him if he was cold, or hot.

At Bill's urging, Mary, Red's wife, called Judy. Since they only lived less than a block apart, it took her only minutes to arrive. With her, she brought several non-prescription Qualudes for the pain and Red sprayed Bill down with Solarcane. For awhile, Bill was numb with pain. Nothing in his life had ever hurt this bad, nor could it -- this was sheer hell, Bill thought.

Within the hour, Frank Kalita arrived at Red's. Tears filled his eyes when he saw how badly Bill's face was burned.

"You've got to go the hospital," Frank said.

"That's not happening. I would rather die than go back to prison."

"It's your choice. Either you go to the hospital or I'll call the police and turn us all in," Frank threatened.

Bill compromised by agreeing to go to his sister, Sharon, who was a registered nurse. Swathed in blankets, Red and Frank carried Bill to Frank's van.

Sharon cried at the sight of her brother. Both her and her husband Ken, who was also a registered nurse, insisted that he go to a hospital. They explained that he had lost so much body fluid that the only chance of his living was immediate hospitalization. Finally, Bill agreed to go to a hospital out of state, in West Virginia.

Judy called her ex-boyfriend, Odell Hall, and he agreed to drive Bill's car to the hospital. Wrapped in blankets, passing in and out, Bill asked that they stop at McDonalds and he ate two hamburgers and drank a Coca-cola.

"What do we do if you don't make it?" Judy asked Bill.

"Throw me in a ditch alongside the road and go home," Bill replied smiling.

He told the doctors that he'd been camping. As he poured gasoline from a can onto a fire, the can exploded, dousing him with the burning gas. Ten days later, Bill was released from the hospital and returned to Baltimore.

Upon his arrival in Baltimore, he discovered the police were looking for him. Joyce, the barmaid at the Bolero Club, hid him at her place for two weeks, nursing his wounds.

* * *

Bill's mind snapped back to the present as he pulled into the driveway. Judy was beside herself when Bill reached the apartment. "They want you for a bank robbery in Spruce Pine, North Carolina. Did you do it, fucker?"

"No, Lil Bit, I didn't rob a bank in North Carolina. Don't worry, baby. There's nothing to be worried about," Bill assured her. He didn't like to give Judy any reason to worry, especially now that she was pregnant with his child. He spent a few minutes calming her, telling her that H. Thomas Moore was just fishing.

Red called, telling Bill that Moore and another F.B.I. agent were at his front door. Bill ran out the door telling Judy that he would be right back.

Moore and Red were seated at Red's kitchen table as Bill bounced up the stairs in leaps and bounds. O'Neil was standing.

"O'Neil, stay the fuck away from my house!" Bill snapped as he entered the kitchen.

"I have a right to investigate. No, I have a duty to investigate suspected felons. And, you are most definitely a suspected felon," O'Neil replied, pointing a finger in Bill's face. Bill slapped his hand down. and said, "I don't fuck with your family - don't fuck with mine!" Red and Moore jumped up from their seats stepping between the two men.

"Now, now," Red said, with a silly grin plastered on his face. But beneath the grin you could see the fear; fear of what Bill might do if pushed too hard.

"I ought to arrest you." O'Neil said,

"If you've got a warrant, arrest me."

"Billy, Billy, Billy." Moore grinned, "At this stage, we are only asking questions."

"If you want information, dial 4-1-1. Leave my family alone," Bill said as he left the apartment.

H. Thomas Moore became Bill's worst nightmare. No doubt about it, he was after Bill's ass. He was always there, always smiling. A confident, 'I can wait as long as it takes' smile. Every so often, Bill would catch Moore following him. Once, at a stop light, Bill got out of his car and waved a friendly gesture just to let Moore know that he knew he was there. Moore just smiled confidently, the smile that Bill would never forget. In a strange, yet not uncommon way, they had a mutual respect for each other. The same kind of opposing generals -- locked in battle where neither had a decisive victory might feel for one another. All the same, Bill would be glad to leave Special Agent H. Thomas Moore behind.

* * *

"Wake up, partner," Red urged in a slow southern drawl. As the car slowed, Bill rubbed the sleep from his eyes, halfheartedly stretched, and sat up straighter in the seat. They'd found their bank.

Red had an uncanny way of sniffing out banks. It almost seemed as if he could sniff the air blindfolded and point the way to a bank. The particular lending institution in question was in a small shopping center. A Texaco gas station sat cattycorner to the bank in an L-shaped plaza. The brick building was newly constructed and well kept. A few shrubs were carefully placed in white gravel beds and, most importantly, the bank had a side entrance.

"What do you think?" Red asked hopefully, as he pulled into the black asphalt parking lot.

"I don't know. I'll check it out." Bill ran a comb through his hair, exited the car, tucked his shirt in, and walked into the bank surveying his surroundings with each step. Noting there was nothing in the immediate area that posed a threat, he entered the bank. The vault was to his left behind the teller's counter. The manager's office was windowed, the blinds open, was to his right. A couple of large desks, the chairs behind them unoccupied, filled the rest of the room. Bill figured the front entrance, facing route 301, was rarely used.

Three tellers, all women, were behind the counters. One at the drive-in window at the rear of the bank, the other two at the main counter in the front. There were two surveillance cameras, one in each corner, mounted on the wall behind the tellers counter. So far, so good, Bill thought.

"May I help you?" a teller asked politely as Bill stepped up to her window.

"Yes," reaching into his pocket, he pulled out a twenty dollar bill. "I'd like twenty one's, please."

The teller opened her drawer, removed a handful of bills, and swiftly thumbed through them, counting as they sped by at machine gun speed, She's certainly no novice, Bill thought. But, then again, neither am I. He smiled his pleasure. She handed him the bills. He thanked her and left the bank.

Red was opening another beer when Bill opened the car door and seated himself. Red started the car, took a gulp of beer, and asked. "Well, what do you think?"

"It ain't got no money in it," Bill replied flatly.

The black Monte Carlo shot back onto highway 301 heading south squealing tires, leaving a cloud of blue smoke from the burning rubber in its wake.

Red guzzled the rest of his beer, wiped his mouth with the back of his hand, belched, and snapped, "Goddamn it, you just don't want to rob no fucking bank!"

"It ain't got no money in it," Bill repeated.

"Whaddya mean, every bank's got money in it. That's what banks are for!"

"We'd be lucky if we got five grand."

"I'll tell you what. If that's all we get, you can have every fucking dime," Red swore. Bill didn't reply and the silence stretched out uncomfortably. Bill stared straight ahead and asked himself silently, "Why me, Lord. Why always fuckin'me?"

As they came upon a shopping center, Bill pointed for him to pull in. A broad grin spread across Red's face. They cruised the lot until Bill found the car that he wanted to steal, a 1968 white Ford Galaxy. It was customary to steal a car opposite the color of the one they were driving. They'd change back to their car as close to the bank as possible, then drive right back by the bank, leaving the cops searching and setting up roadblocks in the wrong direction. To be safe, they needed to be in and out of the bank in three minutes, or less. The closer to two minutes, the better. Time was their greatest enemy; the clock started the second they stepped through the door.

When Bill went to prison in 1968, he was just a desperate kid with a wife and kids, trying to survive in a hostile world he didn't understand. After his release, he made every conceivable effort to be reunited with his family. On his fifth trip to Florida in 1974, he found his ex-wife, Dayle, remarried. A burning hatred for authority grew in his heart. Better educated, skilled in the law. It was time to 'play the game'. Nothing else mattered, until Judy came into his life, then it all changed. Now he wanted a future, a life, to be like other normal men. But he wasn't a normal man. Not any longer. He was a bank robber, and he had work to do.

"Are you ready?" Red asked.

"As ready as I'll ever be," he replied. Bill checked the parking lot, then stepped out of the car carrying a gun, gloves, mask, screw-driver, and a dent puller. Using a metal door opener, he unlocked the driver's door and quickly closed it behind him. Within a minute, the car's engine came to life and Bill pulled out of the parking lot, following Red.

A half mile down the road they passed an oncoming police car. When Bill glanced in the rear-view mirror, his heart dropped down to his stomach. The cop had hit his brakes hard, turned on his overheads, and was broadside in the road making a U-turn.

Bill floored the gas pedal. Blue smoke poured from the exhaust and the six cylinders engine main bearings rattled. Adrenaline ran through his veins, making him shake uncontrollably. "Why always me, Lord?" he asked. The car had no power, no guts. A kid on a skateboard could catch him, he thought. "A turn, a fuckin' turn. Where in the hell is a turn?" he asked the old Ford. But it just farted loudly and lost a little speed.

There it was, a side street. Bill turned right, wheeled around a bend, slammed on the brakes and pulled to the side of the road, not bothering to shut the engine off or bringing the car to a complete stop. He was out of the car and running over a hill. Into an orchard he ran, through more woods, and finally slowed to a walk with his heart beating so fast that he thought it might burst. Sweat covered him and his breath came in short painful gasps. Stopping to catch his breath, he buried his gun, mask, shirt, and gloves under a rock in a small stream. If they use dogs, they won't be able to smell anything underwater beneath the rock, he thought. Bill believed a lawyer was only as good as his client; and he wasn't about to give some country bumpkin prosecutor an iron clad case. Not in this lifetime. Bill kept walking at a brisk pace, conserving energy in case he needed to run again.

"Damnit," Bill cursed, for ignoring his gut feeling about the bank. Red had goaded him into this shit. What irked him more than anything was letting Red goad him to rob a bank. He walked on, alternatively mad and hopeful. His thoughts turned to Judy. She had no way of knowing what was happening now, and he was glad of that. Then he saw in his mind's eye, Special Agent H. Thomas Moore's sardonic grin and thought, not this time Tom, not today.

The air was cool and his sweat quickly dried. Then, he was cold. Bill walked on for a few more minutes and came out of the woods behind a large building. He paused to brush of dust from his jeans and to pick the cockleberries from his socks.

The building was large, the rear at least, consisted of unpainted concrete blocks. Large trash dumpsters were carefully spaced along its length, to allow trucks to empty them. Bill walked around the side of the building until he reached the front. A large grin spread across his face as he spotted 'the bank' and an Army Navy store. He thanked whatever gods watched over thieves and walked inside the store.

From a rack of jackets at the back, at random, he selected a dark blue windbreaker that cost eighteen dollars, and he paid for it with one dollar bills, trying not to look at the cashier. Rule number one, he told himself, 'never attract attention to yourself'. Don't look anyone in the eye or strike up a conversation, unless you want to be identified later.

A black Monte Carlo drove by twice on highway 301. First south, then north. Certain it was Red, Bill walked out to the road. A two-toned blue Chevrolet Blazer pulled up next to Bill and out stepped Cowboy Joe. The tall man wore jeans, western boots, a designer western shirt, and a white cowboy hat.

"Take your hands out of your pockets, real slow," he ordered.

Rule number two, Bill thought, never walk by the fuckin' road. Standing before him, was the Sheriff for Buncombe County.

CHAPTER TWO
LUCKY NUMBER FIVE

"You got some identification on you?" The Sheriff asked.

"Sure," Bill replied. Grabbing his wallet from his back pocket, he offered his Maryland driver's license to the big man.

The Sheriff examined his I.D. for a moment, then asked, "Why are you standing next to the road?"

"My partner had a few beers, and he's an asshole when he drinks. We got into an argument and I told him to stop the car and let me out, rather than listen to his shit."

"What were you arguing about?"

"I really don't recall."

"Okay. So, you just jumped out of the car, as cold as it is..."

"That's correct. Then, because I was cold, I walked into that Army-Navy store," Bill pointed, "and I bought a windbreaker."

"So, why are you standing next to the road?" the Sheriff repeated.

"I thought that I had seen my partner drive by a couple of times and figured that he had time to simmer down."

"What kind of car is he driving?"

"A black 1975 Monte Carlo that has Maryland license plates. It's registered to me."

"You got out of your own car?" the Sheriff asked, bewildered.

"Yeah. He's really an asshole when he drinks."

"Right. Get in." the Sheriff said, pointing to the Blazer.

"Am I under arrest?" Bill asked.

"Get in!" the Sheriff repeated.

"What am I under arrest for?"

"Just get in the goddamn car," the Sheriff nearly shouted, pushing him towards the Blazer. Bill sensed that he was getting under the Sheriff's skin, and it pleased him. The man was practically bursting with arrogance and authority, and Bill was enjoying playing head games with the good old country boy.

It was a short ride to the Buncombe County Jail; only two blocks away, on top of a hill. No signs marked the way. Nothing indicated the nature of the two story brick building, and Bill's Monte Carlo sat in the parking lot.

"That's my car!" Bill announced.

The Sheriff stopped the Blazer dead in its tracks, glared at Bill with cold menacing eyes, and said, "No shit."

Acting as if he didn't understand, Bill repeated, "No, no. That's my car!" he nodded and smiled. The Sheriff's face went beet red.

He's hotter than a two pecker Billy goat, Bill thought, grinning. But he knew when to shut up. He knew when not to press his luck too far.

Once inside the jail, they walked down a long corridor lined with doors. When they reached the Sheriff's office, he steered Bill through the door. Everything was pale green. The walls, the floor. Everything was pale green except for the gray metal trash can. There were a few knick knacks on the desk; a calendar, a small globe and a picture that Bill assumed to be of the Sheriff's family. A couple diplomas hung loosely on the wall. On the opposite wall there was a poorly placed bookshelf. Altogether, it wasn't a very impressive office.

Red sat in a chair with his back to the door. "What did they get you for?" Bill asked Red.

"D.W.I. Do you know anything about a gun? The cops supposedly found one under the front seat."

"No, I don't know nothing about a gun being under the front seat of my car," Bill replied, giving Red a glare. They both knew whose gun it was. When the cops left the room, Bill told Red what he had told the Sheriff.

One of the cops returned, carrying a gray, metal toolbox.

"Do you want to open this?" the Sheriff asked.

"Where'd you get that from?" Bill asked.

"Out of your trunk," the Sheriff replied and, for the first time, grinned broadly.

"Who gave you permission to search my car?"

"Red did," the Sheriff said.

"Then it must be his," Bill chuckled.

The Sheriff was visibly upset. No longer smiling, he threatened, "Open it, or I'll get a warrant."

"You should open it, Bill." Red spoke up.

"Why should I open it. It's not mine!" Bill retorted.

The Sheriff stormed out of the office. A few minutes later, the teller from the bank peered around the door frame. Bill pretended not to recognize her, but deep inside he wanted to scream -- what kind of fuckin' line-up is this? But good sense prevailed. Then, he heard her say: "I think it's him, but I couldn't swear to it. I'm not sure." The Sheriff cursed, then obtained a search warrant. The warrant was vague, it merely authorized him to inspect the contents of the tool box and seize any illegal items.

In 1968 Bill had learned how to look for loopholes in the law, how to research, how to draft motions and writs, and how to use the law to his advantage, as opposed to having it used against him. The search and seizure fell far below the standards required by law.

The Sheriff pried the lock open with a large screwdriver and said, "Well now, what do we have here?" With a flip of his hand, the box sprang open. The contents were itemized. Procedure was, more than likely, about the extent of the lawman's capability and understanding. Bill ruefully relished the thought, H. Thomas Moore would not be proud of him. The items seized were:

1. Ten (10).357 Magnum shells

2. Assorted Tools

3. One (1) Glass cutter

4. One quarter (1) ounce of marijuana in plastic baggy.

Red had been sitting quietly in a chair, until now. He shouted, "I ain't taking no drug rap!"

Bill glared at him, wondering if that was an act, or if he really was that stupid. The marijuana was the least of their worries. The Sheriff read Bill and Red their Miranda warnings.

"What are we being charged with?" Bill asked.

I'm not sure. I'll leave that up to the prosecutor. But, for starters, I'm guessing for carrying a concealed weapon, possession of marijuana, and possession of criminal tools."

The Sheriff escorted them to holding cells, slamming the steel barred door behind them. With the twist of a key they were locked away and it seemed, forgotten. There was a row of cells to chose from and wall to wall bars provided an open area for visitation. Each cell was furnished with a stainless steel combination sink and toilet along with a concrete bed. Against the bars there was a metal table with an attached bench.

Red paced back and forth, nervous and upset. They talked openly and shared the series of events that led to their arrest. The police car was after Red, not as Bill had thought, him. Someone at the bank was suspicious and Red's driving recklessly, prompted them to call the police with the description of the car; a black Monte Carlo with Maryland license plates. That was it, the police had no case whatsoever.

Red went to one of the cells and laid down on the concrete bunk. Bill, alone with his thoughts, wondered if he'd ever see his friends again.

Frank Kalita, one of Bill's very best friends was a happily married man when they'd met. An honest, hard working, bread winner with aspirations beyond his limits. Frank was one of those men who wanted to exercise control in every aspect of life; family matters, business, and even friendships. He dressed casually but he was always neat in appearance, and he took great pleasure in puffing on large stinking cigars which he never inhaled. His round face was saved plainless by a broken nose, adding character. While camping in Camp Lake Sebago, Maine, over an open fire, with several drinks warming his belly, Bill confided to Frank his criminal activities. He desperately wanted to rob a bank with Bill. To that end, although not a drinker, he began to hang around the Bolero Club when they returned to Baltimore. Frank was attracted to the glitter and notoriety of bank robbery. But you wouldn't be so hot to rob banks if you'd ever been through this before, Bill thought. And what would you do, Frank my man, if a man like Special Agent H. Thomas Moore was on your ass the way he's on mine? Could you handle that, Frank? I don't think so. I don't think you'd be able to handle knowing that Moore was trying to lock you up for the rest of your fuckin' life.

About three hours later, the Sheriff gave Bill and Red a copy of the charges against them.

"Damn, I don't believe this. Conspiracy to commit bank robbery, felony possession of a handgun, possession of marijuana, and possession of criminal tools. They also charged you with D.W.I." Bill told Red.

They were immediately arraigned and bail was set at fifteen thousand dollars, ten percent. Bill was pleased with the bail, he'd expected it to be much higher.

Over the years, Bill had endured many disappointments and he'd learned how to eliminate most of them; hope for the best but anticipate the worst. If he looked for something bad to happen, he couldn't be disappointed when it did.

* * *

The girls were attending to their chores when the phone rang. Mary, Red's wife, was hanging clothes in the closet. Judy had a roast in the oven and was trying to decide what to serve with it.

"I'll get it," Mary yelled out, as she walked to the phone.

"This is the A-T and T Operator, will you accept a collect call from Bill Hooker?"

"Yes, I will," Mary replied. "Where are you?" Mary asked Bill.

"In jail."

"Oh, no you're not. Now, where are you?"

"I'm in the Buncombe County jail in North Carolina."

"For what?" she asked dubiously, still not sure Bill was being truthful. Briefly, Bill explained the charges, and Mary went from happy to tearful in time it took for him to finish. She sobbed, broken hearted at the prospect of Red and Bill being taken from them.

"Jesus, Mary. Will you stop that," Bill said, remorseful because he'd once again caused someone he cared for pain. Damn, a woman can make a man feel lower than whale shit on the ocean floor, without saying a fucking word, Bill ruefully mused. They just turn on their god given waterworks to make men miserable.

"Mary, listen carefully. Call Earl Murphy, and tell him that we need a lawyer and fifteen hundred dollars apiece to make bond. Okay, can you do that?"

"Yuh-yuh-yes. I'll cuh-call him ruh-right now," she sobbed. "I just want you guys to come home."

* * *

Bing, bong. Click, click... the metal ball bounced from bumper to bumper, set to life at the touch of a flipper. Earl was playing the pinball machine gambling with the Budweiser delivery man when Joyce called him to the phone. When she heard Mary crying, she immediately knew that something was wrong.

"Who is it?" the big Irishman man asked gruffly. He was totally absorbed in the game and didn't want to be bothered.

"It's Mary. And, she's crying."

It wasn't like Mary to cry, and Earl knew that. He abandoned the pinball machine and went quickly to the phone.

"Hello?"

"Earl, this is Mary. Red and Bill are in jail. Bill told me to call you," she began, going on to explain what was needed.

"Okay, honey. I'll take care of it. Stop crying, everything will be fine," he assured her before hanging up.

Joyce, unable to stand the suspense asked, "What's wrong? Are they okay?" She didn't have to elaborate on who 'they' were. Among their friends, it was a badly kept but seldom mentioned secret that Bill and Red were bank robbers.

"They're in jail," Earl replied, with a sigh of regret.

A tear came to Joyce's eye. The people closest to Bill and Red loved them dearly. Their ongoing and flamboyant personalities captured all of their hearts. Earl picked up the phone and started making calls.

Within an hour, an attorney made an appearance at the Buncombe County jail. He was the best in town and known to be a straight shooter. A family man with values and no love for criminals. But being an honest and ethical lawyer, he would represent them to the best of his ability.

"Okay, before we get to what happened today, I need to know if either of you robbed a bank in Bristol, Tennssee, or Spruce Pine, North Carloina?

"Why are you asking?" Bill wanted to know, questioning the man standing before him. Bill was unimpressed with his casual attire of brown Hagger slacks and a white pullover sweater. He was tall, thin, with well groomed brown hair. Bill guessed he was in his early thirties.

"They want to put you in a line-up. If you fight it, it's going to drag on for weeks. If you agree, they will hold it immediately."

Bill knew the line-up was inevitable, so they agreed to appear in one right away.

It was a long and sleepless night. There was no clock, no window, nothing by which to tell time. Bill closed his eyes, trying to sleep, but when he heard a shuffling noise, he opened them again to find Red on his hands and knees, crawling around on the floor.

"What the hell are you doing?" Bill asked.

"I lost my goddamn handcuff key," Red whispered.

Bill chuckled. Every time they left Baltimore to rob a bank, Red took a handcuff with him. When he was arrested, he had popped the key into his mouth, concealing it.

Red was proud of the fact that he'd once been in a magazine, True Detective, for 'a daring escape' from Virginia state prison. The writer had speculated that it must have taken months and thousands of razor blades to cut through the manacle that chained him to the bed. Bill seriously doubted the story was true. More than likely, Red had used a hacksaw blade to make good on his escape. But Red definitely saw himself as 'an escape artist'. Hence, the handcuff key.

Bill rolled over trying to ignore the cold concrete bunk penetrating his clothing. He reminisced about his younger days when he was in the Baltimore City jail for the shooting of Johnny Campbell, and the song he'd wrote and sang - over and over.

> I ain't got a towel
> I ain't got a sheet,
> Get three meals a day
> and none fit to eat.
> Lose a little weight
> and I worry a lot,
> can't get to sleep
> on this worn out little cot.
> Walk around my cell
> Six square feet,
> Sitting on the floor
> in the middle of the heat,
> Didn't do wrong
> you'd have done the same.,
> If'n my place,
> then you would be to blame.

On Saturday morning, at nine a.m. Bill's bond money was sent bank to bank by Earl Murphy, as suggested by the attorney. But the man hadn't considered that most banks are closed by noon on Saturdays, and the transaction wasn't completed in time for Bill to be released. He would have to wait until Monday. Mary sent Red's bond via Western Union, so he stood in a line-up by himself on Saturday.

Two women tellers from the bank in Spruce Pine, North Carolina viewed and failed to identify him. Red's bond was posted and he was released. Bill released his car to Red, planning to fly home to West Virginia on Monday. The partners shook hands, and Red departed, leaving Bill alone with his thoughts.

When Bill called home Sunday, Mary answered, sobbing. "What's wrong?" Bill asked.

"Red's in jail, and this time he ain't got no bond," she cried.

"What? What happened?"

"He wasn't home fifteen minutes before the F.B.I... them rotten no good bastards, kicked in the door. They had a search warrant and were looking for one hundred thousand dollars in thousand dollar wrappers and machine guns…"

Bill interrputed, asking, "What did they charge Red with?"

"I don't know, but he ain't got no bond." Mary was a pure breed hillbilly, born and raised in the hills of West Virginia. She lacked a good education, but a sweeter woman would be hard to find.

"Did they take anything from the trailer?"

"Yeah, they got about fifty cartons of cigarettes and they took all of the meat from the freezer." She went on to tell Bill that Red was being held in the Pineville County jail. He had a lawyer, and she was going to see him in the morning.

"Do you want me to tell him anything?" Mary asked.

"Yeah, tell him to keep his mouth shut."

* * *

Bill's uncle W.A. once told him that nothing could be so good that it couldn't be better. And, nothing could ever be so bad that it couldn't be worse. He was beginning to understand what that meant.

Monday morning, at ten o'clock the attorney visited. His bond money had been transferred and everything was in motion, the line-up was scheduled for eleven.

"One more thing," the lawyer said. "There's going to be some eye-witnesses from the robbery in Bristol, Tennessee. Any problems with that? Is there anything that I need to be made aware of?"

"No. But why are there more eye-witnesses for me than there were at Red's line-up?"

"They had more time in which to put your line-up together," the attorney answered earnestly.

"How many eye-witnesses are going to be there?"

"Five. Three from the bank in Spruce Pine, and two from Bristol." The lawyer pulled no punches, spelling everything out clearly. Bill paced the floor, wondering who would be there from Bristol? It could be a number of people; the man he grabbed at the door and forced back into the bank or, the woman who blocked their getaway car with hers. Jesus, who would have ever thought of that happening? What are the chances of something like that ever happening again? Bill's mind ran rampant, thinking, starting from the beginning. They'd left Baltimore early in the morning on 'a fishing trip'. Bill referred to a bank robbery as 'fishing in a federal reserve'. In North Carolina, they had stopped at a gun store, owned by a friend of Bill's, and purchased a variety of guns; two Charter Arms .44 Bulldogs, two Charter Arms snub nosed .38's, and one seven shot .22 automatic. After a week of aimless wandering, they crossed from Virginia to Tennessee entering Bristol at one o'clock in the afternoon. They were running low on funds and getting desperate. They picked a bank, but it wasn't a chosen one (one cased in advanced). But when desperate, professional judgment plays a very small role in deciding whether or not to rob a particular bank.

From a local shopping center, Bill stole a blue 1965 Ford Galaxy, then followed Red as he parked the dark green 1970 Pontiac GTO behind an abandoned gas station. The GTO had a lime green vinyl top with lime green leather interior. It was what Bill called 'a sleeper' because at first glance it looked like Grandma's car. Bill's friend, Pete Grimes, owned a car lot on Fort Smallwood road in Pasadena, Maryland. Bill had purchased the vehicle from Pete to be used as 'a getaway car'. The only disturbing thing was the white temporary tag taped in the back window.

At the bank, Bill backed into a parking space and looked at Red questionably.

"You ready?" Red asked.

"Ready as I'll ever be," Bill grinned.

They walked swiftly across the parking lot. Nearing the door, it sprang open and a father and son emerged from the bank. Bill yanked down his mask while seizing the man's elbow.

"Back inside," he ordered. The man meekly complied, his son following close on his heels.

As they entered the bank, Bill shouted, "You know what this is!"

Red leaped over the counter, shopping bag in hand, screaming, "Get it up! Get it up! It better be ready when I get there! "

Terrified bank tellers stacked money on top of the counter in large, untidy piles, Red was moving too slow to suit Bill.

"Move, move, move," he urged, feeling the weight of time pressing down on them with every second they spent inside the bank.

Red disappeared from sight, reappearing moments later with the brown paper shopping bag brimming with bundles of cash, leaving piles of money stacked on top of the counter. He came from behind the counter using the teller's door, and they ran from the bank. As they crossed the parking lot bundles of money fell from the bag and Red stopped to pick them up. No sooner than they jumped into the car and Bill put the car in gear, a woman pulled up and stopped in front of them, blocking them in. Bill honked the horn, twice. She looked at them, and moved. The back bumper of the Ford missed her car by less than an inch as Bill sped out of the lot.

When they realized they could see the bank from where their getaway car was parked, it was too late to worry about it. They switched cars, made a U-turn in front of the bank, and headed for the state line. Police cruisers were coming over the median, passing them, and the sirens in the distance were closing in fast. Bill was on the floorboard in the front seat. Red hung an arm out the window, looked at Bill and yelled, "Get down! You're not down far enough!" With every second Bill wished that Red would turn down a side street. After passing several streets, Bill yelled, "Get off the fucking highway!"

Finally, Red pulled into a shopping Mall, and parked. They split up, both going in opposite directions. First, Bill went into a grocery store and purchased a box of large dark green plastic trash bags. Returning to the GTO, he put the money and incriminating evidence in two trash bags doubling their strength. Then, he placed the bag in a dumpster alongside of side of the shopping center, and spent the next two hours killing time, never venturing far from the dumpster. He walked into a barbershop, got a haircut, then walked to the front of the shopping center, to a Captain Long

John Silver's restaurant, where he ordered a plate of fish and chips with a Coca-cola. One police car after another flew up and down the highway, while umarked car's patrolled the shopping center's parking lot, leaving Bill without an appetite.

After a couple of hours, Bill and Red met at the car. They decided to take a dry run to the state line. When that went well, they picked up the trash bag and drove from the area. As they entered Virginia, Bill began counting the miles. Ten, twenty, fifty, a hundred. Two hundred miles away from the robbery, they stopped and rented a motel room. As Red showered, Bill counted the money out loud. "Twenty thousand, forty thousand, sixty thousand. Red flew out of the shower, grinning from ear to ear, as Bill continued counting, stopping at one hundred and four thousand dollars.

"Not too shabby for two minutes work," Bill said, sharing Red's grin.

* * *

The attorney entered the room and asked, "Are you ready?"

"I guess so," Bill replied.

The attorney looked at Bill's waist and asked, "Did you wear that belt..." Dismissing the question, he suggested, "Trade belts with me."

Bill was placed in a line-up with five other men. After drawing numbers, he was number five. He was further instructed to read from a card, 'Merry Christmas' and 'Have a nice day'. He had forgotten that he told everyone in the bank in Bristol "to have a nice day" as they ran out the door. His face had been covered with a nylon stocking distorting his features, but that was of little comfort as he stood under the harsh glare of the overhead lights. Spruce Pine was his first bank robbery. He robbed the Pepsi-cola employee as he was making a deposit, then bid everyone a "Merry Christmas" as they ran from the bank. His throat was dry and his stomach full of butterflies as, one by one, the eyewitnesses were led into the room on the other side of the two-way mirror. The six men in the line-up took turns stepping forward and reading from the card. Bill was asked to read the card a second time, louder this time.

While the attorney and the prosecutor questioned the eyewitnesses, Bill was taken back to the cellblock to wait, for what seemed like an eternity.

Finally, the door opened and his attorney said, "You're out of here just as soon as the bondsman arrives. Come by my office," he smiled, giving Bill directions.

Bill breathed a sigh of relief. How good it was going to feel to be free. When he was released, he walked to the attorney's office, the fresh air just felt too good not to.

"It was a close call," the attorney began, "Two people picked you, but they weren't sure enough to make a positive I.D. Two others agreed the robber had the appearance of number five and the voice of number two. There was an employee of Pepsi-Cola who was robbed in the Spruce bank while making a deposit. He picked a Deputy Sheriff and was willing to swear to the identification in court."

Handing Bill his next court appearance, the attorney added, "Out of the three banks in town, you picked the worst apple on the tree."

Bill took a cab to the airport. Earl Murphy sent an extra thousand dollars, along with the bond money.

Fifteen minutes later, Bill arrived at the Asheville City airport. After paying the taxi driver, he stepped through the large glass double doors leading to the terminal. As he stepped inside the doors, he was surrounded by detectives in plain clothes.

"Do you have any identification?" a detective asked.

"Who are you looking for?"

"You!" the detective grinned, reading a description of the clothes he was wearing.

Bill was arrested on a felony warrant issued by the prosecutor in Pineville, West Virginia.

The charge -- Breaking and Entering. Here we go again…

CHAPTER THREE
VEGAS ON MY MIND

Arrested at the airport, Bill was taken to the Asheville City jail, booked, and housed on the seventh floor, pending extradition to West Virginia. The authorities told him two things, One, that it would be in his best interest to sign a waiver of his right to a hearing. And two, there would be no bond set for a warrant of extradition.

Bill was somewhat familiar with the requirements of extradition. (1) Establish that a felony had been committed, and (2) establish the identity of the person named on the warrant. Concerned that once he signed the waiver, the authorities could leave him sit in the Asheville City jail for up to six months. And, with the real possibility of that happening, he refused to sign the waiver.

When he was permitted a phone call, Bill called the trailer, and told Judy and Mary what had happened. They weren't at all surprised.

Alone with his thoughts, he wondered how it was that he was being charged when the stolen merchandise came from Red Miller's trailer. Did he snitch? Bill dismissed the thought, the warrant had been issued.

From the prison library, Bill ordered the Prisoner's Self-Help Litigation Manual. From that he found cases, ordered those, and began his research - coming up with nothing of value. Pertaining to the extradition warrant, he found nothing at all to argue. It was on solid ground, air tight.

Among the prisoners in the jail, there was a young Indian boy who had been extradited back from Canada for fishing in a federal reserve. What a waste of taxpayers money, Bill mused. But it was fortunate for Bill the government had gone to that expense. One day, while in conversation, the Indian boy haphazardly mentioned that the airport was not on city land, that it was county property.

"Are you sure of that?" Bill asked, with a broad grin.

"Sure, I'm sure. The reservation sits right next to the airport."

Bill questioned some of the other prisoners, just to be certain. The last thing he wanted to do was file a Writ of Habeas Corpus that had no merit.

If deemed frivilous, the Writ would be dismissed.

Two days later, Bill's Writ of Habeas Corpus was presented to the court:

IN THE CIRCUIT COURT OF COMMON PLEAS
CITY OF ASHEVILLE,-ASHEVILLE, NORTH CARLOINA
CIVIL CASE_____
WILLIAM DANIEL HOOKER
VS
STATE OF NORTH CAROLINA
This is a demand for the issuance of a Writ of Habeas Corpus
pursuant to Title 28 USC Section 2254 and North Carolina revised
statute...
Now comes William Daniel Hooker, herein after Petitioner.
COMPLAINT
Petitioner deposes and says that he is a prisoner of the
City of Asheville, Asheville, North Carolina.
Petitioner contends that he is being held illegally.
Petitioner verily claims he is entitled to redress:
1) On July 10, 1074 Petitioner was arrested by the Asheville
City Police at the Asheville County airport.
2) The City authorities have no priority interest and lack
proper jurisdiction.
3) The City airport is on 'county' property, thereby making
the arrest and subsequent detention illegal under the color of
both federal and state laws.
4) Petitioner respectfully moves the court for a hearing
on the merits presented and/or his immediate release.
Respectfully Submitted,
William Daniel Hooker
Prose

Accompanying the Writ, Bill filed a Pauper's Oath asking the court to allow him to proceed without paying fees or courts cost. He also filed a separate motion requesting counsel be appointed.

The judge granted Bill's motion, appointed counsel, and expedited the hearing.

Bill's court appointed attorney's first question was, what was his reason for filing the Writ?

Bill was confident that, by law, he had a winning Writ. Of course, all the Asheville City police would do was release and re-arrest him the moment he stepped out of the courthouse. It wasn't likely that he would be awarded any money for false arrest should he file a civil case. Besides, all he hoped to accomplish was to force West Virginia to pick him up before the hearing. "I will not sign the waiver a second time," he told the attorney. If he won the hearing, it would void the extradition warrant.

It was obvious, at least to Bill, that the feds particularly Special Agent H. Thomas Moore didn't want him out of jail. The attorney found the situation humorous, and further agreed one hundred percent with Bill's plan.

Two days before the hearing, two policemen picked Bill up and transported him back to Pineville, West Virginia by car. They were happy to get the overtime, and for Bill, it was a welcome ride.

"By the way, what am I being charged with?"

"Breaking and entering, and receiving and concealing stolen property," the younger cop answered.

"Hooker, you're the most sought after person we've seen in awhile." the older cop added.

"Yeah, I've certainly got a lot of friends," Bill responded sarcastically. "Were you there when the trailer was searched?"

"Sure was," the driver replied, smiling at Bill in the rearview mirror.

"How about you?" Bill asked the other cop.

"Yep. And so were the F.B.I., A.T.F. Damn, just about everybody was there for the party."

"How about Red, did he get out of jail yet?"

"Don't know for sure. He had a bond hearing set for yesterday, but I don't know what happened," the driver said.

"I assume that, being such an important person, you guys were told to feed me. Probably steak and ale?"

"Oh yeah. Butch Goode said V.I.P. treatment all the way," the younger cop chuckled.

"Who's Butch Goode?"

"The state prosecutor."

"Well, at least he knows how to treat an important person," Bill grinned.

"Yeah," the driver replied, "We were up late washing and waxing the car. Can't you tell?"

"I was expecting a Limo." Bill sarcastically replied. The police car was dirty, the windows streaked. Dust covered the back seat, except for where Bill sat, and trash littered the floor board.

"Can I smoke?" Bill asked.

The cops looked at each other, then the driver answered. "Sure, go ahead. But don't get any ashes on the floor," he snickered.

"I'll be real careful about that," Bill replied, grinning.

It was a beautiful day, one of many that Bill was not fully able to enjoy. His heart yearned to be with Judy. But now, with even greater appreciation, he lived with his memories. He thought about Las Vegas, the glamour, the lights, and the abundance of beautiful women.

* * *

After the robbery in Bristol, they divided the money in the motel room, then Bill dropped Red off at his apartment and drove to Pete Grimes' home at 202 Georgia avenue in Glen Burnie. He whistled a cheerful tune as he navigated the suburban streets. It was barely after noon when he parked, rushed up the steps leading to the red brick rowhouse, and knocked on the door. Mike Newman was there. He was Eddie O'Neil's partner, and they were professional gamblers. Mike also ran a legitimate laundry business in Aberdean, Maryland. Eddie, on the other hand, never made an honest dollar in his life. He was a gambler, a card shark, a gigilo, a pool huster, and a jack of all trades. It was Eddie who introduced Bill to the Ace pick and how to rip off laundromats. Pick one lock line on a washer or dryer, then walk down the line opening the coin boxes. On the average, Bill made three hundred dollars on a laundry-mat, and he hit ten per night traveling from Maine to Florida. It was a good hustle.

Eddie and Mike ran a poker game inside a pool hall in Dundalk. They used infrared ink, infrared contact lenses, premarked decks of cards, and cold decks. But Eddie could also stack a deck as he shuffled.

Mike said Eddie was in Las Vegas, that he was there to get married.

"I don't fuckin' believe it," Bill laughed.

Seeing Bill's bag of money, Mike asked. "Would you like to attend the wedding? I think that I can get us a free trip."

"It won't cost us anything?" Bill asked.

Mike explained his plan. Casinos, especially the big ones, offered junkets to gamblers. For the pros, they would pay all expenses including airfare, lodging, and room service.

"If we post ten thousand dollars apiece to play, I'm pretty sure that one of the casinos will agree to pay for all of our expenses."

After a few calls, Ceaser's Palace agreed to underwrite the trip.

"Here's the scam. When we gamble at the dice table, I'll place a wager opposite your bet. One of us will win whatever the other loses, and we will get a free vacation. Plus, you will be laundering your money. Laundering money is exchanging money that might be marked for new currency."

Pete loaned Bill a travel bag and he quickly packed it with cash. Dressed in blue jeans and a tee-shirt Bill headed for the airport with his friend, Mike.

When the female security guard opened Bill's bag she could not believe her eyes. After a second inspection, she smiled. Heading for Las Vegas, she was convinced that Bill was a big time gambler.

Once airborne, they laughed, drank champagne, and played with the stewardesses. If either man had a care in the world, it wasn't evident in their behavior.

On their final approach to McCarren International airport, Bill gazed out the window of the DC-10, fully enjoying the adventure. The neon city was lit up like a Christmas tree, visible from fifty miles away.

After landing, Bill and Mike took a taxi to Ceaser's Palace. The full range of the spectrum was represented in the bright lights that flashed and glittered on the facade of casinos. The city was alive in a way few American cities are; the streets were packed with stretch limousines, Ferraris, Porches, Mercedes Benzes, and every expensive exotic car imaginable. The sidewalks were filled with ladies and gentlemen dressed to the tens, reminding Bill of tropical fish gliding through the water.

"The lower class must drive Caddies," Bill chuckled, more to himself.

"Yeah, it sure doesn't seem as though anyone is hurting for cash in this town," Mike smiled, looking out the window.

The sign flashed 'Ceaser's Palace'. Below that, in large black letter's read 'Tom Jones, tonight only'. Bill's head was spinning like a top, around and around. Everywhere he looked, there were beautiful women. His heart fluttered. He was sure that he was in love, he just wasn't sure with which one of the beautiful ladies.

Dressed in blue jeans and a yellow tee-shirt, sporting white tennis shoes, Bill's appearance left much to be desired. He stuck out like a sore thumb, but no one seemed to mind.

The female desk clerk was well mannered when Bill confirmed the reservations.

"Yes Sir, Mr. Hooker. You are in room 522 and 523." Mister? Mr. Hooker? Bill's head swelled with pride. Yes, indeedy, he thought. This must be the good life.

Bill passed the twenty thousand dollars to the clerk, and she smiled, passing him the room keys and vouchers.

"Ron," she turned to the bellhop. "Would you please show Mr. Hooker and Mr. Newman to their rooms?"

"That's okay," Mike intervened, adding, "We traveled light, no luggage."

"Well then, I hope that you find everything satisfactory. If not, please call the front desk. Ceaser's Palace will be featuring Evil Kenevil's jump over Snake River Canyon on closed circuit tv tomorrow afternoon. It's an exclusive viewing, no other casino will be offering it." They were welcomed, catered to, and treated like kings. Bill opened the door to his room, stopping dead in his tracks.

"Unfucking believable!" Bill said, as he gazed at the opulent digs. "Just unfucking believable." The blue carpet was soft, and plush. The walls were blue with gold spirals. One wall was mirrored, and a crystal chandelier, aglow and sparkling, hung above a king sized bed. The bathroom was lime green, richly enhanced by soft blue lights and gold trim. The bathtub/shower was also a combination Jacuzzi/steam bath, enclosed by mirrored doors. The toilet seat was soft, and a telephone was thoughtfully installed next to it.

Bill opened another door and, breathlessly, stared at yet another opulent room. It was much larger, two levels, with full length windows on the upper level overlooking the fountains, and allowing the bright Nevada sun to shine in. There was a dining table on the upper level, and in the middle of the table, sat an enormous bowl of fresh fruit. The couches and chairs on the lower level were first class, with coordinated coffee and end tables.

A fully stocked bar occupied the back wall, and another door opened to Mike's room. Bill made himself a drink, then called Jean.

"You'll never guess where I am?" he teased her.

"I don't give a fuck where you are, probably in jail."

"Nope, guess again."

"I really don't give a shit," she retorted haughtily.

"Okay, I'm at Ceaser's Palace in Las Vegas."

"Are you?" She asked, excitedly. "Are you really?"

"Yes, I am."

"That's not fair. You know that's my dream. Can I fly out and join you?"

"Not this time. I'm only here for a few days. Mike and I flew out for Eddie's wedding."

"Asshole!" Jean spat, slamming the receiver down hard in its cradle.

At the blackjack table, Bill quickly won six thousand dollars. He stopped to shop in a men's apparel store, purchasing two suits, two pair of dress shoes, shirts, socks, underwear, and a few other items.

Returning to his room, he showered, shaved, dressed in newly purchased clothes, and ordered room service. A t-bone steak, baked potato, salad, and a bottle of wine. Reading the menu, he saw the Ceaser's salad, the fruit salad on the table, cost one hundred dollars. Feeling like a king, he sat down at the table, looked out over the fountain, and enjoyed his dinner.

Twenty minutes later, Mike was at the door. "C-mon, big spender. It's time to gamble."

Slowly, Bill closed off the blackjack table by placing bets at each seat when a less unfortunate player left. The pit boss changed dealers repeatedly, to no avail. Bill was on a roll.

The pit boss and cameras watched closely, trying to catch Bill cheating or counting cards.

Bill played the odds. If the dealer's card was showing was a six or less, he wouldn't hit twelve and risk busting. And, he doubled his wager when his hand equaled ten or eleven.

Bill's system, based on the odds and judgment, still depended on a lot on luck.

The pit boss offered Bill free tickets to the show of his choice, and scantily clad cocktail waitresses offered him free drinks, cigarettes, and idle conversation in an attempt to distract him from playing. Still, Bill continued to win.

* * *

When Eddie O'Neil was married at the White Chapel, Bill and Mike bought several bottles of champagne, two bags of white rice, rented a white stretch Limo. Pleasantly surprised, there were warm embraces, slaps on the back, and firm handshakes. Eddie sported a tuxedo. His bride to be wore a long white wedding dress with a lot of lace, and a matching veil. The wedding was short, but charming. And Bill and Mike showered the newlyweds with rice as they emerged from the chapel. After seeing Eddie and his bride off on their honeymoon, Bill and Mike headed back to Ceaser's.

Bill walked through the casino, in search of a poker table, stopping at the Showboat Club for a drink. He asked the bartender where he could find a poker game?

"All of the poker games were on the outskirts of the city in smaller casinos," the bartender replied.

Leaving a generous tip, Bill decided to try his luck at the dice table.

"Place your bets, ladies and gentlemen," the bowtied croupier called out. The croupier was dressed in the standard uniform of black pants, a white shirt, and a black bowtie. Bill watched the play carefully, but after a few minutes he placed a bet. Wedging his way into the crowded table, he claimed his territory. First, he bet heavily on the numbers six and eight. Those numbers could be rolled three different ways. The odds were in his favor. Those numbers were more likely to be rolled before the number seven which is called 'craps' because you lose.

He might have done okay, had he stayed with his plan. But he did what the majority of people do when they have a gambling addiction, he became 'a high roller'. Despite the odds, he covered the field, betting on all of the numbers. On every roll of the dice, he would either lose big, or win a little. When he lost, he would double the bet. Theory overcame logic. Logic was reality. By the end of the weekend, Bill lost thirty-one thousand dollars.

* * *

"Pete, send cash," Bill sighed.

"You're kidding me? You're broke?" Pete asked in astonishment.

"Yeah. I need some money."

"You're nuts!" Although it was Bill's money, Pete only agreed to send one thousand dollars. Gun shy, Bill avoided the casino and stayed in his room.

Mike ordered a couple of Call girls, as if he was ordering a pizza. "And, if they don't meet my approval, I'm sending them back," he told the person on the other end of the line.

Forty-five minutes later, there was a knock on the door, and two of the most beautiful women Bill had ever seen were standing in the doorway. One was a stunning blonde, the other a Korean girl with jet black hair that fell to her waist.

After agreeing on a price of three hundred dollars each, Bill and Mike would have sex with one of the girl's, then switch the girl for the other. As Bill left the bar with the blonde, the other girl was giving Mike a blow job while he laid on the couch reading a newspaper.

For the first time since arriving in Las Vegas, Bill crawled into the huge king sized bed. With very little foreplay and no conversation, the blonde placed her lips around his cock and began sucking. She was trying to bring him to a quick orgasm, and Bill couldn't see his spending three hundred dollars for a blow job.

"Whoa, slow down Sugar. You're not getting off that easy," Bill said, guiding her to a squatting position, her pussy over his shaft. Slowly, she eased her pussy down on him. And he couldn't believe how tight her snatch was. When she began contracting and relaxing her pussy muscles, it drove Bill wild. He quickly came to an orgasm, shooting his load deep into her.

When Bill commented on her performance, the Call girl said that it was just a matter of exercising vaginal muscles. Then, she went to the bathroom. freshened up, and the two men switched girls.

The little black hair Korean beauty spoke broken English, and she moaned saying, "Fuck me, baby...oh, yes... fuck me, baby... Oh, it feels so good," and terribly faked having an orgasm. Finally, when Bill couldn't stand her act any longer, he told her to shut the fuck up.

"But," she said in her defense, "Most American men like that."

"Darling, if you put all of that energy into screwing, I'd like you a lot better."

"Can we have a tip?" One of the girls asked as they were walking out the door.

"Don't cross the street without looking both ways," Mike said.

"Sorry, honey. I dropped more than thirty grand this weekend." Bill offered, when the girl looked in his direction for a tip.

"Honey, how do you think they keep building these highrises?" the blonde said with a smile.

"Yeah. They're going to add another wing onto Ceaser's and call it the Hooker wing," Bill chuckled.

The phone rang, and Bill answered it.

The female clerk at the front desk began, "Will you be checking out before noon? If so, please stop by the front desk and pay your phone bill."

"I thought that was included," Bill retorted, wondering what happened to the 'sir' and 'Mr. Hooker'.

"Your package only included lodging, meals, and air-fare." Las Vegas. You gotta love the place. Yeah, right!

CHAPTER FOUR
COUNTRY JUSTICE

Pineville, West Virginia. As Bill walked down the courthouse steps escorted by two Deputy Sheriffs, a photographer snapped his picture, The evening newspaper headlines read: BANK ROBBERY SUSPECT NETTED IN LOCAL INVESTIGATION.

Bill tossed the newspaper to the corner of his cell, disgusted with himself, the media, and the world in general. People believe this shit, he thought. In today's day and age, society thrives on other people's misery. And when it's in bold print on the front of a newspaper it somehow becomes the truth.

"Guilty until proven innocent," he mumbled, discontented. Butch Goode was the big man in town, the king of the roost.

Not only was he a partner in a prominent law firm, he was the state's prosecutor. The best way to describe him would be to say that he was Telly Savalas, 'Kojak' in real life. Bald, solidly built, compact. His bald pate was accented by gold frame eye-glasses. There was always a sucker protruding from his mouth, which he replenished from a jar filled with tasty suckers sitting on top of his mahogany desk.

"Hooker," he began, "I've got your ass cold." He held a sucker in one hand, "But," he continued, cocking his head thoughtfully, "I'm not really interested in you."

Talk about being skeptical. Sitting before him was the man who sent two cops all the way to Kentucky to extradite him; and he was now telling Bill he wasn't interested in him.

"Oh, I've got you." he said assuredly, reaching in a desk drawer, he pulled out a manila folder and tossed it on top of the desk. "Have no doubt about that." In the folder Bill soon discovered seven signed statements.

"Read those," Butch Goode offered. He stood, walked to the window of his office and gazed over the sleepy town. "I don't want you to doubt me. In those statements Mary's parents spoke at some length about what a nice guy you are. They said that what you gave 'em was out of the goodness of your heart. All kinds of meat, groceries, cigarettes, and money."

"Stupid hillbillies," Bill mumbled, more to himself.

"What's that?" Butch Goode grinned.

"Nothing."

"Yeah. Well, anyway. Mary said the room the stuff was found in was your bedroom. Your good buddy Red backed her up on that, and said he's willing to testify to it."

"He's full of shit!" Bill snapped.

"Could be. But word is he's trying to cut himself a sweet deal on the bank job in North Carolina."

"So, why are you telling me all this?"

"I'm not sure. But everybody that I've talked to has told me what a nice guy you are. I guess I'm just curious."

"Curious about what?"

"About why you broke into my I.G.A. store, stole everything in sight, then gave most of it away. Would you care to make a statement?"

"I don't give statements," Bill replied flatly.

"That's what I hear, but I want one all the same."

"If I give you a statement, then what?"

"I haven't decided. One thing for sure," he said with a gleam in his eye, "I'll frame it and hang it right there!" He pointed to a bare spot on the wall.

"That doesn't sound like very much incentive for me to tell on myself," Bill said dryly.

"Okay. How 'bout this. I won't send you to prison. If you do any time, it will be in my county jail."

"Can I think this over?"

"Sure, take all the time you want. I'll be more than happy to provide you with one of my jail cells, free of charge. While you're there, ask the other prisoner's if I'm a man of my word."

* * *

Back in his cell, as Bill thought of it, his dungeon. With little to do but stare at the old cracked stone walls, his mind wandered to Baltimore, to Las Vegas, and finally, to his hometown in Florida. He thought of Judy and their unborn child.

She was probably still unpacking boxes at their new trailer, which they shared with Red and Mary. This was to be their retirement. West Virginia was certainly a beautiful place. The scenery, the clear blue skies, the mountains, and the fresh air.

He wondered if he was ready to leave the hustle and bustle behind. Was it time to hang up his guns and get down to the business of raising a family.

It was a sudden decision, as sudden as his choosing to leave the bright lights of the city for the mundane life of the West Virginia countryside.

No doubt, he'd miss Baltimore....

* * *

Five times, Gus, the owner of the Wee Hours, had been before the judge dressed in his three-quarter length black leather coat looking as despicable as they come. Yet each time he's received only a small fine for running a disorderly house. The prostitutes paid ten dollars for every 'trick' they took out of the club.

The upstairs, barred by a heavy steel door, was the club's real source of income. Nightly poker games, as well as the hard liquor sold to known customers, made the small fines well worth the risk.

Before Judy, Bill lived with three girls. Two sister's who were go-go dancers, and Ellen who was a barmaid. The only ill-feelings came from Ellen. One night Bill left with one of the sisters to go get chicken from Jack-in-the-Box, a fast food restaurant. One thing led to another, and they ended up making love on a blanket in Atlantic City. The following night Bill presented Ellen with a bucket of cold chicken, and she wasn't amused.

The day that Bill was released from prison, he unexpectedly knocked on the door of Jean's apartment. Gene Litz, her latest beau, was asleep on the couch. Bill sat his clothes outside the door along with his bird in its cage, then woke Gene up and told him that it was time for him to go. The scene was short and unpleasant, but Gene left in a huff; unwilling to stand up to Bill hardened by prison and bitterness.

Bill took Jean into the laundry room, sat her on top of the washer, and for the first time, made love to her.

As time passed he learned that Jean had not been truthful with him. Neither had Gus. Jean had been turning 'tricks' out of the Wee Hours, against his advice. He was troubled, not because of the morality of her actions he was the last person who would sit in judgment of another but because of the life he's seen most hookers end up in. Once respectable Call girls, earning over a hundred dollars an hour, they were now whores standing on a street corner taking their shoes off for ten dollars. The drugs, cocaine and heroin, had turned them into pitiful caricatures of womanhood. Seeing this happen deeply saddened Bill, who liked all of the women who worked at the Wee Hours, and other clubs, whether they'd been hookers, dancers, barmaids, or waitresses.

In the year Bill came home from prison, the city was crazy, in constant turmoil. Guns were everywhere. And when one mixes guns and liquor, accidents happen regularly. Buddy Butler, a crazy Indian accidently shot Gus in the head at the club. Tommy Polis, Gus' cousin, shot a man five times in front of the Wee Hours. Bill, in a barroom brawl with Gene Litz and two of his cronies dropped a .357 Derringer; which discharged shooting him in the knee. The bullet passed through his knee, set off the alarm at the Eagles Nest in Sparrow's Point, and lodged in the ceiling. Bill was barred from the bar for a year. He was later charged for carrying a concealed weapon and discharging a firearm in the City limits, the charges were dismissed.

Domonic Coroza, a.k.a. 'Crowbar' had taken one of Dick and Jerry Everhart's prostitutes out of the Wee Hours, shot her in the head, then dumped her body in the harbor.

Dick and Jerry owned Hector's, another after-hour club in Baltimore.

Crowbar was a hitman for the Mob. Not overly big, but very ugly, with the personality of a dead fish. He killed the prostitute because he paid her to attend a party and she didn't show up.

It was in the middle of the afternoon when Gus opened the door to the Wee Hours. No sooner had he unlocked the steel gate, cars began to line up and park on both sides of Fleet Street. Dick and Jerry Everhart, owners of clubs on Baltimore Street, along with familiar faces from the restaurant Little Italy, trooped through the door. Everyone who was anyone attended the meeting at the Wee Hours, and it was decided that something had to be done about Crowbar. The murder of the prostitute was unjust, and the Everharts' couldn't let people run around killing their girls anytime the whim hit them.

Several weeks later, an explosion rocked the town of Essex. Crowbar's Cadillac exploded when he turned the key in the ignition. The explosion was so great, it blew the doors off the car; catapulting Crowbar from the wreckage before it burst into flames. He lost an eye, a leg and arm. Domonic was disfigured for life, a cripple.

An unemployed plumber was later charged for the attempted murder. He was acquitted.

Gus was leaning on the counter, with Bill standing next to him behind the counter flirting with Rose, the barmaid, before the 'bang' rang through the club. Moments later, Gus was laying on the floor, bleeding profusely from a head wound. At first, Bill had thought Gus had thrown a firecracker, being the jokester he was. Then, the blood squirted from the wound, and Buddy came running from around the corner, dropped to his knees, and cradled Gus in his arms. Tears filled Buddy's eyes and he wept. "Gus, Gus, I'm so sorry!"

Rose was screaming, everyone was in a panic; except Gus.

"Get Buddy out of here before the police get here," Gus whispered to Bill.

The shooting was an accident. Buddy was passed out drunk in a corner table when Craven, another patron, slapped him in the chest and ran. Startled, Buddy drew his gun, and fired on instinct, the bullet hitting Gus as Craven ran past him to the back room.

After getting Buddy out of the club, Bill rode with Gus in the ambulance to the hospital.

"Come on, Gus," a cop at the hospital said, "You might as well tell us who capped you. You're gonna die anyway."

"Fuck you!" Gus snapped, "All I want is a cigarette."

Gus lived. But he lost his equilibrium and had to learn to walk.

After the first operation, there was seepage from Gus' right ear, and he had to endure a second surgery. This time, he cried. Accidental or not, he grew to hate Buddy Butler and wanted him dead.

* * *

Yep! I'm glad to be out of that rat race. I'm ready to retire, Bill thought. Of course, this isn't exactly what he had in mind, he mused, as he looked around his cell.

"Why in the fuck did you rob the I.G.A.?" he asked himself. "Out of stupidity, that's why," he answered.

West Virginia's beauty glistened with the morning dew. The mountains, the winding endless roads. The beautiful scenery, and the wildlife at your backdoor.

The people, so friendly, were out of an earlier time. It was if somebody had turned the clock back a hundred years.

Mary's parents were poor, but good earnest, down to earth country folks. Their home was a wooden shack in a hollar. It was well kept, and heated by a wood burning stove that doubled as a stove. It was atop that stove some of the best meals Bill had ever eaten were cooked. Biscuits and gravy, potatoes with creamed corn, black-eyed peas and fatback. Mary's mother made everything taste good. At the rear of the house was a smokehouse and an outhouse.

Mary's father, somewhat a religious man, ruled the home with an iron hand. Though strict, he was a fair man. He grew the vegetables in the family's garden and the girls canned them for the winter. Clothes were washed by hand and hung out to dry on a line tied between two trees at the rear of the house.

At night, the rocking chairs creaked as the family gathered to talk, and sing good old-foot-stompin'-hoe-down-country music.

Driving up the hollar, crossing over a wooden bridge, and winding up the road for the first time, Bill had felt uneasy. But before the sun has set, he had been accepted into their home, and into their hearts.

It was easy to love these people, and he knew they meant him no harm in talking to Butch Goode.

They had simply wanted to impress upon him what a good man he was. They lacked a formal education, and incriminating Bill was never their intent. What's more, Butch Goode knew what kind of man Bill was; it troubled him to use Mary's parents' statements. Country justice is different from the city where the cops will use any means possible to convict their man. On the other hand, some things often went unnoticed or were hidden deep with the hollars of West Virginia.

It wasn't until after Red purchased the bar that Bill started meeting the locals and the police.

The bar, called the Log Cabin, was actually two bars in one. One bar served only 3.2 beer and sandwiches. Hidden beneath the counter of the bar was a stamp machine. But instead of receiving a stamp, you inserted a quarter to try to win fifty dollars. The bar also sold fifty cent and one dollar punch cards. The main bar was a club for members only. It served hard liquor. The walls were knotty pine, the hardwood floors well preserved. In one corner, there was a jukebox. A full size pool table dominated the middle of the room.

A 'sputnik' globe, that glowed red and white, hung in front of the bar. Appropriately named 'the Log Cabin' it was built on stilts on the side of a mountain and catered to the miners who dug coal in the local mines. The bar, in a good location, was on a main road with ample parking did a fair business.

"Good afternoon," the cop said, entering the bar. He was polite and quite candid, something Bill was not accustomed to in a police officer.

"I assume that you boys know that you cater to coal miners," the cop began. "They're good old boys, but a tough crowd. That Johnny Brash, he's as mean as a two headed rattle snake when he takes to drinkin'. Cut him off early, and save us both a headache." He went on with a laundry list of names for the partners to be wary of, then added. "Ninety percent of the coal miners carry knives, the other ten pack pistols. Better keep yourselves some protection behind the bar," he suggested, with a slight grin. As he turned to leave, he added. "If you boys need us, don't hesitate to call. Have a nice day now, you hear." Bill and Red looked at each other for a moment.

"I'll open in the mornings," Bill quickly offered. It wasn't a hard decision, and he was amused by the look Red gave him.

But they may never open, the state was giving them problems. In order to obtain a liquor license required their being a resident of the state. And to become a resident of the state required living in the state for a period of one year -- something neither of them had done. They applied for a license a second time, this time in Mary's name. It was granted.

The coal mines threw massive amounts of dust into the air causing Bill to wash his customized 1974 white Dodge van at least twice every day. He tired of that, and traded the van in on a 1975 Monte Carlo, bronze with a matching vinyl top, fully loaded. Tilt steering wheel, power windows, seats, and brakes, air-conditioned.

For entertainment, there was a skating rink and a drive-in theater. Bill gambled. On Friday night, there was a card game in a hotel room in Oceana. On Saturday night, there was a game in the back room of a smoke filled bar on Coal mountain, where everyone there carried guns. A man had to be crazy not to. Bill came to the conclusion that all these hillbillies did was drink, fuck, and fight -- not necessarily in that order. For them, it was a way of life. It was all most of them had ever known. The vast majority were illiterate, yet possessed a surprising native intelligence.

The sense of country justice was evidenced by the number of dead bodies found in the hollars and hills of that part of the country. An eye for an eye, a tooth for a tooth. Country justice was swift, and the expense of costly trials and funerals were spared.

Life in West Virginia was a frustrating experience for Bill. When a customer walked into the bar, bought a thirty-five cent draft beer, then talked 'bitch' for two hours; about politics, taxes, cost of living, and when he was done expected Bill to say "Thank you, come again" when the truth was, Bill wished he hadn't come in the first place. The bar had been Red's brainstorm. Bill wasn't keen on the idea then, and it wasn't becoming a bit more appealing.

* * *

Red visited Bill at the county jail. After listening to every thing he had to say about the search, he noted there was no mention of his, or anyone else's, statements. So, Bill made no mention of his conversation with Butch Goode either.

Two days later, Bill called the trailer and Mary told him that Red wasn't there, that he was on his way to North Carolina. Worried about what Red was up to, Bill asked the other prisoners if Butch Goode was a man of his word. Every prisoner that he talked with spoke highly of Butch Goode.

So Bill made the call. "Mr. Goode, do you still want a statement? If so, there's a condition."

"What's that?"

"I want to be released today."

"Why today?"

"Red Miller is on his way to North Carolina." Within ten minutes, Bill was escorted to Butch Goode's office.

"Why did you break into my I.G.A.?"

"I was bored." Bill replied, flatly.

"Bored? You were bored?" He laughed like it was the best joke he'd ever heard. When his fit of merriment subsided to a chuckle, he shook his head and repeated, "bored."

"Yep," Bill answered.

"When you get back from North Carolina, come back and see me." Butch Goode leaned back in his chair, stuck a lollipop in his mouth, and once again repeated, "Bored? If that don't beat all."

"That's it. I can go now?" Bill asked.

"One more question. Was Red with you?"

"No!"

"Was anyone?"

"No! I'd been drinking. I drove by the store every day going to and coming from work. I knew that it would be easy. So, that night I decided to go shopping."

"Shopping?"

"I twisted the lock out of the front door, grabbed a cart, and went shopping, walking up and down the aisles."

"That's it. You simply walked into my store, grabbed a friggin' shopping cart...just like a Saturday trip to the market?"

"Pretty much."

"And no cops came by, the entire time that you were there?"

"Of course they did. But they weren't bothering me, so I didn't bother them."

"What surprises me is that you didn't ask them to help you load your car." Butch commented dryly.

"I didn't need any help," Bill grinned, closing the door to Butch Goode's office behind him.

The air was crisp, cool, and clean. Bill breathed deeply, enjoying his freedom. He hitched a ride home, rejoicing in his new found and unexpected liberty.

Things were certainly looking up, he thought. A few days ago, sitting in the Asheville City jail, he wouldn't have believed he'd be on the street this quickly.

He returned to the trailer, threw a few clothes in a bag, kissed Judy goodbye, walked from the trailer to the Monte Carlo, and drove to North Carolina.

CHAPTER FIVE
WEST VIRGINIA BLUES

On the way to North Carolina, when Bill stopped for gas, he called his attorney. The lawyer told him there was a preliminary hearing scheduled for 9 a.m. the following morning. "I'll meet you at the courthouse," Bill said, then hit the road again.

"How're you doing?" The lawyer asked, as they shook hands on the steps of the courthouse.

"Better than I was this time yesterday," Bill replied with a slight chuckle.

"Your partner, Red, has retained his own counsel, so I will be representing you.

"In other words, there's no conflict of interest if one client decides it's in his best interest to make a deal?"

"Something like that," the attorney sneered, nodding his displeasure.

Red, strolling down the hallway with his attorney, watched as Bill and his lawyer entered the building. Red's eyes widened in surprise. He obviously hadn't called the trailer. He had no idea that Bill was out of jail.

"When'd you get out?" Red asked, grinning.

"Yesterday. They gave me an O.R. bond," Bill replied, grinning back at Red.

"So, how did you like the Pineville jail?" Red asked, for a lack of anything better to say.

"I had a nice view," Bill said flatly, then asked. "Why did you hire another attorney?"

"I, ugh," Red did some quick mental footwork. "I figured we'd be better off with two attorneys. Two heads are better than one, right?"

Bill thought to himself, you little fuckin' slime ball.

But he kept smiling, revealing nothing of his thoughts.

The lawyers met with the prosecutor, while Bill and Red waited in the hallway of the courthouse. Forty five minutes later, the lawyers returned saying, "We've worked out a deal, dependent upon your approval. Plead guilty to attempted bank robbery for a one thousand dollar fine."

"That's it?" Red asked, "Just a fine? No jail time?"

"That's right." Red's attorney beamed.

"No deal!" Bill retorted, leaving no doubt that he would not be persuaded.

"Now, wait a minute…" Red began, but Bill cut him off.

"If we take that plea, the feds could pick up the charges. Do you want to spent the next fifteen years in a federal prison?"

Bill's lawyer spoke up, "That could happen."

The lawyers returned to try to negotiate a better deal.

Ten minutes later, they emerged again, both smiling broadly. "Okay, this is the final offer," Bill's attorney began. "Plead guilty to temporary use of a stolen automobile for a one thousand dollar fine, and walk. The other charges will be dismissed."

"Without hesitation, Bill quickly replied, "We'll take it!"

* * *

The last few weeks had been a strain on Bill, both emotionally and physically. Anxious to see his friends, he was excited about being free and he longed to go to the Bolero club and hear Earl Murphy sing 'Danny Boy'. But, most of all, he just wanted to sleep.

Las Vegas is for suckers, Bill mused. The odds favored the house. Eddie O'Neil, Mike Newman, and the country singer Ronnie Dove thrived on gambling and dreamed of winning big in Viva Las Vegas. The beautiful girls, the glamour, and the bright lights... Ceaser's Palace had catered to Bill, making him feel respected, important, on top of the world. And when the chips were down, the bets placed, the dice rolled it was nothing short of thrilling. When it was over, the last card dealt, the last dice rolled, the last chips gone...stuck in his mind was the Call girl's words, "Honey, how do you think they keep building these highrises?"

Bill and Red went for long drives, casing banks. As a precaution, they took no tools or guns. After the line-up, the stocking masks were also a concern. Driving around with a stocking mask -- for him, was nearly as bad as driving around with a gun.

The answer came unexpectedly one day. While looking through his closet for a misplaced shirt, Bill pulled a toboggan hat from a shelf and, because it struck him to do so, put it on his head and stood in front of a mirror. When he pulled it down it covered his face, he couldn't see through it. An idea bloomed, and he went to the bathroom in search of a razor blade. He used it carefully to cut the seam around the crown of the hat. The loosened material dropped down, extending the mask to twice its length, making it one layer thinner. When he covered his face, this time -- he could see through it. Standing in front of the mirror, he chuckled and said, "How do you like me now, Tom?"

* * *

Red had been introduced to Bill by a friend of a friend. Gobel, was a friend of Bobby and Mary Jenkins. Bill had been out all night committing burglaries and was asleep on a couch downstairs in the living room, surrounded by stolen color tv's, microwaves, and other appliances when Gobel stopped by with Red Miller.

"Hey, wake up!" Gobel urged, shaking Bill. "I want you to meet someone." Gobel was a huge man. Six two, two hundred and ninety pounds. He sported a beer belly and lived to bet on the horses. When he wasn't driving a truck, or working at his vegetable stand on highway 301, south of Glen Burnie, you could find him at the race track.

"Go'way," Bill mumbled.

"Hey man, this is Red. He wants to talk some business with you."

"Hello Red." Bill said, acknowledging his presence.

"Get up, you lazy bum," Gobel chuckled, then turned to face Red, and said. "Don't pay him no mind, he's always like this in the morning."

Seeing that Gobel intended to harass him until he talked to Red, Bill struggled to a sitting position.

"I'll leave you two to talk," Gobel offered, leaving the room.

"What's on your mind?" Bill asked, wiping the sleep from his eyes.

"Ever rob anything?" Red asked.

"Once, a jewelry store," Bill lied. He had never robbed anything.

"Ever think about robbing a bank?"

"Ever since I was a little kid," Bill chuckled.

Red laughed, and said. "I'll tell you what. Why don't you meet me at the Bolero club tonight say nine o'clock. We'll have a few drinks and talk about it."

"Sounds good."

"Do you know where the Bolero club is?"

"Not exactly."

"It's in Brooklyn," Red replied, and gave directions.

"See you tonight," Bill replied, laying back down. Red smiled, and left.

Bill didn't show up for the meeting as planned. It was two weeks before he finally made it to the Bolero club. Red was there, but when Bill asked if he still wanted to rob a bank, he replied that he wasn't sure, pointing out that Bill wasn't very dependable.

"I'm here, ain't I?" Bill snapped.

Red laughed, and ordered drinks, "When do you want to do a job?" Red asked.

"Whenever."

"Are you sure?"

"One hundred percent."

"Meet me here tomorrow night. Bring a change of clothes and a pistol."

They left the Bolero club at closing, driving all night to Spruce Pine, North Carloina. Red had cased the bank previously. Bill stole an older Ford from a nearby hospital to use as the getaway vehicle.

That's where it all began, Bill thought to himself, as he served the miner's beer and whiskey from behind the bar of the Log Cabin.

* * *

Saturday night, Bill and Red were on their way to Coal Mountain to play cards. Bill was driving, talking, drinking beer, and not paying much attention to the road.

Suddenly, Red screamed, "Turn!" But it was too late. Bill yanked the wheel a hard left, but when the tires hit the gravel, the car slid, and it went airborne off the side of the mountain.

There had been no signs of a turn, the ninety degree curve came as a complete surprise and it was impossible to make the turn going sixty miles an hour. The Monte Carlo skimmed across tree tops, rolled four times, then slammed hard against a tree. It came to rest with the driver's window against the ground. It was the wildest ride Bill had ever experienced. He was, amazingly, only slightly injured a cut on his head and Red fared well with only a broken finger. The smell of gasoline fumes spread through the car, and both men were keenly aware of a possibility of a fire or explosion. The ignition was still on, and a single spark could send them to the Great Beyond faster than a New York pickpocket could lift a wallet from a drunk. The car, resting precariously against a tree rocked gently with each movement the men made.

"We're still alive," Red announced.

"So far," Bill replied, with a trembling voice.

Red began kicking wildly at the windshield, thinking about the long drop just a few feet away from the car's front bumper. The long drop the car inched inexorably towards with each movement.

Bill wormed his way out the driver's door window, a tight squeeze. It was pitch black and he had to work by touch alone.

Red yelled, "How did you get out?"

Bill reached back into the car and helped pull him to safety.

The two men sat on the hillside and listened to the sound of approaching sirens.

Bill received six stitches, while Red's finger was placed in a splint. The insurance company replaced the bronze Monte Carlo with a new one, black with a black vinyl top and white leather interior. The new car wasn't fully loaded. It had only air-conditioning and cruise control.

* * *

One night Bill walked into the Bolero club ready to do some serious drinking, the botched would be robbery in North Carolina was still fresh in his mind.

News of Bill and Red's misadventure had preceeded him, as he discovered when Earl Murphy asked. "What the hell happened down there in Tar Heel country?"

"Well, Earl. You know how Red is? His philosophy is there's a bank on every corner. We picked a bank and the cops were on us before we ever got to it." Bill went on to tell Earl about the raid on the trailer, the charges still pending, but the worst was over, he added.

"What do you think you will get out of the charge pending in West Virginia?"

Bill shrugged his shoulders, "I don't know." He didn't see any reason for him to tell Earl about Red's statement, or the deal that he made with Butch Goode. Some things are better left unsaid.

"How'bout a game?" Bill asked, motioning to the pinball machine.

"Sure, why not," Earl smiled. He flipped a coin into the air and said, "Call it!"

"Heads." Both men watched the coin fall and roll around, finally settling on tails.

"Your quarters," Earl reported, then asked. "How much do you want to play for?"

"Make it easy on yourself, old man."

"A hundred it is." Earl grinned.

Cling, clang… The steel ball rocketed out of the shoot, landing in a hole scoring a thousand points -- and the game was on. Earl was a master at work.

It felt good to be home, Bill thought. He dreaded the thought of going back to West-By- God-Virginia. But he had to; tomorrow. As night fell, the bar filled with loyal customers. At eight o'clock the band came in and set-up. The P.A. blared as they tested their acoustics. The first song they played was "Take me home, country roads" and Bill thought sarcastically, "Yeah, right,"

* * *

The next morning, Bill woke up on Bob and Mary's couch with Mary screaming at her son, Billy, to quit banging on his damn drums!"

"Kill him! Someone kill him, before he multiplies," Bill shouted, which caused his already aching head to ache more.

"Oh, Bill. I'm sorry. He's just a kid," she smiled, entering the room.

"At the rate he's going, he's never going to get a chance to grow up," Bill grumbled, burying his head beneath a pillow.

His feet left the couch. First the right, then the left. He sat up, holding his head in his hands and moaned.

"You want some coffee?" Mary asked,

"No, I just want a shot of whiskey and a beer."

"You're joking. You can't be serious," Mary giggled.

"You're right. I'm not serious."

Bobby walked in to the room, saw Bill's sorry state, and grinned. "What's wrong son, did you have a rough night?"

Bobby was like a father to Bill. When he was younger, they had worked at Wilson's Amoco together on Mountain road. Bobby still worked there. He was a mild mannered jovial man, who was totally devoted to his family and the best friend Bill had ever had. Their relationship had lasted many years.

"How do you like West Virginia? " Bobby asked.

"I don't!"

"I thought you bought a bar and a mobile home there?"

"We did, but it's boring as hell. All those hillbillies do is drink, fuck, and fight."

"Bill Hooker! Such language," Mary scolded, her eyes going to her son, who pretended not to hear.

"Oops!" Bill apologized. But he wasn't the slightest bit regretful.

"Well, I have to go or I'll be late," Mary said, rising from the table. She drove a school bus for John Wilson, the owner of Wilson's Amoco. Mary was a fine woman, who strongly resembled Loretta Lynn with her long brown hair flowing down to her waist. She was a bargain hunter and she knew the value of a dollar. Bobby often said that if it wasn't for Mary, they wouldn't have nothing.

"Do I have to go to school?" Billy asked.

"Yes, and you know better than to ask," Mary hissed. "But why?" Billy whined.

"Because I said so! Now, go get ready."

Billy stomped out of the kitchen, accompanied by Bill and Bobby's laughter.

Mary walked out the door, returning quickly. "Who's Monte Carlo is that parked in the driveway?" she asked.

"Mine," Bill grinned.

"It's nice, but you've got me blocked in."

Bill walked outside into the bright sun, shirtless and barefoot.

"When did you get that?" Mary asked. But before he could answer, she asked another question, "What happened to the van?"

"That's a long story."

"You're so lucky. I wish that I had your money."

Money?! Pinball machine? Earl? Jesus! Bill's hand dug deep into his right pocket; keys and some loose change, nothing else. He tried his left and back pockets with the same results. Earl had cleaned him out.

"Ah, speaking of money. Can you loan me some?"

"How much?" she grimaced.

"A hundred dollars."

"Bill, you go through money faster than anyone I know, and Bobby and I work hard for ours," Mary said, exasperated. "Tell Bobby that I said to give you a hundred dollars from the envelope under the lamp next to our bed, but I need it back before the first of the month; it's our mortgage money."

Mary backed her little orange Pinto out of the two-car carport, waved with her fingers, and was gone. Mary loved her little Pinto, and boasted that she had never seen another one with factory air-conditioning. Bill turned and walked back inside the house, grateful for both Bob and Mary's friendship.

As Bill entered the kitchen, Bobby, was sitting at the custom counter sipping a cup of coffee. "Bobby, Mary said that I could borrow a hundred dollars."

Bobby nearly choked on his coffee. "I ain't got any money!" he sputtered.

"It's in an envelope beneath the lamp next to the bed."

"That's news to me. Yesterday she told me that we were broke."

"It's the money for the mortgage. I have to repay it before the first of the month."

"I'm not concerned about that. I know you'll pay me back! I'm just put out with her telling me that we're broke all the time. Well, you know where the money is, help yourself. I've got to get to work." Bobby said, as he headed up the steps to the front door. "See you tonight."

"No, you won't. I'll be leaving for West Virginia this afternoon, but I'll be back before the first."

"Well, have a safe trip."

The white colonial house at 587 Riverside drive was the only real home Bill had ever known. He was grateful for the friendship Bobby and Mary showed him. They accepted him for simply being himself, something few, if any, of the other people he knew could do. He laid back down on the couch and dropped quickly into a deep sleep.

Sandy, Bob and Mary's second oldest, came home from school, and when she slammed the door behind her it roused Bill from his sleep. He looked at his watch. Three o'clock. Damn, he thought, I'm running late. He fetched his bag from the car, showered and shaved, and hit the road at three-thirty.

Bill tooled down the highway, the radio playing country music; half listening to the chatter of the C.B.

"Breaker, breaker one-nine. Anybody got a copy on Youngblood? Kick it back." Bill called over his Citizen's band radio, C.B.'s, radar detectors, and police scanners had become an integral part of his life. He believed in evening the odds and avoiding any contact whatsoever with the police; believing that the less they saw his face, the better. Besides, the drive never seems as long when you have a C.B. radio.

Bill thought about his life as a boy. At the age of five his father, who was the manager of Firestone in Jacksonville Beach, Florida, had brought home a display case filled with seeds. All varieties - vegetable, flowers, shrubbery. The seeds weren't a good fit for a tire store, so the entire rack was being thrown out. Bill' s father thoughtfully decided that he would divide the seeds between his children. Bill's older brother Freddy; his younger sister, Sharon. And, of course, Bill - who was then called 'Danny'. Freddy took his seeds door to door and sold them at half price. Danny's mother helped his sister Sharon plant a garden in the backyard. That night, Danny went to the hardware store with his father which was about a half mile from the house in a shopping center. While his father purchased a hammer and some penny nails, Danny noticed a rack of seeds identical to the seeds his father had given him. Later that night, Danny helped himself to the empty bag from his father's purchase. The following afternoon he returned to the Hardware store, bag in hand, filled with packets and boxes of seeds, and returned them for a full refund.

By the time he was six years old, Danny's scams had improved. At the I.G.A. grocery store, in the same shopping center as the hardware store, he would pick up an item, usually a bag of candy that costs less than two dollars. Then, he would target a female shopper, and ask, "How much is this? Do I have enough money?" He held the bag of candy in one hand, and his small amount of change in the palm of his other hand.

"No, honey. I'm sorry, you don't," came the response - every time.

Danny would start crying, "I've been saving my money. Today is my mother's birthday." And, every time, the sympathetic women would offer to give him the rest of the money needed for the purchase.

The scheme worked like a charm, until one day he ran up to the same lady - twice. She chased him out of the store yelling and screaming - ending his career.

Perhaps the most memorable con, was the incident with a silver dollar and Danny's best friend, Butch Carlisle. One sunny afternoon they were sitting on the concrete porch in front of the white stucco home where Danny and his family lived. It wasn't much of a porch, more of a concrete slab at the front entrance. Butch pulled a shiny silver dollar from his pocket claiming bragging rights.

"Awe, that's nothing." Danny quipped, dismissing the value. "I've got something worth a whole lot more than that."

"Bet you don't," Butch challenged.

Danny walked to the side of the house, picked up two rusty nails and a termite eaten aged piece of wood and returned to sit on the step beside his friend.

"This is from George Washington's rocking chair, and one day it's going to be worth a whole lot more than that old silver dollar."

After much pleading, Danny swapped his items for the silver dollar.

Within the hour, Butch's mother was on the phone to Danny's mother, mad as hell. Danny claimed that he had spent the silver on candy and shared it with his friends. His father wanted to whip his ass while his mother found it humorous. That night, Danny slept with his shiny silver dollar tucked safely beneath his pillow.

Bill grew up with older men; mostly thieves. They'd taught him well.

When fisherman parked their cars alongside the sand dunes and walked to the ocean, most of the time they left their wallets under the front seat or in the glove compartment of their car. And vacationers, when they went to the swimming pool, they would leave their wallets and valuables in the motel room. It was easy to open a car door, or the door to a motel room.

But the most important thing they'd taught him was this; Keep your enemies close and your friends at arms length...which brought his thoughts around to Red. At least, he knew where he stood with him.

When Bill finally reached the trailer, he was exhausted and headed straight for the bedroom. In the morning, Red woke him asking, "When did you get in?"

"Late last night."

"Did you see Earl?"

"Yeah, I filled him in on what's happened."

"I think I found us a bank to rob," Red said, smiling. "When you feel up to it we'll go check it out."

"Where is it at?"

"It's about four hours from here. I think you'll like it." The bank sat on a corner, in an ideal location. They went prepared to rob it, taking with them guns, masks, and the tools Bill would need to steal a car. It was one o'clock in the afternoon when they arrived in town. By the time they had found a vehicle to steal -- a white Ford pick-up -- and stashed Red's red 1974 Ford Torino in a church parking lot, the bank was preparing to close. As they pulled into the parking lot of the bank, a lady stood at the door, turning the key.

"Goddamnit!" Red snapped, jumping from the truck. He ran to the door and asked, "Are you closing?"

"Yes," the woman replied,

"Can you give me just a minute?"

"No. I'm sorry, bank policy."

Dejected, Red climbed back into the truck. He looked at Bill, and said, "Well, I tried."

"That woman probably would have identified you later anyway," Bill pointed out.

"Holy shit. What the hell was I thinking?"

They returned to the trailer in West Virginia without scoring.

* * *

A week later, Bill and Red stayed at the Log Cabin after hours. Bill was playing pool with a patron for twenty dollars a game and winning heavily. At three a.m. Bill announced, "This is the last game."

"No, it's not!" the poor loser replied. They argued back and forth for a few minutes without resolving the issue. Bill felt surely he was going to have a problem on his hands, but when the game was over, the man left without incident.

After locking up, Bill and Red headed for Bill's car when Red stopped dead in his tracks, "Damnit, I think I forgot to lock the door downstairs, I'll be right back," he said, disappearing into the bar. He returned a couple of minutes later and they went home.

At four-thirty a.m. they were awakened by the telephones insistent shrill. The caller was the Sheriff's dispatcher informing them that the bar was on fire.

Twenty minutes later, they arrived at the scene only to discover the bar had burnt to the ground. Bill walked through the still smoldering rubble, kicking debris aside as he did. He found the stamp machine and the Spudnik globe, both burned, twisted pieces of barely recognizable metal.

The next morning, Bill rented a U-Haul, packed his belongings, and departed for Baltimore. There was no reason for him to stay in West Virginia.

The West Virginia countryside snaked the way through the treacherous mountains as he pointed his car eastward. He'd never forget the love of the people he'd met, or Butch Goode's sense of justice. But he was happy to be heading for the bright lights of the big city. He smiled at the thought of Butch Goode's last words as he left his office, "If you tell me where the hundred thousand dollars is buried, you won't have to worry about the feds finding it..."

CHAPTER SIX
GHOSTS OF YESTERYEAR

Bill never enjoyed long trips by himself, it gave him too much time to think. It gave the ghosts of yesteryear too much opportunity to haunt his thoughts.

The ghost that came to visit him the most often, in these moments of solitude, was that of his parents divorce. Up to that point, he had lived a rather happy life. After losing his job with the closing of Firestone, his father accepted a position as manager for Montgomery Wards Service Department in Baltimore, Maryland. The family relocated to Catonsville, Maryland and, for the first time in his young life, he experienced a white Christmas. Then, the family moved to a huge white two story house in Woodlawn, Maryland. From there, his parents purchased their first new home on the outskirts of Glen Burnie in Anne Arundel County, Maryland in Blossom Hills. It was a three bedroom ranch with a basement. He remembered the night his father called him, along with his siblings, to the living room and announced that their mother wanted a divorce. They had decided to allow the children to decide which parent they wanted to live with. As he asked the question, tears fell from his eyes.

Bill's brother and sister chose to stay with their mother. Bill, sharing his father's pain, chose him. He had witnessed his mother's infidelity, and watched as the 'other' man captured her heart while his father was out of town on business trips.

After he and his father moved to Orlando, Florida, they set-up residence in a motel on highway 441. When Bill was hungry he went to the restaurant, ate, and billed it to the room. During the day, alone with his thoughts, in his bitterness, he cried often. Otherwise, he never talked or showed signs of the ordeal he was going through. He decided that he had to be strong. He had to be responsible. In short, he had to grow up.

"No more tears," he vowed. "Never again..."

One day while getting a haircut, he suggested the barbershop needed someone to shine shoes. The barber agreed, and he had his first job.

Two months later, Bill's father rented a house on the outskirts of town. It was a three bedroom ranch with a carport, across the street from a fresh water lake. Upon the move to Florida, he had changed his name from 'Danny' to 'Bill'. His father enrolled him in school, Lockhart Junior High. Bill, already developing an eye for opportunity, joined the neighborhood gang. There was himself, Spike King, Ted Bishop, Tommy Burger, and David Evans. Spike, being the oldest. Ted was the most intelligent. David was Bill's best friend, and Tommy -- he was the last to accept Bill.

Tommy was of Greek decent, built like a linebacker with the swarthy complexion with the curly hair of his Mediterranean ancestors. His hairy, well muscled chest was adorned by a Saint Christopher medal. At school, Tommy would go out of his way to bump into Bill, knocking books from his hand, hoping to goad him into a fight. Then, he'd say his favorite line, "Do you want to do something about it?"

Whenever possible, Bill would try to avoid Tommy. David would say, "Hook, sooner or later, you're gonna to have to fight the asshole. You might as well get it over with." David suggested they fight in the school's gym using boxing gloves. After all, it would hurt less getting hit with those big gloves than it would with Tommy's bare fists.

When Bill's girlfriend broke up with him calling him 'chicken'-- the fight was on. He dreaded the thought of climbing into the ring with Tommy. Bill was only average size. In comparison, Tommy was the size of the Jolly Green giant.

Word of the fight spread throughout the school like wildfire. The atmosphere in the gym was that of a prized fight. The odds of Bill emerging victorious were somewhere between slim and none.

As they entered the ring, stripped out of their shirts and tied on the gloves, Bill looked at his opponent. Tommy was steady as a rock. When he jumped up and down with his hands raised high above his head, the ring shook beneath Bill's feet.

Their eyes met, their gloves touched, the bell rang, and the fight was on...

Tommy charged, throwing a wild haymaker that missed its mark. His size was intimidating, but his timing and reflexes were as slow as molasses. Bill's hands were faster. For every punch Tommy landed, he landed three.

Tommy's face reddened from embarrassment and he instinctively held his hands higher protecting his face. But the only thing hurting Tommy was his pride. When he did connect a punch, Bill went down. Five times Bill found himself flat on his back, seeing stars while staring at the lights of the gym. "Stay down, Hook!" David yelled.

"Had enough?" Tommy asked, after Bill's last fall.

"Have you?" Bill countered. They stared at each other. Tommy looking down, and Bill up at Tommy from the floor.

Then, they both laughed. From that day forward, Bill was an accepted and respected member of the gang.

* * *

David Evans, toothless and carefree, wore his hair slicked back with a curly-cue hanging on his forehead. His wardrobe consisted of faded jeans, white tee-shirts, black biker boots, and a black leather jacket. Like Bill, David lived alone with his father. Once, they decided to run away. They hopped a freight train ending up in a stockyard in Jacksonville, Florida. Three days later, dirty, hungry, and exhausted, they returned home.

The following morning, Bill's father awoke him for school. "Where've you been?" his father asked.

"At David's."

"Well, next time tell me where you're going to be."

"Sure, dad." Bill replied.

Ted Bishop was five feet eleven, a hundred and seventy pounds, with blue eyes and well groomed brown hair. He was always colorful and neatly dressed. He parted his hair right down the middle and kept it neatly combed.

Late one evening, Bill, Ted, and Spike drank a fifth of Wild Turkey Whiskey, and ran the roads rampant, horsing around. Spike stopped the car in front of Lockhart Junior High and the drunken threesome decided that it would be fun to swing on the branches of the palm trees. Fun for them - that is. But it was hell on the palm trees. Bill told one person of his escapades, his friend, Roger Pickett.

The following Monday, a day that Bill decided to stay home, the principal offered a five dollar reward over the P.A. system for information regarding the destruction of the palm trees. Five of Bill's best friends stepped forward to collect the reward.

A Sheriff's car parked in front of Bill's house, the officer stepped out, knocked on the front door, and when Bill answered, he told Bill to bring his father with him to school the following day, that the principal was aware of the nasty little deed he had done.

When Bill's father arrived home, Bill told him what had happened.

"Did you do it?" his father asked.

"Yes, but they can't prove it!"

The next day his father accompanied him to school demanding Bill admit to his wrongdoing and accept the consequences for his actions. The principal wanted to know who the 'other' culprits were who was with Bill. He refused to say. Regardless of the consequences, Bill refused to snitch on his friends, fully accepting the responsibility for his actions. He was suspended for three days and made to pay restitution for the fallen palm trees.

The Rymar Drive-In was the gang's favorite hangout. The benches in the front of the theater was their domain, the girls who sat there, their possessions.

For the next two years, Bill stuck his chest out proudly as he grew into manhood. During their second year living in Florida, Bill's father hired a housekeeper, Ms. Davis. She kept the house sparkling clean, prepared home cooked meals, and made the best cookies in the world. She often offered Bill advice, taking on the role of a motherly figure. But, never once, did she interfere with his life.

Then, Bill's father remarried, and Miss Davis, like Bill's mother, became a part of his past. Bill's world was once again shattered. Along with his father's marriage came two stepsisters. Peggy, being the oldest. And Shirley; she was a cheerleader and always on the honor role at school.

Bill made passing grades and he was content with that, unlike his step-sisters who were straight A students. Shirley made a B once and cried for days. Then came Rules, subject to change at any time. Bill did what came naturally, he rebelled.

The new family moved to a larger house on Prarie Lake drive in Altamonte Springs, Florida. Evalyn, Bill's stepmother bought all of her daughters clothes, while Bill mowed lawns and sold magazines door to door to buy his clothes. Bill mowed the lawn, carried out the trash, and did whatever other chores Evalyn found that needed to be done.

At the age of fourteen, Bill's father co-signed for him to buy a motorcycle, a brand new 1964 80cc Yahama, built for hill climbing and motorcross racing. Impressed with his ability on a dirt bike, Goodman's Yamaha sponsored him to race on the local motorcross circuit.

For Bill, the races were thrilling. When he powered through a turn, or jumped the bike over a stream, the adrenaline rushed through his veins, pumping into his body the strength it took to muscle the bike through the course. The roar of the engines, the cheering crowd. For the first time, Bill discovered the thrill of competition. Nothing short of winning would satisfy him. That summer was a joyful one for Bill, despite the changes at home. Then came high school and family meetings. If Evalyn held a family meeting, it would be centered on something Bill did or didn't do.

The school was Lyman High, the principal Mr. Henley. Bill was dating his secretary's daughter, Donna McCoy. After school one day, Bill and four of his friends stepped outside the back door of the school and lit-up cigarettes. Principal Henley caught the smokers in the act and ordered them to his office. Four boys were given stern warnings, and released. Principal Henley decided to make an example out of Bill.

"Bend over and grab your ankles," he said, grabbing a wooden paddle from its place on the wall.

"That's not going to happen. Not today, not ever. You're not my father!" Bill retorted angrily. It wasn't fair that he let the others go and wanted to single him out to make an example of, Bill thought.

"Suit yourself. But it's either five licks or five days suspension."

"That's fine," Bill replied, flatly.

"You will lose fifteen points off of your six weeks average."

"Can I go now?"

"Not yet. You won't be able to participate in school events or come onto the school grounds to attend any school events while on suspension."

"Are you sure that you don't want to strap me in the electric chair, pull the lever, and be done with it?" Bill asked, sarcastically.

"Okay, for that young man, bring your father with you when you return to school. Is that clear?"

Bill walked out of the principals office, went directly home, and he told Evalyn exactly what happened. As he expected, she was less than sympathetic. They never did see eye-to-eye.

There was an unspoken resentment from the start. As far as she was concerned, Bill was a rebel without a cause. Evalyn told Bill to go to his room and stay there until his father came home.

Bill heard his father's car park under the carport, the door slam, and his heavy footsteps corning down the hallway. Then, the door opened and his father stood framed in the doorway. Bill stood to face him, only to be shoved back onto his bed.

"I ought to beat the hell out of you," his father said, shaking his fists. "You're nothing but trouble. What am I going to do with you?"

For once in his life, he wanted his father to stand up for him, but it wasn't to be. How could he justify Principal Henley letting the other boys go, and his making an example out of him, Bill wondered. But arguing with his father, as he'd learned from past experience, did no good. So, he sat on the bed and took the verbal thrashing his father administered.

The fifteen points deducted from the quarterly average failed Bill for the year. Instead of returning to school, he quit.

The newest girl in the neighborhood was Mary. She and her family had recently moved from Columbus, Ohio. Her boyfriend, Al Zill, a stocky Italian boy fifteen years old ran away from home hitchhiking rides to Florida to be with Mary. At night, Bill sneaked Al into his bedroom through a window, then fed him. Caught by his father, a call was placed to Al's father in Columbus, and he agreed to allow his son to stay for a week, and sent money for bus fare for his return trip home. Everyone gathered around the television at Mary's house to watch the Beatles debut on the Ed Sullivan Show. When Al returned to Columbus, Ohio, he sent Bill a record that his father recorded. On one side of the forty-five record was 'Big Man - Big House' and on the filp side, 'Little Lies - Big Heartaches'. Pat Zill, Al's father, owned a nightclub in Columbus, Ohio.

Watching Al try to row an aluminum boat was the highlight of his visit. Bill found it so amusing that his new friend had never rowed a boat before.

As a parting gift, Bill gave the record to the first love of his life, Donna McCoy. She was two years older than him, and when she left for college, his well intended plans failed miserably.

Less than a month passed, Bill's father told him, "Son, Evalyn has given me an ultimatum. Either you leave, or she does."

"Do you love her, dad?" Bill asked, anguish in his voice.

"Yes, I do. But either you are going to have to go live with your mother, or you and I are going to find another place to live."

"I'll leave. But I'm not going to live with my mother." Bill said, flatly.

"Where will you go?"

"I have friends."

Bill packed a few articles of clothing in a bag, strapped it onto the back of his motorcycle, and his father reached into his wallet handing him a twenty dollar bill, and said, "Call me."

As Bill rode over the railroad tracks by the side of his house, the wind whipped around him, but it wasn't the wind that brought tears to his eyes…it was the fact he had chosen his father, and his father had chosen Evalyn over him. With a quick swipe of his arm he brushed away the tears, remembering his vow to himself, "I'll never cry again."

At the tender age of fifteen, he was on his own, alone against the world.

* * *

As Bill drove through the winding mountainous roads of West Virginia he thought about Bob and Mary, and the place he called 'home' at 587 Riverside drive. The burnt Sputnik and the melted stamp machine would soon be distant memories.

He had traveled this road many times since that long ago day when his father told him that he had to leave. Every time he pointed his car to Maryland his heart swelled with happiness. This was the only place that felt like home, the only place he felt accepted for simply being who he was. He had made many mistakes, but they were his to make, and he'd learned from them. Well, mostly.

Bill pulled into a 76 Truck Stop just inside the Maryland line, gliding into the full service lane, he came to a stop.

"May I help you, sir?" the young pump jockey asked.

"Fill it up with regular, and check under the hood." Bill replied, turning to walk to the diner. He ordered a cup of coffee to go, black. As he approached the checkout counter, there was a rack of 8-track tapes. Skimming through those he found one he liked.

Back on the highway, he popped the tape into the in-dash tape deck and the sounds of The Beach Boys singing 'Little Deuce Coupe' filled the car. He snapped his fingers and beat a tattoo on the steering wheel as he cruised toward s home.

Bill never felt he was any different than other men. He put his pants on one leg at a time, just like they did. If nothing else, they all had that in common.

Over the years, Bill learned that he didn't resent authority, he merely resented the abuse of authority. There were two detectives that were okay in his book; Ken Puritan, a detective at the Anne Arundel County Sheriff's department, and 'Pen' from the Baltimore County Sheriff's department. Pen had pleaded with Bill to return a bag of golf clubs to a man, promising no charges would be filed, explaining they had belonged to the man's deceased father and they had sentimental value. Bill couldn't return the golf clubs, they were gone. But he vowed to himself that he would never commit another house burglary, that he would not steal from the working man. But Special Agent H. Thomas Moore of the F.B.I....well, he was of another caliber altogether.

Dawn was breaking as Bill pulled into the driveway of the white pillared two-story pillared house on Riverside drive, parking next to Mary's two toned orange and white Pinto. He opened the front door and walked into the house. Standing in the dimly lit foyer, he announced his unexpected arrival.

Sandy, then fourteen years old, was blossoming like a wildflower, and as teenagers have a tendency to do, experiencing life on her own terms. She didn't adhere to rules and placed no limitations on herself.

"Hi Stuff," Bill greeted Sandy as she walked into his sight. "Don't I get a hug, or something," he asked smiling.

Mary greeted him with a smile, "What are you doing here?" Before he could answer, she asked another question. "Do you have my money?"

Bobby, sitting at the kitchen counter, chuckled.

"Have you got my money?" Mary repeated, hands on her hips.

"Not exactly -- "

Mary interrupted, "We've got to have it."

"By the first," Bill reminded her.

"Oh yeah, and I haven't forgotten that you still owe me a diamond ring."

Bill laughed aloud.

"Oh, funny, is it?" Mary laughed in mock severity.

"No, it's a very serious matter," Bill assured her, then burst into laughter again. The diamond ring was a promised gift to her. Many years ago, when he was still committing burglaries, he had hit a jewelry store and sold the diamonds to a local fence, Doug and Patsy McQuire. Mary was offended that he hadn't offered the diamonds to her first. To make amends, he promised her a diamond ring.

Doug and Patsy McQuire, Butch Tetso (Patty's brother-in law), Pete Grimes, Pat Dunn, and Sam Panutti, all owned car lots. Sam also owned a junkyard on Mountain road. They were all gamblers. Bill would never forget the night Butch won a new Cadillac in a poker game. He would never forget that because it was his Caddy -- and Bill had to walk home.

When Bill started running with that crowd, he had stopped committing burglaries. That's why Mary had never gotten her diamond ring.

"I'm bushed. I think I'll hit the sack," Bill announced. Bobby chuckled at his escape.

After only a few hours sleep, Bill showered, shaved, and changed clothes. Then he called Judy at her mother's.

"Ginge!" she squealed in delight at the sound of his voice. "Where are you?"

"I'm at Bob and Mary's, but I'm getting ready to leave to go see Earl at the Bolero club." He explained that he'd only been in town for a few hours, that he had some business to take care of, and assured her that he would see her tonight.

"You better, Ginge, or I'll cut your balls off," she threatened.

"I'll meet you at Bill and Joanna's." Judy's parents didn't like Bill, and any meeting there would be uncomfortable in the extreme.

Okay, baby. I'll see you tonight," Bill replied, hanging up the phone.

On his walk to his car, Bill noticed an unfamiliar light beige four door Plymouth parked just around the corner, but still in sight of the house. He paused to unhook the U-Haul trailer, pushing it backwards into the grass at the side of the house. Then, he started the black Monte Carlo, backed out of the driveway, and drove by the car as though he didn't have a care in the world. But he couldn't resist the temptation. He braked, put the car in reverse, backed-up stopping next to the Plymouth. He cranked the driver's window down and said, "Hi Tom. Nice day, isn't it?"

"Could be better," Special Agent H. Thomas Moore replied, giving Bill a grin. "Heard you boys had a little problem down south?"

"Word does get around, doesn't it?"

"It's a small world, Billy. And, you're big news." Still the grin, the grin that haunted Bill's sleep and shadowed his days.

"Sure would hate to have you ruin my day to make yours better, but as long as you're sitting here, if you don't mind, keep an eye on that U-Haul trailer for me."

Moore shook his head. "Billy, Billy, Billy. It's only a matter of time and we're going to get your ass."

"That's never going to happen, unless you find a better place to park," Bill chuckled.

Moore grinned from ear to ear, continuing to shake his head. "Bye, Tom." Bill grinned, waving as he pulled away.

Wilson's Amoco had been remodeled adding a third bay. And the name had changed from Wilson's Amoco to Wilson's American. John Wilson was a sensible, sensitive man. Some people felt that he was born with a silver spoon in his mouth; the truth was simply he was a good man and a hard worker. He was a big man with a purposeful stride, shoulders down and chin up. When Bill was sixteen, with a wife and child, John had taken him under his wing, treating him like the son he never had. He gave Bill a job, opened a savings account for him, and he did his level best to teach Bill how to be responsible.

John's second business interest was school buses. He had a fleet of buses, as did his friend and competitor, Bobby Brooks. Mary drove a bus for John; and, years earlier Bill's mother drove one of his buses. That's how she met Mr. Scott's children. And, through them, Mr. Scott himself. At first, it had been strictly a platonic relationship. But it had -- as Bill feared in his young heart -- bloomed into love.

For two years, Bill walked from his small apartment in Lake Shore to Wilson's Amoco. A man named Herb Sappington, a customer at the gas station, had given him his first (legal) car. The first two cars he'd owned didn't count, as he hadn't had a driver's license. Neither of his parents would sign, taking responsibility, for him to obtain a driver's license. So, Bill forged his father's name, had the document notarized, and presented it to the Department of Motor Vehicles himself.

John had a habit of calling Bill 'boy'. It was "boy do this" and "boy do that." It tickled him because it got under Bill's skin. And when Bill would bark back, John would look at him and say, "You heard what I said."

Bill had the utmost respect for John Wilson, and he sorely missed him when he retired, leaving the station in the hands of the manager, Norman Huffman.

When John and his family visited Bill's mother in Florida, he told her that he had a feeling their boy wouldn't be there when he returned. And, he was right.

When the Monte Carlo was refueled, Bill looked at the young attendant and wondered what life held in store for him. He shrugged off the thought, and pulled out of the station's drive, easing the Monte Carlo into the traffic on Mountain road.

Two miles further up the road Bill drove by a huge brownstone on his right, Annelo's place. The old gray hair man who drove a big black Cadillac, kept a cigar in his mouth, and sported a large solitaire diamond ring on his left pinky finger was reputed to be Mob. He owned Annelo construction, but everyone in the loop knew that he was the Godfather of Organized Crime for the East coast. It had been a well kept secret -- only the gangsters knew -- until his death.

Directly behind the brownstone was Blossom Hills, the neighborhood he and Butch Geoheigan grew up in, the house he lived in at 108 Dupont avenue when his parents divorced. Behind the brownstone there was a field where a much younger 'Danny' picked strawberries and the Schmidts' (the previous owner of the brownstone) paid him ten cents a pint.

A shopping center was in construction across from the Annelo's place. As Bill cruised down the road of the place where he'd lived and loved, cried and hurt, he wished in his secret heart that he could turn back the hands of time.

CHAPTER SEVEN
THE BOLERO CLUB

It was four o'clock in the afternoon when Bill arrived at the Bolero club. Traffic was just beginning to stir, with everyone getting off work. And within the next half hour the roads would be jammed with drivers anxious to get home and end another day.

Bill parked in front of the club, his preferred place. Through the opened door he saw Joyce, honked the horn, and waved. She looked up from behind the bar. Seeing who it was she smiled, and announced, "Bill's here."

As he entered the club, Earl Murphy, the owner, was carefully removing chairs stacked on tables in preparation for the night's opening.

"How's it going, Earl?" Bill asked, seating himself at the bar.

"Not bad," the big Irishman said, then shook his head and added, "I wish that I would've never remodeled this place."

Earl's business, once lucrative, catered to the working class. Before the remodel the bar had a rustic look, with peanut shells scattered on the floor. It was like a second home to the family men who gathered to tell stories and share a brew. With the upgrading, it was simply too nice, the atmosphere was too rich. The band still drew in a hefty crowd. But during the day his old bar crowd frequently other places.

"How're you doing darlin'? Bill asked Joyce.

She placed a Seven & Seven drink in a talk glass in front of Bill, leaned across the bar and kissed him softly, and said, "Good. And you?"

"If I was doin' any better I'd think something was wrong."

"Seriously," she asked. "How is everything?"

"I've had better days, the bar burned down."

"You're kidding?" Joyce asked, dumbfounded.

"Nope. It's history."

"Oh Bill, I'm so sorry to hear that."

"Don't be! I hated it there."

"Earl!" Joyce shouted, to get his attention, "Did you know that Bill and Red's bar burned down?"

Earl continued with his task of unstacking chairs. When he was finished, he sat down at the end of the bar, ordered a drink, and asked Bill. "What happened? "

As Joyce poured Earl a glass of Wild Irish Rose, he told her to give Bill another drink."

Earl listened intently as Bill told him about the events of the night leading up to the fire; about the man he'd played pool with, the phone call in the middle of the night, and his sifting through the ashes.

"Did you have insurance?" Earl asked, with a slight grin.

"Nope. We never got around to buying any," Bill replied, then reached across the bar and pulled Joyce close to him, whispering something in her ear.

She laughed, and said, "No!"

"Is that a definite no, or a maybe?" Bill gave a devilish smile.

Earl chuckled, and said. "She's got a new boyfriend."

From behind the bar, Joyce added. "He's tall, dark, and handsome. And, he has a steady job!"

"Ouch!" Bill shot back, then snickered and asked, "Since when did you start dating the garbage man?" he teased. She didn't reply, but Earl got a big kick out it. Joyce shook her head and walked away. Then, out of nowhere came a hail of ice. As she reached for a second handful, Earl laughed so hard it hurt.

"I'm sorry, I'm sorry!" Bill pleaded.

"You better be!" she warned.

"Wanna kiss and make up?" Bill asked, with the devilish grin.

"No!"

"Just one little kiss, for old time's sake."

"Why don't you go back to West Virginia," she asked testily.

"Cause I'd rather stay here and pester you."

Joyce stomped off to the end of the bar, while Bill leaned over the counter and said, "Nice ass." Joyce just looked over her shoulder and half frowned, half smiled.

As the night wore on Billy, Jabo, and Frank came into the bar.

Jabo sat on a stool next to Bill, bought a round of drinks, and talked softly to Bill about his wanting to rob a bank. At first, Bill was apprehensive, not liking the thought of his being the one repsonsible for introducing anyone to bank robbery. But Jabo was persistent.

"If you're serious, I know where there's a nice one in Annapolis. I will furnish everything, steal the car and drive for you. I'm taking half the risk. I want half the money. Take it, or leave it."

"When do you want to do it?" Jabo wanted to know.

"Tomorrow afternoon."

"Sounds good to me."

"Don't say a word about this to anyone, understand? Not to Billy, Frank, or your girlfriend."

"Okay, no problem."

"I'll met you here tomorrow at noon."

Bill left the bar at eight-thirty, just as the band began to set-up. When the lights dimmed and the band picked up their instruments something mystical occurred, and Bill knew that if he didn't leave he would be trapped, body and soul, until closing. Jabo followed him outside, "I'll be here by eleven o'clock," he said, as Bill slid into the front seat of the Monte Carlo.

"If you're not here by noon, I'm not waiting."

"Okay, later," Jabo said, lightly slapping the roof of the car with the palm of his right hand. He watched as the Monte Carlo pulled from the curb and sped down the street. Bill entered onto the freeway on-ramp and headed for the Harbor tunnel.

The lady attendant at the toll booth was drop dead gorgeous. Long red hair flowed to her shoulders. She had captivating blue eyes, so pretty it hurt to look at her. As she collected the money, Bill tried to think of something to say. He was at a loss for words, so he simply stared at her luscious breasts.

She raised a finely sculptured eyebrow, and asked, "And?"

"And?" he stuttered. "And I think I'm in love...do you have a phone number?"

"I do."

"Can I have it?" Bill smiled.

"No."

"Pretty please."

"I don't think my husband would like that."

"I promise not to tell," Bill pleaded.

"No!" she said flatly, and laughed.

The toll booths ran lengthwise across the freeway. To the right there was a long brick building, with a vault on a floor that was below ground. Several years before his going to prison, he'd received inside information on how the money was transported to the bank. An older man, with gray hair and a pot belly, driving a white Ford station wagon loaded several Army duffel bags filled with currency into the rear of the vehicle, drove off the exit ramp and to the bank. Bill's plan was to use two stolen vehicles. Stop halfway down the ramp, blocking the station wagon in with the second car. Its high concrete walls would make any escape impossible. The man didn't carry a gun. It would be simple to capture him, drive the vehicles to a deserted area, take the money, and leave the man unharmed for the cops to find. A holiday weekend would produce the most money. He'd ended up in prison before he implemented his plan and, upon his release, he discovered that an armored car now picked up the toll money.

Bill drove away thinking about what he'd like to do with the redhead in the toll booth. Then he thought about Judy, and chuckled. The little shit would be throwing things at him if she had an inkling of his bad behavior.

At night, the lights of Sparrows Point rose skyward. If he hadn't known better, Bill would've sworn they were the lights of a roller coaster in some amusement park.

Sometimes, the stench from the dump at Curtis Bay was nauseating, depending on the humidity and the wind. But at other times the bay was a beautiful place to be.

Bill exited the freeway onto route 40 and drove east through Essex, past the Community Club where Eddie O'neil and Mike Newman frequently gambled. He drove through Middle River, turned left at the red light in White Marsh, then right onto Gunpowder road. Within minutes, he pulled into the driveway of Bill and Joanna Smiths house.

Judy, sitting on the couch in the living room, jumped up to look out the window. Then, she ran to the front door yelling happily, "Ginge!"

"Did you miss me?" he asked, walking up the sidewalk. "Get in here, you asshole."

"Asshole. Why do I have to be an asshole?"

"Because you are!" Judy giggled.

"But you love me, don't you?" he asked, grinning, and took her into his arms.

"You know I do," she said, hugging him hard. "That's why you're an asshole."

After a long passionate kiss, she asked. "Where' s Red?"

"In West Virginia."

"Good. I hope the fucker stays there!"

Bill pulled up his shirt, and took the holstered Charter Arms .44 Bulldog from his belt and placed it on top of the mantle of the fireplace.

"Everyone in bed?"

"Yeah," Judy replied. "Bill has to get up early for work, and Joanna has a doctor's appointment.

Bill sat down on the couch, stretched and yawned, then reported that he was tired and leaned back against the cushions.

Judy straddled his legs and ground her ass against his cock. "Too bad," she whispered in his ear, following the words with her tongue. In two minutes, they were both naked and making mad passionate love.

"Morning Bill." His eyes blinked, uncooperative. Like a window shade that couldn't decide which way to go. Before him stood Joanna, a full-sized woman if there ever was one. She wore a gaudy blue floral patterned dress, her mouse brown hair was curled and waved, her cheeks rouged, and her eyes were made-up of several shades of blue. Bright red lip gloss completed the picture.

"Coffee?" she asked, with a smile.

"Black, no sugar."

"Looks like the two of you had a fun night,'Joanna giggled. He and Judy were both naked, their clothes strewn across the floor, and their legs entwined like two pretzels.

Bill Smith peered around the corner. He was tall, thin, dressed infaded jeans, a blue plaid shirt, and carrying a lunch box. He raised one hand in greeting and said, "I'll see you tonight," and rushed out the door, running late for work.

Joanna served the coffee, setting it on the oblong glass coffee table. "You'll be here tonight?" she asked.

"Hopefully," Bill replied, thinking about the bank in Annapolis.

"Hopefully?" Judy asked, wiping the sleep from her eyes.

"Oh, we're alive."

"Are you going to be here tonight, or not?" she snapped. "I can see you're not a morning person."

"Just answer the goddamn question."

"Well, I don't know. Let's put it this way; I plan to be."

Judy looked at Bill, studying his face carefully. "Okay, what's up, Ginge?"

"Nothing," Bill lied. Judy looked at him, suspiciously for a moment, then she looked at Joanna, growled, and buried her head back in the pillow.

"Asshole," came a muffled comment. Within a minute, she was back asleep.

Bill awoke a second time to the sound of the front door opening and closing. It was Joanna, coming from her doctor's appointment.The sun shined bright through the half closed drapes. He gestured for Joanna to be quiet, hoping not to wake Judy. She smiled nodding her understanding. Bill looked at his watch, it was 9:45 a.m. Jesus, I've got to get moving, he thought. Slowly, he sat up.

"Just where in the hell do you think you're going?" Judy snarled, coming to life.

"Huh?"

"You heard me, asshole. Thought you were just going to slip away without telling me, didn't you?"

"The thought did cross my mind," he admitted.

"You're an asshole!" Judy declared. Joanna laughed heartily. Bill, having no defense, dressed, and left for the Bolero club.

* * *

Jabo was sitting at the bar, nursing a hangover, and sipping on a Coca-cola when Bill walked into the bar.

"Are you ready to make some money?" Bill asked, smiling.

"Sure am!" Jabo grinned.

"Did you bring a change of clothes?"

"No, you didn't tell me to."

"No problem. I have a windbreaker in the trunk of the car. You can wear that."

Bill grabbed a napkin from the counter and drew the layout of the bank, showing Jabo where the teller cages were, as well as where the camera was.

"Go to the first teller, announce that this is a robbery, and have her gather the money from the other two tellers. There's only one camera, and it's on the wall at the far end. Do not go near it!"

"Okay."

"Any questions?"

"No, I got it," Jabo grinned, anxious and excited about robbing his first bank.

"When you leave the bank, walk. Don't run! Running draws attention that we definitely don't need."

"I got this!" Jabo said, with confidence.

Once you announce the robbery, you will have two minutes to leave the bank. Not two and a-half minutes, not two minutes and fifteen seconds. Two minutes! Is that clear?"

Jabo looked dubious, as if two minutes wasn't much time.

"Get up!" Bill ordered. "Now, walk to the back door of the bar, look out the door, and come back."

Jabo did as he was told. When he sat back down on the bar stool at the counter, Bill announced, "Forty-five seconds. That's how long it took you to walk to the back door, look outside, walk back and sit down."

"It seemed longer…"

"When you're standing there waiting for the tellers to put the money in the bag, it's going to seem like an eternity, but you have to be out of the bank in two minutes."

"I've got this!" Jabo assured Bill.

Leaving the club, they drove to Annapolis and Bill stopped at the bank.

"Okay, let's do a dry run. Here's a twenty, go inside the bank and ask the first teller for a roll of quarters. If you're not comfortable with doing this, that's fine."

Jabo returned with the roll of quarters, grinning from ear to ear.

"Was it just like I told you?" Bill asked.

"Sure was!" Jabo beamed.

Bill pulled out of the lot, turned right, then left into an apartment complex that was within a half block of the bank. At the end of the dead end street he pulled into a parking space facing a row of apartment buildings.

"Is this where we're going to switch cars?" Jabo asked, not liking the one way in, and out.

"Not exactly," Bill pointed, "See that fence?"

"Yeah, what about it?"

It's overlapping sections, just enough to squeeze through. On the other side of the fence is another apartment complex where we can park the Monte Carlo and leave by another road."

"I like it!" Jabo grinned.

Bill stopped at a shopping center and bought Jabo a baseball cap and a pair of dark sunglasses. The dark blue windbreaker from the trunk of his car would complete the disguise.

"How do I look?" Jabo asked, donning the outfit.

"Best damn bank robber I ever saw," Bill chuckled.

For the getaway car, Bill stole a 1968 red Firebird that was parked in the front lot of a bowling alley. He instructed Jabo to park the black Monte Carlo on the other side of the fence, put the keys under the front floor mat, then squeeze through the fence and meet him at the other apartments.

"I parked as close to the fence as I could," Jabo announced, proud of himself, as he opened the passenger door of the Firebird and seated himself.

Bill handed Jabo the Charter Arms .44 Bulldog pistol, a folded-up plain brown shopping bag, and then gave last minutes instructions.

"You ready?" he asked Jabo.

"Yep, I'm ready."

"Let's do this," Bill said, putting the Firebird in reverse. When they arrived at the bank, Bill backed the Firebird in near the front door.

"Two minutes!" he reminded Jabo as he opened the car door and stepped out.

"Right!" Jabo replied.

As he entered the bank, Bill looked at his watch and began the count. It was 1:45 p.m. Then it was 1:45 and forty-five seconds. His fingers ran through his hair and down the back of his neck as if they had a mind of their own. 1:46 and ten seconds. Time seemed to be standing still. "Come on, Jabo. Come on," he whispered.

A police cruiser sped past in the same direction they would be leaving. 1:47. "Come on, Jabo...Come on!"

Bill looked over his shoulder, in the mirror, up and down the street, and then at his watch again. 1:48 and thirty-five seconds,

Jabo came out of the bank fast, yelling, "Let's go, let's go!" He was shaking so bad, the bag rattled in his hand.

As the pulled away from the bank, his excitement took over,

"I did it. I did it!" He looked into the bag of money, showing it to Bill. "How much do you think we've got?"

"I don't know," Bill smiled, making the first turn. Sirens were approaching fast. When they parked the stolen Firebird, Bill reminded Jabo to walk, don't run.

Bill walked ahead of Jabo by a few steps, squeezing through the fence first. When he got to the Monte Carlo, he grabbed the driver's door handle and pulled. It was locked. He looked through the car to the passenger door, it was locked too. Jabo's face turned deathly white.

"Give me the gun!" Bill demanded, walking to the passenger door.

"Wha-wha-what?" Jabo stammered.

"Give me the fucking gun, and lean against the front of the car."

Using the butt of the pistol, Bill shattered the passenger window, praying as he did that nobody was looking out of a window. Opening the door, he told Jabo, "Get in, and open my door."

Bill sprinted around the car, grabbed the keys from under the mat, and pulled from the lot.

"Clean that glass out of the frame, fast."

The sirens were much closer as he pulled out into traffic. Bill turned left, then right. He rolled the driver's window down, hung his arm out, trying to look less conspicuous.

"Get down on the floor and stay there!"

Making the final turn onto the main road and here they came, the boys in blue. Sirens blaring, lights flashing, speeding towards the bank.

Whish ...whish.... whish. Three cruisers flew by.

Whish ... whish.... two more cruisers passed, going in the opposite direction.

Sweat poured from Jabo's forehead.

Two more miles. Just two more miles, and they would be on the turnpike.

"God, just help me out this one more time, and I'll never do it again," Bill lied.

"What's happening?" Jabo asked, trying to raise his head and peek.

"Stay down, stay down!" Bill yelled. "I'll tell you when it's safe for you to get up."

More sirens, more cruisers. Bill's heart beat wildly, his stomach turned over and over, and adrenaline poured through his veins. Twice, he had to slow down and pull to the side of the road to let the oncoming cruisers pass.

The expressway ramp was in sight, just up the road. Another cruiser whizzed by...whish...and dirt and gravel spewed in through the open window. In the rearview mirror Bill watched as State Trooper's drove across the median and over the grassy knoll, blocking the exit ramp. Bill merged into the northbound traffic with a sigh of relief, feeling safe for the first time since leaving the bank.

"Thank you, Lord," he said a silent prayer.

"Can I get up now?" Jabo asked.

"Not yet!"

The miles on the odometer clicked by - five, ten, fifteen.

Turning onto 301 South, Bill told Jabo that he could get up now. "Your hand's bleeding," Jabo observed, sitting up.

Unknown to Bill, he had cut his hand breaking out the window.

Jabo opened the glove compartment and handed Bill a rag to wrap around his hand.

"What took you so long?" Bill asked.

"Nobody would wait on me! The teller at the last window kept asking, 'May I help you, sir?' The other two tellers were just standing there, talking. It was either go to the last window, or forget about it."

Jabo ran his hand through the bag of money, and proudly announced, "I did good though, huh?"

"Except for locking the keys in the car. You owe me a window, pal."

"No problem," Jabo grinned.

"How do you like me now, Tom?" Bill thought, as they counted the eighteen thousand dollars.

CHAPTER EIGHT
THE BIG FISH

Bill and Jabo counted their take from the bank, and split it up, in a room at the Holiday Inn in Glen Burnie -- directly across the street from the Department of Motor Vehicles. In the back of Bill's mind stirred the unmistakable air of confidence, and those words, "It's just a matter of time..." accompanied by that grin, that fuckin' grin of Special Agent H. Thomas Moore. Bill visualized Moore standing in front of a bank of computers that fed his office information: Bank robbery in Annapolis. Suspect white male, 5'10", 170 pounds, wearing blue jeans, a baseball cap, dark sunglasses, and a windbreaker. Stolen 1968 red Pontiac Firebird used as getaway car, found a half-mile from the scene of the robbery.

Bill wondered, had anyone seen him break the window out of the Monte Carlo? If not, the description didn't fit him and, it wasn't his M.O. (mode of operation).

Jabo was in his glory. He was content with his share of the loot, exhilarated by his performance, and happy that it was over with. He looked at himself in the mirror and said, "I'm going to buy myself some new duds today."

"Duds? You mean clothes? Bill chuckled.

"Yeah, clothes."

* * *

After dropping Jabo off at the Bolero club, Bill drove back to Glen Burnie, stopping at a furniture store on Ritchie Highway. There were aisles after aisles of furnishings. Having made his selections, Bill beckoned for a salesman to follow him through the store with a note pad as he made his choices known.

"How much for this couch and love seat?" he asked the salesman.

Regardless of the answer, Bill asked. "Is that the best you can do?"

With the order completed, the salesman's best price given, Bill asked to see the manager.

When he arrived, Bill asked. "Can you give me a package offer on this order. I'm paying cash!"

"I believe we can work something out," the manager smiled.

"If it's alright, I'm going to pay for the furniture today. But I just got into town and I don't have a permanent address yet."

"Not a problem. Keep your receipt for the merchandise and you will have 30 days in which to pick it up."

Bill agreed to the terms.

* * *

Bobby and Mary were just finishing dinner when Bill arrived.

"Are you hungry?" Mary offered.

"No, I just stopped by to give you some money,"

"Money?" Mary's eyes brightened. "Bobby and I were just talking about that. If you hadn't been able to pay us back, we don't know what we would have done."

"I told you that I would pay you back before the first," Bill grinned.

"I know. And, we trust you. But with the way you live and all, well, you just never know when something might happen."

"A bank was robbed in Annapolis this afternoon," Bobby added. "When Mary saw it on the news, she was worried."

"Wasn't me," Bill continued smiling.

"I know," Bobby grinned. "They showed a photo of the guy on the five o'clock news." Hearing that, Bill's heart dropped into a bottomless pit.

"It definitely wasn't you," Mary giggled.

"What did the guy look like?" Bill inquired.

"He had on a baseball cap and sunglasses, but he looked right into the camera. He's an amateur, no doubt about that."

"I, ah, I've got to run," Bill said, counting five twenties and handing the bills to Mary.

"Oh yeah, Judy called." Mary remembered. "She wanted you to call right away. She said that it was important."

"Probably checking up on me. You know her…"

"You're not mad at us, are you?" Mary asked.

"Naw. Why would I be mad at you?"

"Well, you know, I thought …"

"You thought that I might have robbed the bank in Annapolis, and you were worried about my getting caught and not being able to pay you back? You had a right to be worried. It's not as though I've never robbed a bank before. Well, I better get out of here. See you later," Bill said, and was gone with a wave.

* * *

On the drive to Bill and Joanna's house a thousand thoughts ran through Bill's mind. He sorted through them as if he was thumbing through the Yellow Pages. What if Jabo is arrested? Would he cooperate? Would H. Thomas Moore somehow connect him to the robbery? Around and around his mind swirled with worry, conjecture, and useless speculation. Finally, he resolved to hope for the best, but prepare for the worst.

Forty five minutes later he pulled into the driveway of the white rancher on Gunpowder road as the sun was slashing crimson fire in the West.

The lights were on, but he saw no movement. Opening the front door he raised his voice, "Hello, anybody home?"

"We're in the living room!" Joanna hollared back.

Judy was perched on the love-seat, like an owl perched on a limb. She was wearing white shorts and a blue halter. Her knees drawn up with her arms wrapped around her legs. A cigarette smoldered in her right hand.

As Bill walked into the room, she said, "You asshole!" Glaring at him, she snuffed out her cigarette.

"Wha-what?" he stuttered, grinning.

"Don't you what me!" she screamed. "I know what you did, asshole. Her voice trembled as she started to cry. "The whole fucking world knows what you did. You, and Jabo."

"What in the hell are you talking about?" Bill asked as earnestly as he could.

"Don't give me that shit. You and Jabo robbed a bank in Annapolis. I saw it on the news."

"The news reported that me and Jabo robbed a bank in Annapolis?" Bill asked, indignantly. "Call my attorney, let's sue the bastards."

Joanna laughed.

Judy lit another cigarette and puffed furiously. Then, she looked away.

"Was I on the news?" Bill directed his question to Joanna.

"Not exactly."

"Was my name implicated in a bank robbery?"

"No."

"Well, is there something that I'm missing here?"

"A brain!" Judy interjected.

"To hear you tell it, I'm involved in every bank robbery on the entire Eastern Seaboard."

Joanna laughed again, louder this time.

"They showed a photo of the bank robber on the news. It was Jabo!" Judy declared flatly.

Judy's interrogation was going nowhere and Joanna was laughing so hysterically that Judy was becoming more and more unsure that it was Jabo. After all, she had only met him twice, and the robber was wearing a disguise.

"The robbery took place in Annapolis, right?"

"Yeah, Judy replied suspiciously.

"Well then, I couldn't have been involved."

"Why's that?" Judy demanded.

"I wanted this to be a surprise, but I guess I've got to spill the beans."

Reaching deep into his pocket, Bill pulled the receipt for the furniture. "I spent all day shopping and picking out new furniture."

Judy gave a grudging apology, which Bill graciously accepted.

That had been some good mental footwork, he told himself. If it hadn't been for that idiot getting himself photographed, he wouldn't be going through this shit. A persistent voice in his mind said, "So, you let him do a robbery? Everybody is entitled to a mistake, but mistakes like that could cost twenty years!"

* * *

The next morning Bill rented an apartment in La Mour Gardens, rented a U-Haul truck, picked up his furniture, and then picked up the U-Haul trailer he'd brought back from West Virginia and left at Bobby and Mary's.

Browsing through the Classified Section of the local newspaper, he purchased two red velvet round beds, one with a footstool that circled the bed in the shape of a quarter moon. Working late into the night, Judy and Joanna unpacked boxes, hung curtains, and made the apartment livable. If either of the women thought about the robbery in Annapolis, they made no mention of it.

In certain circles, however, the robbery in Annapolis was discussed in great detail. Amongst Jabo's friends and close associates at the Bolero club, the robbery and the fact that it was televised became 'the topic' of discussion.

Frank Kalita and Billy Grimes both approached Bill, separately, and announced their desire to rob a bank. They made Bill out to be an employer, and they were handing in their applications.

The difference between Bill and Red was that Bill meticulously picked the banks he robbed, while Red was like a Bantam rooster, "Cockle-doodle-do, any bank will do."

Bill traveled from Maine to Florida, covering the entire Eastern Seaboard. A bank had to meet his specifications, the job was planned objectively, with all odds favoring him. The bank had to be easily accessible, prosperous, and most of all, he had to feel good about it. He had no desire to return to prison. Unlike the first time, it was no longer a game. He was no longer young and naive. And, unlike before, he now housed a huge resentment towards authority.

Bill realized that introducing Jabo to bank robbery was a mistake.

Jabo had not only risen to celebrity status, he glorified in his infamous (self) image. The younger man was unaware, and therefore unafraid, of his shortcomings. Jabo was his own worst enemy, Bill feared. Bill tried to disassociate and distance himself. They spoke politely at the Bolero club, but when Jabo approached Bill about robbing another bank, Bill would make an excuse and brush him off.

Billy Grimes was young and single. He was good looking and charming, somewhat of a ladies man who could, Bill mused, talk the panties off a seasoned prostitute. Billy had long blonde hair, brown eyes, and an infectious smile that attracted women like moths to a flame.

Before Bill started robbing banks, he and Billy were partners committing burglaries, mostly in the daytime. Contrary to belief, night time burglaries posed a much greater risk. Police were more observant at night, and they might use any excuse – weaving left of center, a broken tail light, to pull you over and search a suspicious vehicle.

At the time, Bill drove a 1974 Datsun pick-up that was outfitted with a cap. Custom made curtains covered the windows completely; concealing anything that might be in the back. It was not an exceptionally suspicious vehicle, unless it was spotted leaving the scene of a burglary. Occasionally, they would hit a truck loaded with merchandise at night.

During the day, Bill and Billy had cruised the countryside, smoking pot, and casing potential houses to break into. They looked for tell-tale signs that the occupants were away; newspapers piled on the front porch or scattered about the yard. Mail left uncollected in the mailbox. By the days end they would have compiled a list of likely houses to rob. Armed with the names and addresses of the home owners, they would look through the phone book for their phone numbers. If anyone answered, that residence would be scratched off the list.

Billy respected Bill as a criminal and now he too wanted to rob a bank. Bill trusted Billy. The thin, long hair country boy in the jeans and pocketed T-shirts had earned his respect, and trust.

In 1968 B.P. (before prison) the Anne Arundel County newspaper reported that Bill's yellow panel truck was more notorious than Robin Hood in Sherwood Forest. Night after night, frustrated cops would listen to "B & E in progress" followed by, "Yellow panel truck seen leaving scene." And, like a ghost, Bill would disappear into the shadows of the night. For Bill, it was like a game of tag, only he was 'it'.

* * *

It all began when Bill quit his job at Wilson's American to try to better himself. Bill didn't have a driver's license, so when a customer offered him a position earning more than twice his current salary working as an apprentice carpenter for Maryland Housing Corporation building pre-fabricated apartment buildings with a ride to and from work, Bill seized upon the opportunity. Several months later, his friend Glen announced that he was moving back to North Carolina which meant Bill would have to find another way to work. Since then, Bill had tried his hand at many jobs. He worked as an apprentice printer for Imperial Packaging Corporation. His job was to clean the massive printing cylinders and fill the ink wells. His second day on the job, another employee prematurely pressed a button lowering the press crushing Bill's left thumb between the rollers before anyone could press the emergency stop button.

At the hospital doctors debated whether to remove the thumb at the joint, or sew it back on.

"Sew it back on!" Bill demanded.

"It's unlikely that a nail will grow back," one doctor replied.

"Might as well take it off," another doctor concurred.

"Fuck that!" Bill screamed.

A third doctor examined the thumb, and said, "Sew it! We can always take it off later."

Bill was relieved that at least one doctor had some common sense.

Injured, bandaged, and laid off permanently, Bill arrived home expecting some sympathy from his wife, Dayle. Instead, his young strawberry blonde wife dropped a bombshell on him.

"I informed the landlord that we would be moving at the end of the month."

"Why?" Bill asked, bewildered.

"Their son hit Tina with a stick, and when I told his mother about it she just laughed."

With nowhere to go, and no one to turn to for help, Bill clumsily entered into a life of crime.

Butch Geoheigan had a 1968 Mustang Fastback and he and Bill partnered-up. Late one night, out of desperation, Bill broke into the second floor of a house by stacking trash cans one atop another. He made so much noise a neighbor was alerted and called the police. By the time he exited, laden with booty, the house was surrounded by police. He walked outside putting his hands over his head. He was handcuffed, booked, and questioned. Bill admitted his guilt and he was released on his own recognizance. The scenario was always the same, time and time again. One detective commented, "Our officer's wear uniforms, and ride around in marked cars. What's a criminal look-like?"

The comment lingered in Bill's mind long afterward. In fairness, Bill bought a yellow panel truck, wrote 'thief Wagon' in big black bold letters across the sides and rear doors, then installed a police scanner. And so - the game was on!

From the outset, there could only be one loser. He never considered the consequences. Bill was unfamiliar with the judicial process, police procedures, and especially prison life. He had to learn through bitter experience. And learn he did...

If Billy really wanted to rob a bank, he just happened to have a bank in mind.

* * *

A month passed, Judy was showing signs of her pregnancy, and Bill teased her about having swallowed a watermelon seed.

"Ginge," she began, and Bill knew from the tone of her voice he was about to be lectured, nagged, or both.

"Are you ever going to get a job?" she asked.

"I've got a job."

"No, you don't."

"Yes, I do!" Bill insisted.

"Oh yeah, what is it?"

"I'm a gambler?"

"That's not a job."

"It's a profession," Bill countered. "But you mean a regular nine to five job. Lunch box, time clock, that kind of job."

"Yeah!"

"Naw, I don't see that happening,"

Judy pushed him away, glared at him, and said, "I hate you!"

"No, you don't," Bill grinned.

"Yes, I do."

Bill handed her a gun suggesting that she shoot him.

"I don't hate you that much," she giggled.

"You don't hate me Lil' Bit," Bill said, with a gentleness normally not present in his voice. "You love me. And you're worried about our future, so you think that I should get a regular job."

"Yes," she said, her eyes shining bright.

"I'll consider it."

"You will?" She sat cross-legged in the middle of the bed puffing on a cigarette.

"Sure, I'll consider anything." Bill said flatly.

"I still think I hate you," she said, pouting. Bill just laughed. It was so like her to pout like a little girl.

Like with the fish. Judy had bought a large aquarium and stocked it with an assortment of colorful fish, never taking into consideration the predatory nature of some tropical fish. When they fought amongst themselves she cursed, pleaded, and scolded the fish. When she was fed up with their fighting, she used a small net and tried to spank the aggressive fish. Watching her chase the darting fish all around the tank cursing up a storm, never failed to send Bill into a fit of wild laughter.

Maybe it was Judy's child-like nature that made her such a good mother, Bill mused. She had one child, a daughter named Amy. Amy was very distrusting of men, and she hung pathetically to her mother's leg whenever a man was near, watching them closely with her big, brown, puppy dog eyes. It took Bill months to tease her into accepting him, and still, she never knew exactly what to make of him. But at least she didn't run at the sight of him now.

Then, he thought about Special Agent H. Thomas Moore and his boss, old man O'Neil. It was about a month before Bill and Red had moved to West Virginia, that the police, accompanied by the F.B.I., raided his apartment.

Bill had been laying in bed, thinking of nothing more than what he would do with the day, when there was a knock on the door.

"I'll get it!" Judy yelled from the living room. But she didn't get the chance.

"Wham, wham!" and the cops came crashing through the door.

"Oh, my God!" Judy screamed, then shouted. "He's unarmed ...he's unarmed!"

Bill heard the ominous click of a pistol being cocked, and he sat up in the bed with his hands in the air just before they ran through the bedroom door.

"Morning, guys. What's up?" he said, sarcastically.

"We've got a warrant for your arrest," a detective announced.

"For what?"

"Armed robbery!"

Bill's heart sank. Armed robbery, the feds finally had him. The detective tossed the arrest warrant onto the bed. As Bill read it, to his surprise, the warrant was issued by the Baltimore County Circuit Court.

"Who are you?" Bill asked.

The detective flashed his badge and I.D. card, briefly displaying it.

"Can I see that again?" Bill asked. Looking closely, he saw the detective was from Baltimore County.

"You have the right to remain silent..." the detective read from a card he held in his right hand. "Anything you say ..."

"You can skip that. I know my rights," Bill said.

"I still have to read them," the detective replied. "Anything you say can and will be used against you in a court of law..." When the detective finished, he asked. "Do you understand these rights?"

"I already told you I did," Bill answered, as if he was talking to a child.

Another detective picked up the mattress looking for a weapon, grabbed a stack of money, turned and asked another plain clothes cop, "Do you want this?"

"Who are you?" Bill asked.

"F.B.I." the man responded. "Baltimore County invited us to tag along."

"Have you got a warrant for me?"

"No, we don't."

"Then get the fuck out of my house!"

In Bill's heart, he was bursting with joy. He didn't know where the cops had gotten their information from, but he had only robbed banks, so whatever the cops were charging him with was bogus. He knew that he would walk away from this charge.

CHAPTER NINE
DYE PACKETS

The arrest warrant read that Bill and another unknown person committed a robbery at a residence on Reistertown road in Baltimore County.

As the cops were escorting Bill out the door, Judy was on the phone calling attorney, Harold Glazier. Harold was one of Baltimore's premier attorneys. His flamboyant mannerism and brilliant mind made him a showman in the courtroom. Although he strongly resembled the Great One, Jackie Gleason, he possessed absolutely no sense of humor.

Bill was booked into the Baltimore County jail, his mug shot taken along with fingerprints. By the time he was finished being processed, Harold was there asking to see his client.

A Sheriff's Deputy escorted Bill to a conference room where Harold was waiting, alone with his thoughts.

As the door closed, Harold asked, "Did you do it?"

"Hell no!" Bill laughed.

Bill wasn't surprised when Harold didn't laugh, the man only occasionally cracked a smile.

"Are you sure you didn't do this?" he asked again.

"If it wasn't a bank robbery, I can say without a doubt that I didn't do it!"

"Fifi is posting your bond now. Don't go home. And, call me in the morning. "

Fifi London was a local bondsman. Bill also kept him at his beck and call.

"Don't go home, why can't I go home? Bill asked, somewhat bewildered.

"Just trust me, and do as I say. Call my office in the morning.""

"Okay," Bill said, a puzzled frown on his face.

* * *

Judy picked Bill up at the jail and they drove to Pete Grimes townhouse in Glen Burnie. He spent most of the night puzzling over the series of events. In the morning, still no closer to an answer, he called Harold.

"Come to my office, right away." Harold insisted.

Pete accompanied Bill downtown, parking in the underground parking lot of the Keiser building. Harold's office was on the seventh floor. The two men arrived at Glazier's office at ten o'clock sharp and were ushered by the receptionist straight into Harold's office. She closed the door for privacy.

"Do you know who you are accused of robbing?" the big man asked Bill.

"No," Bill replied flatly.

"Do you know who Lou Richmond is?"

"Yes, of course. He frequented the Wee Hours. Everybody knows who Lou is!"

"You know that he runs dice games?"

"I've heard that. So what?"

"You, along with a partner, are accused of robbing 'the floating crap game'. Every week it moves to a new location," Harold explained. "The robbers made everyone get undressed, then they took their money, jewelry, and clothing." Harold paused for a brief moment, then asked. "Are you sure that you didn't do this?"

"No! Son-of -a-bitch. Somebody is trying to get my ass killed!"

Harold sighed. "Fifi needs to see you at his office. When you leave here, go straight to his office." Harold handed Bill a piece of paper with the bondsman's address.

Cars were parked on both sides of the street. There was not a blade of grass in sight. Just rows and rows of aged red brick buildings and concrete sidewalks.

The Keiser's building facade was polished gray stone. The foyer was imported marble tile, and an elegant water fountain flowed against a rear wall. The corridors featured plush red and black checkered carpet.

Fifi's office, on the other hand, was below ground. Bill and Pete walked down a stairway and stopped at a glass door. Through the glass, Bill saw Fifi sitting behind a large oak desk. With a hand gesture, he motioned for the men to come inside. Fifi was an elderly oversized Jewish man who seemed to have a fixed grin. Behind him was a huge metal door that appeared to be a vault. But, it wasn't. It was the entrance to a furnace and electrical room for the building above. A second man was perched on Fifi's desk. He had one leg on the floor, the other resting comfortably on top of Fifi's desk. The man was dressed casual and wearing a sport coat. He was tall, thin, with no other distinguishing features. His right hand was questionably inside of his jacket.

As Bill and Pete entered the office, the stranger looked at Fifi and asked, "Do you know these guys?"

"Yeah, they're friends of mine," Fifi replied, with a fixed grin.

The man looked at them a second time, shrugged his shoulders, and left.

"I know that guy from somewhere," Pete spoke up.

"He runs the junket to Vegas for Lou Richmond. And, he was running the crap game the night it was robbed, "Fifi offered.

"Holy shit!" Bill blurted out. That line-up was about as personal as one could get.

The charges were dismissed the following day, but Bill couldn't help but wonder if old man O'Neil and Special Agent H. Thomas Moore were behind his being charged. Had Bill been the average guy. Had his attorney not been Lou Richmond's attorney, the outcome was something that he didn't care to think about.

Someday, Bill swore, there would be a reckoning. He was brought back to the present by Judy's voice as she scolded her fish, net in-hand prepared to spank any she could reach. "You little son-of -a-bitch. How would you like it if I killed you?" she asked. Its eyes bulging, the fish simply looked at her and went back to munching on its tank-mate.

* * *

The Bolero club was filled to capacity. There was standing room only and music drifted out the door when Bill pulled up and parked at midnight. Earl Murphy was on stage singing "from glen to glen, and down the mountain side, the summer's gone....Oh, Danny Boy .." he bellowed.

Billy must have seen the black Monte Carlo pull up. Bill saw him coming through the front door. Billy held his beer bottle high above his head as he made his way through the densely packed crowd. Stepping outside, Billy squatted next to the car, resting his crossed arms on the passenger window.

"What's up?" he slurred, cheerfully drunk.

"I see you're feeling no pain," Bill grinned.

"Let's rob something!"

"Not right now," Bill laughed.

"What's the matter? You don't want to rob a bank with me? You don't trust me?" Billy concluded.

"Hey! Buddy, partner, old friend of mine. It's not like that! I just need to lay low for awhile.

"Okay,' Billy smiled, satisfied with the answer. "You coming in?"

"Who all is here?"

"Everyone! Pete, Frank, Jabo, Raymond, and Red." Billy reeled off a half dozen less significant names.

"Red Miller is here?" Bill asked, surprised.

"Yeah. Come on in and let's party."

"In a minute," Bill said, watching the younger man weave his way back into the bar. Bill removed the pistol from his waistband, stashing it in a secret hiding place.

Red was the center of attention as Bill walked into the bar. Clad in cuffed blue jeans, a colorful Hawaiian short sleeve shirt, and black dress shoes he looked like a strutting peacock, Bill mused. In one hand, Red held a long neck bottle of Budweiser. His other hand gestured wildly as he spun stories to the crowd of men gathered around him.

Bill approached from behind and tapped him lightly on his right shoulder. "Lose something?" Bill asked, grinning.

"Look what the cat dragged in. Did Judy let you out from under her skirt for a breath of fresh air?" he laughed. When Red laughed, his neck turned beet red. A true Redneck, Bill surmised.

"What brought you into town, the wind blowing in the wrong direction?"

Bill countered.

Ignoring the question, Red asked, "Why did you let Jabo rob that bank?"

"I don't know what the fuck you're talking about." Bill snapped.

Bill looked around the club for Jabo. Their eyes met and Jabo bowed his head. Looking back up, he smiled ingratiatingly, but Bill turned back to Red, not acknowledging Jabo's left hand apology for his talking too much.

"I'll see you later," Bill snapped at Red.

"Hey! Wait up!" Red shouted, following Bill from the bar.

Bill stood in the street, fumbled through a ring of keys, searching for the key to unlock the door of the Monte Carlo.

"What's the matter with you?" Red stuttered.

"What's the matter with me? What the hell is wrong with you?" Bill countered. "In front of God and everybody you're just going to front me off?"

"Buh-but, I was here less than five minutes and everybody was telling me about it," Red said, trying to minimize his mistake.

"What they do, and what you do, are two different things. The difference being you know better."

Bill unlocked the car door and slid behind the wheel. Red tapped on the passenger's window motioning for him to unlock the door. Bill popped him the bird, holding up the middle finger of his right hand, and said, "Do you understand this?"

Red laughed again, motioning for Bill to unlock the door. "Didn't mean to get your dander up," Red apologized after Bill unlocked the door.

"You 'know' better," Bill repeated.

"I wasn't thinking, it was Pete who had brought the subject up."

"I have no control over Jabo, just leave my name out of it!"

"Why didn't you tell him to wear a mask?"

"Look! I drew him a map of the bank. I told him where the camera was and 'specifically' instructed him to go to the first teller. He even had the opportunity to go inside the bank and look it over before the robbery."

"Damn," was Red's only response.

"To make matters worse, the dumbass locked the keys in my car. I had to break the passenger door window out to get in."

"He locked the keys in the car?" Red laughed hysterically.

When Red stopped laughing, Bill asked. "What brought you to town?"

"Hell," Red shook his head, "I couldn't stand it anymore either. I took a big loss on the trailer, but I sold it." Red looked at Bill for a moment, then asked the question that had been on his mind. "Did you burn the bar?"

"What? Hell no! I hated living in West Virginia from day one. I had been thinking of leaving. The bar burning was just the last straw."

"How are you fixed for money?" Red asked, changing the subject.

"If it cost a nickel to shit, I'd have to puke," Bill chuckled.

"Yeah, me too. We don't close on the trailer until the middle of next month. But if you want to make a trip, I have enough money to finance that." Red stuck his hand in his front pocket, and said. "At least I think I do?"

"I'm in!" Bill grinned.

"When do you wanna leave?" Red grinned.

"How about in the morning?"

"Hot damn," Red chuckled, smacking his leg.

"Am I ever ready!"

"Just call me Duracell," Bill shot back. Once again, they were a team. Bill had debated on whether he wanted to use Billy Grimes, or Red. But he hoped that Red had learned from his mistakes. And, after Jabo, he was hesitant to believe that Billy would be any different. The old adage held true, loose lips sink ships.

"Come on back inside and I'll buy you a drink," Red insisted.

Leaning against the bar, Bill asked Joyce, "Do you believe in sex before marriage?"

"No," she lied.

"Okay, come see me after you get married," Bill grinned.

"Very funny. I suppose you want a drink now?"

"That would be nice."

Well, I don't feel like being nice," Joyce giggled walking to the opposite end of the bar.

Bill laughed in high spirits. Things were getting back to normal, and he felt that he had the world by the balls. He eagerly anticipated the 'trip' he and Red would take in the morning.

Maybe a little too eagerly.

* * *

Red and Bill departed from Baltimore late in the week, heading south - destination unknown.

After a few beers, Red confided in Bill that Frank had robbed a bank on the outskirts of Annapolis Monday afternoon. The bank sat on the corner of a small shopping center. "It's the first bank that I ever saw that didn't have a camera!" Red announced.

It was Frank's first robbery. Bill had been reluctant to introduce him to bank robbery because Frank was a family man. Jabo was a big enough mistake.

As the days passed without Bill finding a suitable bank to rob, Red's frustration grew.

"If we don't find a bank, I'll rob the same one that Frank robbed by myself," Bill declared.

There, it was done. Red had nothing more to bitch about.

Why couldn't I keep my big mouth shut? Bill asked himself as he donned his disguise: a baseball hat, dark sunglasses, and a dark blue windbreaker.

There was the bank with a store on the side of it, an alley, then a row of stores in the shopping center.

Bill approached the first teller handing her the brown paper bag. "This is a robbery," he announced. "Put the money in the bag and be quick about it."

The teller moved down the line emptying teller drawers, then passed the bag over the counter back to Bill.

Bill walked from the bank, the bag of money clutched in his hand, walking quickly towards the alley. Red had parked the Monte Carlo at the opposite end of the shopping center backing up against a wall.

Bill was almost to the corner of the alley when a man stepped out of the store next to the bank carrying a long object that Bill immediately, and wrongfully, identified as a shotgun. His heart beat furiously as his hand shot to his holstered gun, ready to draw and fire instantly. Adrenaline pumped through his muscles, charging them. Then, he saw the man was only carrying a broom and he breathed a sigh of relief. Two steps and he turned the corner. At the opposite end of the alley when he turned the corner, he sprinted for the car. He was not even half way there when he smelled a foul odor. At first, he thought it was something in passing and held his breath. Rounding the last corner he exhaled and inhaled again. Jesus, it stank!

As he hopped into the Monte Carlo, Red asked. "What's that smell?"

Bill looked at the bag. It was now spotting red and spewing an obnoxious smelling gas.

"Oh shit!" Bill exclaimed, opening the door and tossing the bag out.

"Get the bag! Get the bag!" Red screamed.

Bill leaped from the car, retrieved the bag, wrapped it in his coat, then sat it on the floorboard.

As Red pulled away from the shopping center, Bill ran his hand through the bag in search of the source of the smoke and gas. His fingers brushed against something hot and he snatched his hand from the bag.

"Son-of -a-bitch!" Bill barked, sucking on his singed fingers.

"Throw the jacket out!" Red screamed.

Bill tossed the jacket out the window onto the expressway. Trying to catch his breath, with tears streaming down his cheeks, Bill held the bag out the window. Foul, red smoke trailed behind them in the car's slipstream.

Bill's eyes alternated between the mirror and the windshield, searching for police cars. Once again, he prayed. "Lord, just get me out of this one and I'll never do it again."

As the bag cooled, Bill threw it onto the floorboard. After clearing the area, Red pulled down a back road, stopping next to a lake. He picked up a stack of five dollar bills that were in a brown paper binding and stamped in red $500. "Ah ha," Red said as he thumbed through the stack. Only two of the bills were real. The five dollar bill on top, and the five dollar bill on the bottom. The rest were plain white paper, hollowed out to accommodate a rectangular silver cylinder. The cylinder had two holes. One shot tear gas, the other spewed red dye. And the red dye was all over the white interior of Bill's Monte Carlo.

"That's playing dirty!" Bill growled inspecting the canister. Red tossed the two spent canisters into the lake, and they left for home.

"Easy, huh?" Bill mumbled.

"Well, it could have been worse," Red chuckled.

CHAPTER TEN
POCKET MONEY

It was four o'clock in the afternoon when Bill and Red stopped by the Bolero club for a cold refreshing Budweiser beer. "Did you have a good night?" Bill asked Earl who was sitting at a table at the rear of the bar counting the tally.

"Not bad," he grinned.

Finishing their beers, as they were preparing to leave, Bill turned and asked Earl if he wanted to exchange some money?"

"How much money?" Earl asked thoughtfully, before committing himself.

"I don't know for sure, we haven't counted it. My guess is fifteen thousand dollars," Bill grinned.

"My fee is fifteen percent," Earl smiled greedily.

"That's fine."

Bill rushed out to the Monte Carlo, grabbed the bag, and sat down on the table in front of Earl.

"You count it. We trust you," Bill replied enthusiastically, turning to make a quick exit. He might have got away clean had it not been for Red's hysterical laughter as they headed for the front door.

Earl opened the bag, peeked inside, and hollered, "Hey! Wait a minute!" He quickly closed the bag, and screamed, "I can't do anything with this!"

With one foot out the door, Bill shouted, "You've got to take the good with the bad."

"Like hell I do!" Earl spat.

"But a deal's a deal," Bill retorted chuckling.

"Not today, it isn't," Earl said gruffly, handing Bill the bag.

"You can't blame a guy for trying," Bill grinned.

Stopping by Red's sister apartment, the two men tried everything they could think of to get the red dye off the money. They tried boiling the worst bills in cleaning solution, adding bleach, salt, vinegar, and Drano. The most effective method was to clean each bill with Comet cleanser scouring powder with a damp sponge. They acheived some measure of success rendering most of the bills passable; but it was quite a chore. Bill's end of the stolen loot was slightly more than six thousand dollars.

The white interior of the Monte Carlo had red dye on the front seat and passenger door panel. Once again, Bill bought every cleaning chemical on the market. Nothing worked.

Finally disgusted, he traded the Monte Carlo in for a brand new white Cadillac with red leather interior. Fully loaded.

Three weeks later, the feds impounded the Monte Carlo from the new car dealership as evidence of a bank robbery. No charges were ever filed.

* * *

Pocket money was no longer coins that jingled and wore holes in jeans. Pocket money was green folding bills that bulged from well tailored trousers, a necessary part of Bill's wardrobe. To dress his money up, Bill purchased a solid gold money clip topped with a gold coin stamped Pike's Peak Mint 1883. It set him back over a grand, but even money wanted to dress to impress sometimes.

Like a kid in a sand box, Bill played on the sunny beaches of the East coast and frequented Disney World to revel in the sound of children's laughter...

* * *

As night fell on the bleak landscape of despair, casting its dark tentacles on the men in the Maryland State Penitentiary, the ghost of his lost past haunted the young Bill. Unbidden thoughts of his daughters would creep into his mind to torment for what he perceived as his failure of them.

His oldest daughter, Tina Marie, was two years old the last time he had seen her. She was standing up, holding onto a glass covered coffee table when Bill held out his arms gesturing for her to come to him. Her chubby little legs were unsteady, but she literally ran into his arms.

Kerri Ann was an infant, resting peacefully in her mother's arms.

The saddest day of Bill's life was, facing prison, his standing at the airport watching his wife, Dayle, and his daughters board an airplane for Florida.

"Hooker 108705," the voice of authority yelled.

Bill was locked in his cell and couldn't see very far down the range, but he clearly heard someone calling out his name and prison number.

"Down here!" Bill shouted.

Bill was 'a fish' brand new to prison life, housed on the third floor, which was reserved for Classification.

A well mannered black prisoner appeared in front of his cell holding a clip board in his right hand. His beige khaki pants and matching shirt were neatly pressed and a shine gleamed on his black state shoes.

"Hooker 108705," he repeated.

"That's me," Bill replied.

"Did you check everything in when you came through the bubble?"

"As far as I know," Bill said thoughtfully.

"How about that watch?" the prisoner asked, looking at Bill's wrist. "Did they put your prison number on the back?"

"No!I didn't know they were supposed to."

"Well, you'd better give it to me, and I'll take it to Control and have your number engraved on the back. Otherwise, the first time a hack shakes you down you'll lose it.

"Okay, thanks!" Bill smiled, handing over his watch.

Bill turned to his cell partner and said, "Nice guy!"

"We'll see," he replied, with a goofy smile.

"What do you mean we'll see?" Bill asked.

Once before, Bill had given a black man his watch - and lost it. That incident occurred when he was in the Baltimore City jail charged with the fatal shooting of Johnny Campbell. Bill had sold his watch to a black prisoner who went by the nickname of 'Spareribs' for two cartons of cigarettes and some candy bars. After only receiving a few items, several days passed. One night Bill saw Spareribs in the dining hall. Believing that he would never see Spareribs again, Bill hit him over the head with a metal tray sending them both to the hole. These circumstances were vastly different, but the outcome was the same. He lost his watch to a con game.

Casey was a big friendly black man who celled next door to Bill. He played the guitar and offered to teach Bill how to play. Young, naive, and somewhat foolish, Bill frequented his new pal's cell on a regular basis. Then, one day, Casey asked Bill if his cell partner, Joe Clark, was his 'daddy'.

"No," Bill replied.

That night, Bill told Joe that Casey had asked him if he was his daddy.

"Uh-oh," Joe said, shaking his head. "Kid, don't you know what that means? He wants to know if I'm fucking you."

"Fucking me?" Bill repeated. He had heard of such things, but this was beyond his limited understanding. "What should I do?" he asked Joe.

"Kid, I'll help you. But I'm not fucking you and I'm not fighting any battles for you."

From the weight pit, Joe stole a short iron bar, used to do curls, and placed it on the ledge above the cell door.

The following morning, Casey stood in the doorway and asked Joe, "Is Hooker your kid?"

"Hell no, he's not my daddy-- and I'm not going to have one either!"

"Shut up! " Casey said coldly, asking Joe a second time. "Is he your kid?"

By then, Bill was on his feet. He snatched the iron bar from the ledge, stood even with Casey's shoulder, and stared up at the big, broad, black man. Bill was scared shitless. His fear gave him courage that he wouldn't normally possess. He swung the iron bar fast and hard, hitting Casey squarely on top of his big noggin. Bam!

"You little fucking punk," Casey roared, seemingly unfazed by the blow.

"Shit," Bill mumbled, a second time. This time more to himself, swinging the bar giving it his all, every ounce of strength he possessed.

"Wham!" damn fine shot, he surmised. Blood flowed from the open wound, dripping down the big man's chin. His face turned white. His eyes bulged. But he stood firm, glaring at Bill.

"I'm going to kill you, punk," he growled, staggering towards Bill, who, figured it was a little late for apologies, and ran like hell.

Casey was hard on his heels as he ran the length of the range. As Bill ran through the gate at the end of the range, the guard closed and locked the gate on an enraged Casey.

"I'll kill you, you punk ass honkey mother-fucker!"

Casey went to the hospital, where he received thirty stitches, then he was transferred to a higher security prison. Bill got thirty days in the hole.

Stripped to nothing but his underwear, Bill went into the concrete tomb that was to be his home for the next month. The steel door slammed shut. In the dim, damp hole he was allowed only a bible. There was a trap door in the door, a slot that opened for meals to be served. He was fed bread and water, every third day - a meal. Bill was given a metal bucket to use as a toilet and told that if he beat on the door, they wouldn't exchange his bucket. At night, he was given a wool blanket. At the crack of dawn, it was taken away. He soon learned that seasoned campers counted the times they were handed the blanket, so they knew how many days they had left. For Bill, it had only distinguished the night from the day.

Bill read the bible, four times. Anyone who believed that Jonah was swallowed by a whale and made a seven day journey in three days is an idiot, he thought. Yet, he wondered what made him shiver. What made him feel pain, sympathy, and sorrow. What made him love, and who created the four seasons and the heavens above? There must be a God, he mused. He looked at the dim, wire covered light, and asked. "Why me, Lord. Why always me?" But if God answered, Bill didn't hear him.

Then one day, the door opened and his thirty days were up.

He quickly dressed in his khaki prison uniform.

The white boys were outnumbered by the blacks nine to one. They grouped together, but when it came to a showdown, when five black guys jumped a white boy - it was always the same story. "It ain't none of my business," they'd say, and like a flock of chickens they flew the coup going off in different directions. Nobody saw anything, Nobody wanted to be involved.

"Hey man, I'm doing my own time," was a standard excuse.

"I came here alone, and I'm going home alone," was another often heard excuse.

Bill studied law. He couldn't afford to purchase brand name cigarettes, so he learned to roll his own. The state provided him with two metered envelopes a month. Prisoners weren't allowed to seal their envelopes before dropping them into the prisoner mail box. Given one sheet of lined paper, twice a month Bill wrote a letter and mailed it to his mother to let her know that he was still alive.

Jean visited sporatically. His mother visited once in two years. His wife, Dayle, never visited, but she wrote several times. Then came the 'Dear John' letter. She told him to remember when he took her and the kids to the airport, because he would never see them again. Bill saved the letter, swearing to himself that someday he would make her eat it.

Bill studied law with vengeance. He was determined not to come out of prison an old man. He soon became known as a 'jailhouse lawyer'. A writ writer, a scapegoat (one who finds holes in the law). Other prisoner's sought his help. It became a way of life, and Bill's means of financial support.

Bill, who once couldn't afford name brand cigarettes, now used them to buy food from the kitchen, so he no longer had to go to the chow hall. He loathed the chow hall, where convicts lined up in single file only to have their food slopped onto metal trays. The prisoners had to sit next to whoever was in front and behind them in the line at long metal tables with hard benches on both sides. When one bench reached its capacity, the line of prisoner's continued seating at the next bench. The men drank from metal cups, ate with a metal spoon, and the beverage of the day (usually Kool-aid) was served in metal pitchers that sat on top of the tables.

The hacks walked around dressed in green uniforms with shiny brass buttons on their jackets. Their green hats had a patent leather brim and a band with the Department of Corrections insignia on it. The hacks carried black jacks and mace, stood against a wall in the chow hall rocking back and forth on their heels, and enforced the 'no talking' rule with an iron hand.

The 'Goon squad' was made up six to eight hacks, and when it was necessary for them to be called an ass whipping was coming with it for the prisoner.

When the University of Maryland offered infectous disease tests and to pay prisoners to be 'human guinea pigs,' Bill signed up for every test offered. The prison's hospital was quiet, clean, with comfortable beds topped with thick mattresses. There was a color television to watch, better food, and occasionally ice cream was served. Rocky Mountain Spotted Fever, Malaria, Sugilarosous. Soldiers fighting in the trenches of Vietnam were getting Shigilarosous by drinking contaminated water. The diarrhea lasted for three days, but the researchers were looking for a faster cure.

Malaria paid the most money and required a longer stay in the hospital. Mosquitos in a Maxwell House coffee can covered with a screen allowed the infected mosquitos to transmit the disease to the prisoner by holding the can against his arm. The prisoners were paid three dollars a day and five dollars every time blood was drawn. And, if the prisoner infected other mosquitos that too paid five dollars. The downside was if the prisoners temperature reached 105° he was given a bath in ice.

Released from the hospital Bill paid Slick, the clerk, a carton of cigarettes a month to keep his cell single. He was assigned a job working recreation. The small green oblong building sat in the middle of a fenced recreation yard. On one side of the yard were weights, benches, and chin-up bars. On the other side there was a baseball diamond complete with painted green bleachers. Everything was a putrid green, the cell bars, the recreation shack, and the bleachers.

Men in the Army made 'Mash'(homemade wine) from potatoes.

Bill mastered the art of making 'hooch' (homemade wine). If he made it from apples, he called the hooch Apple Jack. From raisins, Raisin Jack. Plums, Plum Crazy. And then there was Orange Delight and Watermelon wine.

Every afternoon, when Bill rolled out the canopy and shoved the folding door up in its tracks, prisoners would line-up with containers.

"May I help you?" Bill would ask in his best head-waiters voice. A cup of wine sold for two packs of tailor made cigarettes, the larger mugs went for three packs. The baseballs, gloves, and bats were free, but you had to sign them out.

The living conditions were deplorable, the food horrible, and the treatment of prisoners gave rise to cruel and unusual punishment. It was no surprise when the riot broke out. Bill passed out baseball bats to anybody that wanted one, black or white - there was no discriminating.

The Maryland State Police and the National Guard tear gassed the rioters and broke through barracades in grand fashion.

Back inside the prison, Bill slammed his cell door shut, grabbed his towels and blankets, soaked them in the toilet and shrouded himself. Even then, breathing was difficult.

For the next three weeks the prison was locked down and the prisoners were fed bag lunches, mostly bologna sandwiches with a packet of mustard and an apple.

One by one, the prisoners were ordered to step out of their cells, stripped naked and searched. Some were transferred to other prisons. Some were beaten and tested.

Bill, along with several other jail house lawyers, prepared a Writ of Habeas Corpus claiming their Fourth Amendment Right to be free from Cruel and Unusual Punishment was being violated. Another prisoner who worked in the prison library made copies of the Writ and distributed it to any prisoner who wanted to file. The prisoner simply needed to write his name and prison number on the blank lines, sign it, and mail the Writ to the court. Over three hundred Writs were filed.

The first reaction was a cell to cell shakedown. "Hit B-One -Four," the hack yelled.

"Step out!" the hack ordered.

"And strip it," a second hack added.

"You got a problem, boy?" the older hack asked, staring at Bill with angry eyes.

"No sir," Bill replied flatly.

"What's this?" the other hack asked, waving papers."

"Legal work, sir."

"Is your name James Percy Hall?" the hack barked.

"No sir," Bill answered.

"Oh," he said, raising his eyebrows. "You're one of those jail house writ writers, are you?" He kneed Bill in the groin, causing him to double over, clutching his balls to try to stem the agony. The hack slammed a black baton into the back of Bill's head and fireworks exploded in his eyes. "You ain't one no more," the hack screamed throwing papers all over the range.

"You got a problem with that boy?" the hack asked.

"No sir," Bill replied meekly.

Order had been restored, but prisoner's still fought amongst themselves. James Percy 'steeps' Hall was a black man, highly trained in martial arts, a member of the Black Liberation Army and, like Bill, a militant who fought the system with intelligence instead of brute strength. Short, stocky, and well educated, he was an adversary to be wary of. And, he was serving forty years.

Bill's mother went to the former Commissioner for Anne Arundel County, Jack Evertts, and he used his influence to help Bill. Overnight, Bill was transferred to an honor camp on the Eastern Shore. There, in the last months of his two and a half years behind bars, he earned his G.E.D. Then, he was assigned to work in Governor Marvin Mandell's mansion. Bill mopped the kitchen floor, shined the governor's shoes, and curried the families Collie. There were no specific duties, but every morning he would bid the governor a casual "Good morning." The upstairs were off limits, but Bill enjoyed eating the governor's steaks and playing pool in the State Troopers' barracks with the men assigned to protect the governor.

Bill wrote Steeps several times, but the older man never answered his letters. Bill didn't understand it then, but later figured it out. Steeps -- who wanted Bill to get prison off his mind, and out of his system -- was and always would be his friend.

Then came work release. Bill, along with twenty other prisoners, went on a bus to put in applications at Eskay Poultry in Cordova, Maryland. Bill was pulled from the line and asked if he was any good in math.

"Yeah, sure," he replied, somewhat bewildered.

Hired on the spot, Bill was given the position of Quality Control Supervisor. He applied himself with a single minded determination that impressed everyone. Bill learned every phase of the operation, every conceivable cut of chicken, temperatures, weighing vats in and out considering weight loss. Bill reported to work dressed in nice suits, carrying a clipboard and pencil. At first, the hacks resented him, but as time passed he earned everyone's respect. He stood on the line, took a knife in hand, and learned the various cuts. If someone was behind, Bill would step in to help. He became 'a worker' not just a supervisor.

The women workers brought Bill fresh baked cookies and pies.

But the ghost of yesteryear mingled, wandered, and behaved strangely.

When Bill was paroled, he returned to Baltimore. He went to the Maryland Penitentiary and tried to visit Steeps. But, he was turned away.

"Hey Steeps!" Bill yelled, standing on the sidewalk in front of the prison.

"Steeps, it's Hooker," a prisoner inside hollared.

Steeps walked to the window, saw Bill, and yelled.

"Get out of here, honkey. Get a life! Ain't you had enough of this place?"

The last time Bill saw Steeps -- or, more accurately, his likeness - was on a wanted poster in a United States Post Office.

CHAPTER ELEVEN
ARMY BLUES

"A thousand stars in the sky...make me realize...that you are the one girl...that I..I..I..love, -" the singer wailed.

The Bolero club was very much alive when Bill pulled up parking his white Cadillac at the curb. It was as if he was a magnet and the bar made of steel, Bill was drawn to this place.

Living life in the fast lane, the good life. He thrived on his existence like a plant thrives on water, and sunshine. The popularity he'd acquired, the girls that gathered around him. Bill lived for the moment. His easy going nature and personality made him fun to be around. And, tomorrow? Well, tomorrow was promised to no one, he reasoned.

Red was sitting at the bar nursing a bottle of Budweiser when Bill walked up and whispered in his ear, "We gotta talk."

"Sure, what's up?" Red replied, and chugged the remainder of his beer following Bill outside.

Out of ear shot of anyone else Bill reported, "I found a bank. It's a real good one, in Pennsylvania."

Before Bill could finish speaking, Red asked. "When do you want to do it?"

"Broke huh?" Bill laughed.

"Aw hell, ain't I always." Red grinned, a sheepish look on his sunburned face.

"Let's do it next week. But we're going to be doing something a little different this time.

"Different?"

"I want to capture the bank."

"Capture it?"

"There's an Army base at the end of the street and a vault inside the bank. If there's a payroll there, and I believe there is - I want it!"

"Capture it?" Red repeated, speaking more to himself.

"This is the big one, Red, I can feel it in my bones."

"Sounds good, I think." Red laughed, his face reddening.

"Red. Partner, pal - old friend of mine. This one is our retirement."

"Yeah," Red said, catching Bill's mood. "Retirement, or katy bar the door."

"Well, actually, if we get caught they'll probably weld the door shut. But I feel good about this one..."

"Damn, now you got me wondering. Shit! I just don't know." Red hesitated.

"What's the matter? " Bill asked, stomping his foot, mimicking Red's behavior in North Carolina. "God damnit, you just want to rob no fucking bank!"

Bill and Red looked at each other and started to laugh. It started out as a small laugh, but grew with the force of a tidal wave. Soon, they were holding each other up, laughing like two mad men.

They decided to make the hour and a half drive to Pennsylvania to case the bank Friday morning.

On his way home, as Bill drove past a new car dealership, a 1975 canary Corvette convertible caught his eye and he stopped to check it out. The Corvette was loaded with every option available - power windows, power steering, cruise control, tilt steering, and air-conditioning. The 'Vette' boasted a small block 350 cubic, 360 horsepower engine capable of pushing the car to well over 120 mph. Bill took it for a test drive, putting it through its paces. The three speed automatic ran smoothly through the gears and made telephone poles look like a picket fence as they flew by. No doubt about it, Bill thought, this bitch is built for speed.

Bill pulled up in front of the apartment and beeped the horn. Judy looked out of the upstairs window, shook her head, and disappeared back inside, reemerging a minute later at the front door.

"Okay asshole, where did you get this?" she asked suspiciously.

"I bought it." Bill grinned, all innocence.

"No, you didn't!"

"Okay, I stole it."

"Did you?" she asked, her voice raising in preparation for the temper tantrum she was about to have.

"You don't know, do you?" Bill teased.

"Did you steal the damn car, or not?" she snapped.

"Nope, I bought it."

"Where's the receipt?"

"You mean, the registration?"

"Don't play word games with me, asshole."

"It's probably in the glove compartment."

Judy opened the door, sat down in the passenger seat, looked around for a moment, then snapped. "There ain't no fucking glove compartment!" she said in frustration.

"Nice, huh?" Bill said, smiling.

"Did you steal it?" Judy asked wearily.

"No, I told you that I bought it."

Bill reached between the seats and opened the center console. When he reached inside and withdrew the registration, Judy snatched it from his hand and carefully read it.

"So, what do you think?"

"I think you're going to get yourself killed, Ginge," she said in disgust. "Hey," her eyes narrowed in renewed suspicion, "Where did you get the money to buy this? And, where is the Cadillac?"

"Oh shit," Bill mumbled. "I, ah, borrowed the money. The Cadillac is parked at the dealership. It's safe, we can pick it up later."

"Where did you borrow the money from?"

"From the bank, I took out a loan."

"Take it back, we can't afford payments." Judy snapped.

"I'm just kidding. It's paid for."

"Okay fucker, don't play games with me. Is it paid for, or not?" she nearly screamed her frustration.

"Aw, c-mon baby. Have I ever lied to you?"

"That's it! Either you're going to tell me the truth, or I'm going to cut you off for life. '

"For life? That's a little harsh. No pussy for the rest of my life?"

"None. Not even a glimpse."

"But, I did tell you the truth. It's paid for."

"You didn't pay for this with quarters."

"Maybe I did," Bill smiled.

"Where did you get the money?"

"Nonya - "

"What the hell is nonya?"

"None ya damn business," Bill said, and laughed so hard his sides hurt.

"I give up. You fucker!" Judy said jumping out of the car.

"I guess you don't want to go for a ride."

"Yes, I do!" she said, as excited as a kid on Christmas morning. "I gotta go put some shoes on."

"Sure, I'll wait right here for you," Bill snickered.

"Fucker. You better not leave without me," Judy warned.

"I wouldn't do that," Bill grinned.

Judy was halfway up the stairs leading to the apartment when Bill started the car. She looked over her shoulder, stopped, and ran back to the car. "Give me the keys," she demanded.

"Trust me, I'm not going anywhere without you."

Judy looked at him with reservations. "You better not!"

"Have I ever lied to you?"

Judy smirked, ran up the stairs, and into the apartment. She came back down the stairs smiling, anticipating an afternoon out with Bill. As she jumped into the passenger seat, she said, "Let's go."

Bill pulled away from the apartment in low gear gradually bringing the car up to twenty mph. Then, he floored the accelerator. The tires squealed, seeking traction, and the Corvette fishtailed wildly. When the rear wheels finally grabbed the asphalt, the Corvette shot forward, streaking down the street. When the automatic shifted to second gear, the tires chirped. Judy, was plastered back against the seat, her hair slapping her in the face and screaming, "Slow down, you fucking asshole!"

Bill eased off the accelerator and the transmission slid into third gear. "Fast, ain't it?" he chuckled.

"You're fucking crazy," Judy huffed. Then, in a more gentle tone asked, "Is it all right if I smoke?"

"Sure." Bill grinned, tickled that she had bothered to ask.

"Thanks!" she puffed on Winston. They headed away from the city of Baltimore, with the sun shining warmly and a warm summer breeze in the air. The duel exhaust rumbled off of the surrounding retainer walls. Feeling at peace with the world, she looked at Bill; her man, and though he did many things that 'society' considered wrong, she still loved him with every fiber of her being.

"Where we going, Ginge?" she shouted over the roaring of the wind.

"To Bobby and Mary's," he shouted back.

Judy nodded. She understood, and approved, The older couple were good people who had done so much to help Bill when he'd first come to Baltimore. Besides, she wasn't the clinging type who begrudged her man his friends.

When Bill pulled into the driveway of the white house on Creekside, he honked the horn and revved the engine.

Karen, Bobby and Mary's oldest daughter was the first out the front door. "Where did you get this?" she asked, her eyes wide.

"Like it?" Bill grinned.

"Like it?" the adolescent girl gasped, "Oh Bill, I love it!" Then, Karen looked at Judy and asked, "Is it really his?"

"Yeah, but don't ask me where he got the money," Judy giggled.

"Why?" Karen wondered.

"Because I don't know where he got the money," Judy laughed. Bobby, Billy and Sandy stepped outside.

"Wait until mom sees this," Karen smiled.

Sandy was indifferent, car's didn't impress her.

"Take me for a ride, please!" Billy begged.

"Do you remember when you woke me up pounding on drums?" Bill asked little Billy, with a mischievous twinkle in his eye.

"I'm sorry," Billy whined. "Please, please take me for a ride."

"Okay. But next time you better be more considerate."

"I will be!" Billy promised. Both he and Bill knew the skinny little brat was lying through his teeth...

"Pop the hood," Bobby said, as Mary pulled into the driveway in her pumpkin colored Pinto. She looked at the Corvette, smiled, and asked Bill, "Is that yours?"

"It sure is," little Billy answered. "And, Bill's going to take me for a ride."

"Like it?" Bill asked Mary, grinning.

"Is it his?" Mary asked Judy.

"Why is it that nobody ever believes me?" Bill asked, looking at Bobby for support.

"Because you never tell the truth," Sandy shot back.

"Yes, I do!" Bill replied, in his defense.

"You do not," Judy laughed,

Bobby shrugged his shoulders and chuckled.

"C'mon Billy, I'm not going to win this one."

Billy opened the car door and climbed into the Corvette.

The dual exhaust rumbled as Bill backed from the driveway.

After taking Billy for a ride, Bill and Judy spent the evening enjoying the family atmosphere.

Bill wanted to be well rested for the trip to Pennsylvania with Red the next morning, so he bid Bobby and Mary a goodnight, and drove to the new car dealership. Judy drove the Cadillac back to the apartment..

* * *

Bill and Red pulled to the side of the road directly in front of the bank. The canary yellow Corvette was conspicuous, but they weren't planning to rob the bank today. Today they were casing the bank, checking out the surrounding area, and planning their escape route.

The two-story red brick building sat in the middle of an asphalt parking lot. A concrete retaining wall circled the lot in the rear, rising to eight feet at its highest point. A black wrought iron stairway led to an upstairs door at the rear of the bank. A single plate glass door in front was the only entrance at ground level. To the left of the front door, a large picture window faced the street. Clearly visible through the window were three tellers handling customer transactions. On the right of the building there were four windows, two upper and two lower. At the rear of the building there were three windows. Two on the upper floor, one on the ground floor. The windows were wood framed, which to Bill, meant easily accessible with a crowbar. He could enter the bank at night, wait for the employees to arrive for work and capture them. It would be as easy layin' a drunk hooker, he thought.

Only one thing disturbed him. Mounted on top of a pole on the roof was a yellow beacon. Bill wondered if it was some type of alarm or warning device.

Across the road to the left of the bank were two houses that were situated on a hilltop overlooking the bank and surrounding area. Directly behind the bank was a third house that sat atop a grassy knoll. Any one of these houses could be the bank manager's or somebody in the banks employ. Perhaps they periodically checked the beacon, and if they found it spinning around flashing, they called the Cavalry. Directly across from the bank was an open field, railroad tracks, and an isolated dirt access road. It was on this road where Bill and Red parked the following morning to watch the employees arrive for work.

"Where's the Army base?" Red asked.

"Right down there," Bill pointed to where the main road ended at a four-way stop. On the other side of the intersection was a guard shack, a guard, and a gate leading to the Post. The guard shack had a red and white striped barrier leaving little doubt of what lay beyond the gate.

"So, what do you think?" Bill asked.

"What's that beacon for?" Red asked, pointing to the beacon on top of the pole on the roof of the bank.

"I'm not sure."

"Well, how do we know if it goes off?"

"I guess we've just got to take our chances."

"Look!" Red said, watching a cream colored white Ford pull into the bank. It drove around the building and parked against the retaining wall.

A woman stepped out, locked her car, and walked around the left side of the bank to the front door. She used a key to let herself in and disappeared out of sight.

"Bingo!" Bill grinned, excited. "Count my money for me, baby."

"The bank manager should be pulling in any minute," Red guessed.

Sure enough, a few minutes later a green Volkswagen Bug pulled into the park, rounded the building, and parked behind the cream colored Ford. A middle-aged, balding man got out, walked around the side to the front door, and entered the bank.

"When do you want to do this?" Red asked.

"Next week. The Army pays its men at the end of the month. So, if we hit it on Friday, the payroll should be there." Maybe they cash their checks on the base." Red chuckled, a worried frown on his lips.

"Not a chance. I stumbled upon this bank trying to find a shortcut home from Breezewood. It was a Friday afternoon, the end of the month, and the parking lot was packed with soldiers. I damn near wrecked my car rubber necking the bank," Bill chuckled.

"I've never seen a bank like it before," Red admitted.

Arriving back in Baltimore, Bill dropped Red off at his apartment, the two men agreeing to meet for further discussion on the job sometime over the weekend. Red and his wife Mary's apartment was less than two blocks from Bill and Judy's apartment. Red's sister was the manager of the low income welfare apartments. While Red chose to live in the center of the complex because it had grass, sidewalks, and a play area for their young daughter, Bill opted to live in an upstairs apartment that looked like a row-house where he could park his car at the curb in front of the building.

Bill's knowledge of banks and alarm technology was ever expanding. He was familiar with the various types of silent alarms, triggered by a concealed button or switch. Some were triggered when a certain stack of bills were removed from the cash drawer. Still others were wired to a pressure switch in the floor that a teller could step on to set off the alarm.

The newer, high-tech vaults were equipped with motion and heat sensors, time locks, and numerous other devices to prevent theft. But the bank that Bill had his eyes on was at least ten years behind the times. The vault, once opened in the morning, was protected only by a barred gate that opened with a key. The bank manager would be in possession of the key. Bill had a real good feeling about this bank - it felt like money.

The following day, Bill stopped at an Army/Navy surplus store and outfitted himself as a Lieutenant Colonel. Uniform, rank, and all. He took the clothes home and tried them on while Judy was out shopping. He liked the way the uniform fit him. He cocked the hat at a rakish angle, stood before a mirror, and said to his reflection, "Damn boy, you look pretty good. Maybe you should have joined the Army." He turned full circle, looking at himself from every angle, smiling at the results.

"How do you like me now, Tom?" he grinned.

Sunday night, in a secluded corner of the Bolero club, Bill and Red sat down at a table to iron out the details of the job. Drinking beers, they went over the strategy again and again until Bill felt they had it right.

"I think we've covered everything. If there's anything left out, I can't think of what it would be." Bill said, gulping down the rest of his beer.

"We damn sure covered all the bases," Red agreed.

* * *

Thursday night. They left the Bolero club at closing, drove to Pennsylvania, and began their search for a car to steal to use as the getaway vehicle. Bill stole a dark blue Chevrolet Super Sport from a neighborhood twenty miles away from the bank. By morning, they parked Red's red Ford Torino a quarter mile from the bank. Bill had decided that it was best to capture the first female employee when she showed up. Once inside the bank, he would capture the bank manager when he came inside. Once the vault was opened, his plan was to hogtie his captives, take the money, and make good his escape. Red was to come inside after Bill captured the bank manager. The plan seemed to be foolproof. Or, so Bill thought.

Bill put the uniform over his blue jeans and white tee-shirt, placed the hat on his head adjusting it to the proper angle, then put on a pair of black sunglasses. When he was finished, he looked at his watch, 8:20 a.m. The first employee should arrive any minute.

Sure enough, at 8:25 the cream color Ford turned off of the main road into the bank's parking lot. As she pulled in, Red started the getaway car with the turn of a screwdriver stuck in to the ignition, and they pulled out of the service road. As she closed her car door, Bill was opening his. Perfect timing he thought, as the well dressed lady approached. She looked up, saw Bill coming toward her, the Army uniform threw her completely offguard.

"We don't open until nine," she smiled, coming abreast of Bill.

He took her by the elbow and quietly said, "This is a robbery. Do exactly as you're told and no one will be hurt."

"What do you want me to do?" she asked, surprisingly cool for a woman being kidnapped.

"Just do what you normally do," Bill advised her.

As they entered the bank she locked the door behind them. When they headed up the stairway, she reached to turn on a light switch.

"Don't!" Bill barked.

"But you told me to do what I normally do," she replied.

"Except that," he said, grabbing her elbow again.

The steps led up one flight to a small landing, then went at a forty-five degree angle up to a second floor. Reaching the top, the woman said, "I usually make coffee."

"Not this morning," Bill replied shortly. He was polite and courteous, but he used few words and he never smiled. The less he said, the less chance anyone had of recognizing his voice, or him, at a future date.

"If you don't want me to turn on the lights, and you don't want me to make coffee, then what do you want me to do?"

"Just whatever you normally do."

"But that is what I normally do!" she said, exasperated.

"Okay, let's go back downstairs," Bill said, a little put out with himself. When they reached the first floor, he instructed her to sit on the steps, while he took a position where he could watch the front door.

"Can I smoke?" she asked.

"Sure."

She opened her purse and jammed her hand down inside.

"Go easy!" Bill cautioned, the nine millimeter automatic suddenly in his hand.

She froze and looked at Bill, "I'm sorry. I'm just nervous."

"Don't look at me!" Bill snapped, "Look at the floor."

She obeyed without question, looking at her feet as she lit the cigarette. She flicked out the match and looked around for some place to put it. She must have decided it was pretty silly worrying about neatness when she was being held at gun point because she threw the match on the floor. She smoked with quick, nervous puffs, her earlier composure deserting her.

Five minutes passed, then ten. The door opened and Bill looked up expecting to see the manager, but it was another female teller.

"Good morning," Bill said pleasantly. "Please have a seat on the steps with your friend."

The woman looked puzzled, until Bill showed her the gun.

"What is this?" she asked, the beginnings of anger and indignantcy in her voice.

"It's a robbery," Bill said flatly. "Sit down!" he motioned with the gun.

The woman sat down.

"Look at the floor!" Bill commanded. She too, obeyed without further question.

The front door opened and closed again. The manager came inside, set his lunch and a newspaper on his desk, then went back outside.

Jesus! This wasn't going right. Where in the fuck was Red?

Bill dashed out the front door to find the manager backing up, his hands in the air. Over the man's shoulder he saw Red wearing a ski mask and brandishing a gun.

"Freeze mother fucker!" Red yelled, holding his gun in a two handed combat grip.

The manager's Volkswagon was parked at the front door, still running. Red stepped up, grabbing the bank manager's arm, pushing him back towards the front door of the bank.

The bank manager panicked, jerking his arm away from Red. Red hit him in the head with the butt of his gun twice. But the manager, with the strength of a baby bull, broke loose and ran towards the houses across the road.

Bill looked back inside the bank. One of tellers ran behind the counter, obviously to set off an alarm.

"Forget it, let's go!" Bill shouted to Red.

As they jumped into the getaway car, Bill urged, "Move it, move it!" He slipped the uniform pants off, ripped off the shirt and hat, and stuffed them under the seat. As they switched vehicles, the sound of sirens wailed in their ears. Bill's stomach did cartwheels and his heart dropped to his knees.

"Drop me off," he instructed Red. "Pick me up in two or three hours." Bill bailed out of the car diving into the thick woods boardering the road.

Within minutes, U.S. Army helicopters were in the air, running search patterns just over the treetops, Bill found a large boulder with a slight overhang, took off the white tee-shirt, and hugged the boulder.

Below him, through the woods, he could see a cul-de-sac with houses and children playing. He watched as police cars and Army jeeps navigated the street below, heard dogs barking in the distance, and he prayed. "Lord, get me out of this one and I'll never do it again."

A few hours later, Bill heard the sound of tires crunching on gravel, and then a horn honk several times. It could only be Red. Or, at least he hoped.

Bill stood up, brushed himself off, and ran from the woods. "Damn, am I glad to see you," Bill told a grinning Red.

"It's a good thing that you got out of the car. They were looking for a small blue compact with two men in it." Red reported.

"If you had gone into the bank with me, things would have worked. The manager would have never had the chance to walk back out the front door. We had it, Red!" Bill sighed.

"Look at it this way, at least we ain't in jail." Red grinned, his neck turning red.

CHAPTER TWELVE
PET PARTY

"Hooker," the company commander began. "There's a rumor that you're having a party tonight."

"Yes sir." Bill's brother Fred replied, standing at attention before his C.O., back straight, shoulders back, chin up. The portrait of a perfect sailor.

"I suppose you're aware of your medical history?"

"Yes sir."

"You've been treated for gonorrhea twice, syphilis three times, mononucleosis, damn near every sexually transmitted disease known to man," the commander waved his medical report in the air. "And this," he said, brandishing another file. "This says that you've been arrested not once, but twice, for running a disorderly house."

Yes sir."

"Hooker, you're a medical wonder with a bad record. What amazes me is that your cock hasn't fallen off, or that you haven't ended up in the stockade - or both," the man sitting behind the mahogany desk ranted.

With all the respect he could muster, Fred Hooker replied, "Yes sir, I agree." Privately, he thought his C.O. was a boob, but he kept that to himself.

"I understand that you're having a party," the Captain repeated.

"Yes sir."

"Just what kind of party?" his C.O. asked.

"A pet party, sir."

"Pet party," the Commander questioned. "Would you care to explain to me what a 'pet party' is?"

"Yes sir. It's bring your own date, sir." Fred Hooker explained, smiling widely. "Perfectly innocent, sir."

"Hooker, I don't believe that you know the meaning of the word innocent," the Commander said decisively. "But there's not going to be any trouble tonight, right?"

"No sir. Small party, contained to the house," Hooker assured him.

Freddy Hooker, older than Bill by four years, joined the Navy at a young age and was presently in the submarine service, and stationed in Groton, Connecticut. He'd decided early in his military career that living in a submarine traveling the world was the life he wanted. He'd also decided to dedicate his on-shore time to partying his ass off.

Fred, along with three shipmates rented a house and named it 'the House of DOI' short for 'Den of Iniquity'. Their parties had become legendary and twice he was arrested for running a disorderly house. To this end, Fred rented a mansion on the water from the scion of a local newspaper empire, who on his infrequent and brief trips home from abroad, enjoyed attending the legendary parties. The mansion, with its ten bedrooms (rented to a select few officers from other submarines) featured a pool, sauna, and large well kept grounds. It was so enormous that Fred named his new residence, 'the Ponderosa.'

"Where are you going?" Judy asked, as she watched Bill pack.

"To visit my brother."

"So what do you need that for?" she asked, pointing to the Ace pick in his suitcase.

"I always take it - you know that."

"You're going off with Red, aren't you?"

"No!" Bill laughed,

"Are you telling me the truth?"

"Have I ever lied to you?"

"Humph," Judy snorted. "That's it. You're not leaving!"

"But baby, I'm telling you the truth." Bill said, and gave her a whipped puppy dog expression.

"I'm calling Mary," Judy snapped, picking up the phone.

"Okay, I confess. Red and I are planning to rob Fort Knox in the morning."

"Are you," she asked, seriously.

"No. But I wish that it was true."

"I hate you!" Judy retorted.

"No, you don't."

"Oh yes, I do."

"Okay. You hate me," Bill said, prancing off to the bathroom in search of his toothbrush singing 'Puff the Magic Dragon lived by the sea…' in an off key voice.

"You're not funny!" Judy snapped. As she smashed one cigarette in the ash tray, she lit another and puffed wildly.

"Do you still love me?" Bill asked from the bathroom.

"You're too much," she replied, giggling.

"And you're too little to do anything about it," he replied.

"You've got to sleep sometime," she said ominously.

"Such evil little thoughts. I'm surprised at you Lil Bit."

Judy gave an evil little smile, and said. "I'll hog tie your ass to the bed."

"Kinky, I might like that."

"Then, I'll beat your ass with a belt."

"Fuck that, fun's over. I'm outta here."

"Hey!Where are you going?"

"I was all for it, until you started talking about beating me."

"Oh drat!" Judy said, in mock disappointment.

"I'll be back in a few days. If you need me, call my brother's."

"Be careful. Ginge."

Bill bent over and kissed Judy, then he straightened up and said, "I love you."

Judy didn't say a word until he was almost to the front door.

"Be careful!" she said in a small voice.

Bill smiled, waved, and walked out the door, Hell, he was going to party with his brother. What could possibly happen?

Driving through the City of New York on the expressway with the convertible top down was nauseating. The blue smoke and stench from the factories was overwhelming. As Bill drove through the boroughs, graffiti covered the concrete barriers and overpasses. A common sight was vehicles stripped and their bones left by the side of the road.

Bill looked at the fuel gauge. The Corvette was almost dry. Damn, he thought, this bitch sure guzzles the gas. As he entered the State of Connecticut he eased the car to the right and took the next exit off the freeway.

A few hundred yards down the road was a small plaza with a liquor store, a deli, and a gas station. And at the far end of the plaza, low and behold - a bank.

"Fill it up," Bill told the attendant at the American gas station. He emptied his bladder in the public rest room, paid the clerk for the gas, and then pulled the Corvette into a space in front of the liquor store.

Bill drew in a deep breath of clean refreshing air, walked into the store, and bought a fifth of his favorite whiskey, Seagram's Seven. Then, as if drawn by a magnet, he walked towards the bank.

Bill's eyes moved quickly, missing nothing, as he entered the bank. Four tellers, two cameras, and the clock above the vault indicated that it worked on a time lock. The head teller was the farthest to the right, Nobody had to tell him that she was the head teller -- he had a kind of instinct, a second sight, about these things. She would have a second drawer, or possibly a safe under the counter. That's where the money was!

"May I help you, sir?" the teller asked.

"Can I have a roll of quarters, please?" Bill asked, handing her a twenty dollar bill. When she opened her money drawer Bill peeked inside and guessed, at best, there was two thousand dollars. He took his quarters, and left. His mind already thinking of the possibilities.

Leaving the shopping center, Bill turned left. More to satisfy his curiosity than to actually plan to rob the bank. Two more lefts lead to a dead end in an apartment complex. There was only one way in, and out. Not good, Bill thought. Then, he noticed the cars going by on the freeway and he looked in that direction. There was a path leading from the apartments to a rest area on the freeway.

"Another day, another dollar. See ya, Tom!" Bill smiled.

* * *

The pig was roasting over a blazing fire when Bill arrived at the Ponderosa. The mansion was huge. The grounds, beautifully tended, A four foot stone wall ran the perimeter of the property at the road. A paved entrance led to a horseshoe driveway at the front of the mansion. There was a flight of marbled steps leading to the mansion. Double doors at the front entrance were aged oak, with a stained glass fanlight above.

As Bill drove down the newly paved drive leading to the mansion, cars were parked on both sides of the road in the grass. There were tin wash basins filled with ice and beer everywhere. Men in swimming trunks and girls in scantily clad bikinis played volleyball, laughing and having a great time diving for spiked balls, and bounding to the net to spike one in return.

Bill parked next to his brothers 1958 blue and white Corvette convertible. Parked on the other side was Fred's prized emerald blue 1965 Pontiac GTO convertible.

"Excuse me," Bill said, intercepting a couple walking arm in arm. "Can you tell me where I can find Fred Hooker?"

"Hooker?" the man asked, somewhat drunkenly. "Hey Dewey, where's Hooker?"

"Who wants to know?" a voice shouted back.

"His brother!" Bill shouted.

"Hey, all right!" the voice said, sailing a can of Budweiser through the air. Bill barely caught it before it hit him in the head. He popped the top and took a long gulp. "Damn, that's good."

The cold brew was followed by Dewey, who pumped Bill's hand like he was running for public office.

"What's up man. Fred said his brother would be here, Glad to meet you! Come-on, I'll take you to Fred." Dewey put his arm around Bill like they were long lost friends, and lead him into the mansion. "Where are you from?"

"Baltimore," Bill grinned.

"I've been there. Have you ever been on 'the Block?"

"A few times."

"I've been there once," Dewey belched. "Sure was a lot of fun."

"I bet," Bill replied, still grinning. There was no reason to tell Dewey that most of the club owners were his personal friends.

As they walked into the mansion, Dewey stopped to ask some of the other sailors where Fred was.

"Fred's in the back forty playing softball," Dewey reported. "Go through those doors, turn left, and keep walking. You can't miss him!"

Following Dewey's directions, he walked out onto the back lawn. Lawn hell, Bill thought, back 'field' would be more like it. The back forty was to the left of the mansion and it was forty acres. The entire grounds probably covered sixty acres, and the back forty was definitely the lion's share of that.

"Hey Danny," Fred yelled, rounding third base. "Glad you could make it!" he yelled, waving, as he headed for home plate. Bill took one look at his brother and laughed hysterically. He was wearing the ugliest outfit he'd ever seen. Purple and white polka dotted Bermuda shorts, an oversized olive drab fatigue tee-shirt, and dust covered Jesus sandals. But the ultimate in ugly was the World War II German helmet he held on his head as he ran. Crossing home plate, someone handed Fred a shot glass of Schnapps, which he readily downed.

"Hey Danny, Fred slurred, calling Bill by the name he was called as a child. "Ever play 'beer ball' before?"

"Nope. How is it played?"

"There's quarter kegs on first, second, and third base. When you reach a base, you drink a cup of beer. If you hit a double, you drank two cups of beer. At third base, a third cup of beer. And when you reach home plate, you drink a shot of Schnapps."

"What's the object of the game?"

"Stay on your feet," Fred laughed, then asked. Do you wanna play?"

"What happens if you don't drink?"

"You're outta here!" Fred yelled, jerking a thumb over his shoulder in parody of an umpire.

"What happened to a little get together, a few friends, maybe a weenie roast - that's what I was led to believe."

"Aw, I didn't want you to think that I was exaggerating."

"Shit! I came unprepared. I didn't even bring a pair of shorts."

"I'll loan you a pair!" Fred offered.

Bill looked at what Fred was wearing, and quickly said, "No thanks bro. I'll find something," he laughed.

"Hey Hooker, you gonna play or bullshit?" someone yelled.

"I'm not playing unless my brother does," Fred shouted.

Then, he looked at Bill, who just shook his head. "Guess the game's over!" Fred yelled.

Bill looked at the eighteen unhappy people and made a silent vow to kill his brother in a slow and most painful way as he could think of. Then, he smiled, shrugged his shoulders, and said. "What the hell, you only live once."

Someone tossed Bill a glove and told him to take left field. By the third inning, he was feeling no pain and wondering if he would survive the next day's hangover.

It was the bottom of the fourth when Bill knew that he was for sure, drunk. Why else would he be seeing a girl dragging a goat on a leash across the backyard?

"Either I'm so wasted that I'm hallucinating, or there's a girl dragging a goat around," Bill shouted to his brother.

Everyone stopped to look in the direction that Bill was pointing. A wave of laughter rolled across the field as people watched the girl wrestle with the uncooperative animal.

"What's up, Cheryl," Fred asked between bursts of laughter. "Well," she began somewhat embarrassed. "Lori said that you were having a pet party and that everyone was supposed to bring their favorite pet."

People were on the ground, rolling around, laughing so hard tears streamed down their faces.

Fred was beside himself, he didn't quite know what to say. "Ah...what is meant by 'pet party' is --" Fred went on to explain that a pet was 'a boyfriend' or a 'girlfriend'. "In other words," he concluded, "a pet of the two legged variety."

"Shit! I realize that now." Cheryl, Fred's girlfriend's sister, said, redfaced.

"But, that's okay. We'll make him a mascot," Fred assured her. "Play ball!" Fred yelled.

As darkness fell, there was live band taking requests. Couples danced, and bonfires were set. Some couples sat by the waters edge, while others played beneath blankets. Some looked for an available bedroom. And Cheryl, she continued to drag the goat around wherever she went.

It was around nine o'clock when Fred suggested that she tie the goat up to the door handle of her car.

"Good idea, thanks Fred," she said, and off she went.

Cheryl soon discovered that her Chevette didn't have door handles, it had latches. So, she tied the goat to the passenger door of Fred's G.T.O.

Bill and Fred were sitting beneath a tree at the back of the house drinking beer and talking about old times. Neither was in any condition to drive, and Fred's girlfriend Lori was expecting him to pick her at Fiddler's Three at midnight. She tended bar there. Cheryl offered to pick her sister up. When she went to her car, she found it blocked in. So, Fred tossed Cheryl the keys to his G.T.O. One good deed deserves another.

Bill and Fred toasted each other again, and again.

"Hey Fred. Do you remember when we lived in Pensacola, Florida and you painted Dad's car. '

"Twice!" Fred laughed.

"Which one of you are the oldest?" some girl asked.

"He is!" Fred said. "I just call him my little brother because he's smaller."

"If you believe that, I've got a bridge to sell you." Bill retorted. They went on telling stories about their youth until someone called Fred to the phone.

Bill heard his brother say, "Holy shit! Settle down. I'll be right there!"

Fred turned to Bill and said, "We've got to get to Fiddler's Three fast!"

They hopped into Bill's Corvette and he smoked the tires all the way down the driveway. Bill spun the steering wheel to the right, barely slowing for the turn, and they rocketed down the main road. The wind whipped around making it damn near impossible to hear anything.

Bill managed to shout, "What's up?"

"It's Cheryl," Fred yelled back, holding his German helmet on his head. "She's in some kind of trouble and her driver's license is suspended."

They arrived at the bar just scant seconds before the police. "Who was driving this car?" a police officer asked, standing beside Fred's G.T.O.

"I was," Fred spoke up.

"How do you explain that?" the cop asked, pointing at the rear tire.

Fred looked at where the cop was pointing, and hung his head.

By this time a crowd had gathered to see for themselves what all the commotion was over. Some turned their heads and looked away, while others eyes filled with tears.

"You son-of-a-bitch!" an elderly woman screamed at Fred.

"What is it, Fred? Bill asked. Then, he looked too. But all he could see was a length of blue nylon rope leading from the passenger door to the rear wheel and what looked like a dirty fur coat laying under the wheel. Then, it dawned on both men that Cheryl had tied the goat up to Fred's G.T.O.

"Guess that poor goat just couldn't run seventy miles an hour," Bill chuckled.

As Fred bent down to try to disengage the hapless animal from the wheel well, a camera flashed. The photographer had caught Fred bending over in his purple polka dotted shorts, Nazi helmet, and Jesus sandals tugging at the mangled goat's carcass.

Pet party. A few friends. Contained to the house. No problems. Suddenly Fred could visualize, all too well, the next morning's headlines: DRUNKEN SAILOR KILLS GOAT!

Fortunately, the reporter worked for the man Fred rented the mansion from. The story was squashed, and Fred's Naval career saved.

* * *

Earl Murphy laughed until it hurt when Bill told him the story about the goat and pet party.

"Hey!" Earl leaned close and whispered. "Did you know that Red and

Frank robbed a bank yesterday?"

"No, that's news to me," Bill chuckled.

CHAPTER THIRTEEN
TRUE LUST WITH LOVE

Florida was forever on Bill's mind, particularly Daytona beach. The only thing he enjoyed more than the sunsets of his childhood were the sunrises over Daytona beach. In his troubled youth, Bill would drive sixty miles or more just to stand on a concrete overpass to gaze out over the ocean and watch the magnificent sunrise over the crashing waves. His heart would forever yearn the mystic moment when the great orange globe would sneak over the distant horizon. It was a moment of tranquillity. Over the years, Bill would try to recapture that sense of peace and well-being, but it was never the same. It was as close to God as he ever felt. In his later years, he wrote a poem to try to capture that moment, that very special moment.

BY THE SEA

As I breathe the oceans breath
and cast my eyes upon the sea
beyond the reef's the gull's are ill-tempered
in the nights maturity.
A coat of arms surrounds the shore
and froths with ebbing tide
its roar increases as the night
falls calmly to the side.
Ghostly is the great seas spirit
Aw, for she is the buccaneer
still yet, in her senility
she cannot seduce my fear.
For the sound of sudden terror
thrashes in her wake
and the calmness of still essence
is all that I forsake.
In the distance the dark lagoon

casting silhouettes
of a fervent moon.
With arms stretched out
and opened wide
it illuminates the oceans depths
and journeys with the tide.
Aw yes, when I gaze upon the sea
I marvel at her fertility.

* * *

Bill entered the Bolero club, seeking the shadow of that former tranquility, or as close as he'd come to it nowdays.

"How are you doing, Earl?"

"Not bad," the big Irishman answered, "and yourself?"

"Can't complain. Life's too short to bitch about it. Looks like they 're having fun." Bill gestured with a nod to the group of men sitting on stools at the back of the bar, Red, Frank, Billy and Pete Grimes, Skinny, and Jabo were drinking and laughing.

"They've been drinking all day. Say, before I forget, what's happening with you and the charge pending in West Virginia. Is that over with?"

"I wish it was."

"When do you have to go back?"

"I'm not really sure. Pretty soon, though." The fact of the matter was, Butch Goode had never set a specific date. It was something Bill still had to deal with. But, not now, and today he'd rather not think about it.

"Hey Danny!" Pete yelled from across the room, waving him over to the table.

"Excuse me," Bill told Earl, making his way towards the group of men. He spotted a beautiful young blonde in passing, and bid her a cheery, "Good evening."

"Hi," she replied, and their eyes locked. Time froze for Bill. "I'm Kathy," she introduced herself. Bill's heart beat faster.

"I'm Bill Hooker. I'm single and available. And, I think I love you!"

"Leave her alone, Bill. She's a nice girl." Joyce interjected.

"I like nice girls," he shot back, smiling at Kathy. She was beautiful! Long platinum blonde hair, with a face straight out of a fashion magazine and a full, sensuous body. No doubt, it was lust at first sight.

"He's a whore!" Joyce shouted.

"I am not," Bill replied. In his defense, he said, "I don't charge a dime."

"Do you come on to all girls like this?" Kathy giggled.

"No!"

"What makes me special?"

"Well, to tell you the truth, I'm a prince. And if I don't find my princess by two o'clock I'll turn into a frog."

"Well, that wouldn't be too bad. If I were to turn myself into a lily pad, you could jump right on me, Mr. Frog."

"Nah. I'd rather be Prince Charming and rescue the beautiful princess."

"My fifteen minute break is up. If I don't get back to work I'm going to need rescuing," Kathy giggled, making her way behind the bar.

"Where have you been all my life? Will you go out with me?" Bill pleaded.

"I've got to work." Kathy smiled.

"That's a damn fine quality. I like that in a girl."

"You're wasting your time," Pete yelled. "Billy's been after her all day."

"Good-gog-a-mogga!" Bill said as Kathy walked away. "That's one damn fine split-tail."

"Wanna drink?" Skinny offered.

"I'm buying!" Frank announced, a smelly cigar stuck in his mouth.

"Somebody want something?" Kathy asked, approaching the table.

"You," Billy answered.

"Besides me," Kathy said, with a giggle.

"Give Danny a drink," Pete ordered.

"Who's Danny? And, what's he drinking?

"Am I really that easy to forget?" Bill chuckled, ordering a Seven and Seven in a tall glass.

"I thought your name was Bill?" Kathy said in puzzlement.

"It's a long story. Maybe I could explain it to you over drinks sometime."

"Maybe," Kathy answered with a smile.

"I'll give you ten to one odds that you don't make her," Pete grinned.

"No bet. God is shining on me and I don't want to jinx my luck."

Ever since Bill had taken Billy to Florida and introduced him to his family, who all called him "Danny" both Billy and Pete started calling him "Danny" too.

When Kathy returned with the drinks, Bill told her, "I know of a great after-hour spot. Good music, dancing, soft lights...."

"Maybe," she smiled, as if giving it some thought.

"Thanks for the drink, Frank. Did you run into some money, or something?" Bill asked, grinning,

"Something like that. I want to talk to you later, whenever you've got some free time," Frank said, puffing on his cigar.

"Hey Danny, you got a minute," Billy asked with a grin.

"Sure."

Billy motioned for Bill to follow him outside, stood, and walked out the door. Nobody was offended. These men knew there were things not to be discussed in public, Once outside, standing next to Bill's Corvette, Billy asked. "What's up? Are we going to rob a bank?"

"I've been thinking about it."

"Give it to me straight." Billy said, eyeing Bill closely. "I know about the bank that you and Red fucked up in Pennsylvania, and I know about the bank that Frank robbed in Pennsylvania. Red drove for him, and Frank discharged the gun in the bank by accident," Billy laughed.

"How do you know about the bank that got fucked up?" Bill asked, bluntly.

"Don't say anything," Billy said, "Frank told me."

Bill and Billy went back a long way. When Bill set fire to Frank's store and was badly burned in the arson, Billy introduced him to Demoral and, later to heroin. The burns healed, but Bill remained a weekend warrior, or 'chipper'. Throughout the week he took care of business, but come the weekend he bought a couple 'sacks' of heroin, a syringe, and 'chased the dragon'.

Billy's main source for heroin was in an all black neighbor hood, in an all black bar called Lu Lu's. One night, when Billy went to make a buy, a black man wearing a tan trench coat stepped in front of Billy's Datsun 280Z and pulled a shotgun. Jabo saw the man first and screammed, "Billy!" shoving him against the driver's door, the sawed off shotgun roared, and Billy and Jabo thought they had bought the farm.

Over the sound of shattering glass, Billy yelled, "Put it in gear! Put it in gear!" Jabo had caught a great deal of the shattered windshield in his face and eyes.

"I can't fucking see!" Jabo screamed. His hand groped for the shifter, "Clutch, damn it, clutch it!"

Billy was bleeding profusely from a wound in his shoulder, the blood spurting out in a great torrent, covering both men,

Billy stomped on the clutch and Jabo's hand finally found the shifter, dropping it in low gear. Billy let out the clutch and mashed the accelerator to the floor. The 280Z leaped forward like a Panther pouncing on its kill. The gunman never had a chance to get off a second shot.

A half block away Billy steered the car to the curb and told Jabo to hit the breaks. Almost before the car slid to a stop Jabo had the door open and was pulling Billy to the passenger seat. He got behind the wheel, restarted the Datsun, then hauled ass.

"Hold on, partner, hold on!" Jabo kept repeating to Billy as he sped towards the nearest hospital. Just keeping the car on the road was a challenge, Between the shattered windshield and the glass in his eyes Jabo was almost blind.

At the hospital, Jabo gave the nurse Pete's phone number and asked her to call him. Pete's wife Jackie called Bill's apartment. Judy answered the phone. Then she called Bill at the Bolero club telling him what happened. Bill was the closest, and first, to arrive at the hospital.

* * *

"That mother fucker! That sorry, black-ass mother fucker," Bill said over and over, pacing the hallway just outside of the Intensive Care Unit, where Billy was listed in critical condition with only a forty percent chance of survival.

Pete and his wife Jackie arrived next, then Billy's girlfriend Pam.

The doctors cleaned the glass and blood from Jabo's eyes, but they still burned terribly. He constantly wiped them, cursing all the while.

"I'll kill that sorry mother fucker. I swear, I'll kill him!" Jabo swore before God to Pete.

Pete was Billy's older stepbrother. They had grown up together in Ellicott City, Maryland.

Within two hours everyone was at the hospital, sitting, waiting. Waiting to see if tomorrow would bring a celebration, or a wake.

Judy knew what Bill was feeling and she was concerned for his freedom. "Let it go, Ginge," she begged. "It's not worth it!"

"Fuck that! Let's go for a ride," Bill nearly screamed.

"Let's go!" Jabo snapped, without a seconds hesitation.

"Oh no-no-noooo!" Judy wailed. "Pete, stop them! Don't let them do something stupid."

"Let's hash this over at my house later," Pete said, and tipped a wink at Bill.

Bill looked into the room where Billy lay, swathed in bandages, his right arm in a cast. Wires ran from his chest to a heart monitor and a respirator helped him breathe.

"It ain't over," Bill silently swore. "It ain't nearly over."

* * *

There wasn't much he wouldn't do for Billy; wasn't much he hadn't already done. But he wasn't into drugs anymore, and Billy was. They were a bad influence on each other.

"Look, Billy." Bill said hesitantly. "If you really want to rob a bank,

I can show you where there's an easy one. You and Jabo can take it down with no trouble."

"Where's it at?"

"It's in Connecticut. I'll draw you a map. Or, better yet, I'll take you there myself."

"If it's such an easy mark, why haven't you robbed it yourself?" Billy asked with a grin.

"That's a damn fine way to show your gratitude." Bill chuckled. "It doesn't have enough money in it for me. If I go to prison again, it will be for a long time, and I'm not going to take that risk unless the payoff is extremely attractive."

"Okay, I can accept that. But I don't know about Jabo. I'd feel more comfortable doing it with someone else."

"Jabo's alright, if he listens."

"Think we can pull it off. Me, and Jabo?"

"I think so. Like I said, it's an easy hit."

"I wish you would have let me in on the one in Pennsylvania," Billy countered.

"So do I." Bill sighed. "Red fucked that one up, not me!" If he would have come inside with me, it would have went down right."

"That's what I figured," Billy grinned.

"Let's get back inside, before somebody steals my girl."

"Your girl?" Billy arched an eyebrow at this pronouncement.

"Just hang around and see who she leaves with," Bill replied, with confidence.

"Would you have breakfast with me after work?" Bill asked the blonde waitress when he was seated once again.

"I usually have breakfast in the morning," she replied cooly.

"That's okay. We can get a room at the Holiday Inn and wait until morning."

"Breakfast in bed?"

"Amongst other things, yes."

"We'll see -- "

"Well, I'll be damned," Billy said, as they watched Kathy drive off with Bill in the Vette. "She did leave with him. What's he got that I ain't got?" he asked the group in general.

"A new canary yellow Corvette convertible and a pocket full of money," Pete answered,

"We'll soon be even on that score," Billy mumbled,

"Say what?" Frank asked.

"Oh nothing," Billy replied, with a secret little smile. "Just talking to myself."

* * *

It was a beautiful night to cruise with the top down, and Kathy loved it. Bill was high in spirits and pretty much inebriated as he tooled down Ritchie Highway. In conversation, he learned that Kathy lived in the apartment building directly across from Red and Mary. As a matter of fact, she often watched their daughter. So entranced was he with his companion that he didn't see the Pontiac Bonneville stopped at a red light directly in front of him.

Kathy screamed, "Bill!" but it was too late. Bill locked the brakes up, but the Corvette slid into the rear end of the Bonneville.

"Oh shit! Are you alright?"

"I'm fine, but I think your car is wrecked," Kathy announced. Bill and the driver of the Bonneville surveyed the damage

There wasn't a scratch on the Bonneville. The nose of the Corvette went beneath the rear bumper crumbling the fiberglass. One headlight was laying on the pavement, the other was damaged, and a couple of pieces were missing. Neither driver wanted to call the police.

"Hell, it's a mess," Bill concluded after the examination.

"What should we do?" Kathy asked.

"I think we can make it to the Holiday Inn, that's only a mile away. But we'll have to wait until daylight before driving it any further."

Kathy smiled, and Bill nearly danced his way around to the driver's seat, quietly mumbling to himself, "Good-gogga,mooga, there's going to be some rocking going-on tonight,"

Bill discreetly hung the 'Do not Disturb' sign on the outside door of the motel room behind them.

* * *

The following morning, Bill ordered room service and served Kathy breakfast in bed.

At noon, they checked out at the front desk and walked out to the parking lot to survey the damage to the Corvette. It sickened Bill's stomach to see the damage in the daylight.

After dropping Kathy off, he drove around the corner and parked at the curb of the apartment that he shared with Judy.

"Where you been, asshole? And, don't lie!" she shouted.

She was sitting on the couch with both legs tucked beneath her, puffing irritably on a Winston cigarette. A cloud of smoke filled the room, as he walked up the steps into the living room.

"I wrecked the Corvette last night, and I couldn't drive it. So, I spent the night with a friend."

Judy hopped up like a Jack-in-the box, running to the window to look outside. Seeing the car was wrecked, she relaxed.

Bill showered, changed clothes, and headed for the door. "Where are you going now?"

"I've got to get the car repaired."

"Well, give me some money. I'm not sitting here by myself all day. I'll go shopping."

Bill quickly peeled off some cash and handed it to her. It somewhat eased his feelings of guilt.

At the Chevrolet dealership, Bill was arguing with the Service Parts manager wanting the Corvette repaired immediately.

"I would if I could. But like I said, it's going to take three weeks just to get the parts."

Bill, seeing that all the cajoling in the world would get him nowhere, went off in search of the showroom. After two wrong turns and directions from a perky secretary with a truly gorgeous ass, he found it.

"May I help you, sir," a sharply dressed, polite, salesman asked, as Bill entered the showroom.

"Yeah, I need a car."

"Well, we have many fine models in stock. Is there any particular model that you're interested in?"

"Actually, if you don't mind, I'd just like to browse. I'll let you know if I see anything that I like."

"Very well. I'll be at my desk," he said, pointing it out.

Bill walked around the showroom, mentally weighing the pros and cons of each car he came to. This one was much to sedate, that one was the wrong color. The one over there looked like someone carrying a lunch box would drive to work. He began to despair over finding anything he liked, when he rounded a corner and fell in love with a black Corvette Stingray. It was black on black with t-tops, and Goodyear racing tires on chrome Cragger rims. The car had a mirrored shine that you could see your reflection in, and the soft black leather interior combined to form the perfect automobile. No doubt, he had to have it.

The salesman looked up from his desk. "Have you found something you like?" he asked politely, half expecting Bill to be one of those car buyers who looked but never bought.

"Yep, the black Stingray. How much will you take for it?"

The salesman looked dumbfounded for a moment, then said. "Yes sir, I'll be right with you," and almost ran for the sales manager's office. In a minute he was back, with his boss in tow."

"Hello," the sales manager extended his hand. "Don't I know you?"

"I was here two weeks ago. I bought a canary yellow Corvette convertible. I wrecked it, and it's now in the service bay. I'm told that it will take three weeks for the parts needed for the repair. So, I'd like to trade it in on the black Stingray."

"Certainly. But the value offered on the trade-in will depend on the extent of damage to the Corvette."

"No problem," Bill grinned.

The sales manager beamed. "Well then, step into my office. I believe that we can work something out."

"Did the service manager give you an estimate on the repairs," the sales manager asked.

"No, he didn't. He simply said that it would take three weeks just to get the parts needed."

"Ron, ask Dave for a written estimate." Turning to Bill, he said. "You will need that for the insurance claim."

"I didn't make a police report," Bill replied.

"Why not," the sales manager asked, more out of curiosity.

"To tell you the truth, I was drunk. The other car wasn't damaged and, well, I was with a very pretty blonde and I was more interested in getting to the motel than I was talking to the police.'

The portly sales manager laughed heartily, "Well, I can certainly understand that,"

"Dave's writing the estimate now," Ron reported, peering in the door. "He said that it would be about fifteen minutes."

While they were waiting, the sales manager offered Bill a cup of coffee and made a cup for himself. When the estimate for the repair arrived, the manager looked at it, and then passed it to Bill.

"Twenty-five hundred. For a headlight bucket and a few cracks?" Bill gasped.

The managers fingers flew over the calculator, then he wrote a number on piece of paper, passed it to Bill, and said, "This is the best that can do."

"Damn! I had fun last night, but I didn't have 'that' much fun." He looked at the price a second time, and asked. "Is Ron standing behind me holding a gun, because this is a robbery - plain, and simple. Hell, I just bought the Corvette two weeks ago..."

"I understand that. Believe me, I do. But --"

"We've got a problem," Ron announced, standing in the doorway.

"What would that be?" the sales manager inquired.

"Someone has a deposit on the Stingray and their credit application is pending approval."

"So, what's the problem. I'm paying cash!" Bill retorted.

"Well sir, by law, when someone places a deposit on a vehicle pending credit approval, we are required to hold the vehicle until the credit application is approved, or denied," the manager explained.

"Can you check on the application? " Bill asked.

"Ron, see if you can find out who's buying the car and where things stand?"

"Tell the guy that I'll give him five hundred dollars not to buy the car," Bill offered in desperation.

"I'm sorry, sir, but we can't do that."

Steve, the salesman who'd sold the car entered the room, "Hey, my guy's solid. He's a doctor at John Hopkin's hospital," he announced, dashing Bill's hopes of his getting the Stingray.

"I'm really sorry, Mr. Hooker. If I could sell the car to you, I would. Please feel free to look around the lot. If you see anything that you like, I'll do my best to see that you get it.

"Do you have anymore Corvettes?"

"No, the Stingray was our last one. The dealership only receives ten Corvettes a year."

"Hey! I've got something that you may be interested in. Do you like convertibles?" Ron asked, smiling.

"I've got to have something, and if it's not the Vette, then it really doesn't matter."

"Come with me." Ron grinned, "I'll sell you Steve's demo and I'll give you one hell of a deal."

Ron was irritated with Steve for blowing his deal, and his commission on the Stingray. He was determined to sell Steve's demo - a 1975 Chevrolet Caprice convertible. White with plush white leather interior, red carpet, and loaded with extras. FM stereo, air-conditioning, tilt wheel, cruise control. Power seats, steering, brakes, windows, and mirrors.

Within forty-five minutes the deal was done. Bill drove the Caprice convertible off the lot, much to Steve's irritation. Judy was sitting on the front steps of the apartment with her young daughter, Amy, when Bill pulled up in the Caprice convertible.

"Is that a rental?" she asked.

" No, I bought it."

"How much did it cost?"

" Nothing, really. I traded the Vette "

Judy's eyes widened as she pinched his neck, hard. "Where did you get the hicky?"

"Hey! Wait a minute, I can explain. I…"

"Shit, shit, shit, shit!" Judy yelled.

"C-mon, Lil bit!"

"Shit, shit, shit!"

"This isn't what it looks like –"

"Shit, shit, shit, shit, shit, shit!"

Bill gave up, walking into the apartment and then the bathroom. He looked into the mirror and, sure enough, he had a large purplish red love bite on the right side of his neck.

"Damn you, Kathy," he thought. He didn't remember her giving him the hicky, but it was like having a smoking gun in his hand, proof positive.

Shit! This wasn't on his agenda. Bill knew that he had to make-up with Judy, he just didn't know how he was going to go about it.

"Lil bit," he began, entering the bedroom. But, she was having none of it.

"Damnit, you fucker. You lying fucker! Shit, shit, shit, shit!" she screamed, tears running from both eyes.

The doorbell rang, and Bill took the opportunity to exit. At the front door, he found Bill and Joanna Smith standing on the porch.

"Hi Bill," Joanna smiled, "Where's Judy?"

"In the bedroom, shiting," Bill replied, deadpan.

"Wha -?" Joanna obviously thought Bill had lost his mind.

"She thinks this is a hicky?" he said, pulling his collar down.

"Did we come at a bad time?" Bill Smith asked.

"No, It's not a hicky!" Bill lied.

Joanna frowned, skeptical of his assertion.

"It is not! I wrecked the Corvette last night. It must have happened then.

"Did you tell Judy that?" Joanna asked.

"Are you kidding me, I can't get past, 'shit, shit, shit.'"

Bill and Joanna laughed heartily. "I'll talk to her," Joanna offered.

"Good luck!" Bill said.

"Got a beer?"

"It's in the fridge, bottom shelf. Help yourself."

The phone rang, and Bill walked into the kitchen to answer it. "Bill's morgue. You stab 'em, we slab 'em."

Frank laughed, "Heard you wrecked the Vette?"

"That's not really a good subject right now."

"Trouble on the home front?"

"You might say that, can I call you back?"

"Sure, but I need to talk with you. It's important."

Frank understood problems with women. After all, he was married to Judy's sister, Linda.

"I'll get back with you as soon as I'm sure that I'm not going to get my throat cut in my sleep," Bill promised, and cut the connection.

"You've got enough beer to open a brewery," Bill Smith announced.

"Would you care for something harder? A shot maybe?"

"Sure, why not." 'Both men poured themselves a shot of whiskey, and took their drinks to the living room.

"You okay?" Bill Smith asked.

"Who, me? Sure, It's Judy who's having the shit fit." He took a sip of Wild Turkey. "When you're suffering, this has got to be the best cure known to mankind," he said, raising his glass in a toast.

"Amen."

Judy peeked around the corner, looked at Bill, and said, "I want to talk to you? "

"Has she got a gun?" Bill asked Joanna, as she walked into the living room and sat next to her husband.

"Very funny," Judy spat. "Are you going to talk to me, or not?"

"Sure, I'll talk. Shit, shit, shit, shit, shit!"

"Go ahead, show your ass!" Judy said, and stormed into the bedroom. She slammed the door, yelling, "Fucker!"

"I think she's mad," Bill commented dryly.

"Whatever gave you that idea?" Joanna giggled.

"Well, I guess I better go kiss and make-up, or else it won't be safe for me to go to sleep tonight,"

"Hello, somebody in there," Bill asked at the door of the the bedroom. There was no reply, so he knocked hard. "Open the door, or I'll kick it in! This is the Sheriff of Buncombe County and I have a warrant for the arrest of Judith Gaye Osborn."

"For what?" Judy sobbed and giggled simultaneously.

"Uh, for spouse endangerment and, ugh, cruel and unusual punishment."

Bill opened the door and peeked in. Judy was sitting in the middle of the round bed, legs crossed, wiping her eyes with a tissue.

"You'll never make it as a comedian," she frowned. "And, I told you never to use my middle name."

Little Amy, now two and a half, hugged her mother's waist tightly.

"I'm sorry, Lil bit. I looked in the mirror, and it does look like a hicky "

Bill raised his right hand and said, "I'm telling the truth, the whole truth, and nothing but the truth. I honestly do not know how it happened." That was true, he didn't know anything for sure. He was simply too damn drunk to remember.

"I'm sorry, Ginge. I guess I overreacted." Judy rested her head on Bill's shoulder and whispered in his ear, "I love you."

"I love you too," Lil bit. And, in that, Bill felt that he was telling the truth ...

CHAPTER FOURTEEN
THE ESCAPADE

Frank, clad only in shorts, was washing his blue Dodge window van in the driveway when Bill arrived at his house. Alongside the house, with its door propped open so it could air out, was a well kept travel trailer. Linda, Frank's wife, and mother of his two young boys, was tending to her small flower garden in front of their two bedroom red brick ranch style home. Ryan, their oldest son, was keeping his brother, Dennis, occupied in a sand box behind the house.

"Who's this, the Pillsbury Dough Boy," Bill teased, pointing to Frank's stomach hanging slightly over the waistband of his cut-off denim shorts.

"He needs to go on a diet," Linda laughed.

"What I need," Frank said, with a leer, "is more extra curricular activity," and eyed Linda's ample rear as she bent to pull weeds from her garden.

"You're an asshole, Frank." Linda shot back, embarrassed.

"Yeah, Frank." Bill laughed.

"So are you!" Linda spat.

"Don't pay her any attention. PMS, you know."

"I bet someone would pay attention if I started talking about your 'other' extra curricular activities, Frank." Linda said scornfully.

"Sheesh woman, put a lid on it."

Linda just giggled under Frank's withering stare. She stood up, brushed herself off, and headed for the backyard to check on the boys.

Frank finished washing the van, then turned to Bill and asked, "Do you want a beer?"

"Sure."

The two men walked inside the house. Frank opened the refrigerator, grabbed two beers, and handed one to Bill.

"Sitting on Fat City now, ain't you?" Bill grinned, sitting down at the kitchen table.

"I wish!" Frank replied, looking at Bill.

"I heard that you and Red did a job."

"Me, and Red?" Frank said irritably. "You mean me. I stole the car. I robbed the bank. I drove the getaway car to where Red was parked, and then I gave him half of the money."

"How did you make out?"

"Shit! My half was eight grand. I paid bills, and I still need ten thousand just to get my head above water."

"What about the insurance money from the store?"

"The fire is still under investigation. I haven't received one red cent. What I wanted to talk to you about is this: I heard what happened in Pennsylvania. It bothers me that you did it with Red when you knew that I wanted to rob a bank. If I have to give someone half, I'd rather it be you."

"Thanks. But the reason that I haven't robbed a bank with you is because you're a family man. When we met, you helped me get on my feet. I haven't forgotten that, and I never will. But I couldn't find it in my heart to introduce you to bank robbery. I'd rather give you the money than for you to take a chance of going to prison."

"I don't want charity, or a loan. I want to rob a bank with you," Frank insisted.

"If you're interested, I know where there's a jewelry store in Port Ritchie, Florida."

"I'm interested."

"I've never robbed anything but a bank, but this jewelry store is loaded with expensive diamonds and I want to capture the manager when he opens the store, make him shut off fthe alarm, and empty the safe."

"When do you want to leave?" Frank asked impatiently.

"Monday. I've been on the road a lot lately and I need to spend some time with Judy."

They agreed to meet Sunday night to finalize their plans, and Frank walked Bill to his car.

"Nice car. Is it a rental?"

"No, I bought it."

"Yeah, we see who's rolling in the dough. By the way, how did you make out with the blonde?" Frank grinned.

"We had fun."

"Did Judy find out?"

"No, but don't breathe a word around her or I'll shoot your sorry ass."

"Mums the word," Frank chuckled.

As Bill drove away from Frank's, he pulled the gold money clip from his pocket and checked its contents. It was a little on the thin side, he thought. Less than a thousand dollars, and he would need more than that to take Judy to Atlantic City for the weekend. Driving down the road he went over his options for getting some fast money. The Ace pick? No, that would take too long. A card game? No, too time consuming. And winning wasn't a sure thing. Rob a bank, solo. Why not, he pondered the thought.

It took Bill the better part of a half hour to purchase all of the items needed - hat, sunglasses, road fares, duct tape, band-aides, razor blades, raisins, glue, a dent puller, screwdriver, wire, a small box, and a coat hanger.

Bill parked in a McDonalds fast food parking lot to prepare for the robbery. First, he put four road flares together and wrapped them with duct tape, leaving a large portion of the red showing. He examined his work carefully, making sure the lettering was either turned in or covered with duct tape. Satisfied with that, he wrapped the small box of Irish Spring soap with duct tape, completely covering it. He attached the box to the flares using duct tape. Then, using a razor blade he slit the ends of the flares, cut a wire and inserted it into the flare and ran the other end to the box. He repeated the process four times, looked at his handy work, grinned broadly and said, "It looks like dynamite to me." The orange and yellow wires were impressive too.

"Damn fine job," he said dropping it into the brown paper shopping bag, which he tossed onto the floorboard.

He drove to a nearby Mall and cruised the aisles, parking next to a light blue Cadillac he quickly bent a coat hanger straight, then made it into a door opener. After looking around to make sure the coast was clear, he opened the door of the Caddy. Above the visor, he found what he wanted, an electric garage door opener. He took it!

Bill cruised Ritchie Highway for about fifteen minutes before selecting the bank. He drove by it once, checking the layout. Two blocks down the street he found a good location to both leave his car and steal a vehicle to use in the robbery. It was a indoor theater that was showing two movies and both had over an hour to run. An older green Ford pick-up truck parked in the lot was ideal, the ignition was in the dash and easy to pull out with a dent puller and the steering wheel didn't lock as newer models did. In a matter of thirty seconds, Bill was driving away in the truck with the shopping bag on the seat beside him. He parked on a side street a block from the bank and finished his preparations.

He opened the box of raisins, threw a handful in his mouth, then took a single raisin and, using a razor blade, carefully cut it in half. Using the glue, he glued it to the left side of his face, just above the cheekbone. Bill looked in the rearview mirror of the truck. He was pleased with 'the mole'.

Bill put on a hat, dark sunglasses, and took 'the bomb' from the bag and pulled back onto the highway. Damn! He'd nearly forgotten. As he drove, he rummaged through the bag and pulled out the band-aids. He opened one using his teeth and placed it on his chin, further obscuring his features.

He put 'the bomb' into a smaller bag and placed it in his lap as he pulled into the line at the drive-thru window of the bank. There were two cars ahead of him, so he took the opportunity to check the area one last time for anything he might have missed. It looked good.

Now, there was one car in front of him. He waited impatiently for his turn. He was in the line closest to the bank. The teller's window made him clearly visible, but he needed the drawer that opened. The small tubes at the islands weren't an option. As the car in front moved away he eased the truck to the teller's window. The drawer slid open and she said, "Good afternoon, sir. May I help you?"

Bill placed the bag in the drawer, and waited. The teller pulled the drawer closed, opened the bag, and nearly dropped it. Bill held the garage door opener in view with his thumb on the button and said, "You have one minute to fill that bag with large bills. If you don't, as I drive away I will detonate the bomb blowing you and half of the bank away. Now, get moving!"

"What do I do with the bomb?" she asked, trembling.

"Leave it in the drawer. Now, get moving!"

Within a minute, she was back. The teller quickly placed the bag of money in the drawer and slid it out. Bill snatched the bag. As an after thought, he added, "There better not be any dye packets in this bag, or I'll be back. And next time I won't be so nice, I'll just send you the bomb and push the button as I drive away."

Bill pulled away moving swiftly, but not so fast as to draw unnecessary attention.

When Bill pulled into the theater parking lot, he parked at the far end of the lot. He pulled of fhis sweatshirt and used it to wipe down the cab, obliterating any fingerprints. He placed the shirt, hat, and sunglasses into the bag, removed the raisin and band-aid, and got out of the truck walking casually to white Caprice. He opened the door, climbed in, put the convertible top down, and drove out of the lot in less than a minute. Two minutes later he was a half mile away, passing the first police cruiser's on their way to the bank.

He pulled off Ritchie highway onto Route 100, turned the radio on and hung his arm out the window.

Then, he grinned from ear to ear, and said, "Figure that one out, Tom."

CHAPTER FIFTEEN
SECOND TIME AROUND

It was one o'clock Wednesday afternoon when Bill drove the once familiar streets of Glen Burnie, now changed by time. It had been more than two hours since he robbed the bank and, so far, he had seen no marked or unmarked police cars. Everything was quiet, it looked as if he'd gotten away clean.

Bill pulled into line at the McDonalds drive-thru, hungry after the adrenaline rush of the robbery. As he waited to order, his mind drifted to the past as it often did. He could see the old theater where movies like 'Psycho'and 'Gone With the Wind' showed. Across from the theater was Tony Panutti's bar, the Lamp Light.

Bill had been at Tony's brother's house at a poker game when the phone rang. Sam answered it, and his face paled.

"I'll be right there!" Sam said, and ran for the door. "What's wrong?" Bill asked.

Sam stopped at the door, turned, and replied, "Tony's been shot."

"You want me to come with you?" Bill offered.

"No, stay here and answer the phone," he instructed.

Sam ran out the door. A minute later his car started and he sped away into the night.

The card game ceased and everyone sat around drinking beer, coffee, and soft drinks, waiting for some word on Tony's condition.

One hour later the phone rang, it was Sam. Tony had been shot in the arm by a jealous boyfriend, who'd walked into the bar, shot Tony, and fled into the night. Some patrons of the bar had chased after the man, disarmed him, and beat him nearly to death. Both Sam and Tony were at Riverside hospital.

Bill was jolted from his memories by a honking horn. He pulled around the corner to drive-thru window, picked up his order, and pulled out of McDonalds. A block away he passed another bank, and thought: Two in one day? Two hours apart? Why not? This was a one time thing. When word got out that he was using a phony bomb, the gig was up. By morning, every bank in town might know. The F.B.I.'s experts would not be easily fooled.

From the employee parking lot of Sears, Bill stole a red Ford Mustang. He sliced a raisin in half, stuck a Band-Aid on his chin, and donned the hat, sweat shirt, and sunglasses.

At the bank he pulled through the first line, just as before. The drawer was pushed outward and he placed the bag with the bomb in it inside the drawer, just like before. But when the teller opened the drawer and saw the bomb, she screamed, "Oh, my God!" and ran.

"This is a... Damn!" Where'd she go? Shit, this wasn't supposed to happen. After all, bank tellers were trained to cooperate. They were instructed what to do in the event of a robbery. Remain calm, cooperate fully, press the alarm, and give up the money. Under no circumstances were they to endanger themselves or bank customers.

Bill's thoughts were of desperation. His fingerprints were on the bag. Another teller appeared at the window. Bill held up the garage door opener to where she could see it, put his thumb on the button and asked, "Do you see this?"

"You've got one minute to fill the bag with large bills. No die packets. And, no tricks, or I will level this fucking bank. Understand?"

"Yes, sir." She grabbed the brown paper bag from the drawer and briskly walked out of sight. When a minute passed, Bill started to get nervous. When two minutes passed, he was going into full panic mode. He revved the engine impatiently. This bitch was intentionally stalling, but if he drove away, he could be traced through fingerprints. If he stayed, he might be apprehended at the scene. He tapped the horn, twice. His heart was racing and sweat poured down his back. But, he waited. Finally she returned to the window and placed the bag in the drawer. Bill's foot hit the gas even as he grabbed the bag.

In the rearview mirror he watched a police car pull up to the front door of the bank. Sirens blared and cops were coming out of the woodwork.

"Oh my God. Get me out of this one and I'll never do it again," Bill pleaded. He spun the wheel and hit Crain highway doing sixty. Amazingly, the cop at the front of the bank didn't notice him.

Bill couldn't go back to the Sears store, it was in plain sight of the bank. Instead, he took the first right, pulled the Mustang into a Texaco service station and pulled around back. Sirens screamed as he frantically searched the car for something to put the bags and clothing in. On the back floorboard he found a white shopping bag, the heavy duty type with string handles. Bill dumped its contents on the floor and stuffed the bag with the bag of money, the bomb, the sweatshirt, hat, and sunglasses. He wiped the car clean for fingerprints, closed the door behind him, and walked swiftly to the Sears employee parking lot and to his Caprice. As he walked, a police cruiser pulled into the customer parking lot and cruised the perimeter. Finding nothing of interest, the cop pulled out and drove away.

Bill opened the trunk of the Caprice, tossed the bag inside, hopped in the car and drove off. About a mile down Ritchie highway he stopped at a bar, ordered a couple of drinks to try to get his heart to slow down to its normal pace. When he'd succeeded, he left the bar and drove to Bob and Mary's house.

Bill parked in the driveway next to Mary's Pinto. He opened the trunk of the Caprice and whistled happily as he transferred the money from the two robberies into one bag and walked through the front door, unannounced. Bill trotted down three carpeted steps and rounded the corner leading to the living room following the sound of a vacuum cleaner.

"Hi!" he said to Mary's back.

Mary jumped, startled. "Oh, you scared me!"

"Sorry, come here. I have something to show you." Bill headed for her bedroom.

"What's in the bag?" she asked,

"I'm going to show you," he answered mysteriously. In the bedroom, he dumped the bag on the bed, the green of the money a nice contrast to her gold colored bedspread.

"Oh, my God!" Mary exclaimed, sitting down abruptly in a chair next to the dresser. "Where'd you get that? Never mind, I don't even want to know."

"Why not? I won it playing cards."

"No, you didn't."

"Sure, I did."

"How much is there?"

"I don't know for sure."

"You don't know how much money you won?" she asked doubtfully, eyeing the money.

"Well, I put the winnings in with money that was already mine."

"Really?" she stared hard at the money on the bed. Something caught her eye and she said, "You're lying! Why does some of the money have wrappers on it?"

"Because I took an I.O.U. At the end of the game, I escorted the guy to the bank to get my money."

"I still don't believe you, but that's your business. Has Judy seen it yet?"

"No, and don't you tell her."

"I can be bribed," Mary giggled, eyeing the money.

"How much do you think is here?"

"A lot!" she giggled.

Mary helped Bill count the money, it was just a little more than nine thousand dollars. About two thousand was tens and twenties with numerical sequential serial numbers, which troubled Bill. It could be they were simply new uncirculated bills. But they could be 'bait money' or marked bills. Taking no chances, he placed those bills in a separate bag.

Bill replenished the money clip, gave Mary some money for herself, then gave her five thousand dollars to hold for him. Then, he called Judy and told her to get a baby-sitter for Amy and pack a bag for each of them. They were going to Ocean City for the weekend. She needed to be ready when he got there.

"Who am I going to get to baby-sit on this short of a notice?" Judy asked.

"I don't know, call Mary."

The bags were packed and waiting on the porch when Bill pulled to the curb.

"Did you get someone to watch Amy?"

"Mary called her babysitter for me."

Kathy walked down the stairs leading from the apartment, looked at Bill, and smiled.

* * *

Atlantic City was nice, in its own way. But it couldn't compare to Daytona Beach, Florida, Bill thought. He rented a room at a small motel less than a block from the ocean. Its rectangular shape had an upper and lower floor, with doors opening to the outdoors. Bill asked for a room on the second floor because it had a view of the ocean and boardwalk. The room was modest, but clean. Two double beds were covered with matching flowered bedspreads. There was a color television, a phone on a bed stand next to the bed, a vanity with a sink, and a bathroom with a toilet and shower. Bill dressed in a pair of light blue Bermuda shorts, an Italian loose knit white short sleeve shirt, and brown sandals. Judy wore a pair of cut-off frayed jeans, no bra and a light yellow tank top with a blue Dolphin on the front, and dark blue flip-flops.

Bill and Judy strolled hand in hand along the boardwalk.

"I rented the room for two nights. Sunday we have to leave, because Monday I will be going to help my brother paint his new house. Frank offered to go with me."

"Whatever," Judy replied. Whatever meaning she wasn't believing a word of it. She knew Bill, and she knew there was no way he would volunteer to paint a house. He never got his hands dirty! But she also knew that it made no sense to argue. This was 'her' time and nothing was going to spoil it!

The sweet salty ocean air, the warmth of the sun, and the sound of waves breaking at the waters edge was mystical. The sand was covered with colorful towels, blankets, and umbrellas. People were everywhere, laughing, joking, and showing off their well tanned and muscular physiques.

One little girl turned to look at Judy's belly. She had a bucket and shovel in one hand, several finger's in her mouth, and her bottom was slightly exposed.

"Look!" Judy giggled, "It's the Coppertone baby!"

"Hey Judy, look at that one." Bill pointed to a girl wearing a tiny string bikini.

"You're sick! What do I want to look at her for?"

"If God didn't want me to look, he wouldn't have given me eyes." Bill chuckled.

"This wasn't a good idea, Ginge."

"Why's that," Bill asked, somewhat bewildered.

"Look at those girls, I can't compete with them." Judy looked at their sculpted bodies and her swollen stomach.

"Lil bit, to me, you're the most beautiful woman in the world. You're carrying 'my' child, so it's okay to look like you swallowed a pumpkin."

"Swallowed a pumpkin? You fucker!" Judy said in mock anger.

"Yep, that's me, the fucker. Of course, if I weren't a fucker you wouldn't look like you swallowed a pumpkin."

"Let's have some fun this weekend, Ginge."

"Okay. You're the boss. What would you like to do, boss lady?"

"Let's walk down the boardwalk, eat popcorn, and play games," Judy said, eager as a child at a county fair.

"Okay, but I need to stop at the car first."

The long planked boards creaked beneath their feet, while a long pier extended out into the ocean. For the adventurous, there were tube and raft rentals.

They walked a short distance to the car, and Bill grabbed a handful of money from the bag he suspected of being marked money.

They spent the afternoon stopping at every game and concession stand. Each time, Bill pulled a ten or twenty bill from his pocket, and put the change in his right pocket. "What are you up to?" Judy asked.

"What do you mean?"

Every time we stop at a stand, and we've stopped at every one, you cash a ten or twenty dollar bill."

"I like small bills, they make me look like I have a lot of money. See the bulge in my pocket, it makes me feel important!"

"Bullshit! You're up to something. Is there something wrong with that money?" Judy asked bluntly.

"Not that I know of."

"Is it counterfeit?"

"No, it's definitely 'not' counterfeit."

"It better not be, she pronounced. "Let me see one of those bills."

Bill handed her a new crisp ten dollar bill, and she examined it closely.

"Look real?" he grinned.

"Let me see another one."

Bill handed her a second crisp ten dollar bill, and asked. "What are you doing?"

"Just checking."

"Checking what?"

"The serial numbers. They aren't the same," she giggled.

"I could have told you that,"

Judy frowned. "I know you're up to something," she said with complete certainty.

"Why do you always doubt me?"

"Because you're you," she retorted. Then she stared at him as if those three words were all the explanation needed. "What do you want?" Judy asked changing the subject. "A boy, or a girl?"

"As long as the baby is healthy I'll be happy."

"Well, if you had a preference, what would it be?"

"A boy."

"How come?"

"So I don't have to mow the lawn or carry out the trash." Bill laughed.

"Can't you ever be serious?" Judy asked, laughing with him. Saturday night, while Judy showered, Bill called Frank. "Everything okay?" Bill asked.

"Linda's being her normal self," Frank chuckled.

"I'm not coming back until Sunday night, so if you're still good with things, I'll pick you up at your house Monday morning."

"See you then," Frank said, flatly.

Bill and Judy spent the weekend laughing and playing like children. It was a good time for them...

* * *

Frank was anxious and ready to leave when Bill picked him up. The weekend had been fun, but it was time to get back to work.

"Don't come back, you son-of-a-bitch!" Linda screamed at Frank as Bill pulled into the driveway.

Frank walked out the door, grinning at his wife's antics. In his left hand, he carried a blue tote bag. With his right hand, he directed an obscene gesture at Linda.

"Fuck you, bastard!" she yelled at the top of her lungs as Frank tossed his bag on to the back seat and climbed in.

"Trouble on the home front?" Bill grinned.

"Let's get out of here," Frank begged,

"Oh. I'm not in a hurry, are you?" Bill chuckled.

Frank glared at Bill, while Linda stepped out onto the concrete porch and stood with her hands on her hips, staring bullets at both men.

"See you in a few days," Frank shouted as the car pulled from the drive.

"Don't bother!" she screamed and stomped a foot on the porch.

"Isn't love grand?" Bill laughed,

"Fuck you!" Frank mumbled.

"Hey, we don't have to make this trip," Bill offered.

"No, I'm good. It's just that I told her yesterday that I was going to Florida with you, and she's done nothing but bitch ever since."

"She'll get over it, but if she talks to Judy and tells her that I went to Florida I'm going to have to tell Judy that you lied to Linda."

"Why would you do that?"

"Because I told Judy that we were going to Connecticut to help my brother paint his new house."

"How was Atlantic City?" Frank asked.

"Fantastic! We had a lot of fun, but you'll never guess who baby-sit Amy?"

Frank looked puzzled. "Kathy!" Bill chuckled.

"The blonde from the bar?"

"That's her."

"That had to be awkward." Frank grinned, expecting to hear a juicy story.

"Not really. When Kathy saw me, she simply smiled."

"What happened when you returned home from vacation?"

"I dropped Judy off at the apartment and went to Bolero club."

"You chicken shit," Frank said, chuckling. He pulled a cigar from his pocket, lit it, and puffed wildly. "We've got to come back with some money," he added, with a gleam in his eye.

"I don't see that as a problem," Bill smiled.

CHAPTER SIXTEEN
MOMMA'S BOY

WELCOME TO FLORIDA, THE SUNSHINE STATE, the sign read. In just three and a half hours, they would be in Port Ritchie, Florida at Bill's mother and stepfather's trailer.

"Had my mother known we were coming, she'd fried-up a mess of chicken, made mash potatoes with rich brown giblet gravy, and baked fresh homemade mouth-watering dinner rolls. Um um.." Bill bragged, smacking his lips. "My mother is the best cook in the world. She peels orange, apples, and grapefruit, adds a little coconut and fruit cocktail, and makes the best damn Ambrosia salad that I've ever tasted. For breakfast, she makes fresh homemade biscuits, sausage gravy, and she makes her own marmalade jelly."

"Shut up! You're making me hungry. Why didn't you call you're mom and let her know that we were coming?"

"I wanted to surprise her."

"How do you know if it's a good time to visit?"

"I'm always welcome at Momma's." Bill assured him.

They arrived in Port Ritchie at two-thirty Tuesday afternoon, and wasted no time driving to the rural area where Bill's parents mobile home was tucked amongst tall pines and thick underbrush on a cobbled road. His parents enjoyed the country living, surrounding themselves with Mother nature, enjoying the peacefulness they found amongst God's creatures. His step-father never failed to be moved at the sight of a white-tail deer flashing through the under-brush, or a raccoon washing itself at the small lake behind their trailer.

Bill's step-father, a devote Christian, lived by the grace of God. His mother followed suit, but she didn't think the good Lord would object to her smoking a cigarette or drinking a beer now and then.

"The white Caprice convertible stopped short of pulling into the drive, blocked by a brand new chain-link fence and padlocked gate.

"Someone must've heard you were coming," Frank laughed hysterically.

"Cute Frank, real cute."

The fence ran all the way around the trailer. Two signs hung on the gate. One read : NO TRESPASSING. The other : BEWARE OF DOG.

The 'BEWARE OF DOG' sign was unnecessary; for any idiot would be wary of the two vicious looking creatures standing on the other side of the gate growling and barking, looking like they wanted a good meal, and Bill and Frank were just what they were hungry for. The black and tan Doberman snarled and bared its teeth, while the oversized gray and brown German Shepard claimed its territory by woofing and barking.

Bill honked the horn twice to announce his arrival and waited for someone to call off the man-eaters. Bill's stepfather was relaxing in a brown leather Lazy Boy recliner with a brown weiner dog in his lap. At the sound of the horn he shot forward, disturbed from a comfortable nap and looked out the window.

The weiner dog, Moe, ran out the front door barking as Bill's stepfather paused, squinting against the afternoon sun. Moe added his bark to the chorus at the gate. His stepfather smiled, and called the dogs off when he recognized Bill.

"Howdy son." He said, opening the gate. He motioned for Bill to park in a cleared area, next to their red Ford station-wagon. "Momma, Danny's here!" he shouted.

Bill's mother came to the front door, smiled and said, "I thought that might be you, son." She walked down the steps and hugged him.

Frank hadn't gotten out of the car yet. He sat eyeing the dogs warily. All three now sat at his door, quiet but still watchful.

"What are you waiting for, Frank. Come on and meet my folks."

"Sure, just as soon as someone tells these beasts that I'm welcome here," he replied, still watching the dogs.

"Oh, they won't hurt you." Bill's step-father assured Frank with a chuckle, "They're good dogs."

"I sure hope so. I was looking forward to a good meal, but not being the good meal."

Everybody laughed at that. As Frank stepped from the car, the big dogs sniffed his trousers, then licked his hand. Then the dogs stood on their hind legs, planted their feet on his chest, and licked his face.

"Well, either we're friends," Frank grinned, "or they're sampling me to see if I'm worth eating."

"It's good to see you, boy. How've you been?" Bill's mother asked, linking arms and leading him towards the trailer.

"I've been doing okay, Momma," he replied. They all trooped into the trailer, made themselves comfortable in the coolness of the living room, drank ice-tea, and talked, reminiscing about the good times they shared.

Bill's stepfather, Mr. Scott, had been 'Pop' to Bill for a number of years. After Bill's parents divorced and his mother remarried. Bill visited her at their red brick house in Hunter's Harbor, Maryland, where she lived with Mr. Scott, his children, and Bill's sister and brother. With the help of his children, Mr. Scott had built that home with his own hands.

The way his mother had lured him to visit was with the promise to take him on a camping trip in the Catskill mountains of upstate New York. Short of the necessary funds to rent a cabin, they'd bagged up some food and camping gear.

The family, with the exception of Bill, enjoyed the long car ride. Larry, Bill's step-brother, never missed an opportunity to rib his dad about the old 1954 green Ford, making comments like, "You sure that you don't want me to get out and push," as the car labored up a steep grade. Bill said nothing, sitting in sullen silence in the back seat, refusing to be drug out of his shell of hostility. It was no secret that he resented Mr. Scott for his parents divorce. In his young mind he had only one Dad - his natural father. But nearing the end of the trip, watching how well Mr. Scott treated his mother and the other kids, Bill's heart softened. On an especially laborious climb, when it was questionable if the old Ford would make it to the top, Bill pulled a white rabbits foot from his pocket and handed it over the front seat to Mr. Scott, "Here 'Pop', I think you're going to need this."

"Thanks, son." Mr. Scott beamed. They camped out not only in New York, but also Vermont, New Hampshire, Rhode Island, and Maine. In Maine, they visited 'Thunder Hole' and the Black mountains. The trip was everything promised, and then some.

Mr. Scott would never take the place of his father, but he did become Bill's 'Pop', and over the years he'd grown to love and respect the man.

"I think if you had lived with us, your life may have turned out differently,' Bill's mother sighed, "Sometimes I feel as though I let you down."

"Aw Mom, I've never blamed you for the choices I've made. Maybe I haven't always made the right decisions, but they were mine to make, and, I've always stood on my own two feet."

"We love you, son," Pop said.

"And every day I ask God to watch over my boy," his mother smiled.

"That's an awful lot to put on God's shoulders," Frank chuckled.

"Oh, he can handle it. He created the world in six days. If he can do that, he can do anything," Pop grinned.

"But he rested on the seventh day." Frank added.

"Humph!" Pop bellowed, while Bill and Frank laughed.

"You been behaving yourself, son?" his mother asked.

Bill didn't answer the question. Instead he asked, "Do you know what I miss?"

"What's that?" his mother asked, puffing on a cigarette.

"Your cooking."

"Me too!" Pop laughed.

"What, I don't feed you?" Bill's mom snapped.

"Humph, not like you do when there's company."

Moe jumped onto Bill's lap and put his little black toed feet on his chest.

"Get down, Moe boy." Pop ordered.

"What do you want to eat, son?" Bill's mom asked.

"He's all right," Bill told Pop, then told his mother, "We're not hungry."

"Speak for yourself!" Frank protested.

"Are you hungry, Frank?" she asked,

"Starved!"

"Me too!" Pop voted.

"I could fry some chicken," Bill's mother offered.

"Sit yourself down, Momma. We're okay,"

"It only takes a few minutes, and I'd kinda like to have some myself."

"Well then, you might as well make some mash potatoes, giblet gravy, and some homemade sweet dinner rolls," Bill suggested.

Bill's mom smiled, took a puff on her cigarette and snuffed it out in the ash tray on the end table.

"How long will you be staying?" Pop asked.

"We have to leave in the morning."

"What's the rush?" his mother asked.

"We've got a bank to rob."

"You better be kidding." Bill's mom replied, with a stern look.

"Okay, how about if we just look at it and then decide?"

"Don't upset your Ma, son." Pop chided in.

"She knows that I love to tease her," Bill chuckled.

"You better be teasing," she said, making a threatening gesture with a rolling pin.

CHAPTER SEVENTEEN
MORNING GLORY

The next morning Bill showered before waking Frank. As Frank showered, shaved, and prepared for the day Bill dressed in blue jeans, a yellow Cardigan sweater, and black Italian loafers with tassels. He also wore a light blue wind-breaker. Frank dressed in blue jeans, a white dress shirt, and brown laced shoes. He wore a brown checkered quilted jacket.

Bill's mother and step-father woke to say good-bye and watched as the two men left.

As they stepped from the comfort of the trailer, the air was crisp and cool. Within minutes, they stopped at a Seven-Eleven convenience store, bought two coffees, a box of powdered donuts, and a pack of Marlboro cigarettes for Bill.

"Morning," Bill smiled at the cashier as she rang up his purchase. "Will that be all?" she asked with a smile.

"I reckon," he replied.

As they pulled back onto the main road Bill told Frank, "we will be there in ten minutes."

"You've got nice folks," Frank said, sipping his hot coffee. "Yeah, they're good people."

In less than ten minutes, Bill pulled into the shopping center in New Port Ritchie where the jewelry store was located.

"There it is," Bill grinned, turning right into the parking lot. "It's the second store from the end. I'll drive by it, so you can get a good look."

After making the pass, Frank announced. "I'll sit on the bench at the curb and go in with whoever unlocks the front door."

"I'll park in the back. When you open the rear door. I'll come inside and help you bag the loot."

"Sounds good to me." Frank took his gun and the briefcase containing a roll of duct tape and scissors that he intended to use to bind the employees with, walked to the bench and sat down.

The shopping plaza was quiet at this hour, with just a few workers trickling in to open shops. Time passed in slow tense moments as they waited for someone to approach the front door. Bill parked where he could clearly see Frank sitting on the bench. When he captured the manager and went inside, he would drive to the rear of the store and wait for Frank to open the door. He was surprised when Frank stood up and walked quickly to the car.

Frank opened the passenger door, slid in grinning, and asked. "Did you see that?"

"See what?" Bill asked in bewilderment.

Frank pointed to a white Ford Galaxy parked beneath a light pole on the far side of the parking lot.

"So?"

"Do you see that bank?" Frank pointed.

There was a prefab building at the far end of the parking lot. Several steps led up to a glass door and there was a night deposit box in the front.

"A woman got out of that car, walked to the door of the bank, unlocked it, and went inside. I almost grabbed her, but I wasn't sure if you were paying attention. Let's just sit here for a few minutes and watch."

Ten minutes passed and then another car parked. A female teller got out and walked to the bank.

"To hell with the jewelry store. Tomorrow morning I'm going to sit on the bench and I'm going to capture the bank. I'll tie the bank manager up, drive her car across the street, and you can pick me up there."

"Fine with me," Bill smiled. He started the car and drove to a Holiday Inn at Wichie Wachie Springs and rented a room for the night. They spent the day in Wichie Wachie Springs watching the mermaids swim in an under water show and laughed at Peter Pan's antics. That evening, they drank and made the rounds of the local night clubs and generally acted like any other tourists.

Bill decided to call home and let Judy know that he'd be at least a day late coming home.

"Where are you?" she asked.

"At my brother's..."

"Liar! I called him an hour ago."

"Well, I haven't gotten there yet."

"Bullshit, what's up?"

"The sun, the moon, the stars --"

"You ain't funny. You better get your ass home."

"Why is that?" Bill asked, amused as always by Judy's temper tantrums.

"Cause I said, And, Linda's pissed, She's throwing Frank's ass out, clothes first."

After hanging up, Bill turned to Frank, "You've got problems at home, buddy."

Frank sat on the edge of the bed flipping channels manually while holding the remote in his other hand. "You okay?" Bill asked.

"Yeah, why?"

"Oh, I don't know. But it seems strange to hold the remote to the television in one hand and change the channels manually with the other."

Frank looked dumbfounded at the remote for a minute, then said, "Oh, I do it all the time."

"Did you hear what Judy said about Linda?"

"Fuck Linda."

"She's threatening to throw your clothes out."

"So, I'll buy new ones."

"That's one way of looking at it," Bill laughed.

* * *

"Come on, Bill. It's time to rise and shine. We've got to get a move on it," Frank said as he shook him awake. By seven, they were in the Caprice and on their way to the bank.

They stopped at the Seven-Eleven for coffee and donuts, then Bill pulled into a self service gas station and filled the tank.

Ten miles further down the road Frank said. "Make a right."

Less than half a block down the street he said. "Now, a left."

They pulled into a smaller shopping plaza less than a half block from the bank. The back entrance was shrouded by trees and bushes, partially obscuring the street.

"If anything goes wrong, pick me up here." Frank instructed.

"Are you ready to do this?" Bill asked.

"Yeah, let's do it."

Bill dropped Frank off at the corner of the shopping plaza where the jewelry store and bank were located. Frank walked down the paved sidewalk, stopped at a newspaper rack, inserted a coin into the slot, opened the door and took a paper. Then, he sat on the bench in front of the jewelry store, placed the briefcase on the bench beside him, opened the newspaper pretending to read it, and waited. While Bill parked at the far side of the parking lot, where he had an unobstructed view of the bank, having to move once to let a big white street sweeper do its daily chore.

The white Ford pulled into the parking lot and parked in its usual space. The female teller opened the car door, stepped out, and closed the door behind her. She walked briskly toward the bank, digging in her purse for keys.

Frank was up on his feet, walking, glancing around to see if he was being watched. He paced himself with the woman, arriving at the front of the bank at the same moment she did. He said something aloud and she turned and waited until he came up next to her. He touched her arm and they both walked to the door of the bank. She opened it, and he followed her inside.

Two minutes later, a second car pulled up and parked. The woman, presumably another teller, exited the car and went into the bank. Bill glanced around the parking lot looking for any signs of trouble, but everything looked normal.

When a third car parked and two people got out, and a man and a woman entered the bank. Bill began to panic, what in the hell was Frank doing, he wondered. Another minute passed. Still, no Frank. Jesus!

Turning his head, Bill surveyed the street. His attention was off the bank for less than a minute, but when he turned back -- the white Ford was gone. Shit! Where in the hell did it go? Bill started the Caprice and frantically drove to the pick-up spot across the street.

Frank was standing beside the white Ford Galaxy.

"Come on, come on!" he shouted, waving to Bill, who whipped into the small parking space. Frank hopped in, and Bill turned around and hit the highway, going South.

"Where in the fuck where you?" Frank asked, pissed.

"I missed your exit. One minute you were there, the next the Ford was gone." Bill shot back, a little peeved at himself.

"Three more people came in on me. There was no way that I could control them. I sure as hell wasn't going to take the time to tie them all up."

"So, you took the woman's car, huh?"

"Her too!"

"Her too. Where is she?"

"When I parked the car, I made her get into the trunk."

"Are you fucking nuts?"

"I had no choice. I told the other employees that I'd kill her if they called the cops."

"Shit! Down, down. Get the fuck down, fast!" Bill yelled when he saw the police cars coming at them.

"Either she's disliked by her co-workers or they didn't believe you." Bill spat, holding his breath. Another mile down the road and more cop cars were coming, sirens blaring.

"Stay down, damnit!" Bill yelled as Frank started to pop his head up. The police were looking for a lone man, and Bill was the only one visible. But the risk was greater if the tellers had given a description of Frank.

A cruiser was coming up fast from behind. Bill watched closely in his rearview mirror. Bill looked at the cruiser, an upcoming exit ramp, and his speedometer. He was going too fast, and he would never make the exit ramp at this speed. So he did the only thing that he could do, he slowed down.

The cop car shot up beside him and slowed to match his speed. Bill could feel the cops eyes on him and thought about the Caprice's Maryland license plates. He looked directly at the cop, smiled, and gave a friendly gesture with a wave of his left hand. The cop must have believed that he was just another vacationer because he pulled ahead and shot down the highway.

Bill drew in a deep breath, breathing a sigh of relief.

"I've got a cramp in my leg," Frank complained from the floorboard.

"Stay down. We'll be clear in a few minutes."

Bill looked in his rearview mirror and there were two more cruisers coming, lights flashing and sirens screaming. "My leg's killing me," Frank whined.

"Shut up and stay where you are."

The two cruisers stopped, and pulled nose to nose across the road, forming a road block.

"They just blocked the bridge going into Tarpen Springs, but we're over it," Bill reported.

Five minutes later, an eternity to Frank, they passed through Tarpen Springs. "You can get up now."

"Jesus, I didn't think we were going to get through that one."

"We haven't yet. This is Florida, and they don't take too kindly to this sort of thing."

"I hope that lady is okay," Frank expressed his concern.

"Me too!" Bill sighed, dreading the thought of her being locked in the trunk.

"I almost left your ass," Frank declared.

"You couldn't have been waiting for more than a minute. "

"It seemed like an eternity."

"What if the woman would have seen the car, a white Caprice convertible. Where would we be then?" Bill retorted.

"Our gooses would be cooked," Frank said dryly. Both men laughed, relieving the tension.

They drove over the Tampa Bay bridge and stopped at a Holiday Inn. As they pulled into the parking lot, so did a black four door Ford LTD. To Bill, it looked suspiciously like an F.B.I. car. So, he circled the lot and pulled back onto the highway, the back roads to Jacksonville, then took I-95 North to the Georgia state line.

Halfway through the state of Georgia they stopped at a cheap, out of the way, motel to count the money. There was forty-eight thousand dollars in cash and another thirty thousand in American Express Traveler checks.

"Not bad for a mornings work," Frank said, stuffing his overnight bag with twenty-four thousand dollars in cash. "I don't want the Traveler's checks," he added, with a grin.

CHAPTER EIGHTEEN
ALL MONEY AIN'T GOOD MONEY

Arriving back in Maryland, Bill dropped Frank off at his house, then drove to the apartment where Judy was anxiously waiting his arrival. He parked the Caprice at the curb of the apartment building, put the convertible top up, grabbed his bags, and leaped up the stairs that led to the living room. Judy was sitting on the couch, with both legs tucked to her side, puffing on a cigarette.

"I want some money," she announced,

Bill laughed. There was no greeting, no kiss, and no hug. "What makes you think that I have any money?"

"1 ain't stupid. You wouldn't be home if you didn't have any money."

"What do you want money for," he asked, enjoying the game.

"For the baby. I want to buy everything the baby will need now, instead of waiting."

"Okay, how much money do you need?"

"Three hundred dollars!"

"Three hundred dollars?" Bill replied dubiously.

"Okay, two hundred," she lowered her expectations.

"How about if I make it five hundred."

"Five hundred?" Judy's eyes bulged.

"If you need more, just let me know."

"How much money do you have," she asked, giggling.

"Nonya."

"Fuck you and that 'nonya' shit. You know I hate when you say that." Judy spat, puffing angrily on her cigarette.

"Puff the magic dragon, lived by the sea..." Bill laughed.

Judy threw and hit him with a pillow. Then characteristically of her, she changed the subject, "By the way. Red knows that you've been out of town."

"How does he know that?"

"Everybody has been calling for you."

"Who's everybody?"

"I don't know 'everybody'. Billy, Pete, Red, your brother, Uh, oh yeah, and Bobby Jenkins. Red has been calling Frank's house too, so he knows, or figures, that you and Frank were together."

"What did you tell him?"

"I might have told him that you went to help your brother paint his house."

"That's fine. You did good, Lil bit." Bill praised her. He took the gold money clip from his pocket and laid it on the night-stand beside the bed, unsnapped the holster on his left side and laid the .44 Charter Arms Bulldog revolver next to the money clip, then handed Judy the keys to the convertible. "Go shopping, but wake me up at five o'clock. I have somewhere that I have to be." He counted five One Hundred dollar bills and handed them to Judy.

"Thanks Ginge," she beamed.

Judy could barely see over the hood of the Cadillac, so she was very happy to drive the convertible.

"You're welcome. I'm going to take a quick shower and a nap, wake me when you get back."

The spray from the shower was warm and soothing. Just as he relaxed to enjoy the moment, Judy screamed. What the fuck, his mind raced. Fear shot through him like a lightning bolt. Was it the cops, an enemy? He was naked, his gun on the nightstand. Never before had he felt so helpless.

He jumped from the shower and ran to the bed room naked, hoping to grab his gun. Judy was standing in the middle of the room.

"What's the matter?" he asked, looking around.

"How much is there?" she asked, staring at the open travel bag laying on the bed.

"Holy shit. Is that what you're yelling about. Don't you ever scare me like that again," he scorned her.

"My God," she repeated. "Where did it come from?"

"Don't worry about it. Just leave it there, and go shopping." Bill returned to the shower, then layed across the bed and instantly fell asleep. He awoke to someone shaking him and struggled to open his eyes. Judy stood over him announcing,

"Billy's here, and both Red and Frank called."

As Bill sat up, he encountered boxes and parcels strewn across the bed.

"When did you get back?" Billy asked, entering the bedroom, with a huge grin on his face.

"This morning, what time is it now?"

"About three o' clock. Did you have a nice trip?"

"Yeah," knowing what Billy was asking, he added. "It was quite memorable."

"Looks like it," Billy said, eyeing the packages covering most of the bed.

"It wasn't like this when I went to sleep, but it looks as though someone had a good time."

Judy smiled. "Guess what I bought?"

"Looks like one of everything," Bill chuckled.

"Two of everything," Billy guessed.

"Fuck both you guys," she said, but without anger.

"I'm starved!" Bill said, hoping that Judy would take the hint.

"Get your ass up," Billy said. "We need to talk."

Judy headed for the kitchen, while Billy sat down on the couch in the living room.

"Well damn, I guess I'd better get up," Bill mumbled to himself.

"How come there's no fish in the aquarium," Billy asked Judy.

"There's one," Judy replied. "I'm teaching him a lesson. He ate all of the others, so I figure if he's lonely for awhile he will behave when I buy some new fish."

Billy laughed, and asked for a beer.

After searching around for leftovers to feed Bill, she handed Billy a Budweiser.

"Want to smoke a joint?" Billy asked her.

"I'd like to, but that's probably not a good idea," she replied, rubbing her swollen belly.

Bill came around the corner fully dressed, but obviously tired.

"Coffee's almost ready. Do you want breakfast, lunch, or dinner?"

"Just feed me. I woke up with my stomach growling, my head aching, and a hard on."

"You're awful!" Judy tried to sound severe, but she couldn't suppress the giggle. "I could fry some eggs," she offered.

"With crispy bacon, hash brown potatoes, toast buttered with jelly, and a glass of orange juice." Bill added.

"I offered eggs -" Judy countered.

"Damn woman, for five hundred dollars I should be getting fed steak and eggs, in bed."

"Don't press you luck."

"It's no wonder you have a headache," Billy chimed in.

"Sorry, no orange juice," Judy announced looking through the refrigerator. "But I will make the rest of the order, Master. Just don't make this a habit."

Bill laughed, as he walked into the living room to talk with Billy.

"What's on your mind, Billy."

"The bank in Connecticut. While you and Frank were out of town I robbed a bank with Jabo, but it wasn't much. So, now I'd like to get the scoop on the bank in Connecticut that you told me about. Sure wish you would rob the bank with me. Hell, you've robbed one with everybody else."

"Frank and I didn't go off to rob a bank. But we did a little something that made the trip worthwhile. We made some money."

"Big money," Billy quizzed.

"It wasn't a bad lick."

"If you don't want to tell me, that's fine. It's none of my business anyway." Billy grinned to show he had no hard feelings.

"Let's sit down at the kitchen table and I'll draw you a map of the bank, the area, how to leave the bank, and where you can walk through the woods to the rest area on the expressway."

As Bill ate his breakfast, he drew Billy the map. As Billy stood to leave, Bill asked. "How much money did you and Jabo get?"

Billy's face flushed with embarrassment. "A little over three thousand dollars. How much did you make?"

"A lot more than that."

"Come-on," Billy grinned. "I told you!"

"Forty-something-thousand," Bill said, deadpan.

"Goddamnit. You're the luckiest son-of-a-bitch I've ever known," Billy swore, shaking his head. Bidding Judy a farwell, he bounced down the stairway.

* * *

Bill was on his way to Bob and Mary's with his take from the Florida robbery, which he intended to stash there. When the convertible hit some potholes it rattled terribly, irritating Bill. A new car shouldn't rattle like that, he thought.

Leaving Bob and Mary's house. Bill went to the Bolero club for one - and one only - drink he promised himself. He parked in front of the bar. As he walked inside, Red spotted him and waved him over to the bar.

"How are you doing. Red?"

"Not as good as you are." Red grinned. "I was going to offer to buy you a drink, but since you're doing so swell, you can buy me one."

"Sure." Bill smiled. "Hey Joyce, what's a guy gotta do to get a drink around here?"

"Just ask, love."

"I thought we were partners." Red asked, looking solemn.

"We are. But you went off with Frank before I did." Bill reminded him.

"I guess you're right," Red chuckled. "So, when are 'we' going to make another trip?"

"I dunno," Bill shrugged his shoulders. "I'm pretty set for awhile."

Frank walked over to the bar, puffing on one of his nasty cigars. "You're up, Red." Frank motioned to the pinball machine with a nod of his head.

"Okay. I love to take these chumps money." Red strutted his way to the machine. His cuffed blue jeans and red plaid shirt reminded Bill of a true redneck.

"I tried to call you." Red called the house while we were gone and talked to Linda. She told him that we were in Florida. So, I told him that we robbed a Savings and Loan in Georgia and got twenty thousand dollars and a bunch of American Express Traveler's checks."

"That'll work," Bill grinned.

"I was hoping to tell you first. I didn't want you to think that I had a big mouth."

"Hey guys! I'm stepping up in the world," the voice came from the front doorway. Bill looked up, but because of the afternoon sun, he could only see a silhouette. As the man stepped further inside, Bill saw that it was Skinny, Pete's repo man. Normally wearing blue jeans and black motorcycle boots, Skinny was attired in a three piece suit, complete with a folded silk handkerchief stuffed in the pocket of his coat. His hair was neatly cut and his shoes shined. Without asking, everyone present knew, Skinny was now a bank robber.

Pete, Billy, Jabo, and Raymond (Pete's salesman) came in. One drink turned into two, then three - and pretty soon the band took the stage. The liquor flowed freely and it wasn't long before the men were as drunk as Lords.

"Can I get anybody a drink here?" a familiar voice asked.

Bill turned to face Kathy. She was as beautiful as the night they met, standing behind him.

"Hi Princess," Bill smiled.

"Hi Mr. Toad. Would you like a drink, or would you care to place another wager?"

Oops, Bill thought, obviously someone had told her about the bet.

"That's not fair," Bill said, trying on his best smile.

"I'll decide what's fair for me," she snapped.

"But I didn't place any bets!"

"Are you married?" she asked, changing tactics in midsteam and temporarily throwing him off balance. But, he recovered quickly.

"No, I'm not married."

"You're not?"

"I swear," Bill held his hand in the air.

"We'll talk later. Do you want a drink?"

"Seven and Seven in a tall glass. Make it a double."

Returning with the drinks, Kathy said, "Not even close, huh? You live with Judy, she's you're pregnant girlfriend."

"That's true, but we aren't engaged. Would you have gone out with me if I told you that I live with someone?"

"Probably not."

"My point exactly, and, I'm glad that I didn't tell you."

It was around midnight when Bill asked Earl if he would be interested in purchasing stolen American Express Traveler's checks. Earl asked Bill to stop by tomorrow afternoon and they would discuss it.

At the end of the night, Kathy decided that she had a long day and went home, by herself. Bill went to Pete's house and got into a serious game of craps. By morning, he lost twelve thousand dollars.

* * *

It was mid afternoon when Bill returned to the Bolero club. Earl was behind the bar, as usual, and Bill took a seat on a barstool at the far end of the bar.

"Earl," Bill began. "I've got twenty thousand dollars in American Express Traveler checks. Can you do anything with them?"

"Where did they come from?"

"Between the two of us, from a bank in Florida three days ago."

Earl made a phone call, then sat on a stool next to Bill. "I can get you fifteen cents on a dollar. That's the best that I can do."

"I'll take it!"

"The sooner that you can get them to me, the better."

"I'll be right back," Bill promised. He walked outside, opened the trunk of his car and removed a small brown paper bag.

"How's that for quick, efficient, service?" Bill slid the bag to Earl, then asked. "Now, when can I get paid?"

"Be right back," Earl chuckled. He returned a few minutes later with a plain white envelope filled with cash, which he handed to Bill.

"Pleasure doing business with you." Bill thanked him.

"Don't mention it."

As Bill stood. Earl held up a hand. "Wait a minute, I need a favor. I need for you to find a place to rent in the country with a large dry basement, or a heated attached garage. It has to have a good source of power."

"What are you going to use it for?"

"A printing press."

"A printing press...." Bill inquired further.

"I've got some guys that print money. So far, they've managed to stay one step ahead of the authorities. They've never been caught. Don't breathe a word about this to anyone."

"Are these the same guys..." With a quick gesture Earl cut Bill off short. Billy and Jabo had just walked through the front door.

"Hey, Bill. Heard you lost a bundle last night?" Jabo grinned.

"Easy come, easy go." Bill chuckled.

"Twelve grand. I'd hang myself," Billy said.

"Jabo and I just stopped in for a drink. For luck, then we're off on a little trip." Billy winked at Bill.

"Give everyone a drink on me, for luck." Bill chuckled. As Billy and Jabo were leaving, Frank walked in. He spotted Bill at the bar, and laughed.

"Don't say it," Bill warned.

"Say what?" Frank grinned, unwrapping a cigar.

"Must you," Bill asked, pointing at the cigar. Frank sniffed the cigar, and smiled. "Ummm, baby."

"You're crazy."

"I'm crazy? I'm not the one who lost twelve grand in a craps game."

"Yeah, I woke up yesterday morning and said to myself, self, why don't you go over to Pete's house after the bar closes, and you're good and drunk, and lose twelve thousand dollars. Shit, I didn't plan that!"

"Well, how would you like to make up for your losses."

"What do you have in mind?"

"Another trip. Another day. Another dollar."

"I'll talk to you about it later. Right now, I'm beat. I just want to go home and get some sleep."

"Oh yeah, Judy called looking for you."

"And?"

"Linda talked to her. I think she told her that you were probably out with Kathy again."

"She what? Frank, how in the hell could you tell Linda that I took Kathy out. You stupid --"

Bill didn't finish because Frank was laughing hysterically. "Just kidding. Damn, you looked madder than a wet hen."

"Asshole! I'm outta here. I'll talk to you later. Bye, Earl."

"See ya," Frank said.

"Take it easy, Bill." Earl added.

CHAPTER NINETEEN
THE GOOD, THE BAD, AND THE UGLY

"Where have you been?" Judy asked, irritated.

"Don't start, please. I'm beat, and all I want to do is get some sleep." Bill pleaded.

"Can I use the car, the convertible?" she clarified.

"Sure." He tossed her the keys. As she hustled to gather her things, Bill took a closer look at Judy. Her face, especially her cheeks were fuller. Her belly now looked like she had swallowed a beach ball. But there was a certain glow about her, something that made her altogether beautiful as only a pregnant woman can.

Before walking down the steps and out the front door, she bent to kiss him, and asked. "Do you need anything?"

"Sleep, just sleep," he mumbled already halfway there.

* * *

When Bill woke up, Judy still wasn't home. He wondered when the people Earl was talking about were coming to town, and if it was the same bunch of counterfeiters he'd met years earlier. If it was, they were professionals. The last time they were in town they had printed the City of Baltimore's employee paychecks, as well as Maryland driver's licenses and Social Security cards as identification to use for cashing the bogus payroll checks. Bill recruited five people providing them with a Maryland driver's license and a social security card. Creating false names, Bill paid people that he trusted to sign the driver's license and checks, and then handed them to his workers pre-signed. If a worker was caught passing a check. Bill instructed them to say they found a wallet with the check inside, already signed. They could only be charged with uttering and publishing - which carried a far less penalty than counterfeiting or forgery. To this purpose, the person cashing the check was only allowed to have one check and one I.D. on his person at a time, and, after cashing three checks, the I.D, was changed. The Mayor and City Counsel of Baltimore and its employees were paid every two weeks, so Bill made the checks out for around seven hundred dollars. To authenticate the look, Bill rented an IBM typewriter and used a check machine to stamp the amount of the check in perforated red numbers. Bill provided his workers with everything needed, and for that he received half of the amount of the check.

The counterfeiters charged Bill twenty-five dollars per check and the Maryland driver's license and Social Security cards were free. On the first day, Bill profited ten thousand dollars.

Billy Grimes had recently purchased a 1966 Chevrolet Super Sport, dark blue with black interior. Under the hood was a 327 cubic engine pushing 350 horsepower with a four speed transmission geared for speed. Billy was younger then, and his long blonde hair, unshaved baby face, and pearly white smile made him a hit with the ladies.

Greedy Bill decided to cash some checks himself. Why split the profit when he could have it all. Billy drove Bill to a shopping center on the far side of the city, parked in an aisle, and Bill proceeded to walk into a Radio Shack. After selecting a pair of two-way radios, he approached the male cashier, sat his purchase on top of the counter, and handed the cashier his paycheck and identification. The cashier paused, looked at the check, then back at Bill.

"I'll be right back," the cashier said.

Bill watched. As the cashier picked up the phone and dialed a number, he promptly bolted for the door. The cashier hung up the phone and gave chase. As they ran down the aisle towards the waiting getaway car, the cashier stopped dead in his tracks, and screamed. "Stop!"

Bill looked over his shoulder to see the man standing in a perched position with his hands held forward, as if he was taking aim to shoot.

Bill stopped, prepared to surrender.

"He ain't got no gun!" Billy yelled out the window, as he started the car and put it in first gear.

The race was back on. Bill ran for the car with the cashier hot on his heels. There wasn't time to open the car door, so Bill dove in head first grabbing hold of the seat. He secured a tight grip with one hand at the bottom of the seat, the other at the top. The cashier grabbed Bill by the legs as Billy popped the clutch dragging him across the parking lot until he could hold on no longer.

With that last check, Bill quit. There were no arrests, no charges, and no convictions for anyone involved.

His reverie was interrupted by the slamming of the front door. Judy was home.

"Don't get comfortable. I'm hungry," Bill announced.

"I bought stuff to redecorate the bathroom." Judy smiled, proud of herself.

"Let's go get a pizza," he suggested.

"Okay, Ginge."

Bill and Judy set at a booth in the small pizza parlor. She was still talking about her purchases, the items to redecorate the bathroom.

Bill signaled for the waitress. When she appeared at the table, he said. "I'll take a pitcher of Miller's to begin with."

"I don't want beer," Judy spoke up.

"That's fine. Order whatever you want, the beer is for me."

"A whole pitcher? "

"Yeah, that's enough to start with, don't you think?"

Judy rolled her eyes and ordered a Coca-Cola.

"There's a special on pizza today, two for the price of one," the waitress suggested, smiling.

"Okay. I want mushrooms, pepperoni, hot peppers, and black olives on mine," Judy ordered first.

"Are you sure the baby wants all that?" Bill grinned.

"Yeah, she's just like me."

"She, huh? What makes you think the baby is a girl?"

"It is," she said with assurance.

"Well, if it's a boy, he'll probably take after me --."

"I sure hope not!"

 "As I was saying before I was so rudely interrupted, if it's a boy he wants pepperoni and sausage."

"I don't think so," Judy giggled.

"I'll get the drinks," the waitress said, walking away shaking her head and laughing.

"Nice ass," Bill said admiringly.

"What am I going to do with you?" Judy asked with a frown.

"How about you order whatever your little heart desires, and I'll do the same."

"You'll order whatever my little heart desires?"

"No. I'll order what I want, and you order what you want. But I still don't think the baby likes mushrooms."

* * *

They were at home, redecorating the bathroom when the phone rang.

"Hooker's whore house. No muff's too tough," Bill answered.

"Suppose that was your mother?" Judy snapped.

"What?" Frank laughed.

Bill's eyes widened and he motioned for Judy to take the receiver. "I think it's your mother," he whispered.

Judy shook her head, bit her lip, and said, Then she cautiously put the phone to her ear and said, "Hello?"

"How tough is 'your' muff?" Frank asked,

"Damn you!"

Judy threw the phone down and glared at Bill. "You're not funny, fucker."

Bill laughing, picked the phone up and asked." Frank, are you still there?"

"Yeah. Is Judy pissed?"

"No, she thinks that I have a wonderful sense of humor."

"I'll bet. I was just wondering if you're ready to make another trip?"

"Not at the moment, I have something else going-on right now. But hold that thought and check back with me in a few days."

"Business?"

"Of course," Bill replied, surprised at his asking.

"I'll see you tomorrow," Frank said, hanging up the phone.

* * *

"I can't get the coat hanger in the door without it bending," Billy bitched.

"Let me try it," Jabo said, taking the hanger,

"I sure wish Bill was here, that son-of-a-bitch can steal a car in less than a minute." Billy swore.

"Oh shit, duck!" Jabo saw the car coming before it's headlights illuminated them kneeling next to the gray Pontiac. They crawled to the rear of the car as the late night motorist drove past and parked at the far end of the lot. An older man dressed in a blue uniform, probably a factory worker, got out of the black Trans Am and quickly went into an apartment.

"You want me to try the Trans Am?" Billy asked.

"Yeah, let's go." Jabo scooted up to the car and tried the door, it was unlocked. He used a heavy screwdriver to peel the steering column exposing a metal rod which he broke with the screwdriver.

"I sure hope I'm doing this right. I only watched Bill do it once."

"Oh shit!" Jabo mumbled. "Now you tell me."

* * *

Bill awoke the next morning with thoughts of calling the prosecutor in West Virginia. Butch Goode. If he didn't take the initiative to call him, it would only be a matter of time before a warrant would be issue for his arrest, he surmised.

"Pineville police department." the switchboard operater answered.

"Butch Goode, please."

Moments later the line was connected, and the voice on the other end said. "Hello?"

"Butch Goode, this is Bill Hooker. Just thought I'd call and check-in with you."

"Hey, Bill. I half expected you to be in jail by now."

"Nope, in North Carolina I pled guilty to Temporary Use of a Stolen Automobile for a one thousand dollar fine."

"I've never heard of such a charge," Butch chuckled.

"Me neither! But it was good by me. When the bar burned. I moved back to Maryland."

"That's what I heard."

"Have you given any thought to what you're going to do with me?"

"I have given that a lot of thought. The people who gave the statements did so with intentions of helping you, they all said what a nice guy you are. These are the same people that voted me into office, but I can't just let you rob my stores. I'm going to issue a capias, do you know what that means?"

"Not exactly."

"It's a warrant for your arrest on the charge of Breaking and Entering. But it's only good in the State of West Virginia and it has an expiration date of five years. Does that sound fair?"

"Sounds fair to me." Bill replied, in his best country accent.

"By the way, if you'd like to tell me where that hundred thousand dollars is buried. I can assure you the feds will never find it," he chuckled.

"I wish that I could do that. Butch. I really do. But if there ever was any money, consider it poorly spent."

"Gotta run, Bill. Good luck to you."

"You too, Butch. You just made my day!"

CHAPTER TWENTY
TROUBLE BY THE NUMBERS

Bill hung up the phone and laid back, happy that the business in West Virginia was finally over. He was thinking about coffee when he smelled its fragrant aroma drifting into the bedroom. Suddenly, he remembered the previous day he'd bought a coffee pot with a timer, and the coffee was brewing.

"Hot damn." he said, jumping out of the bed. He quickly pulled his pants up and headed for the kitchen.

"What are you doing up so early?" Judy asked, dressed in pink panties and wearing one of Bill's shirts, still wiping sleep from her eyes.

"Admiring my new coffee pot." Bill grinned. "Automatic coffee pots, microwave ovens, dishwashers. It won't be long and you'll probably be replaced too," he teased.

"Only if they make something else that you can stick your dick in." Judy mumbled on her way back into the bedroom.

"Well, at least there won't be no nagging," Bill retorted.

"Fuck you!" Judy called out over her shoulder while giving him the finger.

Bill walked down to the front porch, recovered the morning newspaper, then retreated to the kitchen table. After pouring himself a cup of hot coffee, he thumbed through the Classified Real Estate section. An ad immediately caught his attention: Farmhouse. 3 bedroom. 2 baths. Spacious, large closets, fireplace. Three out buildings. Charming country setting on 20 acres. Immediate occupancy. Owner relocating. Rent, with option to buy.

Bill dialed the number for the Real Estate agent and made an appointment to view the rental that afternnon.

* * *

"Wake-up Jabo." Billy urged. The sun was shining brightly through the window of the shabby little motel room. The sound of heavy footsteps, children's laughter, trunks slamming closed, and cars driving through the parking lot had disturbed Billy's sleep. It was ten o' clock.

"Come-on." Billy urged. "Haul your ass outta bed. We've got to get on the road."

Jabo opened one eye about a millimeter, and moaned. His brown hair was ruffled. His face, suffering from a bad case of acne twisted.

"Go away." Jabo replied, adding. "Check out time ain't for another two hours."

Billy grabbed a foot and pulled him from the bed. "We've got work to do!" Billy said sternly.

Jabo stumbled to the shower, brushed his teeth, ran his fingers through his thick hair, and dressed.

* * *

Billy opened the door to the bank, stepped inside, making a mental note of his surroundings. There were two cameras, four tellers, and it appeared to be an easy hit. He strolled up to the nearest teller and asked for a roll of quarters, handing her a twenty dollar bill. Billy guessed this was the head teller, the one Jabo would be sure to rob.

"Anything else, sir?" she asked, handing him the roll of quarters and two five dollar bills."

"No thanks." Billy grinned, exiting the bank.

"What do you think?" Jabo asked, as Billy climbed into the driver's seat of his red 1959 Corvette convertible.

"I don't know."

"Did you see any cameras?"

"Not that I noticed."

"Did you check out the tellers drawer?"

"I didn't have time."

"Well, what exactly did you do?" Jabo bitched.

"I got a roll of quarters and checked out the teller's tits," Billy grinned. "The head teller is the last one on the left. She's wearing a blue jacket over a white sweater. "

The stolen Trans Am backed-up to the front door of the bank.

Billy put in park, leaving the engine running.

"You ready?" Billy asked Jabo, who had already climbed out of the car donning a rubber mask and headed for the front door of the bank with a pillowcase in one hand, a gun in the other.

Jabo ran through the door and jumped the counter. Billy, three steps behind him, stopped in the lobby, and yelled, "Nobody move!"

"You." Jabo said, pointing his gun at the head teller. "Open the money drawer." When she hesitated, he screamed. "Move bitch, or I'll blow your fucking head off!"

"But sir..."

"Move!"

"Sir. I…"

"I know you're the head teller, now open the drawer."

"I'm not the head teller. It's uh-only muh-my thu h-third day, she stammered, her face a sickly shade of gray. Then, she fainted.

"Shit!" Jabo jumped over her and started grabbing money from teller drawers and stuffing it into the pillowcase.

"Let's go. Let's go!" Billy yelled as Jabo went from one teller drawer to the next.

After four minutes passed. Billy yelled frantically, "Let's go!" Jabo jumped back over the counter.

They hopped into the Trans Am, still masked, and sped away from the bank. There was a line of cars waiting to exit the shopping center and turn onto the main road. Billy wanted to speed by them, but he waited in line. He gritted his teeth as sirens approached in the distance.

The line moved, but before Billy could move, a woman pushing a stroller with a small child walking by her side walked in front of the car.

"Look. Mommy," the child said, pointing to Jabo. "It's Donald Duck."

Jabo raised his gun and motioned for the woman to move out of the way. She looked at the mask, then the gun, and screamed, snatching the baby stroller back away from the car.

"Move!" Jabo yelled at Billy. The tires screamed as the sports car fishtailed from the parking lot onto the main road.

They tore their masks off as they rounded the corner heading into the apartment complex. The first responders shot into the shopping center parking lot as they turned the corner off the main street. Before losing sight of the shopping center, five police cars had pulled-up in front of the bank.

The Trans Am bottomed out as it entered the apartments parking lot, sending off an array of blue, white, and red sparks. Billy pulled into the double above ground garage, shoved the car into park, and didn't bother to turn the ignition off.

"Shut the door!" he yelled at Jabo, but Jabo continued running for the woods. Billy cursed, and turned back to close the garage door. He yanked hard, and as it slid towards the ground he heard sirens approaching.

"Shit!" Billy mumbled, and headed for the cover of the woods.

Just as he reached the tree line, out of the corner of his eye, he watched a police cruiser pass through the parking lot. He dived into the woods and laid still, praying. Jabo was sitting in the passenger seat of the Corvette, anxiously waiting for Billy to show up. As he hopped into the car and started the engine, he announced, "That was too damn close!'

"We're in the clear now," Jabo smiled.

"Not yet, we're not, We have to get out of this state before I'll feel comfortable."

* * *

Having found what he hoped to be a suitable house for the counterfeiters, Bill called Earl Murphy to give him the news.

"Afternoon Earl, how are you today?"

"Not very good," the big Irishman replied.

"What's the problem? "

"Have you talked to Red lately?"

"Not in the last couple of days."

Not wanting to be the bearer of bad news, Earl said, "I suggest you watch the news, talk to Red, and stop by afterwards."

"Sure, Earl. I'll talk to you later."

Bill dialed Red's apartment and let the phone ring twenty times, but there was no answer. Next, he grabbed the remote, turned on the television and flipped through the channels until he found the news. The lead story was about a woman apprehended at Baltimore International airport carrying three hundred thousand dollars in uncut counterfeit ten dollar bills. The following story brought Bill to the edge of his chair. The news anchor reported. "...Meanwhile, the F.B.I. and local authorities are continuing their search for this man (a photo of the person robbing the bank flashed on the screen) who has been identified as Gary 'Jabo' Wandrum. If you have any information...."

"Jesus-fucking-Christ," Bill said, unable to believe that so much could go wrong so fast. Why can't someone just hit me in the head with a big rock, he wondered.

Still sitting in the chair, lost in contemplation, someone entered through the front door. His first thought was, cops. He tensed, expecting the worst, but then Frank asked, "Do you always leave your front door open?"

"Do you always walk into houses without knocking?" Bill countered.

"Have you heard the latest?"

"I just watched it on the news."

"The news?" Frank replied, his eyes bulging with fear.

"Yeah, the photo of Jabo robbing the bank in Annapolis, his name - the whole story."

"Jesus, that's the first I heard about that."

"What in the hell were you talking about?"

"The robbery in Florida. The Money Orders that you sold Earl Murphy. The feds are investigating you, and Red. You sold those damn Money Orders to Earl. He sold them to the Mob, and the Mob gave them to a guy named Bill Murphy, who is no relation to Earl. But he was busted at a casino in Las Vegas trying to cash the American Express Traveler checks, and, guess what?"

"What?" Bill asked, almost afraid to hear the answer.

"Bill Murphy, by a freaky fucking coincidence is your neighbor. He lives right down the street. What drew the feds attention to you was the 1974 white Cadillac and the white 1975 Chevrolet Caprice convertible parked at the curb of welfare housing. The feds have already been to visit Red. They think it was you and him who robbed the bank in Florida."

"I just tried to call Red."

"He left last night to go visit Mary's folks in West Virginia. "

"Jesus, this day is a fucking nightmare."

"It could get worse," Frank reminded him.

"What's on your mind?"

"Let's go get some money while we still can."

"Alright, but there's a couple of things that I need to take care of first."

* * *

"We did it!" Billy grinned, excited and relieved to drive out of the state of Connecticut. "How much do you think we've got?"

"I don't see any fifties or hundreds," Jabo reported, looking into the pillowcase. "But there's sure a lot of tens and twenties."

"Goddamn, I feel good. I think I'm going to buy myself a guitar."

"I thought you said the woman in the blue jacket was the head teller?"

"I thought she was," Billy grinned.

"Did you knock her out?"

"No, the bitch fainted," Jabo laughed.

"Did you see the cop pull into the apartments?"

"No! And if he saw me all he saw was asshole and elbows."

"You fucked-up by not closing the garage door. If I hadn't ran back and closed it. I seriously doubt that we would have made it past the first exit."

"Yeah, okay - I fucked up," Jabo admitted.

After renting a room. Billy sat down on the bed, dumped the money on it, and started counting money into two piles. "A hundred for me, and a hundred for you." The total take was sixty-two hundred and fifty dollars each.

"Hooker is the luckiest son-of -a-bitch I know. He always gets the 'big' money!"

"Shit. I'm good with this," Jabo grinned.

"Yeah, but just once I'd like to get a big score." Billy picked up the phone and dialed a number.

"Who are you calling." Jabo asked, more out of curiosity.

"Pete. I want him to go to a music store and buy me a guitar before it closes. I'll pay him for it when I get home," Billy explained.

"Grime's Auto Sales." Jackie. Pete's wife, answered.

"Where's Pete?" Billy asked.

"Oh God! Billy, hold on." Billy heard her yell for Pete, who was outside talking with a potential customer. In seconds Pete was on the phone. "Billy. Jabo's photo of him robbing the bank in Annapolis is all over the news. They have his name, and the feds and local police are watching his house. This phone may even be tapped. If you're with him, haul ass right now!"

"See ya!" Billy said slamming the phone in its cradle. "The F.B.I. are looking for you big time. We've got to get out of here, now.

"Looking for me, for what?"

"The Annapolis job. Your photo along with your name has been all over the news.

"Shit!" was all that Jabo could think of to say.

* * *

Later that evening, Bill went to the Bolero club. Earl was sitting in his normal spot, on a stool at the end of the bar. Bill sat next to him, ordering a Seven and Seven in a tall glass.

"I can't believe this shit," Bill said disgustedly.

"Neither can I," Earl replied.

"The girl arrested at the airport, did she have anything to do with our guys?"

Earl took a deep breath. "She was exchanging uncut counterfeit ten dollar bills for twenties."

"Our guys?"

"They're gone. Ten minutes after she was arrested, they packed-up and left town."

"How did they get onto her?"

"It looks as though it came from the other end."

"Did you hear about Bill Murphy getting busted in Las Vegas at a casino trying to cash the American Express Traveler checks?"

"Pure bad luck. Red left town. I think it might be a good idea for you to leave for awhile, at least until the heat falls off.

"I intend to do just that. I found a farmhouse, made an appointment to look at it this afternoon. But, I never made it."

"That's just as well."

CHAPTER TWENTY-ONE
THE GREAT OUTDOORS

Bill tossed and turned, all night, contemplating his next move. Beside him, Judy slept like a baby, curled up in a fetal position.

By eight o'clock. Bill was up, showered, shaved, and dressed. After only one cup of coffee and two slices of buttered toast, he left the apartment driving away in the Cadillac. He drove from one car dealership to next looking to sell the car for the best price. Finally, settling on a price, he sold the Cadillac and was given a ride back to the apartment.

Without going inside, he hopped into the Caprice, put the convertible top down, and drove down Ritchie highway. Parked on a grassed knoll at a Ford dealership a new 1975 emerald green Thunderbird. The car sported a dark green half vinyl top. It had plush green velour seats and power everything, within an hour, Bill traded the convertible in on the Thunderbird and drove it out of the parking lot.

Still tired, Bill returned to the apartment to take a nap.

"Can I use the car?" Judy asked.

Bill tossed her the keys, removed his holster, and placed the money clip on the bed side table, then fell across the round bed exhausted and was instantly asleep.

Only to be awakened by an irate Judy. "God damnit, where's the car? I walked around the block looking for it."

Bill walked to the front window, looked outside, and saw the Thunderbird was right where he had parked it. Then, it dawned on him that he hadn't told Judy about the new car.

"Oops. Sorry, honey. I forgot to tell you that I sold the Cadillac and traded the Caprice in on a new Ford Thunderbird."

Judy left in a huff. When she returned several hours later, she complained. "It's too damn big! I can barely see over the hood, and it goes all over the road. Besides that. I don't like the color.., and, it ain't my fault."

Bill yawned and stretched. Then, it struck him -- all over the road, ain't her fault.

"What ain't your fault?"

"I'd rather not discuss it," Judy said primly.

"What did you do to my car?" Bill asked, dressing quickly, determined not to lose his temper.

"Nothing. But it made you get out of bed fast, didn't it? she giggled.

"Why you little wench." Bill growled in mock anger, chasing her around the bed.

* * *

Leaving the motel. Billy and Jabo drove down the road discussing the problem at hand. Jabo suggested that he lay-low by camping out, and Billy had the perfect place in mind. So, Billy and Jabo went on a shopping spree. Jabo bought a tent, lantern, Coleman fuel, cooler, Bowie knife, a radio, batteries, and a sleeping bag. Then, they stopped at a grocery store and purchased can goods. Luncheon meat, mustard, potato chips, bread, and a six pack of Coca-Cola.

Five miles outside of Ellicot City. Maryland Jabo set-up camp in the woods. He dug a shallow pit with his Bowie knife and encircled it with stones. From an abandoned refrigerator he spotted alongside the highway he scavenged two wire shelves, and used one for a grill. Now, all he needed was something to cook.

In the stillness of the night, crickets churped and a distant love sick frog croaked. Next to a placid lake, Jabo rested uneasily.

By morning, the bologna was gone and the canned beans weren't appetizing. He looked at the lake, deciding to catch a fish for lunch. On second thought, he remembered that he didn't have any fishing tackle. He picked up the other shelf and studied it intently. From the ground he spotted a gray rock that looked like granite. He picked the rock up and started banging on the metal wire shelf, attempting to knock one of the thick pieces of wire loose. His plan was to fashion a hook that he could use for fishing. After fifteen minutes of futile labor, he gave up.

What I need, he thought, is a list of supplies. He tore a piece of paper from one of the shopping bags and looked for something to write with - a pencil, pen, or even a crayon. He did not have a single writing instrument. So, using his knife he carved the list into the hard clay ground.

As night descended over the camp-site, he fueled the lantern and built a roaring fire. He put batteries in the radio and tuned it to a rock station. He found a green twig and chewed on it while listening to the radio. After a couple of hours, he decided to count his money. After counting it three times he quickly became bored.

"Screw this," he announced into the night and crawled into his sleeping bag.

He awoke to the sound of footsteps crunching through the dry pine needles around the tent. He jumped from his sleeping bag and grabbed the Bowie knife. If anyone tried to enter the tent he would stab them through the flap when they reached for the zipper, then he'd slash the back of the tent and make good his escape.

As Billy made his way through the woods pushing branches aside, the branch sprang back, slapping Pete in the face.

"Damnit. Billy. Quit that shit!" Jabo heard Pete growl as they neared the tent.

Billy chuckled. Inside the tent, Jabo grinned.

"I wasn't home for ten minutes and the F.B.I. knocked on my door," Billy told his friend.

"You were on the news again last night. They've been to the car lot, to your girlfriend's, every place they think you might show up," Pete added.

Jabo threw more fuel on the fire and stepped back as it flared up.

Billy looked around, spotted the carved message on the ground, and asked. "What's that?"

"It's my shopping list," Jabo grinned.

Pete and Billy looked at each other and laughed. "It's going to get lonely out here?" Pete said.

"It's better than being in jail," Billy countered.

"Not by much, it ain't," Jabo groused. It's difficult for people to relate to something they've never experienced, he thought.

"You may have company soon," Billy laughed.

"What's that?" Jabo questioned.

"The F.B.I. are investigating Bill and Red for a bank robbery in Florida. Red took off for West Virginia."

There was a brief moment of silence, while Jabo stoked the fire. Then, deciding to say what was on his mind, he turned to Billy and asked the question. "Do you want to rob another bank?"

"You're crazy!" Billy replied, without given it any consideration.

"May as well. One, two, or five, what difference does it make?"

"He's got a point there," Pete agreed.

"I've got to think about that," Billy grinned.

The following morning, Jabo's eyes opened and he examined his surroundings, momentarily confused. But in a moment it came to him, the tent. The blue vinyl floor was tracked with dirt. He had left the zipper partially open to let in some of the coolness of the night, and now the tent was full of bugs. He groaned and burrowed deeper into the sleeping bag. But after several minutes of tossing and turning, he decided that sleep would evade him. He wondered what time of day it was, and wished he hadn't left his watch at home.

* * *

Billy was awakened by a persistent knocking at his front door.

"Who is it?" he asked, through the closed door.

"F.B.I. We have a warrant for the arrest of Gary Wandrum. Open the door!"

As Billy opened the door, he said, "Jabo isn't here."

"Then you won't mind if we look around," the agent said, stepping through the door.

"Look for yourselves," Billy grinned.

* * *

"There's some things going-on that you don't need to concern yourself with. But we're getting rid of the apartment, and moving. I've already talked with Bill and Joanna and they said that you and Amy are welcome to stay with them until I get back."

"Get back. Where are you going?"

"Nonya."

"Damnit, you know that I hate that nonya shit!"

"When I get back, we'll rent an apartment closer to White Marsh."

"How long are you going to be gone?"

"Less than a week."

"Be careful. Ginge."

Bill dropped Judy and Amy off at Joanna and Bill Smith's house giving her a wad of cash. Then, without calling, he drove directly to Frank's house.

"How do we case a bank over the weekend," Frank wanted to know.

"We don't, but we can size it up."

"How in the hell do you size a bank up?"

First, you find a bank that is centrally located. If it doesn't have more than one escape route, it's no good. Secondly, since we intend to capture it, we want to make sure that it has a safe, not a vault. Last, it has to be in a commercial area or heavy industrial area. A bank in the country isn't likely to have the kind of money that we're looking for."

Frank packed a duffel bag, told Linda that he would be back in a few days, and a block away from the house they could still hear her yelling and screaming.

Sunday night. Bill picked a bank in Wilson, North Carolina located on highway 301. To the left of the bank, there was a Dairy Queen, with picnic tables topped with blue and white umbrellas.

Two miles further down the highway was a Ramada Inn, where Bill rented a room. Monday morning they watched the bank parking lot. A white Pinto drove into the parking lot, backed-up to a curb, and a female employee stepped out, walked to the bank, unlocked the front door and disappeared inside.

By noon, they had checked the getaway routes and finalized their plan.

This time Frank would wear a disguise, a wig and false beard that Bill purchased in a novelty shop.

That afternnon Bill broke into a car and stole a C.B. radio.

Then he stopped at a Radio Shack and bought an aerial. Within an hour, he had the C.B. hooked up in the Thunderbird. All truckers used channel 18 and reported on the 'smokies' location.

Knowing where the police were was always nice to know, Bill thought.

While Bill and Frank were preparing to rob a bank Billy was sharing a bed with his girlfriend Pam. Jabo was in the woods tossing and turning in a sleeping bag. Red was sipping coffee at his in-laws in By-God-West -Virginia. Pete was preparing for work. Skinny was dreaming of his next heist, and Judy was puffing on a cigarette with her feet folded under her while sitting on Joanna's couch.

Bill awoke to find Frank shaking him.

"Let's go, Bill," Frank grinned. He was wearing a light brown wig with the false beard glued to his face. He topped his head with a wide brimmed hat and dark sunglasses. Convinced the chances of his ever being identified were slim to none, he was prepared to go.

Frank sat on the bench in front of the Dairy Queen waiting anxiously for the manager to arrive.

A black man, presumably waiting for a bus, sat down across from him and made idle conversation. Frank looked straight ahead, hoping the man wouldn't know that he was wearing a disguise. He told the man that he was the C.P.A. for the bank and that he was waiting for the manager to arrive.

He looked at his watch, it was three minutes until eight when the white Pinto pulled in and parked. Frank was quickly on his feet and walking across the parking lot, carrying a briefcase containing strand tape, scissors, and green heavy duty garbage bags. He timed it perfectly. Just as she stepped out of her car, he smiled, and said, "Good morning. This is a robbery. Leave your car keys on the seat of your car and come with me." Seeing the small.25 caliber gun in his right hand, she offered no resistance.

As Frank and the manager reached the front door, a second car entered the parking lot, and the light blue Ford Fairlane back-up to the curb directly in front of the bank.

Bill started the Thunderbird anticipating Frank's flight. But Frank, cool as a cucumber, told the bank manager to stay where she was, walked over to the other female teller and captured her. A minute later the three entered the bank.

"Son-of-a-bitch," Bill grinned, thinking that either Frank had the balls of a brass monkey or he's in serious need of a straight jacket.

The plan was for Frank to take the manager's Pinto and meet Bill on a street behind the bank. Bill parked the Thunderbird alongside the road and nervously waited.

The white Pinto rounded the corner, sped up, and pulled in behind the Thunderbird. As Frank climbed out of the car, Bill opened the passenger door. Frank came running with a briefcase in one hand and a large green trash bag in the other. He flopped on the back floorboard, poured water from a canteen into a bucket and began removing the false beard. "Go, go!" Frank urged.

As Bill turned the corner he glimpsed in the rearview mirror. The Pinto was parked. So far, no cops. He hung a second right turing back onto highway 301.

"Oh fuck!" Bill said.

"What? What's the matter?"

"Just stay down!" Bill slowed as a police cruiser shot across the median directly in front of him and pulled into the bank parking lot.

"What's going on?"

"Just stay down!" Bill repeated, stepping on the accelerator. In the rearview mirror he saw a second then a third cruiser.

At the first light, Bill turned right to get off the main road, but this was the same right as Frank had taken. On a street to his right he could see the white Pinto parked alongside the road. Oncoming police cruisers forced Bill to pull to the right of the road, yielding the right of way. As they approached, he held his breath. As they passed he breathed a sigh of relief and pulled the Thunderbird back into traffic.

"Man. I gotta get out of this car," Frank announced.

"Just stay down!" Bill ordered, driving a few minutes in total silence. He broke the silence with a prayer. "Lord, just get me out of this one and I promise I will never do it again."

"Me too!" Frank said.

Bill took a left turn into an apartment complex. Frank got out of the car with a green garbage bag filled with cash, guns, and clothing in his hand, walked to a big green dumpster, opened a door, and sat the bag inside. Then he proceeded to fade into the woods behind the brick buildings. Bill knew that Frank would stay near the tree line and keep one eye on the dumpster. Bill pulled away in search of a place to spend the next two or three hours.

Two hours, a haircut, and a shave later, Bill picked Frank up. As he entered the complex Bill spotted him, playing basketball with four or five black kids.

After retrieving the garbage bag, Bill reached into the glove compartment and pressed a button opening the trunk. Frank tossed the bag in, and quickly shut the trunk.

"Having fun?" Bill grinned, as Frank climbed into the Thunderbird.

"Fun, hell. You dropped me off in an all black neighborhood.

"Why didn't you go into the woods?"

"What woods? Standing in the middle of the trees, you can see the apartments on both sides."

"Good thing that you can play basketball," Bill chuckled.

"Very funny," Frank griped.

"What took you so long inside the bank?"

"Have you ever tried hogtying two women using strand tape?" Frank chuckled.

"I thought we were about to bite the bullet. Man, I was scared." Bill admitted.

"Think I wasn't," Frank grinned.

* * *

Beans, ravioli, corn, tuna. Jabo rummaged through his meager supply of canned goods in search of his breakfast. But there was nothing to quench his thirst or satisfy his hunger, He stepped from the tent, drew in a deep breath of fresh air and exhaled. Life in the great outdoors was definitely palling. He tasted something foul in his mouth and it took him a moment to realize that it was his breath. He wrinkled his nose, and muttered, "That's it, I gotta get the hell out of here."

CHAPTER TWENTY-TWO
THE HUNT

"All the good things in life are free..." Bill sang.

"...but you gave them to the birds and the bees..." Frank chimed in.

"...I want mu-uh-money...."

"...That's what I want!" Frank sang bass, grinning.

The Thunderbird was rolling down the highway on cruise control, the stereo was pumping loudly, and the two men were thumping to the old Beatles song. If either man had a care in the world, it wasn't evident.

One hour ago, in a small motel room in Virginia, somewhere off the beaten path, they had stopped to count their take and divide the money. The total amount came to sixty-two thousand five-hundred dollars.

Yes sir, life sure is grand, Frank thought.

How do you like me now, Tom? Bill mused, smirking at the infamous grin captured in his memory.

* * *

"The feds were at my house at seven o'clock this morning, that dumb ass Jabo stirred up a hornets nest," Billy bitched to Pete.

"They were at the car lot three times, and Jackie says they came to the house once," Pete replied disenchanted.

"Why were they at the car lot three times?" Billy asked, deep in thought.

"Because Pete wasn't here," Raymond, Pete's salesman answered the question.

"Where were you?" Jackie asked archly, staring at Pete for any sign of deception. Everyone in the room knew that Pete was a womanizer and he treated Jackie badly.

"I was at the auction, bitch. You want to make something out of that?" Pete growled at his wife.

"Nuh-no." she said trembling, and fled to the safety of the kitchen.

"I'd hate to be in Jabo's shoes, they want that boy bad," Raymond concluded.

Bill never understood what made Raymond such a good car salesman. It certainly wasn't the large scar on his right cheek, or his gangster demeanor. He dressed casual, and wore a sportcoat.

* * *

Jabo stood at the waters edge filling empty beer cans and throwing them as far out into the water as he could. He'd spent the day trying to keep busy and fight the loneliness of the deep woods. When he tired of chucking beer cans, he used the Bowie knife to cut down a sapling and fashioned it into a crude bow. He notched the ends and strung a piece of twine, then carved arrows from twigs and set off on his hunt for dinner. Jabo soon discovered that arrows without quills wouldn't fly straight.

But he stalked through the woods with a vision of a rabbit roasting over an open fire. He shot at several rabbits, but his arrows were too erratic.

Discouraged, on his way back to the camp, he came upon a turtle crossing the path in front of him. He discarded the bow and arrows, and picked the turtle up by its shell deciding to keep it as a pet. What the hell, he figured, talking to a turtle wasn't nearly as crazy as talking to 'a nobody'.

"We're going to be pals, what do you think of that?" he asked the turtle.

The turtle turned its head and bit Jabo.

"Ouch. You little bastard. How would you like to be soup?"

Returning to the camp. Jabo put the turtle inside the tent and zipped the entrance closed. He gathered sticks and using the Bowie knife sharpened one end to make stakes, then used a rock to hammer the stakes into the ground placing them a half inch apart, creating a circular corral for his pet turtle.

"Be good and I'll find you some food," he told the turtle as he placed it in his new home. Then, to himself, he mumbled. "I wonder if turtles like pork and beans?"

Jabo squatted near a tree, pulled his pants down around his ankles, swatted flies, gnats, blood sucking mosquitoes, and cursed his lot in life.

Finished, he built a fire and heated a can of pork and beans. When they were hot, he made a plain Spam sandwich and ate enthusiastically.

Things had to get better, he mused, because they damn sure couldn't get much worse.

* * *

In the privacy of their homes, everyone gathered around their television to watch the six o'clock news.

"...And the F.B.I. continue their search for bank robber suspect Gary Eugene Wandrum," the anchorman reported.

Pete, Jackie, Billy and Pam, Raymond, Judy, Joanna and Bill Smith, Bobby and Mary: all across Baltimore people sat ith their eyes fixed on the TV, keeping abreast of the hunt. Depressed by the events, sickened by the knowledge that they or their loved ones could be next, they watched, and waited.

* * *

Returning home, as Frank walked through the front door of his home with Bill close behind, they found Linda vacuuming the living room. "Anyone call for me?" he asked.

"No. I hope you guys had fun," her voice dripped with sarcasm.

"Fun? Honey, we've been working," Bill chuckled.

"I'm not Judy, my head doesn't screw on and off," Linda snarled.

"I'll see you two love birds later," Bill grinned, making his exit.

But before he got to the door, Linda asked. "Have you guys seen the news?"

"Why?" Bill asked, flatly.

"Do you know a guy, Gary Wandrum? He goes by the nickname, Jabo."

"Never heard of him," Bill lied.

"Well, the F.B.I. are looking real hard for him. That's been all over the news. Apparently, the F.B.I. are investigating a series of bank robberies."

"Say that again?" Bill said, stopping dead in his tracks.

"The F.B.I. are investigating a series of bank robberies they believe can be connected to this guy." As Linda repeated herself elaborating further, Bill could have sworn there was a gleeful gleam in her little piggy eyes.

"Fuck them," Bill said dryly.

"You fuck em. I'm not," Linda snarled.

Both Bill and Frank laughed, then walked outside to talk privately.

"The F.B.I. can investigate all they want. If we did our job right, they're not going to find jack shit. But don't try to call me. I'll see you at the Bolero club," Bill suggested.

"Why can't I call you at home?"

"I moved. Judy and I are staying with friends, Bill and Joanna Smith, in White Marsh until I find a new apartment. Besides, you do not want to be connected to me. Keep your head low until this shit blows over."

On the drive to the white sided rancher on Gunpowder road a thousand thoughts ran rampant through Bill's mind, none connecting. By the time he arrived at the Smith's residence everyone was in a rotten mood, including Judy.

Joanna and her husband Bill were fighting. The minute Bill pulled up, Judy lit into him.

"What are you doing?" she snapped.

"Well, I was, ugh, about to get out of the car. Why, don't you want me to get out?"

"No."

"Why not?"

"Bill and Joanna are fighting."

"Bill bad," little Amy, Judy's two year old daughter said, clinging to her mothers leg.

"Me?" Bill asked, pointing a finger at himself. Amy nodded.

"Yes, you," Judy agreed.

"Bull not bad, Bull good," he told Amy.

"Ugh, ugh," Amy said, shaking her head.

Bill shook his head, resigned. "What's Bill and Joanna fighting about this time?"

"Stupid shit."

"Well, let's go break up their little party," Bill grinned. Bill Smith looked at Bill as they entered the house,

"Doesn't look to me like you kicked his ass," Bill chuckled.

"No, but I'm going to kick 'your' ass if you don't shut the fuck up," Joanna snapped.

"Ain't love grand. Damn, I guess it looks like I'm going to spend this all by myself," Bill said, pulling his money clip from his pocket. He thumbed through the thick roll of One Hundred dollar bills.

"Oh no, you wont!" Judy made a quick grab for the cash as Bill snatched it away.

"You're an asshole," Judy reported.

"Yeah, but you love me."

"Sometimes."

"Oh, this is so fucking touching," Joanna sneered.

"What are you guys fighting about?" Bill asked.

"What would you do if Joanna threw your dinner across the room?"

"I'd kick her ass!"

"Oh yeah, you wanna try?" Joanna asked with a gleam in her eye.

"Wasn't my dinner." Bill replied, chuckling.

"Would you like for me to make you a plate?" she offered, with a sadistic grin.

"No thanks, I just ate with Colonel Sanders."

"Are you sure?" Joanna offered a second time.

"Oh yeah, I'm sure. I heard the last time you cooked, when you fed the leftovers to the dog, he turned around and licked his ass to try to get the taste out of his mouth."

Everyone laughed. Bill Smith threw his head back, and roared. Judy giggled behind her hand.

"You're pressing your luck, Hooker." Joanna shook her fist at him.

"Hey! It's just a rumor, I never believed it for a second."

"Fuck you!"

"Just when I was ready to fight, you make 'another' offer."

"Kiss my ass." Joanna laughed,

"A little foreplay, works for me."

* * *

"Look! There's the big dipper." Jabo pointed with a twig. "and there's the little dipper." he told the turtle, then stuck the twig in his mouth and chewed on it. The turtle stood on its hind legs and clawed at the stakes that held it in captivity, completely ignoring Jabo.

"I wonder what I'm going to look like with a beard?" Jabo said aloud.

The turtle offered no opinion.

"You need a name." Jabo said, decisively. "What are you, a boy or a girl?"

He picked the turtle up by its shell turning it over looking for clues of its gender. When he got too close, the turtle extended its neck and snapped at Jabo's hand.

"Close, but close is only good in horseshoes and hand grenades." Jabo chuckled. "You must be 'a bitch' because you ain't got no dick or the good sense not to bite the hand that feeds you, so, I guess I'll call you, Snapper. Yeah, that fits. There you go, Snapper." Jabo said, tossing a piece of Spam and bread into the corral. The turtle didn't seem very enthusiastic about the evenings meal.

"Well, you'll eat it if you get hungry enough."

Jabo wasn't the sharpest tack in the box. He often didn't know what day of the week it was, and he forgot names constantly. So, it was no surprise that he would carry on a conversation with a turtle, but though the turtle never listened to his questions, it was too busy trying to tunnel under the stakes that made up its prison. With thoughts of Jabo living in the woods, Bill later wrote a poem:

Futurity

As God created the galaxy

with his heavenly touch of reality
a star spangled aurora clustered gallantly,
and somewhere within the celestial sphere
our Father's home we know is near.
With tongues well-oiled we fluently
named each shining star construently,
Pluto, Venus, Neptune, and Mars
and the goddess of love among the stars.
The big dipper, the little one and Leo the Lion,
the falling star our wishful sign.
The cosmic system and the Milky Way
and the northern star that shines its ray
radiates the night of the worldly dome
the abode of Saints
our eternal home.

CHAPTER TWENTY-THREE
THE GREAT ESCAPE

The rectangular red brick building in Towson, Maryland was ambiguous if not for the F.B.I.'s emblem to the right above the front entrance. There was a paved asphalt parking lot, a small yard with grass, a sidewalk, and a stainless steel pole where the American flag proudly waved in the air.

Inside the building, Special Agent H. Thomas Moore stood in a room of agents at the head of a conference table expressing his optimism. "It's time to move this investigation forward. We have spent all of our time, resources, and energy, searching for Gary Wandrum, aka. 'Jabo'. Now, I believe that approach was a mistake. It appears that our Mr. Wandrum is more elusive than we first thought. However. I am confident that by the week's end we will have him in custody."

"Good luck," a young agent mumbled.

"What's that, Agent Sweeny? We don't need luck. In fact, we possess all of the ability necessary to catch our elusive thief."

Flustered, the young agent said. "Quite frankly, sir. Unless you're in possession of information not known by the rest of us, or you have a crystal ball, it's difficult for me to have more confidence."

"I believe we have all shared your frustration at one time, or another. But we have a job to do. Each of us have four years of criminal science and two years of rigorous training at Quantico, Virginia. If we gave up every time we became frustrated few, if any, suspects would ever be apprehended." Moore smiled knowingly and tipped a wink in general. "Besides, we have one thing on our side, that makes all the difference."

"What's that?"

"Time. Our fugitive will get tired of hiding before we get tired of looking for him. We have information there's a group of men believed to be bank robbers that hang-out at a bar in Brooklyn called, the Bolero club. I suggest that we spend some time there ourselves."

"Is that your plan?"

"We know where Mr. Wandrum isn't. It's time to regroup, release an updated report to the media, turn up the heat, and wait for the rats to start scurrying."

"Ugh, you lost me, sir."

"I have set-up a listening post in Ellicott City. Presently we have four phone lines tapped; Wandrum's girlfriend, Billy Grimes, Wandrum's closest known friend. Billy's brother Pete Grimes. and, Grimes Auto Sales, owned by Pete Grimes."

"How did we obtain warrants to monitor those phones?"

"We didn't."

"Is that legal?"

"Well, it's questionable. But, I'm an investigator, not an attorney."

No charges will be filed as a result of the wire taps, so the legality should never become an issue.

"Do we step on toes?"

"No, but make your presence known."

* * *

"Asshole!" Jabo screamed. Two stakes were bent and the turtle had escaped. Jabo ran his fingers through his long brown stringy hair, and cussed, "Damnit, I'll find you, you little asshole." He pulled on his faded denim jeans and headed off into the dense undergrowth.

"When I find you, you're ass is going to be turtle soup," he mumbled, as he pushed his way through bushes and tree branches, following a non-existent trail through the woods. Every once in awhile he'd see a bent blade of grass or a broken bush and tell himself he was hot on the turtle's trail.

Meanwhile, the turtle was enjoying a cool dip in the lake not twenty feet from Jabo's tent.

Hell bent on finding his pet turtle. Jabo wandered nearly two miles through the woods when he heard a familiar sound, an approaching auto. He heard the car slow down, and he rushed forward, crouching low among scrub bushes. An older green Ford Maverick pulled into the parking lot of a country store, the sound of crushing stone beneath its tires.

A Budweiser sign hung in the window. His mouth watered in anticipation of the taste of a cold brew. Jabo walked from the woods and approached the store. He hoped there weren't many other customers in the store, the less people who saw him, the better.

"Good afternoon," the elderly gent behind the counter greeted Jabo as he walked through the front door.

"Good afternoon, nice day isn't it?"

"Sure is. I didn't hear you pull in."

"I walked."

"You look familiar, are you one of John Day's boys?"

"No sir, I'm not from around here. I'm just camping out and doing a little fishing."

"There's some good fishing spots around here," he paused, "but most of them are on private property."

"I'll keep that in mind, and be sure to get permission before I throw a hook into the water."

"Most folks around here don't mind, they just don't want no fusses."

"You got any fishing hooks?"

"Second aisle, first shelf."

Jabo began to pile his intended purchases on top of the counter. Soap, deodorant, bread, fishing hooks, fishing line, a hat, two towels, razor blades, toilet tissue, eggs, milk, beer, potato chips, bread, bologna, and some canned goods.

"That be all," the old man asked,

"I reckon so," Jabo grinned.

"The old man added the purchases on an old National cash register. The total amount popped up, thirty-two fifty.

A small black and white television on a shelf behind the counter caught Jabo's eye. He looked up and saw a rerun of Leave it to Beaver.

"Beats watching Soap Operas," the old man chuckled.

Jabo nodded.

As the groceries were being bagged, Jabo reached into his pocket, pulled out a roll of cash, peeled off a crisp fifty, handed it to the old man, collected his change, and bid the proprietor a good day.

"Oh little red riding hood...you sure are looking good..." Jabo sang as he descended upon the woods.

Forty-five minutes later he wandered into his camp, looked at the abandoned turtle corral and said, "Fuck you, asshole."

Stepping into the tent, he stripped down, grabbed the soap, razor, towel, and ran naked to the lake. As he waded into the shallow water he held his breath, then plunged beneath the icy water. He came to the surface sputtering from the cold, and got down to the business of bathing.

* * *

Joanna, would you mind if I borrowed your car today?" Bill asked as he finished breakfast.

"I've got things to do, what am I supposed to drive?"

"You can drive my car."

"I don't know. My husband would divorce me if I was to get him into any shit."

"I don't want to do something wrong."

"You sure." she questioned.

"I promise."

"Why do you want to trade cars?"

"Because mine is known and yours isn't."

"Be back before my husband comes home from work!"

"I'll try," Bill promised.

"Judy and I are going shopping. Do you need anything?"

"No, I'm fine."

"Well, I need some money, and speaking of money, where did all that money come from?" Judy asked.

"What money?" Bill played stupid.

"You know damn well what I'm talking about, the money in your travel bag."

"That's not mine, and, what are you doing snooping?"

"I wasn't snooping. I looked to see if you had any dirty laundry. If it's not yours, whose is it?"

"Nonya."

"Don't give me that shit."

"I wish it was mine, but I'm just being paid to deliver it."

"Are you buying dope for someone?" Judy asked, alarmed.

"No," Bill laughed.

"Ginge?"

"Look! I can't tell you everything. But this is legal. Besides, I told you when we first decided to live together that we're going into the Iron and Steel business together. You do the ironing, and I'll do the stealing."

Bill drove straight to the Bolero club, to arrange a business deal with Earl Murphy. Earl regularly laundered money for Bill, taking fifteen percent for his commission. At this meeting, he would be laundering twenty-five thousand dollars.

"My business is suffering badly. There's been so many off duty cops in here lately my regulars are going elsewhere."

"How do you know they're cops?"

"C-mon, do you think I don't know a cop when I see one? I can smell one! I think it's so obvious that it's driving my patrons away."

"I'm sorry to hear about that, Earl. I really am."

"It's not your fault," Earl said, shrugging his shoulders.

"Let me buy you a beer," Bill offered.

The two men drink several while they wagered fifty dollars on a game of pinball.

"Bing, bong," the steel ball sounded as it struck against the intended targets. Bill bumped the machine with both hands urging the ball to bounce back and forth. "Ping, ping, ping," the points scored. But he was no match for the master, Earl. With a hundred and fifty dollar loss, he left.

"Another day, another dollar," Bill said happily to himself as he strolled to the car.

At four fifteen Bill returned to the house on Gunpowder road. Bill Smith pulled into the driveway fifteen minutes later.

Dinner was on the stove, so the two men grabbed a beer and relaxed in the living room.

Neither man had seen the noon news, so it was with considerable surprise that they viewed the latest story about the search for Gary 'Jabo' Wandrum.

* * *

"Pete, the feds have been parked across the street all day," Jackie announced, as he returned to the car lot.

"Goddamnit, I don't want to be involved in this shit! Get Billy on the phone."

"Yeah," Billy answered.

"The feds are parked across the street from my business."

"So, what do you want me to do about it? They 've been here four times today."

"Tell everybody involved to stay away from this lot. I can't run a business like this!"

"You saying that you don't want me to come around?" Billy asked, angry and hurt.

"No, Goddamnit. It's just that I can't have the feds parked in front of my business all day. Word gets around, and I won't be able to sell a go-cart."

"You act like this is my fault."

"Let's not go into that. Have you seen Jabo lately?"

"Hell no, I'm scared to go anywhere near him."

"I wouldn't if I were you."

"No shit, they want that boy bad."

"You got any reefer?"

"Not much. What are you looking for?"

"An ounce."

"I'll probably have that tomorrow."

* * *

"That's nice," the agent monitoring the call chuckled. "How are we doing," Special Agent Moore asked.

"The Grimes brothers smoke pot. Pete Grimes is upset about the feds having his car lot under surveillance, and, Billy Grimes 'knows' where Jabo is staying, but he hasn't mentioned a location yet.

"We will get him. It's just a matter of time."

* * *

The proprietor of the country store stood gaping at the television in amazement, "I knowed I'd seen that boy before!" he yelled, as he looked at Jabo's picture on the evening news. He reached for the phone, and dialed the number flashing across the screen for the F.B.I.

"We got him!" Special Agent Moore grinned broadly as he hung up the phone. He's living in the woods in Ellicott City. It pays to advertise," he added gleefully.

"When are we going after him?" Agent Sweeny asked.

"At daybreak."

"I want a helicopter equipped with infra-red on standby."

"What about the local authorities?"

"I'm not chancing any outside agency blowing this. We will notify the local police when we're on site.

"I want an airplane to fly over the area at daybreak, in the hopes of spotting his camp. Helicopters are too noisy for that."

"Yes sir."

"We will coordinate the search from Wymer's grocery, the store where Jabo was spotted."

CHAPTER TWENTY-FOUR
BAD DAY RISING

The white single engine Piper Cub lifted off from a runway thirty miles north of the area where Jabo was camping out. Having drank himself into a stupor, Jabo had no idea what was coming. He was deep asleep inside the tent.

"Airborne One to base," An excited agent Sweeny called from the small plane.

"Base, go ahead."

"We are airborne and in route to the search area, over."

"Copy, what is your E.T.A?"

After consulting with the pilot, Sweeny replied. "Approximately ten minutes."

"Copy. We will be standing by. Over, and out."

"Out," Sweeny replied, and sat back to enjoy the flight.

"What are we looking for?" the pilot, an ex-military flyer asked.

Sweeny looked at his newest associate, he was in his late forties, with gray hair and a slight beard. There was nothing distinguishing about the man other than his tough, no nonsense, demeanor.

"A tent, a camp site, a car parked in the woods. Anything that our fugitive may be hiding in."

"A desperado, huh?" the pilot grinned.

"A bank robber."

"The one that was on TV last night?"

"You got it," Sweeny replied smugly.

"Do you want to fly over at tree top level?"

"No, let's try covering the lake with binoculars first. We don't want to spook this guy."

"Gotcha!"

* * *

In the parking lot of Wymer's grocery store, the largest congregation of law enforcement officers the area had ever seen convened. Thirty-four local police, twenty fatigue clad state troopers and half a dozen F.B.I. agents including H. Thomas Moore. He was certain that Jabo was his ticket to nailing Bill Hooker, and nothing was going to deter him from that one, single goal.

"Mr. Wymer, we appreciate your assistance. Do you think that you can identify the man you saw yesterday again?"

"Oh, yes sir," the old man said most assuridly.

Moore spread six photo's on top of the counter, and without a seconds hesitation Mr. Wymer picked Jabo's from the line-up.

"Are you one hundred percent positive that this is the man who was in your store yesterday?"

"Yes sir. I'm absolutely positive. This man," he pointed to Jabo's photo, "came into my store yesterday morning and bought a mess of supplies. He spent exactly thirty-four dollars and fifty cents, and he paid with a crisp new fifty dollar bill. He had a pocket full of money and peeled it off as if it was nothing."

Moore grinned. "Thank you, Mr. Wymer. You've been of great assistance."

As Moore left the store, an agent met him in the parking lot.

"Well, we have a positive I.D. As soon as the plane arrives, it's a go," Moore announced.

"Yes sir," the agent replied, trotting off towards the gathering of law enforcement officers at the far side of the parking lot.

"We got an anonymous tip after you left last night. The caller reported that Hooker and an associate, Frank Kalita, made a trip down south recently."

"Down south?" Moore repeated, pondering the information. "Yes sir. we're following up on that now,"

"Son-of-a-bitch. Why doesn't he quit."

"What's that, sir?"

"Nothing. Never mind..."

"Airborne One to base, over."

"Base, go ahead."

"We are inbound to your position, please inform us when you have a visual."

"Copy. We have a positive I.D. on the fugitive. It's a 'go green' for the fugitive."

"Airborne One, copy. Over, and out."

"Base, out."

"What's a 'go green'?" the pilot asked.

"Red means it's a false alarm. Yellow means that it's 'a possible' and to proceed with caution. Green is a license to hunt, it's 'a definite'. In this case, the fugitive is believed to be armed and dangerous."

"Base to Airborne One."

"Copy, base."

"We have a visual. You're just to the right of us."

"Roger, base. We 're going to circle and sweep the perimeter of the lake first."

"Copy. Over, and out."

Five minutes later, an excited agent Sweeny rattled the radio's speakers, "Airborne One to base, we have a visual of a tent maybe a hundred yards back from the lake. Repeat, we have a visual of a tent." Sweeny gave a map coordinance to the location.

"Base to Airborne One, do you see any activity?"

"Negative, base. It appears to be quiet."

"Roger. Stay on location, and observe. We 're going in..."

Deep in the woods Jabo slept blissfully, burrowed deep in the comfort of his sleeping bag, unaware his impending capture.

With the dawn, the woods were coming to life. The birds churped merrily hopping from one branch to another, and squirrels scampered about gathering food for the new day. Even the turtle emerged from the lake to sun itself on a tuft of soft grass.

"Airborne One to base," Sweeny called. "Base, go ahead."

"Be advised that your best entry to the location is via, route 40. The camp is approximately two miles west of base."

"You mean Wymer's store," an amused agent asked.

"Affirmative. Airborne One, out." From the air, agent Sweeny watched as F.B.I. agents, state troopers, and local police cordoned off the tent, and slowly, cautiously, moved in.

"Gary Wandrum. This is the F.B.I. Come out with your hands in the air," Moore announced through a bullhorn.

Jabo's eyes popped open wide, He wondered if he was having a bad dream. Then, he heard the announcement a second time.

"This is your last chance, Wandrum. Come out, or we're coming in!"

Jabo jumped from the sleeping bag and looked around wildly. The tent glowed an orange-red in the dawn and was sweltering in the morning heat. He pulled on a pair of jeans, falling in his haste to get dressed. "Damnit. I'm coming out," he hollared. "I'm coming out!" He unzipped the flap to the tent, put his hands out first, and slowly stepped from the tent. Several F.B.I. agents rushed forward, threw him to the ground face first, and slapped handcuffs on his wrists behind his back. Another agent frisked him for weapons, then jerked him to his feet.

"The fugitive is in custody," Moore announced over the radio. A cheer went up from the surrounding woods, and Airborne One flew away, returning to its hanger.

"How did you find me?" Jabo spat at agent Moore.

"You should pick your friends more carefully," Moore answered, with that infamous grin spreading broadly across his lean face.

* * *

By noon, news of Jabo's arrest had been released to the media, and the word spread like wildfire.

After Jabo was finger printed and his photo taken, he was allowed one phone call. He called his best friend, Billy Grimes.

After a late night of partying, Billy and his girlfriend Pam, were still in bed. Pam answered the phone, somewhat perturbed about having her sleep disturbed. "Hello."

"Is Billy there?"

"Jabo." Pam snapped, sitting up straight. "You know better than to call here, the feds were here four times yesterday looking for your ass."

"I'm in jail. I need to talk with Billy."

"Oh, shit! Hold on a minute. Wake up. Billy, wake up." As he opened his eyes, she said. "Jabo's on the phone, he's in jail."

"Shit! Give me the phone." Rubbing the sleep from his eyes, Billy asked. "Where are you? "

"In jail, the feds arrested me early this morning."

"Where?"

"I was asleep in the tent in the woods."

"How'd they find you?"

"That's what I'd like to know. You, Hooker, and Pete are the only ones who knew where I was camping out, and Moore told me that I ought to pick my friends better. What does that tell you?"

"Hooker? I don't belive that. I've known Danny for years, and I know he's not a snitch."

"Did you tell 'anyone' where I was staying?"

"You know better than that!"

"Do you think Pete did? I didn't tell on myself."

After a moment of silence, Billy said. "Danny may have confided in someone, but I know he wouldn't have intentionally told on you."

"If I find out he did, if it takes me twenty years I will kill that mother fucker, and you can tell him I said that."

"Don't jump to conclusions, bro. Not until we have all of the facts. How much is your bond?"

"I don't have one. My arraignment is tomorrow. After I'm appointed an attorney I'll find out if they intend to try me as a juvenile or an adult."

"Do you need anything?"

"Tell my sweetheart to come see me."

"Take care of yourself, Jabo."

* * *

Bill and Judy had spent the night at the Holiday Inn on Ritchie highway in Glen Burnie. Consequently, they'd missed the news of Jabo's arrest. when they arrived at Bill and Joanna Smith's house on Gunpowder Road, Joanna met them at the door. "Frank is looking for you. He's been to your old apartment and Judy's moms. She gave him directions here. He said that he needs to talk to you as soon as possible, that it's urgent."

"Are you in trouble?" Judy asked, in a near panic.

"No baby, nothing like that," Bill grinned, trying to calm her.

"Are you sure?"

"I'm sure," he reassured Judy. "I'll be back in a little while."

Bill's first stop was the Bolero club. Earl was behind the bar taking inventory and restocking whiskey when he walked through the door.

"What's up, Earl?"

"You ain't heard?"

"Heard what?"

"The feds caught Jabo this morning. It's been all over the news."

"Jesus! That must be what Frank is so hot to see me about."

"Probably. Him and Red came in after you left yesterday, and they stayed until closing."

"Speak of the devil," Bill grinned, as Red walked into the bar. He sat down on a stool next to Bill and ordered two long neck bottles of Budweiser. One for him, the other for Bill.

"How are ya doing partner?" Red grinned.

"Hear about Jabo?"

"Just now."

"I'm sure glad that he don't know nothing on me," Red chuckled.

"Yeah, well, don't be surprised if he takes the fall and keeps his mouth shut."

"That's mighty generous of you especially considering that he's telling everyone who'll listen that you put the feds on him."

"Is that so?" Bill replied, an edge of anger in his voice.

"I'm just telling you what I heard. I just came from Pete's car lot, and that's what the word is there."

"You know me better than that."

"According to Pete, only three people knew where Jabo was camping out. You, Billy, and himself."

"I don't know who knew, but I know that I didn't tell anyone where he was."

"You sure that you didn't mention it to Frank when you made another trip down south to rob a bank?"

"Who said that I robbed another bank with Frank?"

Red picked up his beer and drained it. "I ain't stupid, I know you and him went down south and hit another bank."

"So what if we did?"

"I thought we was partners. You could have taken me."

"I'm not saying that I took anybody or did anything. But if I did. I certainly wouldn't advertise it. Besides, you were in West Virginia visiting Mary's folks."

"That the way it is?" Red asked, his face flushing in anger.

"Yeah, that's the way it is," Bill answered flatly.

Just then, Frank walked into the bar, sat on the stool next to Bill, and ordered a beer. Red excused himself and went to the restroom.

"Did he ask you if we robbed a bank?" Frank asked.

"Yes, he did, and I told him that it was none of his business."

"That's why I've been trying to find you."

"What did you tell him?"

"That we did something, but I didn't elaborate."

"That's fine." Bill turned to Earl and asked if Red knew about the money he was exchanging for him.

"Not unless you told him," the big Irishman replied. "As a matter of fact, you can pick that up in the morning."

"Thanks. You never know, I may need it soon."

By six o 'clock Bill was back to the house on Gunpowder road. Judy had seen the story about Jabo's arrest on the evening news, but she had no reason to suspect Bill was remotely connected.

CHAPTER TWENTY-FIVE
LADY JUSTICE

At ten o 'clock the following morning, U.S. Marshals escorted Jabo through a wake of cameramen and journalist gathered in front of the federal courthouse into the building to a room where Special Agent H. Thomas Moore waited.

"Good morning, Gary. Are you ready to talk to me yet?" Moore grinned.

"Depends on what you want to talk about," Jabo grinned back.

"We're willing to make you a deal, providing of course, that you cooperate."

"Are you going to release me?"

"No, but we're willing to offer you a five year sentence."

"Five years, do you think I'm stupid," Jabo screamed.

"Well, we've got two or more bank robberies. In Annapolis, you gave us a photo. A damn good one. Then, there's the bank you robbed in Glen Burnie wearing a helmet and making your getaway on a motorcycle," Moore continued grinning.

"I'd like to see you prove that," Jabo chuckled.

"That's no problem," Moore assured him.

"So what? The most you can make me serve is until I'm twenty one. I'm almost eighteen, that's only three years.

"That's not entirely correct. The judge may decide to try you as an adult. In that event, you could be facing up to twenty five years on each robbery."

"But –"

"And assuming that you are tried as a juvenile, you could be tried as a 'special offender' and sentenced up to fifteen years. Of course, with good behavior you could be out in eight years."

"But."

"Oh, there's no provision for parole under the special offender act."

"Fuck you!" Jabo snarled. He sniffled and Moore thought he was about to break down and cry. So, he was caught totally off guard when Jabo turned back and spit in his face.

Moore didn't move. He just looked deep into Jabo's eyes and said. "You're going to regret that."

* * *

"The United States verses Gary Eugene Wandrum," the clerk in toned.
Jabo stood before the black robed judge.

"This is a very serious offense you are charged with young man," the judge announced as he glanced at the charges in front of him. "Do you understand the charges filed against you?"

"Yes sir."

"Do you have means in which to hire a lawyer, or do you wish the court to appoint you counsel?"

"I don't have the money to hire a lawyer."

"Very well then, the court will appoint counsel."

"Your honor," the prosecutor spoke up. "Mr. Wandrum is a juvenile. However, due to the seriousness of the the charges and the possibility that he may flee the state, we ask that defendant be held without bail. We might add, that as a fugitive Mr. Wandrum was found living in a tent. There is no reason to believe that he would appear for any future proceedings."

"Point well taken," the judge agreed. He stirred restlessly, peered over the top of his horned rimmed glasses at the young man standing before him, and said. "Mr. Wandrum. I am going to enter a plea of not guilty in your behalf and the court will appoint you an attorney. At this time, you will be denied bond. That may or may not change in the future. Do you have any questions?"

"Fuck you!"

Moore grinned at Jabo's arrogance.

"Mr. Wandrum, one more remark like that and I will hold you in contempt of court," the judge snapped.

"Whatever." Jabo snapped right back.

By ten o'clock Jabo called Billy's apartment to tell him what happened in court. Pam sleepily answered the phone on the third ring, "Hello?"

"Is Billy there?"

As Billy placed the receiver to his ear Jabo shouted, "It's Hooker! The feds know about the bank robbery in Glen Burnie too!"

"What happened in court?"

"No bond, and they ain't sure if I'll be charged as a juvenile or an adult."

"Okay. Listen. I hate to cut you short but I didn't get to bed until seven this morning, Call back around one o'clock, or so. "

"I'll try, but be careful of Hooker."

* * *

As Bill walked into the Bolero club Earl asked, "Want a drink?"

"No thanks, we'd better get right down to business."

Earl began stacking money neatly on the counter in five hundred and thousand dollar stacks. After a quick count, Bill picked up the stacks and dropped them into a brown paper bag.

"By the way, what's happening with Jabo?" Earl asked.

"I don't know. Since his arrest I haven't heard a thing."

"It's a shame."

"Yeah, but I'm tired of everyone blaming me, had he followed instructions he wouldn't have gotten busted. Besides Jabo, nobody could feel worse about this than I do. But what's done is done, and there's nothing that I can do about it."

* * *

Leaving the bar. Bill drove to Bobby and Mary's, pulling into the driveway simultaneously. He parked to the left of her pumpkin colored Ford Pinto.

"Hi Bill, what's in the bag?" Mary asked, smiling.

"It's full of money."

"No, it's not. Let me see," she giggled as they stepped inside the house.

"Follow me," Bill grinned, walking to the master bedroom.

"Oh, my God," Mary exclaimed as he dumped the bag of money onto her bed. Then she sat down heavily in a chair and said, "Aren't you afraid of getting killed? I know I would be."

"I quit! This was the last one."

"That's good, because Bobby and I do care about you, and you have Judy to think about too. She's going to make you a daddy soon."

"Yeah. I know. It's time for me to settle down."

The next week was, for the most part, quiet. Bill spent a lot of time with Judy and stayed out of circulation. By keeping a low profile he hoped things would soon blow over.

Friday night, Bill decided to stop by the Bolero club and see what the latest news and gossip was. He arrived two hours early, before the band set-up. Earl was busy removing chairs from the top of tables and placing them on the floor.

"Hey big guy, what's happening?" Bill asked Earl with a grin.

"Nothing good," he answered.

"Why? What's up?"

"Sit down, order a drink, and I'll be with you in a minute."

Earl sighed, continuing to unstack chairs.

"Where you been keeping yourself stranger?" Joyce smiled.

"I've been sleeping under bridges and hiding under rocks," Bill chuckled.

"What's your pleasure?" she ased.

"I'll have you," Bill grinned.

"I meant, what do you want to drink?"

"The usual."

"Seven and seven in a tall glass, coming right up."

"Have you seen Red lately?" Joyce asked Bill, as she sat his drink in front of him.

"Nope. I've been staying pretty much to myself."

"Frank was in earlier. He and Earl played pinball. They were playing for a hundred dollars a game. I've got to work all week just to earn two hundred dollars. Makes me want to consider your lifestyle sometimes." Joyce had a wicked gleam in her eye when she asked. "You aren't looking for any help, are you?"

"I'm retired," Bill grinned.

"You won't quit. It's in your blood."

"Then I'll get a transfusion."

"You're not going to like this," Earl said, taking a stool beside Bill. He reached inside his jacket and pulled out several pieces of paper, stapled together.

"Read this."

Bill unfolded the papers. It was captioned 'THE HOOKER GANG'. It read: Beginning in 1974 and through 1975 five white males identified as Frank Kalita, Cleveland Red Miller, Gary Eugene Wandrum, Billy Grimes, and William Hooker, have robbed banks from Maine to Florida. No more than two of the gang members have ever entered a bank at any one time. In most cases, stolen cars have been used and left within a half mile of the scene of the robbery. In at least two robberies, the first employee to arrive for work was accosted and forced to open the bank to the robbers. One individual entered the bank with the hostage while the other waited in the getaway vehicle. To date, the gang is responsible for sixteen bank robberies on the eastern seaboard.... The article listed each bank by name, city and state, specified the amount of money taken, and the mode of operation. (The number of 'known' bank robberies was later increased to twenty-three).

"Where did you get this?"

"It cost me a hundred bucks, but I thought it might be worth it to you. Our friendly neighborhood crooked cop brought it to me. It's marked CONFIDENTIAL and it's been distributed to every police department in a five state radius. Guess who the author is?"

"Special agent H. Thomas Moore?"

"You win the kewpee doll."

"Thanks, Earl." Bill reached into his pocket, pulled out his gold money clip, and peeled off two fifties. They shook hands, and Bill left the bar. He read and reread the report over a dozen times. It was accurate, too damn accurate. The one thing that he questioned was how could the feds possibly know for sure who robbed each bank when they had worn masks, and, something else stood out, the last two banks that Red and Frank robbed weren't listed. But the bank in Port Ritchie, Florida and Wilson, North Carolina were on the list. To Bill, this could only mean one thing. Someone was cooperating, and that someone was 'Jabo'.

Bill left the Bolero club plastered. He awoke the next morning on the couch at Joanna's with a killer headache and little Amy screaming in his ear. "Bull, Bull." She couldn't pronounce his name.

"Whatda ya want?" Bill growled, sure his head was about to explode.

"Mommy, mommy!" the little girl screamed pulling on his arm.

Then he heard an agonizing scream. Bill jumped up and ran to the kitchen, finding Judy laying on the floor doubled over in pain.

"What's wrong?" he asked.

"Do something!" Judy screamed.

"Joanna!" Bill yelled.

"She's not here," Judy snapped.

Bill ran for the phone. "I'll call an ambulance."

"No, wait." Judy gasped. "It's over for now."

"What's over?"

"I'm in labor, dummy. But I think we should get to the hospital before the contractions start again."

"I'll call the doctor."

"Never mind that, the hospital will call him. Just get me there."

Bill stopped dead in his tracks. "Wait a minute! The baby isn't due for another two months. Are you sure that you're in labor?"

"I've been through this before, dummy."

"Okay!"

At the hospital the contractions began again, more intense than before.

"Oh God, Ginge. Please don't leave me. I'm scared."

"Don't worry, Lil bit. I'm right here. I'm going to call someone to come pick up Amy, but I'll be right back."

From the waiting room, Bill called Joanna.

"Hello love," he began. "Have I told you lately how beautiful you are?"

"Cut the crap. What is it that you want?" she asked.

"I'm at the hospital with Judy and Amy. Judy is in labor."

"Cut the crap," Joanna laughed, knowing she wasn't due for another two months.

"I know that...and you know that. But apparently nobody told the baby."

"You're serious, aren't you?"

"I'm as serious as a heart attack. I need for you to come pick up Amy, so that I can be with Judy when the baby is born."

"I'll be there in twenty minutes."

"Thanks!"

CHAPTER TWENTY-SIX
IT'S A BOY!

"It's a boy." the doctor announced as the child, red and shriveled, finally emerged from Judy's womb. He weighed in at two pounds, eight ounces. The baby, though healthy, was born seven weeks premature and as such was whisked off to the Intensive Care Unit immediately.

"He's as healthy as can be expected under the circumstances," the doctor explained to a worried Bill. "But, he is premature and it's standard procedure to keep him in the Intensive Care Unit for awhile."

"He's so tiny," a sleepy Judy said as she was being wheeled from the delivery room. William Daniel Hooker. Jr., fifteen inches long, weighing just two pounds eight ounces was born on November 27, 1975.

Bill quickly filled Judy's room with flowers, fruit, and stuffed animals. He visited their son daily, but from a distance. The tiny infant lay in an incubator, with hoses and tubes in his nose, arms, and mouth! It tugged at Bill's heart to see his son lying there, so small and helpless. Bill decided that when their son was released from the hospital, they would not be living with Bill and Joanna Smith. The house was not clean enough for the baby!

Bill drove to the Chevrolet dealership on Reisitertown road where he had bought the canary yellow Corvette and white Caprice convertible and he traded the emerald green Thunderbird in on a 1979 maroon and white Chevrolet C-10 pick-up truck. He customized the truck with a white fiberglass cap, chrome wheels, and installed the C.B. that he had stolen in Wilson, North Carolina the night before the bank robbery. Then he drove past White Marsh and rented a two bedroom apartment. He furnished Amy's room with a round bed and a red velvet headboard that matched his and Judy's bed. He bought a new living-room set and matching chrome glass end tables. Beneath the glass topped end table he placed a white bear skin rug. In the bathroom, impressed by the one at Ceaser's Palace, Bill had a phone installed next to the toilet. Then he thoughtfully placed a small color tv on on the vanity. It was a beautiful apartment and a nice surprise for Judy.

* * *

Earl answered the phone at the Bolero club with a gruff, aggravated about being pulled away from his sports page.

"It's a boy!" Bill announced excitedly.

"A what? Who in the hell is this?"

"Damnit, you don't know my voice by now?"

"Bill?"

"Yeah. Judy had the baby. It's a boy."

"Congratulations! I didn't think she was due for another couple of months."

"She wasn't, but I guess he was impatient."

"Well that's good news."

"Oh, oh. What's the bad news?"

"The feds arrested Frank."

"For what?"

"I don't know. He was just arrested this morning."

"Jesus! If it's not one thing, it's another. If he calls, tell him that I'm working on getting him out."

"Stop by later and I'll buy you a drink."

Bill called Frank's house, and Linda answered on the second ring.

"What's going on Linda?"

"You son-of-a-bitch! I hope you're happy," she screamed into the phone.

"Calm down and tell me what happened?"

"The F.B.I. arrested Frank, that's what happened. Where have you been? I've been trying to get in touch with you all day."

"I've been back and forth between the hospital and our new apartment. Judy had the baby."

"That's unfortunate. How is she, or me, supposed to raise our children with our men in prison?"

"What do you mean 'our' men? I haven't been arrested for anything."

"Oh, like you haven't done anything."

Bill quickly changed the subject. "Does Frank have a lawyer or a bond?"

"His bond is One Hundred thousand dollars. Cash or surety. Red is working on getting him a lawyer."

"Where is Frank?"

"He's in the Baltimore City jail."

"Okay, listen. Tell him not to make any statements or talk to anyone. I will arrange for a bondsman to bail him out, and I will call Harold Glazier."

"Who's Harold Glazier?"

"He's the best criminal attorney in Maryland."

"I've called five bondsmen and they all want ten percent, plus security.

"Don't worry. I'll take care of this," Bill assured her.

"How's Judy and the baby?"

Bill filled Linda in on the details of little Bill's birth, then hung up. He placed a call to Fifi London, an International bondsman and personal friend. Then, he called Harold. Frank was out of jail two hours later and he and Bill had an appointment at Harold's office at ten o'clock the following morning.

Harold's office was on the ninth floor of the Keiser building, a stately gray granite high-rise on Baltimore's east side. They parked in the underground parking lot and took the elevator.

The receptionist motioned for them to have a seat, but Harold bellowed from behind his massive oak desk, "Come on back, Bill."

Entering the office, Bill noted that, as always, Harold was attired in an expensive suit and smoking a Havana cigar.

"The first question I have is, what possessed you to fuck with the feds? They have a ninety percent conviction rate."

"Well, that's where the money is," Bill grinned.

"Right. I've spoken to my sources and there's a very good chance that you," he looked directly at Frank, "may be charged with a second robbery." "Right now our only concern is the one in Wilson, North Carolina. I will have to retain local counsel because my license only allows me to practice law in the state of Maryland in which I'm a member of the Bar. But I can act as 'co-counsel' in any state. My retainer will be twenty thousand. Thirty if you are charged with a second robbery."

"I only have ten thousand," Frank sighed.

"I'll pay the other ten," Bill offered.

"Thanks, Bill." Frank smiled.

"Don't mention it. If you're willing to go to trial, the least that I can do is help you, with a good attorney I think you have a fairly decent chance of winning."

"Bring the cash to me tomorrow morning and we will discuss strategy."

* * *

Bill found himself in a dilemma. Tomorrow afternoon Judy would be released from the hospital. Within the next three weeks their son would be released. They had no insurance and he no longer had the money in which to settle the bill. He was wrestling with the problem as he walked through the hospital parking lot after visiting Judy and his son. As he neared his new maroon and white Chevrolet pick-up, he saw Red standing next to it. He sensed trouble even before Red opened his mouth.

"What's up, Red?"

"What in the fuck is the matter with you?" Red asked, his speech slurred by alcohol and anger.

"What do you mean?"

"We're supposed to be partners, but you never call me or anything."

"I've been busy. Judy just had a baby for Christ's sake," Bill retorted, angry with himself now in the face of Red's verbal attack.

"Well, do you plan to help Frank out?"

"I already have. He's out on bond and this morning I took him to see a lawyer. I just paid out the money that I intended to use to pay the hospital bill."

"You broke?"

"Flat broke!"

"Do you want to rob a bank?"

"Do you have one in mind?"

"There's a bank on every corner," Red chuckled.

"Judy gets out tomorrow afternoon. I'll meet you at the Bolero club tomorrow night. We'll go to Pennsylvania, rob a bank, and be home for dinner."

"I'll see you there." Red smiled, and walked back to his car. Bill wondered who the brunette waiting in his car was, it wasn't his wife, Mary.

* * *

Bill met Red at the Bolero club. They drank and placed wagers on the pinball machine with big Earl all night. After closing, Bill and Red drove separately to the Community Club in Essex, where Red left his red Ford Torino. They used Bill's new truck to drive to Pennsylvania. Arriving at three in the morning, they checked into a small motel. Bill fell immediately asleep and Red soon followed suit.

The next morning they awoke early and set forth in search of a suitable bank to rob. Bill was looking for a bank with enough money to make it worth robbing, yet small enough not to require extensive planning. In the tiny town of New Freedom they found a bank that wasn't much larger than a postage stamp. It had three tellers, sat on a corner, and had easy access. The bank was a small concrete block building, the front was blank with the exception of a glass entrance door and one plate glass window. "I'm going to park up the block and walk back to the bank to take a closer look. You slide over into the driver's seat," Bill told Red. He parked in front of a hardware store, and said. "I'll be back in ten minutes, or less."

Back in five minutes, Bill reported, "It looks good!"

"Hot damn, we've got us a bank to rob."

"I didn't say that. I just said that it looks good. I'm not going to rob a bank if the police station is on the same block. We did that in Wilson, North Carolina, and the cops were on us like fleas on a dog. They came from everywhere!"

"Okay. But other than that it's a go."

"Yep, other than that, it's a go."

"There's three teller windows and from what I saw they're fat with cash."

"Hot damn. Here piggy, piggy, piggy." Red laughed and slapped his thigh like the redneck he was.

"Drive up the street, let's see if we can find the police station."

They drove around for twenty minutes without spotting a police station. Finally, Bill told Red to pull up next to a woman walking a small dog.

"Excuse me, Ma'am. But could you direct me to the police station?"

"I beg your pardon," she said, unsure of his question.

"We're salesmen and we need to check to make sure there's no local ordinance against canvassing this area."

"Oh, I see. Well, the Sheriff's department serves this area, but that's located in the next town, Quincy."

"And how far is that?"

"About twelve miles."

"Thank you very much," Bill smiled.

They drove out of town, toward a factory they'd spotted on their way in. They would steal a car to use as their getaway vehicle.

"What do you think?" Red asked as they neared the factory.

"Easy pickens, Red. Easy pickins."

* * *

Meanwhile, Frank and Billy had gone to Virginia to rob a bank. The feds followed them. Just as it began to get dark, Frank noticed the car passing them had passed several times throughout the day. Billy took the next exit, turned right, and made another quick right turn down a private road, and stopped. Frank looked over his shoulder and watched as three familiar cars zipped past. "We were damn lucky this time," Frank said, deep in thought.

"What do you want to do?" Billy asked.

"Let's go home and come back another day."

Having shaking their pursuers, Billy drove back to Maryland. It was the second time that he had gotten lucky, though he didn't know it. The feds had followed him and Jabo out of state once before. They were somewhere in Virginia, out in the country, when Jabo pulled into a bank's parking lot.

Billy walked inside to purchase a roll of quarters, and case it. Moments after they left, Jabo pulled the car to the side of the road. Billy jumped out of the car and opened the trunk. Believing they were preparing to rob the bank, the F.B.I. rushed to secure the bank. When Billy and Jabo ran through the door they would be running head first into the F.B.I.'s trap. But Billy was only getting into the trunk to fetch a baggy of marijuana. He rolled a joint, lit it, and passed it to Jabo as they drove merrily down the road.

After shaking their tail, Billy drove back to Maryland and dropped Frank off at his house. The following morning Frank was arrested for violating the conditions of his bond. He wasn't permitted to leave the state.

CHAPTER TWENTY-SEVEN
EASY PICKINS

At ten o'clock Bill guzzled a warm beer before gathering his tools; a coat-hanger bent straight with a loop on one end to open the driver's locked door with, a dent puller to snatch the ignition out, and a screw-driver to start the vehicle with. Stealing a car was the easy part, he'd never heard of anyone getting killed stealing a car. Robbing a bank, however, was a a totally different proposition. The newspapers reported on bank robbers getting killed all the time.

"Where do you want me to drop you off?" Red asked. He was, as usual, eager to get it done. Over the past two years Bill had been doing the thinking for the both of them. He thought of them as batteries. Red was EverReady and he was Duracell. Red was EverReady because he was always ready to rob a bank. Bill was Duracell because he figured that he would outlast Red by many years. Bill contributed his longevity to the careful selecting of banks. Red, on the other hand, would rob anything that looked-like a bank with anyone.

Bill chose a 1969 white Ford Galaxy to steal because the ignition was in the dash and easily removed.

"Drop me off at the top of the hill. I'll steal the Ford and meet you a couple miles down the road." They had picked a place to park the truck in an alley one block from the bank. Their plan was to park the stolen car on a one-way street at the side of the bank. After the robbery, they would drive a block, make a left turn into the alley, walk to the truck and drive away.

Within thirty seconds after entering the Ford Bill pulled the ignition, started the car, and drove out of the parking lot. He drove back towards the town of New Freedom. After a couple of miles, Bill pulled to the side of the road and Red pulled behind him. Bill jumped out of the stolen car and ran to the truck, dropped the tools on the floorboard, and grabbed his toboggan mask and gun. He ran quickly to the stolen car as Red pulled out in front of him.

Red parked the truck in the alley and climbed into the passenger seat of the stolen Ford.

"You ready?" Bill asked.

"Yep," Red smiled.

They parked the car on the side of the bank, leaving the engine running. They ran through the front door of the bank wearing blue knitted stocking masks cut one-layer thin and yellow surgical gloves covered their hands.

"All right everyone, you know what this is!" Bill shouted stepping through the door. He held the Charter Arms .44 Bulldog aloft so that anyone who might be slow would quickly comprehend what he meant.

Red vaulted the counter as Bill surveyed the inside of the bank. There was one lone customer, a female. As Red jumped over the counter. Bill caught a glimpse of a man in a gray suit who ran through an archway into a back room.

Bill grabbed the female customer and held her in front of him as a shield, pointing his gun in the direction the man ran. "What's the matter?" Red asked, stuffing money into a bag.

"A man just ran through that archway," Bill pointed with his gun hand.

"Shit!" was Red's only comment.

'Lord,' Bill thought, 'just get me through this one and I promise I'll never do it again'. The seconds seemed to stretch into an eternity as Bill stood at the door with his captive waiting for Red to finish bagging the money; or for the man in the gray suit to step back into the room with a gun. 'Please don't come back,' Bill silently pleaded.

"Move, move, move!" Bill shouted at Red, who was acting like he was at a local Seven-Eleven store shopping for beer and pretzels. After two minutes passed, Bill was worried the man would return with a gun or, worse yet, the police would pull up in front of the bank. Finally, he heard Red tell the bank tellers to "have a nice day" as he vaulted back over the counter.

Still masked, they ran from the bank and around the corner to where their getaway car was parked. Two of the female bank tellers stood on their tippy-toes to look out a side window. Seeing this, Bill told Red not to take his mask off yet.

With Bill driving the Galaxy they pulled from the curb and nonchalantly drove away, making the first left into the alley. They pulled up behind the truck, stepped from the car unmasked, and walked to the truck. Once inside, Bill started the engine and drove away quietly. At the end of the alley he turned right and within less than three miles they entered the state of Maryland. Driving country roads with no real sense of direction they finally came upon a recognizable highway.

"How much do you think we got?" Bill asked with a grin.

"I dunno."

"Wanna make a bet?" Bill asked, grinning.

"No, but where do you suppose that idea came from?" Red grinned, remembering Bristol, Tennessee, and their One Hundred and four thousand dollar score.

"Who cares? The last time we made a bet, you won, and I didn't mind losing. How much do you think we've got?" Bill asked.

Red looked into the bag, tossed the bills around, and said, "thirty thousand."

"I'd say it's closer to twenty thousand," Bill bet.

"Your ass, the bags half full!"

"Yeah, but there's no money in it."

"What's that green shit then, trading stamps?"

"You know what I mean. There's no big bills."

"I'll bet you a hundred dollars there's more than thirty grand," Red snarled. He pulled a tab from a can of beer and took a big gulp.

Bill leaned his head back and closed his eyes for a few seconds, the long hours were catching up to him and all he wanted now was some sleep.

"You want a beer?" Red offered.

"Nah. All I want is a warm bed and a hot piece of ass."

"You tired?" Red grinned.

"Hell yes, aren't you?"

"I was thinking that maybe we should rob another bank."

Bill sped up, and turned the radar detector on. Telephone poles seemed to get closer and closer together. At a hundred miles an hour the poles looked like a picket fence. The tires hummed and the exhaust roared as their speed increased.

After ten minutes or so they came to a crossroad. Slowing to a stop, Bill asked. "Right, or left?"

"Right. No, left," Red amended, glancing to his right, In that direction a state trooper was approaching.

"I thought you said right?"

"That was before I saw the cop car," Red laughed uproariously.

"Goddamnit!" Red shouted.

"What's the matter?" Bill asked, his heart jumping up in his throat.

"I spilt the damn beer in my lap," Red bitched.

"You asshole. You stupid fucking asshole. You scared the living shit out of me. Did it ever occur to you that we just robbed a bank?"

"Well, I didn't exactly plan to spill beer down my leg," Red said in his defense. His face and neck reddening.

"Lord, just get me home in one piece," Bill prayed. Red opened another can of beer.

"What's the cop doing?" Bill asked for a report.

"Oh, he went by without a glance. I suppose you don't want to rob another bank today?" Red chuckled.

"Fuck you!"

"How far is ten or fifteen thousand going to take you?" Red asked, grinning.

"All the way home," Bill said with a smile.

"Come on," Red pleaded. "Once you get hung up in Judy's apron strings I may not see you for another three months."

"That's if you're lucky," Bill smiled.

"Okay, but promise me one thing."

"What's that?"

"If you do decide to rob another bank, you will call me first."

"I promise. Now, can I go home?"

"Yeah, after we count the money and you pay me my hundred dollars."

In a motel room in Essex. Red and Bill counted the money. It was just over sixteen thousand dollars. Red being the sore loser, begrudgingly paid

Bill a hundred dollars, and Bill drove him to his car where they parted ways.

All the way home Bill rehearsed the lies that he would tell Judy. The truck broke down. He was at the bar, got too drunk, and spent the night on Red's sofa. Aw hell, he thought, she wouldn't believe anything he said. He thought decisively that if he told her the truth, that he robbed a bank, she wouldn't believe that either. He needn't have worried.

He found the apartment empty. A note she left on the kitchen table read: Ginge. Went to the hospital with Bill and Joanna to visit the baby. Please pick me up at their house around two o'clock. Love, Judy.

It didn't sound as though she was too pissed off. Bill drove to the house on Gunpowder road. He grabbed about fifteen hundred dollars from the bag, filled his gold money clip, and stashed the rest of the money in the drop ceiling in their kitchen. Then he laid down on the couch in their living-room and fell to sleep instantly.

CHAPTER TWENTY-EIGHT
THE SEARCHES

"Bull, Bull!" Amy screamed. Bill woke-up, opening his eyes slowly, hoping it was just a bad dream. No such luck. "Bull bad!" Amy shouted directly in his left ear, nearly splitting his eardrum.

"Judy! Get your daughter out of here before I sell her to the gypsies."

"Get him Amy," Judy laughed.

"Please call her off," Bill pleaded.

"Amy, go to the kitchen, and you, get up. I cooked you breakfast."

"I'm not hungry."

"I didn't cook for the sheer joy of it, you're gonna eat."

"But I'm not hungry."

"I don't give a shit. Eat so you don't get hungry."

"Bull bad!" Amy yelled from the kitchen.

"I am not. You're teaching her that shit, aren't you?"

"Hell no, she's just a bright child. Where were you last night?"

"Nonya."

"Ooooh, you know that pisses me off when you give me that nonya shit. I ought to belt you one."

"For what?" Bill grinned.

"I don't know. But, you do!" Judy surmised.

"How's Danny?"

"Don't change the subject. You're not getting out of this one, Buster."

"Buster?" Bill broke into hearty laughter.

"Don't laugh at me, Bill Hooker. You know that I hate that too!"

"I'm sorry. lil bit. But sometimes you say some of the silliest shit, and I just can't help myself."

"Ooooh. I'm really pissed now," Judy announced, with her hands on her hips.

That did it. Seeing Judy is such a huff. Bill wrapped his arms around his stomach and laughed until he thought his sides would split.

"That's it. You're cut off for life!"

"For life? Your life, or mine?"

"For the rest of your life," Judy said decisively.

"Oh hell, just kill me now and get it over with," Bill moaned in mock defeat.

Judy couldn't help it, she just had to laugh. No matter how mad she got, she could not stay angry at Bill. He knew it too, and shamelessly exploited the fact.

"Where were you?" she asked again. Bill knew he'd better tell her something this time.

"Playing cards."

"Where?"

"In Essex, at the Community Center."

"Good story, but I ain't buying it. Mary called last night looking for Red."

"Well, he was there too," Bill admitted.

"Just playing cards, all night?"

"Yep."

"Swear it?"

"I swear to God that Red's red Ford Torino was parked at the Community Center at noon and we left from there together going our separate ways."

"Okay, I believe you."

"Gee thanks," Bill remarked.

"You've got ten minutes," Joanna announced from the kitchen as she began setting the table.

"Okay, thanks," Bill replied to Joanna. "How come you believe me?" he asked a smiling Judy.

"Because you swore, and I can tell when you're lying."

"Yeah," Bill agreed. "I guess I'm not a very good liar. But I didn't think you would believe me, especially since I was with Red."

"I can tell when you're lying."

"Lucky me."

"Get your ass up! Oh, and don't forget that tomorrow is your birthday. Don't make any plans for tomorrow night." Judy said with a lewd wink.

"Hi Bill," Joanna said entering the room.

"You're a bad influence on her," Bill said, nodding towards Judy.

"Me?" Joanna giggled. "What'd I do?"

"For starters, you probably told her to wake my ass up."

Amy reentered the room, walked to the couch, and slapped Bill on his arm. "Bull bad!"

"Bull -- I mean Bill, is not bad. But he should spank Amy's and Mommy's butts for waking him up." Bill sat up on the couch placing his feet firmly on the carpeted floor.

"Mommy! Mommy! Amy screamed, running to Judy and hiding behind her leg.

"He's teasing, honey." Judy giggled. "That's mean, Ginge."

"You shouldn't scare her like that."

"I'm sorry!" Bill apologized. "But it's not nice to scream in Bill's ear to wake him up. Understand?"

Amy had the biggest and brightest brown eyes, he thought. She nodded and ran into the kitchen.

"Linda called this morning," Judy said.

"What did she have to say?" Bill inquired.

"Harold said that Frank probably won't get another bond."

"I kinda figured that."

"She also wanted to know if you have any money for Frank?"

"I'll call her later."

"Why don't you call her now," Judy suggested with a devious grin.

"Why? So you can listen?"

"Well, I do have a right to know what's going-on."

"Hold on!What Frank and Billy did is absolutely no concern of yours, or mine. That's not my problem, do I make myself clear?" Bill asked, in a stern voice.

"Yes. I just wanted to know if you were going to give him any money." Judy snapped.

"I can't afford to. If I could afford to, I would."

"I don't understand. Why would you even consider giving him money?"

"Because we're family. Linda is your sister and she blames me for everything. But no matter how much we fight or argue, we are still family."

Changing the subject, Judy asked. "Did you win or lose last night?"

"I won."

"How much?" she smiled.

"A few dollars."

"Good, cause I want two hundred dollars."

"Can I go back to sleep?"

"No!"

"Then you can't have any money."

"Fuck you!"

"I thought I was cut off for life?"

"Asshole!" Judy snapped, and broke into uncontrollable laughter.

"I do have an asshole." Bill quipped.

"You have two. One that you shit with, the other you talk out of."

"Are you trying to say that I talk shit?"

"More than a television preacher."

"Ouch!"

"The truck is filthy. Why don't you get up off your lazy ass and wash it?"

"If it bothers you so much, why don't you drive it to the car wash?" Bill countered.

"Because I can't reach the damn pedals to drive the damn thing. That's probably why you bought it."

"Smart of me, huh?"

The night passed without incident and, though Bill couldn't know, it was to be one of his last peaceful nights sleep for many days to come.

Bill awoke early and gave Judy money to go shopping for clothes for their newborn. Then, he took the opportunity to drive to his ex-girlfriend Jean's apartment in Glen Burnie. They were still friendly, at least they were on speaking terms. He owed her some money, which he wanted to pay while he had it. She still lived in the apartment they once shared with her son and daughter. Donna, was seven years old and her brother. Roland, was nine. When Bill ended their relationhip, he left with nothing but his clothes. As he drove down Route 40 on cruise control his mind was on bringing Danny Jr. home from the hospital to their new apartment - along with a dozen other things. He was completely oblivious to his surroundings as the exited onto Craine highway, turning left, then right, into the apartments. It was a complete surprise when an unmarked blue Dodge pulled up next to him and literally forced the Chevrolet Cheyenne pick-up off the road. The driver, dressed in a suit, jumped from his car, drew a gun and shouted. "Don't move! "

Bill kept his hands on the steering wheel. He looked in the driver's side mirror and saw a familiar face in the car pulled up behind him. Slowly, Bill opened the door of the truck, stepped out, and turned around in a complete circle to show that he was unarmed. Then, he walked to the passenger door of Special agent H. Thomas Moore's car, opened the door and sat down.

"Good morning, Tom."

"Morning Billy." Moore grinned.

"May I ask what this is about?"

"We know about the nasty little deed, the one in New Freedom, Pennsylvania."

"You must have me confused with someone else."

"I don't think so." Moore grinned, then asked. "Did you know that we were following you?"

"Of course." Bill lied.

"I figured that when you headed for the apartments."

"Why'd you stop me?"

"We couldn't risk you getting rid of any evidence."

"Do you have a warrant for my arrest?"

"No."

"Am I under arrest?" Bill pursued his questioning.

"No."

"Can I leave now?" Bill asked.

"No."

"But you just said that I'm not under arrest and you don't have a warrant?"

"You're being detained."

"For what?"

"We have a warrant to search your residence on Gunpowder road in White Marsh. Agents are conducting that search as we speak. I've requested an additional warrant to search your truck."

"You don't need a warrant for that. You have my consent. Go ahead, search away."

"I've already requested the warrant. May as well wait."

"Damn Tom, this is not how I planned to spend my birthday." Bill opened the car door and asked, "What would you do if I just walked away?"

"I'd shoot you." Tom said seriously.

"Would you really shoot me, Tom?"

"If you left me no choice, I would." he grinned.

"This is bullshit! I've never in my life heard of being'detained' I have cooperated fully, consented to the search of my vehicle, and you are holding me without cause and threatening to shoot me if I leave."

"I didn't threaten you."

"The fuck you didn't. A bullet is a bullet, and you said that you would shoot me if I walked away."

"Calm down, Billy. I'm just doing my job."

"Yeah, well, harassing me seems to be a full time occupation for you."

"What do you have in your pockets?" Moore asked.

"A wallet, comb, cigatettes, lighter, and my money clip."

"Where were you yesterday?"

"I have nothing further to say."

"I've got to read you you're rights anyway."

"Not if I'm not under arrest." One of the first things Bill learned when he began studying law was his Miranda warnings which applied at the time of arrest.

As they talked, Jean drove by in her white 1974 Ford Mustang. Seeing Bill's truck and him sitting in Moore's car, she stopped and rolled down the window to ask what was going-on.

"Call Harold Glazier. Tell him that I am being illegally detained by Special agent H. Thomas Moore of the F.B.I." Bill shouted.

After Jean drove off Moore said, "This is completely legal, Billy. Now, I'm going to read you your rights."

"So, I am under arrest?"

"No, you aren't. The Supreme Court says that when the focal point of an investigation is on a suspect, that suspect is entitled to have his rights read to him."

Bill had a strange admiration for H.Thomas Moore because he played by the rules.That was commendable and to be respected. Bill never resented authority, merely the abuse of it.

"I know my rights," Bill replied.

"Doesn't matter, Billy. I still have to read them to you."

"Doesn't matter, Tom. I'm still not going to make a statement."

Bill waited impatiently for the search warrant for his truck to arrive, his mind wandered to the search going-on at Gunpowder road. Why hadn't he laundered the money immediately, as he normally did? Why did he keep a two dollar toboggan hat? The answer was simple enough, nobody knew where he was staying, or so he thought.

How did they know where he was staying? He searched for the answer. Only Judy, Bill and Joanna Smith, knew about the new apartment. Frank! Frank and Linda both knew that he and Judy had been staying with Bill and Joanna Smith in White Marsh. The feds had probably tapped their phone. That's how they knew that Frank and Billy were going out of town. Stupid, stupid, stupid! Whatever the case may be, he had to deal with the situation at hand. Nobody knew where his money was stashed and he hoped they wouldn't find it.

"Why were you going to Jean's apartment?"

"I had to piss. I still do. Can I go now?"

"No."

"Can I stand up and piss outside?"

"No."

"Can I piss in your car?"

"No!"

"Are you going to shoot me if I do?"

"Don't piss in my car, Billy." Moore grinned.

"Would it piss you off? Cause I'm pissed off, and misery loves company."

"Billy, don't try my patience, The warrant will be here in a few minutes. If we don't find anything in your truck, or at the residence, you will be free to go."

"Is that so?"

"That is my understanding."

"Okay, I believe that I can hold-it for another fifteen minutes."

It was a bright, warm, sunny day. They were surrounded by red brick three-story apartment buildings. The lawn around the buildings was freshly mowed, and the gardens not iceably absent flowers with the coming of winter.

"Empty your pockets, Billy."

Bill followed his instruction. Moore took the money from Bill's gold money clip, pulled a computer sheet from his pocket and began comparing serial numbers of tens, twenties, and fifty dollar bills that were stolen from the bank in New Freedom. Pennsylvania. None matched.

"You're lucky, so far Billy."

"Lucky? You call this luck?" Bill frowned.

"Things could be worse," Tom grinned. That grin, the same one that taunted Bill even in his sleep.

The search warrant arrived and the agents converged on the truck, finding no evidence linking Bill to the robbery in New Freedom.

"Did you play baseball in school, Tom?"

"Yeah. Why?"

"Just curious. I hope you had a better batting average, cause you're striking out today."

"I've got to take this money," Moore grinned.

"Bullshit! You can't take my money. How am I supposed to pay my bills?"

"Sorry Billy, I have to take it. I'll give you a receipt."

"A receipt? Are my creditors going to accept your receipt as payment for my bills?"

"I seriously doubt it."

"Screw that. Why do you want my money?"

"Possible evidence. It's going to the crime lab for analysis. Maybe I'll get lucky and one of the bank tellers' fingerprints will be found on a bill," Tom grinned. But that wasn't to be. Only five prints were found on the money, all belonging to H. Thomas Moore.

"Can I go now?"

"In just a minute. Would you mind stepping out of the car. This will only take a minute. I need to call headquarters."

Bill watched Moore make the call. He frowned and practically slammed the hand mike back in its cradle. Then, he motioned for Bill to get back into the car.

"It's cold out there." Bill rubbed his arms, grinning.

"One more thing." Moore chuckled.

"What's that?"

"I need your jeans."

"You've got to be joking." Bill snapped.

"I'm not, believe me. There's a car in route bringing you another pair of pants."

"Let me get this straight. After I give you my jeans, I will be free to leave, right?"

"That is correct."

"Okay, here." Bill complied taking off his faded Levis. He took off his flannel shirt, wrapped it around his waist, and opened the car to make good his exit.

"You don't want to wait for the pants?"

"Nope. If I'm free to go, I'm gone."

"I have no reason to detain you any longer. By the way, Billy, Happy birthday!" Tom grinned. It was the same grin that sent chills up and down Bill's spine, the one that haunted him.

CHAPTER TWENTY-NINE
THE HONEYMOON SUITE

Bill jumped in his truck, started the engine, turned on the heater, and drove away. He turned right onto Craine highway. At the traffic light in the center of Glen Burnie, he turned right onto Old Annapolis road, crossed Ritchie highway and looked carefully in his rear-view mirrors to make sure that he wasn't still being followed. He drove less than a half mile before turning right onto a dead end street. His friends Greg and Barb lived at the end of the street on the left. He pulled the truck into their driveway, then into their back yard out of sight from the road. When he honked the horn. Greg came to the door.

"Hey Greg," Bill chuckled. "This is a bit of an awkward situation, but do you have a pair of pants that I can borrow."

Greg laughed. He was considerably a bigger man than Bill by at least four inches around the waist.

Bill stepped from the truck holding the black slacks up using both hands.

"I don't suppose you also have a belt that I could borrow," Bill chuckled.

"What happened to your pants?" Barb wanted to know.

"The F.B.I. took them."

"What?" Greg chuckled, handing Bill a belt.

Bill called Judy. She answered the phone tearfully. "What's wrong, baby?"

"The ef-ef-ef-be-eye was here. They said you're going to prison for fuh-for twenty yuh-years," she nearly screamed into the phone.

"Wait a minute, calm down. Take a deep breath." When the crying tapered off to a sniffle, Bill asked. "What happened?"

They searched the house. It was just getting dark and they were about to leave, when one of the agents decided to check the ceiling in the kitchen."

"What did they take?"

"Money from the bank! And they took some guns from the bedroom. But they walked past your gun on the mantle."

"Hide that gun under a bush in the backyard. I'll take care of it later."

"When are you coming home. This place is pretty tore up and Bill Smith is having a fit."

"I've got to take care of some things, but I promise that I'll call you later."

"They're looking for you, Ginge. They have a warrant for your arrest."

"Don't worry, I'll take care of it." Bill assured her.

"What should I do?" Judy asked and began to cry.

"Stay there, and quit crying. Everything's going to be okay."

"You lied to me."

"No, I didn't. Red's car was parked in front of the Essex Community center all night, and we did part company from there."

"Are you going to run?"

"No! I'll call you later."

"Promise?"

"I swear I will. I'm going to call the attorney, then I'll call you right back. Okay?"

"Be careful. Ginge."

"Aren't I always?"

Jean had already talked with Harold at his office, so when Bill called his office he was prepared for his call.

When Harold had checked, there were no warrants for Bill's arrest.

"There is now." Bill explained, filling Harold in on the series of events that led up to the call. Harold asked for a phone number in which to call Bill back at. He told Bill to stay put while he made a few calls. Forty-five minutes later, Harold called.

"This is a serious charge, Bill. I've worked it out. Turn yourself in at the F.B.I. Headquarters tomorrow morning. You will appear before a U.S. Magistrate and bond will be set at less than One Hundred thousand dollars. I may be running late, but I will be there. FiFi will post your bond and you will be out before noon."

"How early?" Bill asked.

"Turn yourself in before nine in the morning."

Harold was like a father figure to Bill. He had always dealt with him squarely and fairly. Neither Bill, nor anyone else, who used Harold as their attorney had ever stayed in jail for more than a few hours. Not in Baltimore, anyway.

Bill called Judy and told her that he couldn't come home tonight, but he would be out on bond before noon the following day.

At seven o'clock Bill woke from a fitful nights sleep filled with dreams of steel bars and concrete walls. He drove to the F.B.I. Headquarters in Towson, Maryland to meet his destiny for better, or worse. He parked his truck in the parking lot, took a deep breath, and walked through the front door.

"Good morning, may I help you," a bespectacled receptionist greeted him.

"I'm here to see Special agent H. Thomas Moore."

"Do you have an appointment?"

"Honey, this appointment has been a long time in the making. Just tell him that Bill Hooker is in the lobby."

The receptionist dialed Moore's office. Twenty seconds later H. Thomas Moore, Sweeny, and several other agents hurried to the lobby.

"I'm here to turn myself in, Tom. You don't need the army."

"They just want to watch the leader of the Hooker Gang turn himself in." Tom grinned.

"Glad that I could provide some entertainment."

"To tell you the truth Bill, we were making bets on whether or not you would show up this morning. How did you get here?"

"I drove myself. My truck's in the parking lot."

"Amazing. There's a nationwide ABP out for you and the truck, and you drive right in. Well, at least you found some pants."

"You won't impound my truck, will you?"

"I have no interest in your truck. You got somebody to pick it up?"

"I'll drive it home this afternoon."

"That remains to be seen. The judge isn't going to release you just because you say you're innocent." Moore grinned.

"Yeah, I know. I've made other arrangements."

"I'm sure you have, but my recommendation will be that you be held without bond."

"Why's that, Tom?"

"You're a flight risk."

"I turned myself in." Bill countered.

"Let's not waste time. Billy, you are under arrest for armed bank robbery. You have the right to remain silent..."

After reading Bill his rights, Moore escorted him to the booking area and processed him into federal custody. Fingerprints and a photo.

"Do you want to make a statement?" Tom asked.

"You know better than that." Bill grinned.

"For the record, who is your attorney?"

"Harold Glazier."

"Okay, now I need a hair sample. You can give it willingly and sign a waiver, or I will obtain a court order. Your choice."

"First, you took my money. Then, you took my clothes. Now, you want my hair. What's next, a couple quarts of blood?"

"That should be it, Billy."

Bill pulled a few strands of his hair, handed those to Moore, who placed them into a plastic baggy and sealed it closed. He labeled it, then sent it to the crime lab.

"Why did you want a sample of my hair?"

"I can't tell you that, Billy."

"Why not?"

"Because it would be very unprofessional of me."

Next, Bill was taken to the federal courthouse, where he appeared before a United States Magistrate Judge. Although Harold Glazier was not present, the court moved forward with the hearing. The Magistrate entered a 'not guilty' plea on Bill's behalf. When the issue of bond was addressed, the prosecutor stood up, "Your honor, it should be noted the defendant is currently under investigation for up to sixteen bank robberies and additional charges are expected to be forthcoming. The government asked the defendant be held without bond."

"Wait a minute. Your honor, I turned myself in. If I was going to flee I would have already done so."

The prosecutor continued. "The defendant's links to Organized Crime makes him a likely candidate to flee the country."

"In light of the possibility of other charges pending bond is set at Three Hundred thousand dollars."

"I turned myself in with the understanding that an agreement was in place to recommend that my bond be set at less than One Hundred thousand dollars."

"My decision has been made, Mr. Hooker."

Bill was led from the courtroom by two brawny U.S. Marshals. Special agent H. Thomas Moore was waiting in the hallway. Standing near him was Joanna, Judy, and William Jr., who was just released from the hospital. Moore had that fucking grin on his face. Seeing his grin, and seeing his wife and infant son looking so abandoned and rejected, Bill snapped. He looked at Moore and said. "I'll never turn myself in again. Next time, you 'll have to kill me!"

"What did you say?" Moore asked walking beside him.

"You heard me." Bill retorted.

"Yeah, I did." Moore grinned.

The words, spoken in anger would haunt Bill for the rest of his life. From that day forward, every time the authorities had a warrant for his arrest he would be considered armed and dangerous - no matter how small the infraction was.

Bill called Judy several times from the county jail. Harold Glazier wanted money, and Bill had none. Worse yet, FiFi London's license only allowed him to write up to a One Hundred thousand dollar bond.

Judy called Red, who gave her a song and dance. She tried to raise bond money by selling their new furniture. But most of what she sold was to shysters who made promises to pay, and didn't. It was a bad experience, especially for Judy, who had never dealt with the judicial system.

Several days later Bill was transported to the United States Penitentiary in Lewisburg. Pennsylvania. He was given a prison number 40151 -133 and locked down in segregation.

The U.S. Penitentiary at Lewisburg was an old prison. The walls were made of huge brown granite blocks.They were more than thirty feet high, topped with razor wire and gun towers. Bill's cell was cold, damp, and poorly lighted. In one corner there a combination stainless steel sink and toilet. The meals were passed through a slot in the door.

For the first two days, Bill was alone. On the third day, the door opened and in walked Tommy Di' Amatto, all six-three, two hundred and forty pounds of him. Tommy was serving a life sentence for a mail truck robbery in which two postal workers were killed.

"This must be the Honeymoon Suite," he rumbled in his gravely voice.

The Honeymoon Suite? Oh God, Bill thought. "What in the fuck do you mean, the Honeymoon Suite. I'm not for that queer shit!"

"Hey, take it easy kid," he laughed. "I was referring to the accommodations. But I'm glad to see a white boy who'll take up for himself. Most of them around here are chicken shits."

Bill told Tommy about how the feds had kidnapped him, explaining that he was taken across state lines, from Maryland to Pennsylvania, without an extradition hearing.

"They are holding me with no visits or phone calls."

That was, until Tommy's gangster friend, Jimmy Burke arrived. Bill and Tommy were cooking steaks on a hot plate, drinking whiskey, and smoking cigars all courtesy of Jimmy. Plus, the guards brought a phone to the cell upon request.

Bill soon learned by talking to Judy, the feds were holding a second grand jury hoping to get an indictment for the bank robbery in New Freedom.

"Bill Smith was served a summons. Joanna's pissed. She's threatening to divorce his ass if he says anything that causes you to get indicted."

"I hope she does." Bill replied. There was a renewed hope. Bill was taken from the prison and appeared before a Magistrate in Harrisburg. The feds argued that Bill owned a car dealership in North Carolina and assured the court that he had the finances to retain counsel. The Magistrate judge refused to appoint counsel, and Bill was returned to Lewisburg where he wrote the following poem :

> Esprit de corps with much esteem
> unveil the path of evergreen
> prunes and prisms I implore
> with good faith the center core.
> Schematic buttons propel the quill
> have the fruits of justice taken ill.
> Somewhere lost in meditation
> is the greatness of our nation.

CHAPTER THIRTY
UNLUCKY THIRTEEN

December 15, 1976. At seven o'clock in the evening, at Tommy Di'Amatto's request, a guard plugged a black phone in to an outlet at the end of the range and passed it through a slot in the steel door.

Bill called Judy, she had just returned home from Harrisburg. The prosecutor presented new evidence to the grand jury to indict Bill on the bank robbery in New Freedom. Pennsylvania. This time, he succeeded.

At Bill's arraignment Authur K. Kusic was appointed as counsel. Kusic immediately filed a motion requesting a reduction in bond. The judge granted the request, reducing the bond to fifteen thousand dollars, cash or surety. Bob and Mary Jenkins posted their home as surety and Bill was released.

Authur Kusic was a small Jewish man with a very annoying squeaky voice, but he defended Bill with passion. His second motion attacked the legality of the search warrant. For the purpose of this hearing, Bill offered testimony.

"Mr. Hooker, was the house on Gunpowder road your residence?" Kusic questioned.

"No, sir, I have an apartment in Aberdeen, Maryland."

"Thank you." Kusic smiled.

"Cross examination?" the judge offered.

"No questions." David Dart Queen grinned.

"You honor, the search warrant clearly states 'to search the residence of William Hooker' at the residence on Gunpowder road. The search warrant is invalid on its face!" Kusic argued, then grinned over his shoulder at Queen.

"I agree," Queen began. "The residence searched does not belong to William Hooker, therefore he doesn't have 'standing' to challenge the validity of the search warrant. The items seized are evidence of the bank robbery in New Freedom Pennsylvania and as such they are admissible as evidence."

The judge agreed with the prosecutor's argument and ruled the evidence 'admissible'.

Kusic tried every loophole in the book, and a few that weren't. He argued that Rule 44 of the Criminal Rules of Federal Procedure states that a defendant is entitled to counsel at every stage of the proceedings, from his initial appearance before a magistrate through the Court of Appeals. In this case, Bill had requested that counsel be appointed and his request was denied. The judge ruled that because Kusic couldn't point to any specific cause of prejudice the denial of counsel was 'harmless error'. The case proceeded to trial.

Unlucky thirteen: Twelve jurors and a judge. The tattoo thirteen and a-half stands for twelve jurors, one judge, and a half ass chance.

The Assistant U.S. Attorney. David Dart Queen, was fresh out of law school and this was his first case. His black neatly groomed hair, rosy red cheeks, three piece dark blue striped suit, and quiet manner attracted the attention of the jurors. And, of course, his mother and father were in the courtroom supporting their son's first trial. H. Thomas Moore sat at the table next to Queen.

Bill sat at the defense table along with Authur Kusic. Behind them sat Judy with the baby, Joanna Smith, and Wiley O' Dell Hall.

"This is going to be a fucking circus." Bill whispered to Kusic.

"Don't be so pessimistic," the lawyer chuckled.

First, the prosecutor called the bank officials to the stand. Their testimony was dry, but necessary. The day passed by at a snail's pace, with no serious damage to either side. On the second day things began to fall apart. On their way to the courtroom Bill and Judy stepped on to the elevator with a group of people. A federal agent looked at Bill and asked. "Hooker, are you ready to get twenty-five years today for robbing the bank in New Freedom?" A woman on the elevator took the stand identifying Bill as one of the men who had robbed the bank.

Kusic stopped the trial, and put Judy on the stand. She told the judge what the agent had said in the elevator. David Queen then called the woman to testify. She claimed that she did not recall the incident in the elevator. The judge ruled that her in-court identification would stand. She lied! With the toboggan hat cut one-layer thin and having no eye holes no one could tell if the robber was black or white much less make an identification.

The next prosecution witness was the mayor of New Freedom, who also owned a car lot near the bank. He testified that on the day of the robbery he had been up on a ladder fixing the sign by the road. He saw a maroon and white truck that he thought belonged to a friend, and he waved as it drove by. Then, he saw that it wasn't his friend behind the wheel, and he identified Bill Hooker as the driver.

"Let the record show the witness has identified the defendant as the man who was driving the truck."

"That's a damn lie," Bill hissed. Red Miller was driving the truck, not him.

The next witness to testify was the female customer that Bill had held in front of him as a shield. In her statement to the police she described her assailant as being no more than five-feet-eight. Bill is six feet tall. To compensate for the difference she testified that at the time she made the statement, she had forgotten that she was wearing high-heels.

"So, the robber could have been taller?" Queen asked.

"Yes, in fact I'm sure he must have been taller. Maybe even six feet," she testified.

"This is bullshit." Bill complained to Kusic.

"She's been coached," he replied.

The judge did rule the guns taken from the residence were inadmissible. But it made no difference. Queen painted a picture of Bill as a man with unlimited access to firearms, able to use and discard them as casually as one throws away a butane lighter. Several poster size photos taken from the surveillance camera sat on an easel throughout the trial as a reminder to the jury of the woman held hostage.

The next person called to testify for the the prosecution was 'an expert witness' from the F.B.I.'s Crime Lab who stated the hair taken from the toboggan hat and the hair samples taken from Bill were 'inconclusive' to a match.

On cross examination, Kusic opened the door, allowing the expert to strongly hint that only professional ethics prevented him from saying the samples did, indeed, seem to match.

Next, the prosecution called 'the fingerprint expert' who testified that six latent prints (fingerprints that can identified) were found on the money seized from Bill during the search of his truck. Five of those prints were identified as those of Special agent H. Thomas Moore. The sixth, was identified as 'possibly' belonging to a female employee of the bank.

On cross examination. Kusic asked. "Just what do you mean by 'possibly'?"

"Well, it takes twelve points to 'positively' identify a fingerprint. The sixth fingerprint that I found only has ten points." He made it very clear the law required twelve points for court indentification. "However, I feel 'reasonably certain' the sixth fingerprint belongs to an employee of the bank."

Kusic argued with the witness for ten minutes, but he appeared to be trying to impeach damaging testimony, and that was a mistake. It only made the jury put more weight on the expert's opinion.

Queen handled himself like a professional. He made his questionable testimony of witnesses seem like they the were honest, sincere working folks.

"Good afternoon, ladies and gentlemen." Kusic began. "Allow me to read from the indictment the charges lodged against my client. Count One states that my client took from 'the person and presence of Susan Ann Kurtz' sixteen thousand and.... Who is Susan Ann Kurtz? She's the teller 'behind the counter'. The robber 'behind the counter' is undisputed five-feet-seven. Five inches shorter than my client." Kusic smiled, feeling a victory at hand. In a surprise showing, he asked the jury to consider Wiley O' dell Hall, Judy's ex-boyfriend. He matched almost perfectly the robber's description. He had access to the Smith's home, and, on many occasions, he had borrowed Bill's maroon and white Chevrolet Cheyenne pick-up truck.

Kusic made a valiant effort, arguing that Bill did not match the description of either of the robbers that was given on the day of the robbery; the most accurate description. He argued that Bill did not live at the Smith residence, nor did he have access to their home.

Once again, however, Kusic had underestimated David Dart Queen. In his summation, he dazzled the jury with his verbal prowess.

"What Mr. Kusic is now offering is an eleventh hour defense," he told the rapt jurors. "Mr. Hooker would have us believe that he's never been in New Freedom. Pennsylvania. Yet we have not one, but two eye-witnesses who have placed him there within minutes of the bank being robbed. Was he just passing through? Not hardly! Mr. Kusic would have you believe that, in order to be convicted, his client had to personally remove the money from the cash drawers. This, too, is incorrect. Mr. Hooker is charged under United States Code Title 18 Section 2103 and 2. U.S.C. Title 18 2103 is the statute for bank robbery, and 2 is the statute for Aiding and Abetting as the judge will instruct. All the prosecution is required to prove is that the defendant 'knew' of the robbery and helped facilitate its commission. We've placed Mr. Hooker in the truck leaving the area of the bank seconds after it was robbed. Was it a mere coincidence? No, it wasn't! The defendant and another man, still unknown, robbed the bank in New Freedom. If you believe the defendant, William Hooker, in any way helped facilitate this crime, then you must bring back a verdict of guilty."

"Wait a minute. First, he argued that I was the bank robber, then he closed to the jury that all I had to do was participate which means that I didn't even have to be in the bank. Object to this shit!"

"Queen is grasping at straws. Don't insult the jury's intelligence." Kusic said confidently.

The judge read the instructions for Aiding and Abetting. He told the jury to select a foreman, review the evidence 'circumstantial' and 'conclusive ', and spelled out in Laymen terms the requirements of what was necessary to convict under U.S.C. Title 18 Section 2103, and 2.

The jury deliberated for less than two hours. As they filed back into the courtroom their faces were blank which Bill did not see as a good sign.

"Has the jury reached a verdict," the judge asked.

"Yes, we have, you honor." Said a portly man chosen as the foreman. He handed the bailiff the jury's finding. The bailiff glimpsed the paper, then passed it to the judge.

"Would the defendant please rise," the judge instructed.

Bill stood, along with his attorney, Authur Kusic, and waited for the jury to announce his fate.

"You may proceed," the judge told the foreman.

"We, the jury, find the defendant William Daniel Burns, guilty on both counts of the indictment," the foreman intoned. To Bill, it was the voice of doom.

"The defendant is remanded into the custody of the U.S. Marshals," the judge ordered, then rattled on about a presentence report and set a date for sentencing.

Bill turned to look at Judy. She was sobbing, holding the baby close to her breast.

Joanna swiped her own tears, and took the baby from Judy, who ran to embrace Bill before the Marshals cuffed him.

The atmosphere at the prosecutor's table was jubilant. David Dart Queen shook H. Thomas Moore's hand, who then stepped out of the way so the young Assistant U.S. Attorney's parent could hug him.

"The end justifies the means, Billy." Moore said grinning as he passed the defense table. For all of his cockiness, Bill thought Tom was basically a good man, and, he wondered if the lies told by the prosecution's witnesses had actually set well with him. Did the end really justify the means?

* * *

"I would have baked a cake if I'd known you were coming?" Tommy Di'Amatto grinned.

"If I'd know that I was coming, I would have brought some hacksaw blades to put in it." Bill chuckled, as he shook his friends hand.

"So, what happened?" Tommy wanted to know.

"They railroaded me, what else? I had a small Jewish attorney, and the only person he outsmarted was himself. The prosecutor was young, fresh out of college. This was his first case and his proud parents sat in the courtroom. His name was David Dart Queen. He had black hair, combed neatly. Rosy red cheeks, and he dressed to impress. Dark blue pinstripe suit, black penny loafers. The jury loved him! This guy could charm the pants off a whore, and my attorney couldn't buy pussy in a brothel."

Tommy laughed hysterically as Bill told the story.

"It was a circus, like entering a plow horse in the Kentucky Derby."

Tommy was stuck between apologies and helpless laughter.

"I know what you mean, kid. Would you like some coffee, or something to eat?"

"I've kind of lost my appetite."

"How did the old lady take it?"

"Hard. She fell apart when the jury found me guilty."

"That's the worst part."

"Don't I know it." Bill sighed,

The days passed into weeks. Judy sent photos of the baby. Kusic filed a motion for a new trial, which the judge promptly denied. One night, with his heart filled with sadness, Bill picked up a pen and wrote a poem :

Prince of Darkness
Oh, Prince of darkness, Lucifer
wicked one, foul fiend
you are the Author of all evil
a Master in your reign.
I treaded close upon your heels,
a faithful follower
and you rewarded me with treachery
it's time that we part friendship, Sir
for I have breached astray.
I loathe your slavish manner
for you taught me by degree
how to hurt the ones I love
and live in misery.
Yes, Prince of darkness, Lucifer

wicked one, foul fiend
you are the Author of all evil
a King in your domain.

In a phone call to Judy, she reported that Red was arrested in Pennsylvania along with another man, whose name meant nothing to Bill. After making bond, Red was arrested for the first bank they robbed, the one in Spruce Pine, North Carolina.

Authur Kusic appealed the conviction, his Brief and arguments giving renewed hope. In fairness, Bill remembered Kusic made a trip to Maryland just to familiarize himself with the scene where the search took place. He had genuinely tried to help!

Tommy hammered Bill with, "What are you going to ask the judge for at sentencing?"

"I want to ask the judge for a (A)(2) number because under that provision I can be released at the Parole Boards discretion."

"Don't forget that. Otherwise, it's mandatory that you serve one-third of your time before you're eligible for parole."

Every day Bill ordered books from the prisons law library. He was deeply disturbed that after his arrest, he was taken across state lines without a hearing, and locked away in a federal prison. From the beginning, the feds had played 'dirty.' He'd been kidnapped (taken across state lines) and held incommunicado. This was America, for Christ's sake, they couldn't do this!

But the federal courts didn't see it that way. The feds actions had no reflection on his trial. At best, it was a civil matter. So, Bill filed suit in federal court naming the F.B.I. and U.S. Marshals as defendents, charging them with acting in a conspiracy to deny his civil rights as secured by the U.S. Constitution.

In his research, Bill found a case Stryker v. United States.

While confined in a county jail in Pennsylvania, facing criminal charges, Stryker attempted to escape and he taken to the federal prison at Lewisburg and placed in segregation. Bill was not an escape risk. Although Bill would, more than likely, win the civil suit there was a question of damages. If he was awarded 'nominal damages' that could amount to One dollar. Other than having his name in a law book, it was a lost cause.

"Hooker. 40151-133," the guard asked.

"Yes, sir." Bill stood at the small window.

"Pack it up!"

"Where am I going?"

"You're leaving on the bus in the morning."

"Where am I going?" Bill asked a second time.

"The bus is going to the federal penitentiary in Atlanta, Georgia."

"Are you sure that I'm on that list. I haven't been sentenced yet."

"Are you William Daniel Hooker, 40151 -133?"

"I am."

"Then you 're on the list," the guard assured him.

CHAPTER THIRTY-ONE
THE TRIP

At five o'clock in the morning the steel door opened and Bill bid Tommy farewell with a handshake and a slap on the back. He soon joined the ranks of other prisoners who lined up to be counted. One by one they were strip searched, handcuffed to a belly chain, and their feet shackled. Then, they were led in a single file to an old army green school bus. Heavy wire mesh covered the windows to prevent impromptu excursions. The seats were caged in, with an armed guard sitting at the front and one sitting in the rear.

Before the trip began, the guard in the front made an announcement. "There will be no standing, switching seats, or rowdiness allowed. For your convenience, there are two plastic jugs. If you need to use the restroom, use the jugs. Do not piss on the floor! It's your property, or the guys next to you, that you will be pissing on." The guard stared around the small area for a moment, a smile playing at the corners of his mouth. Then he added. "Your friend may no longer be you friend if he bites down into a soggy Little Debbie."

"Will we be driving straight through to Atlanta?" a prisoner asked.

"No, sir. We will be stopping at the Reformatory in Petersburg, Virgina, where some you men have reservations for the night and others will be transferring to other transportation for other parts of the country."

"Are you going to feed us?" was the next question.

"Yes, sir. The chef has prepared a delicious lunch for each and every one of you. His sandwiches are individually wrapped and prepared with your satisfaction in mind. I can assure you that our lunches are talked about throughout the prison system. Have a nice trip, gentlemen," he said locking the steel cage behind him.

Once the trip began, the discomfort was magnified tenfold. The green vinyl seats sprang into action and Bill felt as if he was in a rodeo. The radio was barely audible over the rattle and idle chatter, and the vinyl seats either stuck to your back or you slid off them with the slightest move.

The bagged lunches consisted of two peanut butter sandwiches, an apple or an orange, and a orange flavored drink in half-pint milk carton.

By the time they pulled into Petersburg Federal Reformatory in Virginia, Bill was looking forward to a hot meal, a shower, and a good night's sleep. But being as they arrived late, they were fed a variation of the bag lunches they'd ate on the way. In the morning, those who were continuing on to Atlanta were called to the assembly area. One by one, they were strip searched, cuffed and shackled, and put back on the bus. Bill was among them.

The next stop was the Duram County jail in Durham, North Carolina where they left one prisoner: William Hooker. Red Miller must have summoned him to court, Bill guessed. That was the only logical explanation.

At booking, the deputy confirmed that, yes, the U.S. Marshals would be picking him up in the morning and taking him elsewhere. Where and when, he couldn't, or wouldn't say.

Bill had been in his share of jails across the country. In Talbot County, Maryland he'd seen one made of gray granite walls with concrete floors that looked like something from a horror movie. In Pennsylvania, he'd been in a jail that was built of steel - the walls, floors, even the stairs, and everything was painted Army green. But none compared to the old Duram County jail. The white stone structure had long been condemned. The jail itself was a dilapidated hell hole. The second floor had cell-blocks, with rows of cells. On the outside of the steel bars was a walkway where visitors stood. There were huge holes in the floor, large enough to put a fist through, and roaches. Huge ugly cock-roaches claimed whatever food was left unattended.

The following morning a single U.S. Marshal picked Bill up. "I have a writ to take you to the Asheville City jail. You're not going to give me any problems, are you?"

"No sir. I'm just a witness."

"I hate to break the bad news, but I don't believe that's the case." He looked at the piece of paper in his hand and reported. "This writ is issued Ad Prosequendum which means to prosecute."

Bill sat back thoughtfully. The marshal wasn't a bad sort. He'd cuffed Bill hands in front, foregoing the use of belly chains or shackles. It was a nice day, the ride would be comfortable, and Bill wanted to just enjoy the day and worry about Asheville when he got there. The U.S. Marshal removed his coat exposing a .38 Smith & Wesson holstered on his right hip, in plain view and easy reach.

The Marshal stopped at a burger place and bought Bill lunch. "Damn, that was good." Bill said after scarfing down a burger, fries, and a chocolate shake. "It's probably going to be awhile before I eat like that again."

"What do you think the charge is in Asheville?" the Marshal asked.

"I don't know."

Bill thought about Judy and the baby and a tear tried to escape, but he pushed it back. The car slowed to a stop. They were in the down town area of some small town. When the light turned green, the car didn't move. Bill looked at the Marshal and saw he was sound asleep, his head tilted back, mouth open.

"Hey!" Bill said loudly.

"Wha--?" The Marshals head snapped up and he looked around in confusion.

"The light's green. Bill said in a quieter voice.

"Yeah, thanks," the Marshal said, sitting up straight.

"Long night, huh?"

"Yeah. I've put in a seventy hour week. But after I drop you off I'm headed home for three days."

"Wish I was so lucky."

"How old are you, son?"

"Twenty-seven. But, I feel forty."

"Get yourself straight. You've made a wrong turn somewhere along the line."

"Yeah, I suppose."

The Asheville City jail hadn't changed since his last stay. At booking he was told that he had been charged with a bank robbery in Spruce Pine, North Carolina.

Red was asleep in his cell when Bill walked in, kicking the door. "What's the matter, you get lonely?"

"Well goddamn, look what the cat dragged in. What happened in Harrisburg?"

"Guilty! The jury was out for less than two hours."

"What'd ya get?"

"I haven't been sentenced yet."

"Hmm, Seems to me they should've finished there first."

"Nothing surprises me anymore," Bill said, looking pointedly at Red. "Nothing!"

"Frank's on the other side," Red said casually, as if Frank Kalita was just naturally going to be in a jail in North Carolina.

"Frank Kalita?"

"Yep. He lost both of his trials. After his convictions, he cooperated with the cops. He's a witness. You can talk to him through the vents." Red stood on the toilet, cupped his hands, and yelled into the air vent, "Hey Frank, you snitching bitch. There's someone here who wants to talk with you."

If Frank heard, he remained silent. Bill stepped up on to the toilet and repeated the procedure, "Hey Frank, it's me, Bill Hooker. Are you going to put me on the shy? I'm not going to stand on this toilet all night."

"What's up, Bill?" Frank replied, sounding dejected.

"Hey! I was going to help you, but things didn't go so well. I got found guilty."

"Two juries found me guilty."

"How much time did you get?"

"Twenty-five years in Wilson. North Carolina. I havent been sentenced in Florida yet."

"Twenty-five years is a lot of time."

"No shit! How much time did you get?"

"I haven't been sentenced yet."

"When did you get here?"

"Just now, Is it true that you're going to testify against me?"

"I don't know what I'm going to do yet."

"You 're a piece of shit, do you know that, Frank?"

"They offered me ten years to cooperate, and I went to trial. I went to trial on the second bank robbery too. I can't handle fifty years. I don't want to cooperate, but what choice do I have? I have to think of Linda and the kids."

"I have a family now too, Frank. Nobody twisted your arm to do anything,"

"Either you or Red told on me."

"You stupid fucking Pollock. I paid for your attorney and had to go to trial with a court appointed attorney."

"But I'm doing the time."

"You're missing the point."

"I'll talk to you later." Frank shouted.

"Told ya." Red grinned,

One of the trustees remembered Bill from his previous stay, and he asked if he wanted his 'boys' to take care of Frank.

"Don't involve me!" Bill replied flatly.

Two days later the local newspaper headlined: GOVERNMENT WITNESS BEATEN IN ASHEVILLE CITY JAIL. The story named William Hooker and Red Miller as convicted bank robbers and members of an Organized Crime Syndicate. The pending trial was outlined, along with Frank's beating and the alleged connection between the two.

Three black prisoners claimed Frank had initiated the fight by calling them stinking niggers. Frank suffered a few sore ribs, and some bruises and abrasions. The court appointed Bill an attorney and announced a trial date for him and Red to be tried as co-defendants in three weeks.

Robert Pitts, Bill's court appointed attorney argued that three weeks was not long enough time for him to adequately prepare for trial, and the court agreed to severe the cases. Red was to be tried as scheduled in Asheville. Bill's trial was moved to Bryson City, North Carolina. The government offered Bill a concurrent sentence to whatever time he received in Harrisburg for his cooperation against Red. Bill turned the offer down flat.

Red's trial lasted two days. Frank testified that he was cooperating because he believed Red had given the F.B.I. information that led to his arrest and conviction. Frank, therefore, was returning the favor. He added that he had in no way been offered any deals for his cooperation. The jury found Frank's testimony credible and convicted Miller in less than forty five minutes. Red opted to be sentenced immediately. In an effort to gain leniency from the judge his attorney called H. Thomas Moore to the stand. He testified that Red Miller had provided information that led to the arrest and conviction of Frank Kalita and 'other' bank robbers as well.

"Mr. Moore," the prosecutor asked under cross examination. "Wasn't Mr. Miller out robbing banks also?"

"Yes."

"Then, what you're saying is that he was playing both ends against the middle?"

"I guess you could say that." Moore grinned.

Red Miller was sentenced to serve fifteen years. He was moved to a safe area of the jail immediately.

"Hey, Frank. Did you read the newspaper yet?" Bill yelled through the vent.

"Not yet."

"Read page twelve. There's an article you just might find interesting."

The cat was out of the bag. Red had collected rewards for giving information on every one of the Hooker Gang. Bill was now sure that Red had set him up for the robbery in New Freedom, and he wondered if he was a surprise witness who appeared before the second grand jury.

The prosecutor offered Bill a second plea bargain. Plead guilty for a concurrent sentence. Again, Bill turned it down. He hoped the Court of Appeals or a higher court would overturn the conviction in Harrisburg. A guilty plea for a concurrent sentence would negate his efforts.

Judy, along with Bobby and Mary Jenkins offered to testify on Bill's behalf. H.Thomas Moore went to Bobby's place of employment, Wilson's American on Mountain road in Pasadena, Maryland and threatened to charge him with perjury if he testified, but Bobby wasn't so easily intimidated.

He told Moore to arrest him, or get out of his face.

CHAPTER THIRTY-TWO
ONCE BITTEN, TWICE SHY

Once a week Bill was permitted a fifteen minute phone call. He always called Judy, and his guts always wrenched when he heard her voice.

"Is everything alright?" he asked.

"Yeah, kinda." she replied.

"What you mean, kinda?"

"Joanna's threatening to divorce Bill, he's been such as ass lately. I think he's on the rag or something."

"Red was found guilty." Bill reported.

"Yeah, I heard. The snitching bastard deserves it."

"How's the baby?"

"He's so cute, Ginge. He looks just like you. I wish you could see him. Amy loves him, she calls him her brudder." Judy giggled.

"My trial is next Wednesday."

"I know. Bobby is taking off work on Tuesday. He's driving down and we're splitting expenses. So far, it's me, the baby, Bobby and Mary, and their son, Billy. Joanna wants to come, but she's having a hard time finding someone to watch her kids. That's probably why they're fighting."

"Did Bill get his guns back?"

"Hell no! He's too chicken shit to even ask for them."

"Have you talked to Linda lately?"

"Yeah. She's got a job now, and she's selling the house and filing for divorce."

"Does Frank know that?"

"I don't think he knows that she's filing for divorce."

"None of this was ever on the agenda, Lil bit. It just doesn't seem fair to anyone."

"I know." Judy sighed.

Bill's attorney, Robert Pitts, was going to have his hands full. It was difficult -- bordering -- on impossible to prepare a defense. Bill had no alibi and only one person to testify on his behalf. But there were some things that favored him. The government had no eye-witnesses, no expert testimony, and no concrete evidence.

On his day of trial, two U.S. Marshal's escorted Bill to the federal building in Bryson City, North Carolina. As they entered the City limits the deputy behind the wheel asked, "Have you ever been to Byrson City before?" directing the question to Bill.

"Can't say that I have." Bill replied. "Well then, you 're in for a surprise."

"Why's that?"

"It's on the Cherokee Indian reservation."

"So -- "

"They don't much take to outsiders."

"Yeah, or lawmen," Bill grinned. For some reason, the deputies didn't find that amusing.

"You're a real comedian." the driver touted.

The courthouse sat in the middle of a small town square. Then again, the entire reservation seemed small.

The courtroom seemed smaller than most, and juries were selected and seated for more than one trial, which led Bill to believe the judge was a circuit, or roving, judge. If he was right, the judge only came to Bryson City once a month. The room smelled of knotty pine, and a American flag hung limply next to the judges bench. Rows of pews, seven deep, held spectators and defendants not in custody. The prosecutor's table and jury box were on the right, the defense table and door leading to the holding cell on the left.

Judy and the baby sat in the first pew, directly behind the defense table. At the request of counsel. Bobby, Mary, and Billy sat further back so as to be less conspicuous.

At the beginning of the trial, the prosecutor asked the court to sequester the witnesses. This was done so that none of the witnesses called to testify could benefit from hearing another witness's testimony. The defense decided to only call Bobby Jenkins, so he was moved to another room. The government had two prosecutors. One young gun who would handle the presentation, and an older one (soon to retire) who would act as an advisor.

The jury consisted of good old fashion country folks that seemed to be of reasonable intelligence. Robert Pitts, Bill's attorney, felt good about the jury and that engendered a spirit of hope in Bill.

The trial began. One by one, the government brought out their witnesses. Bank tellers, customers, towns people, and Frank Kalita. The first two bank tellers to take the stand told of how the robbery occurred but neither identified Bill as being one of the two robbers. The prosecutor moved to introduce some photos taken by the surveillance cameras.

"Objection, your honor!" Pitts was on his feet. The prosecutor grinned.

"I was not made aware of any such photos during discovery, and I have not had an opportunity to review them."

" I was unaware of that, the prosecution will not introduce the photos, your honor."

"Your honor, may I review the photos?"

"You may," the judge ordered.

After looking at the photos Bill's lawyer withdrew the objection allowing the photos to be introduced into evidence. It was impossible to identify either robber, his attorney surmised.

The third teller to take the stand positively identified Bill as the robber at the door.

"That's bullshit!" Bill hissed into his lawyers ear. She didn't identify me in a line-up two years ago. How in the hell is she going to identify me now? Robert Pitts was not about to inform the jury of a previous line-up.

"Just be calm," his lawyer said.

"Does the defense wish to cross examine this witness?" the judge offered.

"Not at this time, your honor. But I would like to reserve the right to recall the witness for redirect."

"Very well."

Robert Pitts was the kind of man to inspire confidence in country people. He was well dressed, but not flashy, preferring simple slacks and a jacket to a suit. On his feet he wore tan laced Hush Puppies, chosing comfort over fashion. His tie was a modest gray, his brown hair neatly combed, his speech was slow and deliberate, and his words were chosen carefully. The jury liked him, identified with his 'just plain folks' manner. On the other hand, they disliked the prosecutors patronizing attitude towards them, his air of superiority.

The first customer to testify was the Pepsi-Cola driver. He testified how he was robbed while making a deposit, and as to the amount of money taken from him. He looked directly at Bill while he sat in the witness chair. When asked if he could identify the man who robbed him, he responded, "No."

The next witness to testify was a name Bill hadn't recognized on the witness list, but seeing him sent a jolt of fear coursing through Bill's system.

"He works for the Ford dealership where I bought a new 1974 white customized Ford van." Bill whispered to his attorney.

"Do you recognize anyone in this courtroom," the prosecutor asked the sales representative from Valley Ford?" Valley Ford was off of Reistertown road in Reistertown, Maryland.

"Yes, I do."

"Could you point the man out?"

The stout salesman with the curly brown hair pointed a finger at Bill. "The man sitting right there."

"Let the record show, the witness has identified the defendant, Willam Hooker."

"They used this guy to try to indict me for a robbery in Bristol, Tennessee." Bill whispered to his attorney. His lawyer gave him a yellow legal pad and a pencil and asked that he write whatever he felt he needed to say on paper.

"And how did Mr. Hooker pay for this van?"

"In cash!"

The jury shifted restlessly, talking amongst each other. "Did you pay cash for the van?" Pitts asked Bill.

"1 financed a thousand dollars."

"Cash?" the prosecutor repeated, raising his eyebrows in mock surprise. "And what was the total amount the defendant paid for this van?"

"Thirteen thousand, three-hundred, and ninety-four dollars, including taxes."

"No further questions."

"Any questions from the defense?" the judge asked.

"Just a few, your honor."

"Did you pay for the van on the spot?" Robert Pitts asked Bill.

"No, I didn't."

The lawyer stood, approached the witness stand, reached into his pocket, pulled out some money and held it in his hand, palm up. "Did the defendant just reach into his pocket and pull out thirteen thousand dollars in cash?"

"No, sir. He gave a one thousand dollar deposit to hold the van, and left. He returned an hour later and paid the balance."

"No further questions."

"Redirect, your honor," the prosecutor nearly leaped to his feet. "If you recall, was the money loose, or wrapped in something? "

"Oh, I remember. The money was in a paper bag and it was wrapped in white twist ties, like the ones on garbage bags."

"Thank you. No further questions."

"Anything more from the defense?"

"Yes, your honor."

"I believe that you testified Mr. Hooker paid for the van in cash?" the attorney asked.

"That's correct."

"I'm surprised that you remember it so vividly. "

"It isn't everyday that someone walks in and pays in cash."

"I suppose not. But the truth is my client, in fact, financed a portion of the van, did he not?"

"I have nothing to do with transactions made through the finance department. My superior and I counted --."

"Objection, your honor. The witness cannot testify for the actions of his superior," the prosecutor shouted.

"Sustained, Limit you testimony to personal knowledge," the judge instructed.

"Yes, sir."

"I'll rephrase the question. Did Mr. Hooker, to your knowledge, finance some of the van?"

"No."

"But, it's possible, correct?"

"Yes."

"No further questions.

The court recessed for lunch. Bill spent an anxious hour in the holding cell. When the court reconvened, the government called their last witness, Frank Kalita. He testified that he and Bill were friends and associates and that Bill had once worked for him.

"Did Mr. Hooker confide in you?" the prosecutor asked.

"Yes, sir."

"Did he tell you that he and an accomplice had robbed a bank?"

"Yes."

"Where was the bank located?"

"Spruce Pine, North Carolina."

"What did Mr. Hooker tell you regarding the robbery?"

"He stood at the door wearing a mask made from women's stockings while Miller…"

"Objection."

"Sustained. Limit your testimony to the defendant's actions," the judge instructed.

"Okay, Hooker had a Smith & Wesson .357 single action gun. He stood at the door and robbed a male customer who came into the bank to make a deposit."

"Was there anything special about that customer?"

"He worked for Pespi-Cola."

"And did Mr. Hooker tell you how much he made from that robbery?"

"His part was almost sixteen thousand dollars."

"When did Mr. Hooker tell you this?"

"A few days after the robbery. He stopped by the house to show off his new customized van, it had a color television inside."

"Did he tell you that he paid for the van with money from the robbery?"

"No. But he was broke the week before, so I assumed he did."

"Objection."

"Sustained. The jury will disregard the witnesses response. Strike his answer from the record."

"No further questions, your honor. The prosecution rests."

"Cross examination?" the judge offered.

"Yes, your honor. Mr. Kalita, how long were you and Mr. Hooker acquainted?"

"About three years."

"And, in the beginning, he was employed by you."

"That is correct."

"What kind of business were you in?"

"I owned a business on Craine highway in Glen Burnie, Maryland called Stitch and Save. We sold brother sewing machines."

"Was Mr. Hooker a repairman?"

"No, he was a salesman. "

"I'd say that you're quite the salesman," the lawyer lashed out. "Is it true that you were convicted of a bank robbery in Wilson, North Carolina?"

"Yes?"

"In that case, did you take two women hostage using a gun and enter the bank with them when they arrived for work?"

"Yes."

"Did you leave the women hog-tied laying helplessly on the floor?"

"Yes."

"How much time were you sentenced to for that bank robbery?"

"Twenty-five years."

"Were you also convicted for a bank robbery in New Port Ritchie, Florida?"

"Yes."

"In that case, did you take the female manager hostage, leave the bank in her car, then lock her in the trunk and leave her in the sweltering sun?"

"It was early morning."

"Did you lock the manager in the trunk and leave her there?"

"Yes."

"Were you convicted for that robbery?"

"Yes."

"And how much time were you sentenced to?"

"I haven't been sentenced yet."

"And you came forward with information 'after' the conviction in Florida. Is this correct?"

"Yes."

"No further questions."

Frank was excused and the defense called it's only witness, Bobby Jenkins.

"How long have you known Mr. Hooker?" Bill's attorney asked Bobby Jenkins.

"About fifteen years. We worked together at Wilson's Ameican gas station in Pasadena, Maryland." Bobby grinned his boyish all-american grin. Dressed in his light blue Standard Oil uniform he looked every bit the working man. The jury related to Bobby, even before he opened his mouth. Clearly, this was an honest man.

"Do you recall the day Bill bought his new van?"

"I sure do. Not the exact date, but I recall the day."

"How can you be so sure?"

"Cause he had to get money from me. It was about four-thirty in the afternoon when he came to my house."

"How can you be certain as to the time?"

"I get off work at four o'clock. I get home around four fifteen. We had just sat down for dinner when Bill arrived, he rarely misses a meal."

The jury chuckled at his rarely missing a meal, and Bill's spirits soared.

"Did Bill drive the van to your house?"

"Not the first time. Bill is a gambler. It wasn't unusual for us to hold large amounts of money for him. One time, we held thirty thousand dollars. But he lost sometimes, too. I remember his losing a brand new Cadillac in a poker game." Bobby looked at the jury. They nodded almost as one, as if to encourage him to continue this entertaining tale. "Anyway, he came in and asked Mary for fourteen thousand dollars. Mary got the money –"

"From where?"

"From behind the dryer in the laundry room. She gave me a paper sack, a lunch bag, and I counted the money out."

"Objection, your honor. Mr. Jenkins cannot testify to the actions of his wife.

Mary cringed at the thought of her having to testify. "I watched her!" Bobby said, grinning.

"You observed her physically get the money?"

"Yes. I had to move the dryer for her."

"Objection over-ruled. Continue," the judge said.

"Bill left with the money and returned about two hours later with the van."

"Can you describe the van?"

"A white 1974 Ford customized van. It had a mural of a blue mountain scene on the sides. It was carpeted inside with the Playboy bunny emblem on the inside of the carpeted cargo doors. There was a bed in the rear of the van, a refrigerator, and two captain chairs in frent. The van had air-conditioning, cruise control, and a killer stereo system. That's all I can recall. Bill later added a color television, leg pipes, and custom wheels."

"Thank you. Mr. Jenkins. The defense rests."

"Cross examination?" the judge offered.

"You bet! Mr. Jenkins, do you recall your telling F.B.I. agent H. Thomas Moore that the defendant was your friend, and that you were going to testify for him regardless of the consequences?"

"That's not true," Bobby snapped. "You're only telling half the story. Moore came to where I work and threatened to charge me with perjury if I testified for Bill. I told him then, and I'll say it now. Bill Hooker is like a son to me, but I would not lie for him. I came here to tell the truth as I know the truth regardless of Moore's threats."

The prosecutor smirked. "Mr. Jenkins, you testified that you gave Bill fourteen thousand dollars. Is that correct?"

"Yes, sir. I sure did."

"Just answer yes, or no."

"Yes."

"Was the money loose, wrapped, or in anything out of the ordinary."

"Not that I can recall. It was in a paper bag."

"Very well…"

"Wait a minute." Bobby fingered his chin, thinking.

"Yes, it was! I remember. We were out of rubber bands, so Mary gave me some of those.." he made a twisting gesture with his thumbs and two fingers.. "of those twisty things. Twist ties! That's it. I wrapped the money in twist ties," he grinned.

The elder prosecutor sat at the table, frowning. The second Bobby said the money was wrapped in 'twisty things' he snapped his pencil in half. The young prosecutor stopped dead in his tracks, dumbfounded at Bobby's revelation.

"Nuh-no further questions."

"Any redirect?" the judge asked.

"No, your honor."

Closing arguments were brief. The prosecutor recapped the in court identification and Frank Kalita's testimony, stressing that just days prior to his purchasing the fancy new Ford custom van, Bill had been broke. Bill's attorney made a brief statement about the reliability of the statements made by convicted felons. Then, the jury was led from the courtroom to begin deliberations.

While the jury decided his fate, Bill was placed in a holding cell, where Judy and the baby were allowed to visit.

"What do you think, Ginge?" she asked.

"I don't know. There was more evidence here than there was in Harrisburg. If I judge it by those standards, it's a guilty verdict."

"Do you want a couple of Valiums?"

"Yeah." Bill grinned.

"I forgot that I had them. I'm glad the deputy didn't find them."

"How did Bobby know about the twist ties?"

"Little Billy. He told us everything at lunch."

* * *

Forty-five minutes later the jury returned with a verdict. Bill was led into the courtroom and seated at the counselor's table next to his attorney.

"All rise," the bailiff announced loudly.

"You may be seated," the judge instructed the court room, seating himself. Then, he turned to the bailiff, and said. "You may bring the jury in."

One by one, the jury came through the door and seated themselves. Their faces were expressionless. The foreman of the jury passed a slip of paper to the bailiff. He looked at it, then passed it to the judge.

"Would the defendant please stand," the judge ordered.

Bill was feeling the effects of the Valiums, following instructions, but numb in thought.

"How do you find the defendant as to Count one," the judge asked.

The foreman cleared his throat, then replied, "not gulity!"

A silence fell over the court room.

Then the judge asked, "and how do you find the defendant as to Count Two?"

"Not guility!" the foreman declared.

The verdict was drowned out by the cheering from the spectators gallery. Bill grabbed his attorney's hand and pumped it gratefully, then he reached over the wooden partition and hugged Judy. Bobby stepped forward and grabbed Bill in a bearhug, grinning from ear to ear.

Every member of the jury was smiling, pleased with their finding.

The judge pounded his gavel to silence the courtroom. "Order, order in the courtroom!" he shouted.

A silence fell over the courtroom. Bill turned to look at the judge scowling down at him. Then, the judge looked at the jury and said, "That's the worst verdict that I've heard in my history on the bench, however, it is your verdict. You are excused until nine a.m. tomorrow morning. The defendant is hereby released. '

"But, your honor --" the bailiff retorted.

"That is, unless he has other holders," the judge added. "This court is adjourned."

As two deputy sheriff's escorted Bill across the street to the local jail, one looked at Bill and said, "I just want to know one thing?"

"What's that?" Bill asked.

"Did you do it?"

"Can they ever try me for it again?"

"Nope. You're free and clear."

Bill looked up at the blue sky scattered with white powder puffs, sighed, and said, "Naw, I didn't do it."

Bill Hooker was returned to Harrisburg, Pennsylvania for sentencing. Judge Nealon sentenced him to serve 15 years under the provisions of 4205 (B)(2). Remembering what Tommy Di'Amatto had coached, Bill asked the judge for a (A)(2) number.

"4205 (A)(2) has been replaced with 4205 (B)(2)" the judge explained, smiling.

WHY DO I LOVE THEE, LORD
You've given me a song to sing
within my heart to thee
you 've given me one life to live,
you've shown me charity.
When I deserved the least
you've given me the most
when I knew not how to walk,
Jesus died upon the cross.
I cannot count the blessings
that you've bestowed my way
but in Jesus' name
I give my thanks
in each and every passing day.
Lord, thank you for the sunshine
and every blade of grass

thank you for the seven days
especially the last.
Thank you for my fellow men
I pray for their souls too
that through your goodness
may they find -
the truth revealed in you.

ABOUT THE AUTHOR

William Daniel Burns was born in Lakeland, Florida. His family, and those who knew him in his early years called him "Danny." At an early age, he discovered his gift for conning people to get whatever he wanted. At the age of five, he convinced his best friend that two rusty nails and a piece of wood were from George 'Washington's rocking chair and they would someday be worth a whole lot more then his old shiny silver dollar.

When he was seven, his father moved the family to Baltimore, MD. It was a much tougher neighborhood. Danny learned to fight, and hustle. His parents divorced when he was twelve. His younger sister and older brother chose to stay with his mother. Danny chose to live with his father. They returned to live in Florida, and Danny changed his name to "Bill." His father remarried when he was thirteen. Bill quit school, and left home when he was fifteen. He married, and had two beautiful daughters by the age of seventeen - Tina Marie, and Kerri Ann. He was ill-prepared to handle the responsibility, and moved back to the mean streets of Baltimore, where he turned to crime as a means to support his family. The police made a game of that by telling him they rode around in marked cars and wore uniforms, then asked what does a criminal look like. Bill purchased a yellow panel truck and wrote THIEF WAGON across the back and sides in big black bold letters. The game ended with Bill being sent to prison.

Released from prison, he found his wife remarried and his daughters calling another man "daddy." Bill felt that he had nothing left to lose and devoted his life to crime!

Bill returned to federal prison twice. He furthered his education by obtaining his G.E.D., a degree in Commercial Art, and he has the equivalent of a two-year college Associates Degree. Bill has owned a number of successful businesses.

In 1988, Bill worked as an independent contractor for O's Auto Sales in Walbridge, Ohio. In 1991, while the owner vacationed in Florida, Bill was left in charge of the business. Several other guys also used the license, but they weren't registered to buy or sell vehicles at the auctions.

On May 28, 1991 Bill left with his girlfriend on a Florida vacation, returning June 8, 1991. A fire occurred at Adrian Auto Auction May 31, 1991, and a murder occurred in Northwood, OH on June 7, 1991. When questioned in regard to the murder, Bill accounted for his whereabouts for the entire vacation.

In 1993 Bill was charged with stolen vehicles in Monroe and Adrian, Michigan.

On the advice of two attorneys Bill pled guilty. At sentencing, he told the judge there was nothing anyone could do when they are signed, sealed, and delivered. That just because he signed the titles, it did not necessarily mean the vehicles were his!

Bill served his sentence, and in 1998, he was transferred to the halfway House in Monroe, Michigan. Ten days before his release, he was charged for the arson of Adrian Auto Auction. The prosecutor contended that his motive for the arson was to destroy incriminating evidence, the titles to the stolen vehicles. Bill filed three formal motions for discovery - none were complied with! He refused plea offers of 10 years, 5 years, and 2 years with credit for six months served. Bill was convicted, and sentenced to serve LIFE. He still maintains his innocence.

Bill is a strong supporter of prison reform. He wants to let the youth of today know that crime, drugs, and violence is not a "game." Bill thanks God for his love, insight, and guidance as he journeys through life. For more information on him, please contact him via www.jpay.com. He is inmate number #189577.

ORDER MORE EXCITING NOVELS FROM W.D. BURNS!

THE WEE HOURS

Nothing could have prepared Nicole Redman for the brutal murder of her six-year old daughter. Through a cloud of shock and pain, she seeks her daughter's murderer in a world filled with sleazy strip clubs, after-hour joints, and a notorious outlaw biker gang. She is quickly drawn into a life of illicit sex, drugs, and onto the path of a sadistic hitman.

PEACHES: WEE HOURS II

Nicole Redman found herself lost in an unforgiving world of outlaws whom she had grown to love, respect, and understand. Morally bankrupt by the rules of society, the outlaw bikers lived by one rule - an eye for an eye. The brotherhood ran deep, and Nicole 'Peaches' Redman was proud to call the Argots her family. In her wildest dreams, she had never imagined herself becoming a prostitute, a dancer, a biker chick, a murderer, or a reputed drug dealer. When life handed her lemons, she made lemonade.

FLORIDA SNOW: WEE HOURS III

Hoping to escape a trail of blood and death, Peaches arrives in Florida only to discover that the death toll had just begun. The Argots and the Heathens suddenly find themselves pitted against one another in a vicious drug war, forcing Peaches to fight to save her beloved club. Now, in order to survive she must tame a powerful Columbian Druglord, and outfox an F.B.I. and D.E.A. Task Force.

SOME KIND OF CROOK

Baltimore, Maryland, 1974. Special Agent H. Thomas Moore of the Towson Office pursued a group of five men who committed 23 known bank robberies across the Eastern Seabord from Maine to Florida. This story is based on the life of the alleged leader.

OCTOPOOL: SOME KIND OF CROOK II

Alleged to have committed 23 known bank robberies on the Eastern Seaboard and convicted of only on one robbery in the small town of New Freedom. After serving 39 months, Bill was paroled to Cleveland. Ohio. More than anything in the world. Bill wanted a new lease on life. He hoped that his lot in life would change with an indoor 8-men Jacuzzi named Octapool.

FRAMED: SOME KIND OF CROOK III

At the close of June 1992 the Northwood Homicide Task Force has found that William Burns criminal contacts going across the United States and Canada. We have found that there have been investigations from local to federal enforcement agencies.

ORDER THE ENTIRE BAD ASS OUTLAW PUBLICATIONS LINEUP!

Bad Ass Outlaw Publications

Mail: Bad Ass Outlaw Publications
4216 Riverview Lane
Lorian, OH 44055

Name: _____

Address:_____

City/State:_____

Zip:_____

Quantity	Titles	Price	Total
_____	The Wee Hours	$12.95	_____
_____	The Wee Hours II: Peaches	$12.95	_____
_____	The Wee Hours III: Florida Snow	$12.95	_____
_____	Some Kind of Crook	$12.95	_____
_____	Some Kind of Crook II: Octopool	$12.95	_____
_____	Some Kind of Crook II: Octopool Special Edition	$36.95	_____
_____	Some Kind of Crook III: Framed	$12.95	_____

Add $3.95 for shipping and handling (Via Priority Mail) for
1 book, $5.95 for 2 books , $8.95 for 3-4 books, add $1.95 for each additional book.

Total: $_____
FORMS OF ACCEPTED PAYMENT: Certified or government
issued checks and Money Order, all mail in order takes 7-10
Business Days to be delivered.
Or, just order online at http://www.badassoutlawpublications.com!

www.ingramcontent.com/pod-product-compliance
Lightning Source LLC
Chambersburg PA
CBHW071108250626

47159CB00002B/652